EPiTAPH FOR A TRAMP
& EPiTAPH FOR A
DEAD BEAT

The Harry Fannin Detective Novels

DAVID MARKSON

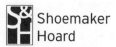 Shoemaker
Hoard

Library of Congress Cataloging-in-Publication Data
Markson, David.
    Epitaph for a tramp & Epitaph for a dead beat : the Harry Fannin
detective novels / David Markson.
    p. cm.
ISBN-13: 978-1-59376-134-9
ISBN-10: 1-59376-134-1
I. Markson, David. Epitaph for a dead beat. II. Title.

PS3563.A67E75   2007
813'.54—dc22

2006030690

Interior design by David Bullen
Cover design by Gerilyn Attebery
Printed in the United States of America
Distributed by Publishers Group West

Shoemaker & Hoard

An Imprint of Avalon Publishing Group, Inc.
1400 65th Street, Suite 250
Emeryville, CA 94608

10 9 8 7 6 5 4 3 2 1

Contents

EPiTAPH FOR A
TRAMP

CHAPTER 1

You know how hot the nights can get in New York in August, when everybody suffers—like the vagrants in the doorways along Third Avenue without any ice for their muscatel? Or all the needy, underprivileged call girls with no fresh-air fund to get them away from the city streets for the summer?

I'd taken a cold shower at one o'clock. Since then I'd recited the line-ups of six out of the eight National League baseball teams from the early thirties, I'd tried twice to make a mental list of every woman I'd ever known carnally, and now I was running through parts and nomenclature of common American hand weapons. I'd even had the light on and read for half an hour, but it was no good. It was still steaming. I was still awake. I was still thinking about her.

Cathy. I did that once in a while. Lying there alone like a chump and remembering. Things like the little cries she'd made, my name the way she'd always said it over and over, and then the way it would come in a gasp and her fingers would tear at my shoulders and—

Me Tarzan, you Jane. It was a recollection you'd cherish, like your first swift hobnail boot in the shins. I wondered how much lower she'd sunk in the year since I'd seen her.

No, I didn't wonder that. All I wanted was to get some sleep. I started doing the linemen of the 1940 Chicago Bears. Stydahar. Artoe. Fortman. Musso. Plasman. Turner. Bray. Wilson. Fortman. Or had I said Fortman? I was almost glad when the phone rang.

I knocked my book to the floor, reaching for it. One considerably bushed private investigator with a healthy dose of insomnia, at your service. "Hello," I said.

There was nobody there. Or rather somebody was, but he wasn't saying anything. Probably just shy. "Take your time," I told him.

I heard one long exhale. Then the steady dull buzz of a disconnected line.

"At the tone," I said to no one in particular, "the time will be sort of damned near three-thirty in the morning."

I put back the receiver, then fumbled for the book and put that back too. Nothing else to do, so I supposed I might as well be neat. Maybe I'd even get up and iron. I took a smoke, rolled over on the damp sheets with my hands behind my head and stared at shadows.

The book was a gay little thing by Thomas Mann called *The Magic Mountain,* another one of the forty-nine thousand and thirteen items I hadn't had time for when I was day-laboring my way through the University of Michigan at left halfback. Or before that, in North Africa. Or for that matter later, when I had been night city editor in too many saloons. I had been slogging through it for weeks and was having a rough time. Hardly any shooting at all.

I heard a car screech around a corner and then pull up abruptly near my building, burning rubber extravagantly along a curb. It had to have come in from Lexington Avenue, since I live on 68th just off Third and the traffic runs one-way east. The car door slammed with a squeaky sound, as if a terrier had had its tail in the way. High heels clicked a few irresolute steps on the pavement, paused, clicked indecisively some more, stopped altogether. The car was very likely something small, probably a foreign sports job. The indecisive lady was very likely potted.

I heard another car door closing, a heavier one this time. And this time when the telephone started I did not lift it immediately. I let it tease me until after the sixth ring, just to give my playful chum an idea of how valuable my time could be.

"Hi," I said then, "this is Judge Crater. Where is everybody?"

"Mr. Fannin? Mr. Harry Fannin?"

"Fannin's dead. Wasted away from lack of sleep. People kept calling him in the middle of the night."

"Oh, please, this is urgent. May I have Mr. Fannin?"

She wasn't one of the names in the little black book. She sounded young and pretty. But then they always sound that way. Also they always think it's urgent.

"This is Fannin."

"Mr. Fannin, you don't know me, but my name is Sally Kline. I'm—"

"You call a few minutes ago?"

"What? No. Please, Mr. Fannin, I started to say, I—"

I lost the rest of it, or at least the next sentence. The doorbell blasted in my ear like time to change to the next classroom. When I caught Sally Kline again she was saying, "—and I think she might be in trouble, Mr. Fannin, in serious trouble."

"Who?" I said. "Listen, Miss Kline, hang on, will you? All of a sudden we've got a Laurel and Hardy two-reeler running up here."

"A what? But—"

"One minute. I've got to get the door."

I left her angled on top of ponderous friend Mann and went

5

to the buzzer. I've got one of those speaker things at the bell, rigged by an electrician who should have been a tuba player, and it sometimes works. "Who is it?" I said brightly.

Another female, but that was all I got out of it. My name and a lot of static. This one seemed to know me, however. She called me something that sounded intimate, like *hlmphlmph* or *phrugg,* instead of formal old Fannin.

I pressed the button and unlatched the door, but I didn't bother to look out. I'm on the second floor in front, and with the stairs moving toward the rear you couldn't see a pole vaulter carrying his gear home from practice until he was almost to the top. I started over to Miss Kline again, and then I remembered that it might be appropriate to greet my guest in something more dignified than common perspiration.

I pulled on G.I. suntans, then leaned down to the phone and said, "Can you hang on there for one more minute?" I went to the door again without listening for an answer. "Who is it?" I called down.

There was no reply but I knew it would be the gal from the sports job, the one I'd decided was drunk. I could hear her using both dainty left feet on each of the steps, taking them slowly enough so that for all I could tell she might have been lugging that little car on her shoulder. I wasn't going to help her with it. "If you've got any friends or pets maybe, bring them along too," I told her. I went back to the phone.

Miss Kline had found some other form of amusement. I put the receiver on the cradle, crossed the living room once more and went into the kitchen, took ice out of the bucket and poured two Jack Daniels on the rocks. There were a couple of steaks in the Frigidaire, but they were frozen solid and I wasn't quite sure they'd be fully thawed before my guest got there.

I decided I wasn't feeling too hospitable anyhow. Snow White was in the outside corridor now, but she was so tight that even on a level keel she was bumping into dwarfs all over the forest. A professional call, no doubt about it.

I could see it all. One of my legion of admirers, alone and bewildered in the night, come to seek succor at Harry's hearth. Eight to five I'd have to listen to some incoherent sob story until she passed out, all the while doing valiant combat with my conscience to keep from taking advantage of her condition—which would be precisely what she would have come up to have taken advantage of. I dropped myself into my one good chair and took a short snort of the sour mash as the door opened.

No one came in. The door had swung inward toward me, so that I could see her shadow where the light behind her threw it on the rug, but nothing else.

The shadow swayed. Whoever it was, she giggled.

I'd expected a belch. So now we were playing guessing games. "Garbo," I said. "Anna Magnani." I couldn't think of any woman with a foreign car, but I decided I ought to be sporting about it. I supposed I'd given out the license when I'd pressed the buzzer to let her in. "Dietrich. Wendy Hiller. Maria Meneghini Callas."

Still nothing. I had a paperback *Book of Quotations* on the stand next to the chair and I tried that, stabbing a page at random. "*The life of man in a state of nature is solitary, poor, nasty, brutish and short.* Thomas Hobbes. And don't ask me who Thomas Hobbes is, because governess hasn't come to that part yet."

"Old Harry," she said then.

I closed the book. I put down the glass. I put down my cigarette also, so there were only my hands left, and since there wasn't anymore room on the table I picked those up and stared at them.

"The same . . . same old Harry."

It was a year. I supposed it was a year, but when I looked up

7

at her everything was the way it had always been. There was the face, there were the eyes. It was all there and it still did it to me, and even if I'd had a last name like Onassis or Getty or Zeckendorf this was still the only counter in the world I could buy it at.

She had one hand on the doorknob. She was wearing one of those white linen summer coats which weigh about as much as an overseas airmail stamp and her other hand was inside of it, holding herself below the left breast so that she looked as if she had knocked aside six or eight old ladies in her breathless sprint to get here. But she generally looked like that. That was just another one of the little things that made her so easy to forget.

She had moved toward me half a step, unsteady on her feet, and then had thought better of it. She stood there, clinging to the knob, and all I could do was flip some more pages in the book.

A mighty fortress is our God, said Martin Luther. *It is better to die on your feet than to live on your knees,* said Emiliano Zapata. *Work out your salvation with diligence,* said Gautama Buddha. Everyone had something right on the tip of his tongue except Fannin.

"You're stoned," I said then. "You're stoned and you ought to be in bed. Go the hell home, won't you? Or wherever it is you're shacked up now."

I didn't want to say it like that, God knows I didn't. But there wasn't any other way. I'd found that out a year ago and I wasn't going to leave myself open for it again.

She was still swaying slightly, the out-of-breath smile still in her eyes, being so lovely you could pawn your poor brains for five minutes of not remembering what had happened. "Old Harry," she said again. "The same tough, hard . . . same old . . . same . . ."

I was out of my chair when she started to buckle, but it came too fast. She hadn't given any sign, hadn't even closed her eyes, just turning a little and then going over as if she'd simply gotten tired of standing there and thought she might like to try the rug for size, and I had to go down on one knee to keep her from hitting. I took her weight with one arm around her shoulders and eased her down, holding her head and shoulders up. And then all of a sudden all of the lovely, lovely toys were smashed and scattered all at once.

"Cathy," I said. "Oh, good God, Cathy—"

The coat had covered it while she was standing. The stain was as big as a six-dollar sirloin below her breast, dark and seeping, and the inside of her hand was soaked with it from where she had had her palm pressed against herself. I saw the slash in the blouse where the blade had gone in, no wider than a man's leather watch band, centered and near the top of the seepage.

Her eyes were open, staring at me, but they weren't smiling now. There wasn't any expression in them at all. They were as empty as two spoonfuls of weak tea.

"Harry. Know what I did, Harry? Real . . . cops and robbers. You would have . . ."

"Easy, baby," I said. "Tell me later. Let me get a doctor. You just lie here and—"

"No!" She had clutched me by the wrist. A four-year-old at his first Hershey bar would have had a hand about as sticky. Or with as little strength in the grip. "Harry, don't let me go. Hold me, Harry, I . . ."

Her hand slipped away. All I could think of were the five minutes I'd spent counting the sterling while she was dragging herself up the stairs.

"Cath, you've got to let me—" I was stretching, trying to reach a pillow from the couch without letting her go. I couldn't make it.

"Cathy, I'm going to make you lie back. Just don't move and I'll—"

"Harry—"

"Yes, baby, yes. Here I am."

"Harry . . . just for a minute . . . both your arms. Hold me, Harry."

My right arm was still beneath her shoulders. I put my other hand along her cheek and it was tearing me apart then. Because it wasn't going to make any difference if I called a doctor now or ever. I could save the dime for my estate.

I lowered my hand to below her breast, cupping it tight against the wound. The blade had missed her heart but it had been close enough. It had to have happened just before she rang the bell. It was seconds before I caught the faint small beat, like a whisper behind heavy draperies.

"Harry . . ."

"Here, baby, here."

"Nobody else, Harry. Rotten . . . so rotten for you. The only one . . . only one it was ever right with. You, Harry . . ."

"I know, baby, I know."

"Harry . . ."

And then there was nothing else. "Cath," I said. "Cath. Baby, I—" Or maybe I didn't say it out loud, I'm not sure. It didn't matter. I knelt there holding her for another minute, feeling her hair against my neck, and then I put her down.

The phone was ringing. I had no idea how long it had been doing that again. I got up and walked toward the bedroom extension to answer it. I had a dead one on the living-room carpet and all my instincts told me there were a dozen things I'd better start doing, but I couldn't think of any of them. Because this one wasn't just silver dollars for Harry Fannin, private cop. This one was about Cathy.

The phone was in my hand. "Yes?" I said stupidly.

"Mr. Fannin, please, this is Sally Kline again. I tried to tell you before, I live with Cathy. I'm worried, Mr. Fannin, and I didn't know who else to call. I think Cathy's in trouble. I think something might happen to her."

I was staring into the other room. The irony of it registered very remotely. "What?" I said.

"Oh, heavens, what's the matter? Are you asleep, Mr. Fannin? I said it's about Cathy, about your wife . . ."

CHAPTER 2

I met her in the summer of '56. It had been one of those weeks when all the business is the kind the competition deserves. On Monday a pleasant Mrs. DiJulio told me that her sweet, innocent, sixteen-year-old Maria was being kept out all night by a not'a so nice'a crowd, and could I perhaps tell'a the boys to leave her alone? Sure. I told'a the boys, although I had to confiscate a few switchblades to do it, and that left me with Maria. Alone in Central Park with charming, innocent Maria. First she ripped off her blouse and screamed rape. No patrolman was close enough to be impressed so she ripped off her skirt too. That impressed *me,* enough to spank her. So then she threw her arms around my neck and wailed that this was what she had wanted all along, a man, a real man. She had lovely arms, only thirty or forty needle punctures above the elbows. I went over there again the next morning and dialed the number myself to make certain that Mrs. DiJulio got through to the juvenile bureau.

That was Monday. Wednesday it was a pharmacist named Heppenstall whose wife had wandered. I found her easily enough, holed up with a Matterhorn-size lesbian and the dregs of a case of rum in a dollar-a-night Third Avenue hotel.

Agnes Heppenstall threw a sheet-shredding tantrum while I booted out her playmate, then turned whisky coy the minute we were alone. She was such a dreadful mess, she said. And it was all psychological. Heppenstall hadn't excited her in seventeen years and so she had been experimenting. And I was such a pretty man, couldn't I help her experiment some more? She was sick four times in the cab on the way home, and not psychologically.

Nice week, nice profession. Friday it was a tavern keeper named O'Rourke from Eighth Avenue whose night-shift barmaid was clipping the payments on a Mercedes-Benz out of the till, but would I go a little easy because the dame was his deceased brother's only child? No thanks, Mr. O'Rourke. Even if the doll didn't have nineteen sailor pals guzzling for free along the rail, there would probably be a light machine gun behind the blackberry brandy. Or a folding bed under the rear booth. No, O'Rourke, sorry, but I was just leaving. I had a date to wrestle a python. Something undemanding, you know?

I locked the office and got out of there fast. Three newspaper guys I knew had rented a shack on the Long Island shore. Ants, roaches, linen that had been dirty when the last of the Mohicans abandoned it and hadn't been washed since, dishes in the sink from one leap year to the next. And no Maria DiJulio, no Agnes Freud, no worldly little barmaid. Just a couple of fifths of Jack Daniels, a little sun, and I was my clean, wholesome old self again.

The newspaper guys drove back into the city late Sunday evening, but I decided to give it another night. I sat around for a couple of hours, disciplining myself by not opening the next bottle until I could manage it without defacing the tax stamp, and trying to make sense out of something called *The Waste Land* by T. S. Eliot which was the only book in the joint. About midnight I decided I'd take a stroll on the beach.

I did not have anything in mind. The tide was out and I went along the edge of the wet sand. I walked for twenty minutes and used up a couple of cigarettes and then I decided it might fill my later years with fond memories if I left my clothes on some rocks and went in.

The water was fine. I took my bearings on a tank tower behind some dunes and swam easily for about ten minutes, going straight out from the shore. When I checked the tower I had not veered off much. I lay there and rode the swells for a while, thinking about original sin and the fallibility of the human intellect and what the Red Sox would do for base hits when Ted Williams finally quit, and then just to impress myself I sprinted back.

I touched bottom with the water up to my chest and stood there waiting for my lungs to straggle on home. That was when it came to me that I was never really going to amount to anything in life. Here I was with an audience, and I hadn't even had the foresight to print up tickets.

She was at the edge of the water. I could not see her face but in the dim light her hair looked the color of Palmolive soap. She was wearing a light-colored blouse and a dark skirt and no shoes, and she was standing with her feet wide apart. The wash went in and churned around her ankles and buried them as it slipped back. She had a cigarette in her hand.

I was still twenty yards out and she spoke quietly but I had no trouble hearing her over the surf. She had a deep, throaty voice and she seemed amused. "The cigarette's yours," she said. "I didn't go through your pockets. I just sort of felt around the outside for the pack."

"I'm glad," I told her. "None of the rest of that stuff is supposed to be opened before Christmas."

"I guess I can wait. But we can have a tree, can't we?"

"I'll tell you what. You turn your back for half a minute and I could maybe get started trimming it right now."

"Don't tell me!"

She was laughing. She walked forward a few short steps, so that the water swirled around her calves. Her hair was tinted more yellow than green now, but her face still might have been Jolson's just after they'd painted him up to do *Mammy*.

She had edged forward even more. When it swelled inward now the water was almost to the level of her skirt.

"Suppose I don't turn?" she said. "Suppose I just camp right here?"

"You'll get a little damp when the tide comes in," I told her. "Me, I'll be home by the fire. I'm coming out just about now."

"Don't."

"Don't what?"

"Don't come out."

"Oh, now look, I know it was probably a dumb stunt, but I just drained out all my anti-freeze last month. If you don't turn your back I'm going to—"

"Turn yours." She was laughing again. And then her hands were at her blouse.

"For crying out loud—"

I decided my only hope was to start swimming around to my clothes the back way, via the Oriental trade routes. I went perhaps a dozen lazy overhand strokes, hearing nothing, and then she came up ahead of me. She took a deep breath and grinned after it and her face caught the light now. I saw the way her hair was flat along her skull and the way her eyes sparkled. I saw how beautiful she was.

"Hello, Harry Fannin," she told me.

We were treading water. "I know you. You're the trustworthy girl who didn't go through my pockets."

15

"Wouldn't you? If you found someone's clothes on the sand?"

"No doubt about it."

"I thought all sorts of things. Foul play, mayhem, drunk and disorderly conduct—"

"Death by water. The fire sermon—"

"I know that poem. Eliot. And I thought all detectives were illiterate. Anyhow I was all set to rush off screaming. You ruined it all."

"I'm sorry. I would have squandered my savings on a heavy meal first if I'd known."

She laughed again, a rich, husky laugh that had nothing false about it. It was as real as the way she'd let her hair get wet like that. Hell, it was as real as her being there. She splashed water at me and then slipped away, going under so that I saw the flash of her back arching just beneath the surface and then the gleam of her long legs, and then coming up ten yards off and swimming out. She did a crawl well, moving with sharp clean strokes and heading off at an angle against the current. I'd decided she wasn't tight after all. I watched her for a minute and then I went in and walked back up the beach to where my clothes were.

I was smoking when she came out. Her own things were scattered along the sand and she stood there at the edge of the water for a long minute before she started to put them on, brushing water from her body and bending over to wring out her hair. Her hair was chopped fairly short. She did not look at me but she did not turn away either. She had a lovely body, with the long legs that I had seen and good hips and breasts that were high and round when she turned into profile against the water.

I think that was when it happened. She was standing there with her legs wide apart and her back half toward me, and she was wearing nothing but her panties. The line of her thighs was turned beautifully and I watched it as she moved. She wrung out her hair again but did it by leaning backward this time, arching her body the way a diver might at the height of a back dive and holding it that way with her arms lifted back and all of her being fluid and lovely in the moonlight, and I felt the tightening along my jaw. Because she was not doing it for my benefit. She had decided she could be just as batty as the next guy, and now she was getting dressed the best way she could without a towel and it was as simple as that.

Sure, simple. So why not run and fetch your zither, Fannin, strum us a little mood music? Come off it, huh? Probably she'd turn out to be an untouched little Bryn Mawr sorority president who'd never had a night in bed worth remembering since the time she'd snuggled up with a hot copy of *Studs Lonigan*. I chucked my smoke into the sand and started walking down the beach away from her.

And then I decided I was nuts altogether. A screwball dame comes prancing into the locker room and offers it to me all wrapped up with a red ribbon and I start acting like some bashful adolescent too mixed up by puberty to kiss his own mother good night. For crying out loud, Fannin.

I stopped when she caught up with me. She'd had to run and she was out of breath. Her breasts were rising and her blouse was tight across them where it had gotten wet. I reached out and touched the wet ends of her hair.

"I tell you you're the prettiest nitwit I've met in months?"

She laughed. "And I haven't had a drink since the V-8 juice at breakfast, that's the silly part of it. I think you're probably pretty nice, Harry Fannin."

We were near the dunes. She was lovely, all right. So make up your mind, I told myself.

"You're staring at me."

"The way you stare at four aces," I told her.

"Because you always think you've misread the hand?"

"Partly. Mainly because you're sure somebody's going to call a misdeal before you get a chance to bet."

She was smiling. Her eyes were dark and bright under her wet lashes. There was something so alive about her it made my throat ache.

"Bet," she said then. "Bet the hand, Harry Fannin."

But I was still looking at her. "The limit," I said. "With four it can't be anything under the limit."

"Suppose I raise? Suppose I've got a straight flush. That would win, wouldn't it? You and your measly four aces."

"Have you? My bet's in."

"God, we're talking. Have you got any idea why we're talking so much?"

There were beer bottles. There were tin cans and chunks of driftwood and seashells. There could have been hot coals.

Her arms were across my shoulders. Her body was warm and damp beneath me and her face was turned against the sand. My face was along her neck where her hair had fallen away and I could feel a pulse, fast at first and then slowing. And after a very long time the sound of the surf came back.

"Who dealt that?" she said then. "Oh, my God, did I deal that?"

I pressed my hand over her lips, turning my head. They were coming toward us along the water's edge, talking, and she saw them and lay still.

One of them was sketching jerky little abstractions against the darkness with a cigarette. His voice was high-pitched and nasal but it carried across clearly as they passed us. "He's a beautiful little boy," he said, "beautiful. But the only person who knows if he's mine or not is my wife. I love that kid, I do. But I tell you, I just don't know if he's mine—"

Surf took the rest of it. I watched them going away, not moving and hearing her breathing softly next to me.

Her voice was distant. "If you go now you won't have to fumble through the talk," she said. "It can be messy to fumble through, particularly when you don't even know the girl's name."

"Mrs. Harry Fannin," I told her.

I could feel her laughing without hearing any sounds or seeing her face. She said, "I did have the straight flush, Harry, and thanks. But it would be kind of silly to think there could be two winners in the same hand, wouldn't it?"

"Marry me," I told her. I didn't know I was going to say that. You've got to think the whole thing was something you'd just invented to say that, and it was something I had had before. But I could count the times. I had had it once in the army in Texas but after a while it had come out that the girl had a husband getting shot at somewhere, and so there was nothing to do but go off with my lip quivering and get shot at myself. I'd had it once at college also but the girl was killed in an automobile wreck and what I did after that I didn't much like to remember. I'd had it those two times and here it was again after six or eight years and how do you know you'll ever find your way back to the same stretch of sand? So I said it again.

I had lifted myself to my elbows and she turned her head, watching me. "I told you I went through your wallet," she said. "I saw your investigator's license and that Sheriff's Association card and the gun permit and, gosh, all sort of impressive things. But I guess I must have missed the release papers from that mental institution. I never did see them at all."

I was kneeling. I dug out two cigarettes and lit them and gave her one, grinning back at her. I picked up her wallet where it had slipped out of her skirt and lit another match. Hawes, it said. Catherine.

"Harry?"

"Let's get out of here, Hawes. Right now."

She had lifted herself slightly, braced on one arm. She took up a handful of sand and let it run through her fingers. "It would be gone before we got to Pennsylvania Station," she said remotely. She was looking past me. "Something like this, so damned quick. What was it, maybe twenty minutes? Old first-glance Cathy. You don't think it's the first time, do you? Go away, Fannin. Take another swim and wash the hayseed out of your hair. I was reading a Dostoievski novel before I came out for my little walk. I'll go back and finish it now, so I can see what it's like when people really suffer things that tear out their guts instead of ten cents' worth of romantic twinge just because there's moonlight and for five minutes you don't have to feel alone anymore or—"

I had taken her by the shoulders. "Hawes, come on."

"Oh, damn," she said. "Oh, goddam." She was chewing her lip and I was sure of it then if I hadn't been before. Because you get so many with whom there's never anything left. But here it was afterward and I was kneeling there and I was still feeling it. It hurt me to look at her. It hurt me the way her voice was, the way the line of her thigh joined her hip.

Which was romantic as all hell, but was still no concern of our two wandering companions. They were coming back up the beach and this time the other one of them was holding forth:

"I'm telling you, Lou, with three kids around you're paying for fifteen meals a day. Fifteen. That's one hundred and five meals a week. And when you're doing it without love, well, brother—"

Her arms slipped around my neck then. "Fannin, Fannin, Fannin, it's insane. Of all the idiotic, impossible, scatter-brained, impulsive . . . and I just don't know *what* I'm going to tell Frank

Sinatra in the morning!" She was trembling, maybe laughing, maybe crying, I don't think it mattered which. Because we came together and it was all there again and it had to be right.

It was. For maybe ten months.

CHAPTER 3

She was twenty-four. She had gone to Barnard College for two years, and she worked as a secretary in the sales department of a publishing house on Fourth Avenue. She had a mother and an older, unmarried sister named Estelle who lived on West 72nd Street, and she had been sharing an apartment in Greenwich Village with two other girls. She had a tiny scar under her left eyebrow from diving into water that was too shallow; and when she was six years old, before her father had died, she'd been lost in the Adirondack Mountains for three days. She'd camped out her share of times since then also.

"Sometimes it's gotten a little messy, Harry," she told me. "But I never knew what I was looking for. Now I don't want anything else, just you and me."

Just us, and Beautyrest made three. Maybe we could have gotten a patent on it after all. Once in a while we also boiled some eggs or went to the films.

Fannin had it, all right, and he had it badly. During his mottled career Fannin had also had several .32 and .38 caliber bullet holes in various inconsequential portions of his anatomy, a knife wound in his right shoulder, shrapnel in his left, not to mention two broken noses and sundry other minor disabilities. Once in a while he has even been known to pick up something which lasts, like smoker's hack.

It happened on the 4th of June.

I'd been to Chicago for three days. I had those out-of-town jobs from time to time. This one was blackmail. I'd been trying to pick up some of the cash my client had paid out before the Illinois law could move in and impound it all. I'd made out well enough, but there'd been a lot of chasing around and I'd missed sleep. It was five o'clock in the morning when I hit LaGuardia Airport coming back, and I took a cab to the place without calling Cathy. She flicked on a small light while I was undressing.

"Baby," she said. She could even look beautiful waking up.

"I was trying to be quiet," I told her.

"Old Harry, the silent sleuth. I'll bet you were."

"I really was. I'm one weary husband, m'am."

"That weary?"

I got into bed. The sheets were crushed and warm and her arms came around me. "I'll live," I told her.

I woke up about eleven and phoned the client to make an appointment. I did not get out of bed to make the call. I kept looking at the mirror across the room and grinning at what Cathy had written on it in soap before she'd gone to the office. It said, "Go ahead, you bastard, sleep while I slave." I called her next.

"Thanks," I said.

"Fine time to be getting up." They should have paid her extra for the way her voice sounded on the phone. "Thanks for what?"

"For saying hello on the mirror. I just called to return it."

"You already did."

"What, talking in my sleep?"

"You said hello this morning, idiot. Most of my men don't forget such things."

"Shucks," I said. "That."

"Ummm, that." She was laughing. "You going to the office?"

I was taking a cigarette, holding the phone wedged against my neck. "Couple hours," I said. I shook out the match and leaned across to drop it into the ashtray on the telephone table. That was when I noticed it.

"Bye, Harry."

I did not answer her. I was staring at the tray.

"Harry?"

"Here," I said.

It must have gotten into my voice. "Harry, is anything wrong?"

I kept looking at it. "No," I told her. "Just thinking about something. I'll see you tonight, Cath."

She hung up. I let the phone dangle in my hand for a minute and then I put it back. The ashtray was one of those big ceramic modern things you could have served chops in. There were ten or a dozen butts in it. Three or four had Cathy's lipstick on them.

I remembered it clearly. The tray had been loaded when I'd been packing to catch the plane three days before. Tidy Harry had picked it up and carried it to the trash basket in the john and dumped it.

Cathy did not smoke much. A pack of short-size Kents lasted her close to a week and frequently she would go another three or four days without buying any, chiseling a few of my Camels. The butts with the lipstick stains in the tray were Kents. The other seven or eight were Pall Malls.

I was sitting there and seeing them, trying not to think what I was thinking. Try that sometime, especially when you're in the trade.

I got out of bed and picked up the thing and dumped it. I got dressed and heated up the coffee she'd left and toyed with a cup. I picked up the phone three or four times to dial her office number. Each time I stared at the receiver and then put it back.

It was just somebody who had dropped in. An old friend. Yes, old. So old he'd been too weak to sit on a chair and had had to lie down on the bed.

No. Cathy had brought the tray out into the living room, put it back without emptying it.

Cathy.

It was no good. I went up to the client's office on Park Avenue and delivered the money and collected what was due on my fee. I walked up three blocks to the bank on the 47th Street corner and deposited the check. It was a bright summer day and there were a lot of women on the streets. All of them were very smart-looking and very chic and not one of them had that quality of being alive that Cathy managed even when she was shaving her legs.

Mrs. Harry Fannin.

I dialed her at four o'clock from the office. She got on and I told her I had rotten news. There was a rush deal and I'd have to be away again for two or three days. Cleveland, I said. I was making a flight in forty minutes.

"Oh, Harry—"

"I'm sorry. Just came up. I'm in a hurry, Cath."

"Harry?"

"Yeah?"

"Harry, you've been so strange on the phone today. So kind of—of distant."

"Cath, look, I've got to scram."

"All right, Harry."

"See you, huh?"

"Bye—"

I hung up. She'd sounded forlorn as hell. The first guy who came along with a tin cup, I was going to buy every pair of shoelaces he had.

I went out and took a cab down Fifth Avenue to the nearest You-Drive-It and I rented a two-year-old Ford sedan. I drove over to Third Avenue and stopped at one of the cheap saloons the fags hadn't decided was quaint yet and I had three bourbons while watching the clock. At 5:15 I left and swung around to Lexington and went back up town. It had started to drizzle. I pulled in at 68th at exactly 5:28 and parked near the end of the block, away from the direction in which she would come home. Four minutes later I saw her make the corner on the double, running with a newspaper over her head. She went inside. I sat there.

I chewed cigarettes, thinking how the one kind of job a legitimate P.I. won't take are those cheap divorce things where you climb through transoms with a fresh load of Sylvania 25's in your flashholder. I could make a couple thousand more a year if I was hard up enough to do that. I could have probably even afforded an electric lathe or a power saw, so that my wife would have had a hobby when I was out nights.

The rain stopped in an hour. No one had gone in or out of the building who I didn't know. There are only four apartments in it. Collins, the architect on the top floor, went in about ten minutes after Cathy. Jojo Pringle came out a little after six. He's a jazz clarinetist and a hophead and I knew he'd be on his way for a light brunch. Three or four patients went into Dr. Salter's private entrance on the ground floor.

I began to dislike myself around seven. By eight o'clock the feeling had become one of contempt. I had planned to park there for three days if I had to, but now I told myself I'd give it one more hour and then if I had any sense I'd go upstairs and apologize.

She came out at 8:33.

She had changed out of her office clothes. She was wearing a tight, candy-striped summer skirt and a white blouse. She was great on white blouses. Her hair glinted under the street lamp.

She began walking away from me, going with the one-way traffic and glancing over her shoulder. I started the engine in the Ford when I spotted the empty cruiser cab in the mirror. It picked her up and went a block and then cut downtown on Second.

Go to a movie, I said. Do that, Cathy. Tell the driver to head over to midtown.

Get rich wishing. The cab went all the way down to 14th before it turned. It went across to Seventh Avenue and then south again into the Village. It stopped at Sheridan Square. The light was green and I had to pass it. I double parked in front of a liquor store, using the mirror while she paid and got out. A panel truck pulled away a little up the block. I waited until she turned a corner and then I eased the Ford into the gap.

There was a small off-Broadway theater over a few blocks. Maybe she was going there. Maybe she was going to Hoboken or Las Vegas or Guam, since they were all in that general direction.

The joint was called Angelino's.

It was one of those seedy basement places some landlord had had to turn into a bar twenty years before because no one would pay United States currency to live in it. I knew the kind of crowd it would get. Guys with a notion they wanted to be artists who didn't shave because they thought you were half-way there if you looked the part. Girls in grimy sweat shirts with the complete poems of Dylan Thomas under their arms when what they needed were cartons of Rinso. Sophisticated young uptown ladies slumming with their toothbrushes in their pocketbooks.

I supposed she'd known the place from when she'd lived in the Village before we were married. I went past the doorway once and saw her standing in the crush at the bar. If she was meeting any one guy in particular he wasn't doing any downhill schuss to get there.

I went back and got the Ford and parked it a few doors down from the entrance. I walked down the opposite side of the street to the liquor store and picked up a pint of bourbon. When I came back past the doorway this time three or four of the guys near her were working on it. It was all palsy enough so that she was laughing about something. I went back to the car and opened the pint.

People drifted in and out or along the street. So did their conversation, and it was too muggy to roll up the window:

"—Look, if you can call *my* mother Jocasta, and *me* narcissistic—"

"—Talk about paranoia—"

"—The really accomplished Mexican painters, like Orozco and Tamayo—"

The bohemians. The intellectuals. Tamayo and Tamayo and Tamayo, seeps in this petty paste from plate to plate. If they stopped that talk for three consecutive minutes the world would blow up.

"—Do I know Willie? Why, he quotes me three separate times in one chapter—"

"—If I saw Heathcliff on the street I'd just die—"

It got to be ten. It got to be midnight and then one o'clock. You can drink a goodly amount of whisky in that time, say a pint. I was saving a buck or two by drinking it out of the bottle instead of across a bar. Be sensible that way for another decade and I could probably even manage that two-week cruise to the Bahamas I'd been dreaming about all those years.

It was 1:49 when I tagged them. He was a tall slender kid with fairly good shoulders under his denim jacket. He was wearing tan slacks and a black knit tie and white sneakers and if someone had told him that the frat was holding a stag beer party he would have trotted off on the spot. Nobody told him. She had him by the arm and when they came up the stairs onto the sidewalk she said something and he laughed.

They came past the car. She never saw me. They were both laughing now but she was not that tight. She walked easily and when they were turning the corner I saw his arm go around her hip.

They walked two more blocks and then they went into a rundown building with a grocery store on the street floor. I was sixty yards behind them on the other side of the street. Next to me a sign in a plumber's window said, IS THERE WATER IN YOUR BASEMENT?

After a minute a light went on two flights up. Third floor front. I lit a cigarette. The grocer was pushing haddock that year. I smoked the cigarette hard. I was still trying to finish it when the light went out again.

I went across.

There were a lot of bells and a lot of names. Lonergan. Goldman. Zachery. Hoy. Cranley. Philkins. When I was nine years old an avant-garde juvenile delinquent named Philkins knocked half the spokes out of the front wheel of my Western Flyer with a baseball bat. Or maybe that was Filkins. There was no lock on the outside door.

There was one naked light bulb for each flight. There was a faint odor of turpentine. The walls were a drab schoolroom brown. The door I wanted was like any other dingy door in any other dingy walk-up anywhere. I wondered what I was doing there.

I rang the bell hard, hearing it blast inside the apartment.

A minute passed. If they had the turpentine I wondered why they didn't get some paint. I heard him padding toward me. "Who is it?" he said through the door.

"Delivery."

"Huh? Here?" The door opened. "You want Cranley, mister?"

He was peering out at me, tying the sash around a blue robe. He was a good-looking boy, no more than twenty-two or twenty-three. The line of his nose was sharp and straight where the light from the hall cut it half into shadow. I would not have had to move my right hand more than ten inches from where it lay near the bell to change all that.

"You sure you want Cranley, mister?"

"Go back inside," I said. "Tell her it'll be cleaner if she's got something on when I come in."

"What? Hey now, what is this? Who do you think you're—"

I took him by the front of the robe, moving close to him. "Maybe you better say you never saw her before tonight," I told him. "Maybe you better get that over with first."

He got with it quickly enough then. I let him go and he edged away a step or two, his eyes going toward a closed door that would be a bedroom and then back to me. He was pushing six-one which made him almost as tall as I am but I had him in all the other ways and he knew that. He was about as thick through the chest as a breakfast lox. He swallowed once, scared.

"Look," he said then, "if you're her husband, honest, I didn't know. I never did see her before, really. She said she was divorced and she—"

"You got a can?"

"What? Yes, sure, right over there—"

"Get in it," I said. "Get in it and lock the door and scrub the bowl or something until you hear us leave."

He didn't argue. He wasn't going to write home about the experience but he went. I waited until he closed the door and then I walked across and opened the other one.

The candy-striped skirt and the white blouse and her underclothes were thrown over a straight-backed chair. She was lying across a rumpled spread with her back toward me, looking at a magazine. One small shaded bulb threw a tarnished circle of light over the bed, and if I'd been Leonardo da Vinci I probably would have started fumbling around in a panic for paper and crayons.

She thought I was the kid. "Aren't you lucky," she said. "People bringing you surprises in the middle of the night."

"What was it, a race?" I said. "Do you get a trophy for it?"

She hadn't moved, not consciously. I saw the muscles tighten beneath the flesh of her shoulders as her arms went rigid to the elbows beneath her. Then her head came around slowly. Her face was the color of ice cubes.

"You had to go marry a cop," I said.

She came apart then. Her lower lip quivered and her eyes filled. I had never seen her cry before. It broke me up real bad. "Wrap it up," I told her. I shut the door on her and went back into the other room.

I stood there, feeling the whisky in my stomach and seeing the place for the first time. She'd found herself an adult one. He collected things. There were lanterns from construction barriers, signs that said *No Parking 8 A.M. to 6 P.M.* Near the door there was a cross-wired Department of Sanitation street-corner trash basket big enough to turn over and cage a walrus in. He didn't have the walrus but it wouldn't have taken more than a word. The kid's jacket was hanging over a chair and the label said *Whitehouse and Hardy, Fifth Avenue,* so good old Dad had paid for that the same way he was paying for the graduate school. There were enough books to repave the Jersey Turnpike.

There was a typewriter with a sheet of paper in it. *G. P. Cranley,* it said at the top, *Comp. Lit. 207, Page 4,* and under that it said:

> *And thus it is my conclusion that* The Recognitions *by William Gaddis is not merely the best American first novel of our time, but perhaps the most significant single volume in all American fiction since* Moby Dick, *a book so broad in scope, so rich in comedy and so profound in symbolic inference that—*

She was dressed. She went straight to the door and out without saying anything and I followed her down. When we got to the street she turned the wrong way and I said, "This way." I said, "Here," when we got to the car. I ran a red light on Hudson Street and said, "Nuts," when some guy yelled at me. So I won. That made four more words than she had said.

Coming out of Central Park I had to wait for a light at 66th. "He didn't even know my name," she said then.

"That's all right," I told her. "I didn't once either. Maybe something lovely will grow out of it for you both."

She sucked in her breath. I found a parking slot directly in front of the apartment and she went in ahead of me with her own keys while I was locking the car. I wondered why I was bothering to do that with a rented job. She was in the good chair with one small light on when I came up, sitting with her head on her chest and her arms dangling, looking like a thrown coat.

I made myself a drink, spilling an inch and a half of Jack

Daniels into a kitchen tumbler and taking it without ice. It had the same effect as a short carrot juice. I went out and sat across from her.

You could hear the busses out on Third Avenue.

"Why?" I said.

She said nothing.

"I thought it was good. Plodding, dull-witted old Harry, I thought nothing could be better. And all the while I—"

"It *is* good. But I'm just—"

"Good, yeah. It must be remarkable. You're just what?"

"I don't know," she said. "I don't know." Her voice was ragged and she looked up at me. I stared at the rug.

"You go away," she said then.

"Good God—three, four times in a year?"

"It doesn't matter. Whenever you do, the minute you're gone, the minute I'm alone I start pacing. I start walking around this room as if I don't belong here, as if I'm a stranger." She was talking from very far away. "It's as if something is pushing me. I've got to get out of here. Just out. And I can't stop myself, I want to be with—with I don't know who. It doesn't make any sense and I can't explain, I—"

"How many times?"

"Almost every time." I heard her swallow. "You were in Phoenix four days. When you were in New Orleans it was five. And just now three when you were in Chicago. Almost every one of those nights."

I didn't feel sore. I didn't feel cheated or betrayed or outraged or anything else. I felt nothing. I was sitting there hearing her say all that and somehow it did not have anything to do with me. I knew it would have something to do with me later but it didn't now. I got up and poured myself another drink and then I came back and sat there again.

"The same guys? How many guys?"

"They're different each time. A different one each night, Harry. I see one and then they want to make dates but I won't. It's all confused, like if it's only one night it's not so bad, as if I'm not really doing anything wrong if I don't let any of them get to mean anything. I go into bars and I meet them the way I did tonight and I . . . Oh, God in heaven, I—"

She had her face in her hands. She was sobbing and saying, "Help me, help me." She said it over and over. And four plus five made nine and three made the dozen. And tonight was thirteen. I stood up.

"Harry, I'm sick. Something's the matter with me. It's all right when you're here, when I'm with you, but the minute you're gone I'm—"

I went into the bedroom. I dug out a suitcase and opened it on the bed. She came into the doorway.

"I'll go," she said. She had stopped crying. "It was your place before I came. I can stay with my mother and Estelle until I find someplace else."

I didn't answer. I did not have a particularly distinct concept of the ethics involved in that kind of thing.

"It will be easier that way," she said. "I'll take one bag. I can come back when you're at the office and get the rest."

I went past her and into the living room. She did not take long. She came out with the suitcase and stood it near the door. She hung there like something wet on a hook.

"It's going to sound pretty silly, isn't it? But I—I'm sorry, Harry."

"Forget it," I said. "You told me all about it that first night on the beach, all about the other ones. I didn't buy anything without a label on it."

I wasn't looking at her. Outside they were running every bus on the line.

"I deserve that and more," she said. "But that was different,

Harry. Before we were married I wasn't hurting anyone but my-self. I didn't want to hurt you. Oh, dear God, I didn't! I—" Her voice broke. She was sobbing again with her head turned, softly now. "Harry, I love you, I—"

"That's swell," I told her. "I'll keep that in mind. I'll remember it every time I think about you in that crummy room down there tonight with your drawers flung over that chair and your bare butt sprawled all over the bed. 'Aren't you lucky, people bringing you surprises in the middle of the night. And, oh, by the way, my name's Cathy. Mrs. Cathy Fannin but don't worry about that, the sucker's gone chasing off someplace and—'"

She missed the best part of it. I hadn't even worked up a light sweat. The door had not swung shut all the way and I could hear her on the steps. Then the downstairs latch clicked and after that there was the sound of a car door closing that would be a cab and then there was nothing.

The glass smashed low against the wall across the room when I heaved it. The whisky left a stain which I finally scrubbed off but there was a small permanent mark where the paint had been chipped. The mark was still there a year later when Cathy came back up the stairs for the first time since that night and giggled once in the hallway and then fell into my arms and died.

CHAPTER 4

I had not seen her in all that time. She had come a day later to collect the rest of her gear, and a few months after that I'd gotten divorce papers in the mail, stamped from a place called Athens, Alabama, where I suppose they peddle those things on the corner newsstands. And that had been the end of it. The end, except that I still had the pail and shovel but all the sand was gone from the sandbox.

And now I stood in the doorway of the bedroom holding the phone and not listening to a girl named Sally Kline who was trying to tell me something she thought was urgent. The Second Coming could have waited.

I wondered how much of it had been my fault. "Help me," she'd said. I wondered if it would have made any difference if we really had talked, if I'd tried to understand it and had had the guts to try and work it out. But I'd had to be one *muy* tough *hombre*. I'd had to let her walk out that night and I'd had to bury the ache in whisky and the job and other women and not once even ask anybody if she were alive or dead.

And now there she was on the floor like the armful of kindling after somebody'd tripped.

It had happened right outside. It didn't take Dashiell

Hammett to figure that much of it without going down. She'd come in the sports car I'd heard, fast, screeching her rubber along the gutter. And then the second car had stopped, the bigger one, probably right behind her, and someone had caught her between third and home and had poked it into her ribs. Here, smack in the middle of Fannin's own ball park.

So whatever kind of mess she'd been in, she'd been coming to me. And then she'd let go without telling me who did it because she'd known she didn't have too many words left and it had seemed more important to her to talk about something else.

But she'd been coming here in the first place because she'd thought she needed me. I kept looking at her, standing there. I'd been as much help as a ruptured aorta. So now all I could do was find out what had happened; and maybe also find out some of the things I should have learned about her a long time before, the things that might have made everything different.

All right, I said, I'll do that, yes. And then I said I was sorry. Cathy, I said. Baby, I . . .

I made myself come out of it. Cop, I said. Be cop again, Fannin. Who did it, cop? I lifted the phone.

It was dead. I took the directory and looked up Kline, Sally. There were two of them. One of them lived on 200th Street. I dialed the one in Greenwich Village.

She must have been poised over it like a kitten at a wounded housefly. The first ring didn't even finish. And then she didn't give me time to say hello.

"Who . . . who is it?"

"Easy," I said, "Fannin."

"Oh, thank heaven! Are you drunk, Mr. Fannin? Is that it? Every time I call you— Oh, please don't be drunk, Mr. Fannin."

"I'll talk now."

"It's Cathy, Mr. Fannin. It's those two boys she went away with yesterday, I think. Those hoodlum ones. Oh, Lord, I told her she'd get into trouble. And the one who's out there watching the house. I don't know if he's one of them or somebody else, but he goes away and then he comes back, it's been all night now, and then the phone keeps ringing and when I pick it up there's nobody there, and—"

I pulled out the plug. She was dialing me every channel on the set. "Look," I said, "I'll come down. Are you in any trouble yourself?"

"Oh, thank heaven. No, I don't think so. I don't know. But I'm scared, Mr. Fannin. That one outside, just standing there. In the alley across the street. I can see his shadow from the window. And I don't know what to do. I wanted to call you earlier. I thought you would be better than the police, but then I didn't know whether I should or not because you're not married to her anymore, but I couldn't think of anything else, and . . . can you do something, Mr. Fannin? Do you think you can?"

"What's your apartment number?"

"Five. We're on the top floor in front."

"Your lights on or off?"

"I've got the bedroom lamp on, Mr. Fannin. But not the ones you can see from the street, if that's what you mean. That's how I can see him. He was there when I came in—that was about eleven—but he must think I'm in bed now. I can look out through the blinds in the dark."

"Keep it that way. Don't put on any extra lights when I ring."

"But won't he see you come in?"

"There's a front apartment below yours?"

"Yes, but—"

"What number?"

"Three, I think. Yes."

"All right."

"But what are you—?"

"Never mind that now. Look, I'll be thirty minutes, more likely forty. You sit tight and keep your door locked. I mean that."

"Gosh, Mr. Fannin, you make it sound so—"

"Never mind how I make it sound." I wanted her to stay edgy and cautious until I got there. The duck outside seemed a pretty good bet to be watching for Cathy, but I didn't know whether Sally Kline might be in any danger from whoever else was involved in it. Whatever in hell it was.

"All right," she told me hesitantly.

I didn't tell her about Cathy. She did not sound like the first girl you'd pick to share a rooftop with when the dam broke. "Sort the laundry or something," I said again.

"All right, Mr. Fannin."

I hung it up. The alarm clock said 3:49. Fifteen minutes. Maybe only ten. That would have been the time to get downstairs, when Cathy had first buzzed. So I'd sat here thinking it was some lush or other. Now I wasn't going to find anything outside but frustrated mosquitoes who'd missed the last open window.

I had to ease her leg aside to get through the door.

There were stains along the floor in the hall, still wet. There were prints of her hand on the wall where she had had to brace herself. None of it looked real. It never does. It always looks like a promotion stunt for a cheap horror film where you follow the painted gore across the lobby to the ticket office. I went down the steps and out.

No one was around. I hadn't been expecting a B.P.O.E. convention.

There was a red MG at the curb with the keys in the ignition, but the blood did not lead to it. It went off at an angle to the edge of the sidewalk about a dozen feet behind it. To where the second car I'd heard had probably pulled in behind her.

There had been a rush of blood when the knife had come out. It had slowed quickly but you could have painted a country firehouse with what had spilled in those first seconds. If she'd fallen it must have been to her hands and knees, because it had hardly stained her coat.

It was as easy to read as a scrawl in a latrine. It just made you sicker.

She'd been in a jam or she wouldn't have been coming here, but she hadn't thought the trouble was the kind you can get dead over. She'd seen the second car and she'd known the person driving it. She'd gotten out of the MG and walked back to talk things over with whoever it was. The poor kid had walked right into it.

I tried to map the rest of it. She must have hung there a minute, long enough for the killer to decide she was dead or dying before he gunned off. Or had he seen her get up and start for my door first? Had he seen that and been just too gutless to go for her a second time?

I hoped that was it. I hoped he had seen her make the door and was having to sweat over whether she'd managed to tell me what it said on his dogtags. Oh, yeah. I hoped he was sweating over that enough so he figured he would have to get me next. I hoped he would try that, the son of a bitch.

Yes, I said, try that. Come on, you son of a bitch.

I was standing there in the empty street. Probably I looked like the neighborhood drunk. I must have, because the drunk from the next neighborhood pegged me for a brother the second he reeled around the corner. He let out a bellow like he'd found out what happened to Amelia Earhart and started circling the sidewalk for a landing, coming on full throttle. I went back to the MG and took out the keys. There was a celluloid case on the steering rod which said the car belonged to an

Adam Moss of West 113th Street. I left that where it was, pocketed the keys and caught the drunk by the shoulders before he nose-dived the sixty or eighty feet to his shoe tops.

"Buddy," he said. "Frien'. Customer. You wanna buy a polishy? Sure, you wanna buy a polishy." He was about fifty. He had gray hair cropped short and he was still very well dressed in spite of the two quarts he'd spilled on his tie. It was an expensive tie and there were probably two maids and a butler watching anxiously for him with a light in the window. "No policy," I said. "Be nice and sleep it off in your own gutter, huh?"

There was no point in asking him if he'd seen anything. He was too far gone. He wouldn't be seeing anything but hideous pink snakes.

"Extra speshal polishy," he insisted. "New kind." I would have let him go but it would have been like letting go of a piano from high up. "New polishy. Group shuishide plan. Why die wish strangers when you can die wish friends? We pick time, plaish, monuments. Monuments won't wilt, won't shrink, won't shiver, Guar'raranteed. Painlish and inshtant death. Torture clause—"

I caught him off balance and stepped away when the sidewalk wasn't tilted. I'd tricked him. He hung there on a cord. "You hate me," he decided then. "Jush how long have you hated me? When did it start? Jush tell me when it started?"

I left that one for his head doctor. He'd have one at about forty bucks a session. The hall had not gotten any prettier but I'd have to leave that, too, for the cops who didn't make forty bucks in two days. I went upstairs and inside.

She did not have a purse. There was eighty-six cents in change in one of the pockets of her coat, plus a lipstick and a tiny chain with three keys. Two of the keys would be for the place on Perry Street, one for the main entrance and the other for the apartment. The third was for a mailbox lock.

Her wallet was in her other pocket. She had twenty-four dollars in bills and an uncashed paycheck from the publishing house. There was a driver's license still made out to Mrs. Catherine Fannin, a beat-up birth certificate for Catherine June Hawes, female, and a single ticket for Row E at the Cherry Lane Theater dated for a week from that night. There were folded sales slips from Bloomingdale's and Saks Fifth Avenue and two deposit slips from her bank for small amounts. These said Catherine Hawes. There was a snapshot of me.

I left everything. I went into the bathroom. I washed quickly, scrubbing the blood from my hands, shaved fast, brushed my teeth. I went into the bedroom, took off the G.I. slacks, changed into a tan suit. I took the modified sportsman's Luger out of the bottom dresser drawer, removed it from its pocket holster, checked it, put it back in the sheath, clipped the whole thing over my belt and into my right rear pocket. I called Dan Abraham.

It rang three times. His wife took it.

"Sorry," I said. "Wake him for me, will you, Helen?"

"Harry?"

"Yes."

"Must I?"

"Yes."

There was a minute and then I could hear him groaning. He was an old Army friend and the only P.I. in town I trusted enough to ring in on it. We worked with each other from time to time when one or the other of us had a job too big to handle alone. He was still making unhappy noises when he found the mouthpiece.

"It isn't bad enough that I'm in the racket myself," he said. "I've got to have friends in it, too. Why don't we take up something where they let you sleep, Harry? Maybe I'll try out for concert violinist someplace. You know anybody needs a good concert violinist who can move to his left? How about Kansas City? Sure. Hell, they got holes all over the infield—"

"Dan, I've got a dead one."

He took his head out of the quilt then. "Yeah? You getting trigger-happy in your old age or did somebody dump it on your doorstep?"

"Doorstep is close enough. It's Cathy, Dan."

"Oh, no, Harry—"

I could hear him telling Helen. We had spent ten or a dozen evenings together the year before. I heard Helen cry out.

"Listen, Dan—"

"Right here. Where are you?"

"Home. Look, I'm going out on it. The girl she'd been living with just called me, worried about her. That's all I've got."

"You want me to take it from over there?"

"Right. Everything'll be just the way it happened. Roughly 3:30, give or take five. Somebody knifed her on the street but she made it up. Give me an hour or so and then try to get Nate Brannigan at Homicide. Rouse him up if he's off, his home number's in the book on my desk. He'll ride with me longer than most. I'll call you when I get a chance. Up till then you don't know where I am."

"You haven't told me anyhow."

"And, Dan, if you see anything that doesn't look kosher, you might square it away before they start pulling up the floor boards."

"Harry, you haven't been seeing her lately?"

I didn't answer him. He knew better than that.

"Delete that," he said then. "Be on my way in six minutes. You going to leave it open?"

"I'll stick an extra set of keys under the mat in the outside hall."

"Right. And Harry—"

"Yeah?"

"I'm sorry, fella. If there's anything else you want me to do? Or Helen maybe—"

"Thanks, Dan. Nothing. I'll leave the lights on. You'll trip over her if you're not looking."

I cradled it, went back into the living room, glanced at everything except Cathy. The two bourbons I'd poured were still sitting on the stand next to the chair. It would be a dumb sort of thing to have to explain, pouring one of them for an unidentified female sot who took five or seven minutes getting up the stairs and then turned out dead. I carried them into the kitchen, dumped them, washed the glasses. The bottle was still out but the cops would find that quick enough anyhow.

I took the extra set of keys out of the desk. It had been Cathy's set. I looked at her then, thinking it was probably for the last time. It was all there again. I bit down hard on it and went out.

It followed me down. She'd be stiff before Dan got there. I was thinking about that and I was outside before I remembered I was holding the extra keys. I told myself to quit it. I turned back, opened the outside door and edged the two keys under the rubber.

It was twenty-five minutes since I'd spoken to Sally Kline. It would probably take the night man ten more to unshuffle my Chevy from the loft in the garage around the corner, and I did not see a cab. I had promised the girl I'd be there in forty. I wondered if Mr. Adam Moss of West 113th Street would mind if I borrowed the MG. I wondered who Mr. Adam Moss was. I expected to find out soon.

I was just contorting my hundred and ninety-seven pounds below the low wheel when she came around the corner. I got out again, fast, because this time it wasn't any drunk's mating call I heard. The cry was sick with agony or horror or both.

She started to run toward me. She was an old woman and her hair was disheveled and it didn't matter to her that her housecoat was flapping loose from the flimsy white nightgown she wore under it. She lost a slipper but she couldn't bend for it, not with what she was carrying pressed against her breast.

It was swaddled in a white blanket. The blanket had blood on it.

I jerked open the door on the sidewalk side of the MG. "Here!" I told her. "Quick!"

"Oh, thank the Lord, thank the Lord! Any hospital, any hospital at all. She fell out of the window. On the fourth floor. She—"

There was no movement in the blanket, no sound. "She *what?*"

The woman had started to get into the car. "Why, she's always out there at night," she said. "She was just playing. She—"

I had taken her by the elbow. I eased her around firmly before she could get seated and lifted a corner of the blanket. The cat was an expensive angora. Its head was bloodied up some but it had a good seven or eight other lives ahead of it. I kept propelling the woman around until I could swing the door shut. Then I ducked around to the other side of the car.

"But—" The woman was gaping at me. "You mean you won't—" She was sputtering. I choked the car and she was shocked. When I released the handbrake she was outraged.

New York at night. You think *anybody* sleeps? The loonies in Bellevue, maybe they sleep.

The woman stuck her tongue out at me. "Get a rickshaw at the corner, lady," I told her. I heard the cat yowl once and then saw it racing along the sidewalk as I pulled out. I went over to Second Avenue and straight down.

Around midtown I remembered Cathy's mother and sister.

That did not make the night any better. Someone was going to have to tell them and I didn't much want it to be any tactful plainclothes cop working overtime with a hangover.

I liked them both. Mrs. Hawes was over sixty and stone deaf. She had taken to me and had been broken up when things did not work out for us. She had not understood Cathy, but then who had?

Estelle was thirty-six or so. She taught grammar school and you wouldn't mistake her for Moll Flanders in the darkest bedroom in town. She wore steel-rimmed glasses and straight plain dresses that had gone out with the N.R.A. I had always suspected that buried under that Iowa-spinster get-up she had a shape something like Cathy's, but she did as much with it as a baker does with last Tuesday's bagels. It was as if she had given up all hope of ever getting a man and did not much care. Or probably she was frigid and had found that out somewhere along the line and did not care about that either. But she worried about Cathy and I was not ecstatic knowing I would have to break it to her and the old woman.

I cut across 14th and then down again. I left the MG in front of a Sanitary Valet shop on 11th, just off Seventh Avenue. It was 4:28. I walked the single short block down to Perry and then the block and a half across. I walked jauntily, tossing my keys as if I made book for every widow in the neighborhood. I did not see anyone to have to convince, however, either on the street or in the alley across from Sally Kline's number. There were no lighted windows in her building, a three-story brownstone.

I rang five, where the card said *Kline—Hawes*. I had intended to ring three at the same time, so that the light would go on in another front apartment, but with no one outside I didn't bother. I glanced at my watch again. I was a half-minute overdue on my promise.

I was about to ring again when the hall door finally buzzed.

I went in. There was a wide stairway that was well carpeted and softly lighted and I climbed the two flights. The place was as quiet as a prairie in the moonlight. I saw Five ahead of me at the front end of the top corridor and I went down and tapped on the door.

Nothing happened. I waited six or eight seconds, tapped again, then tried the handle.

It turned. I eased the door inward several inches, seeing only darkness. I had just decided to unsheath the Luger when someone else's gun nosed through the crack and parked itself cordially against my navel.

CHAPTER 5

It was not a very nice gun. It was home-made, of the sort that enterprising young high-school boys put together in machine shops when teacher is preoccupied with the bottle in the cloakroom. I stared at it, giving it about C-minus for sloppy craftsmanship.

There was a voice behind it somewhere. "Okay, Jack," it told me. "Inside."

The voice was not particularly nice either, nor was it Sally Kline's. Hormones, my dear Watson. Two sexes, don't you know? Elementary. Sure. So meanwhile what do we do now?

We close the door. Because whoever he was, Zip-Gun was not much of a thinker. The rod and the fist holding it were poked out at an angle through the eight-inch crack like roses from a bashful admirer. And my own hand was still on the knob.

There was not much noise, just a quick muted cracking. A broken ulna generally makes that kind of sound. Or maybe it was the radius that went. One of those insignificant bones about two inches above the wrist.

The gun clattered to the floor without going off. I'd heaved myself to the side, but I hadn't seriously expected it to fire. Jam your wrist into a vise and your fingers open, they don't close on any triggers.

My friend had let out a sickening gasp. He let out a louder one when I grabbed the wrist. It made a nifty fulcrum, bent that way. I jerked him forward and shouldered the door inward at the same time, then swung the arm in a fast arc so that his body followed it around. I could feel the cracked end of the bone through the skin when I pressed the arm up between his shoulderblades.

"You may take one giant step," I told him then. He didn't want to so I shoved him. My foot got in his way and the poor slob fell on his face into the room. He lay there clutching the break and sucking air through his teeth like the little choo-choo that couldn't.

I let him lie for a minute. They'd be running off the next few heats without him.

I picked up the zip-gun. It was taped together. I broke it apart, dropped the handle section onto a chair just inside the doorway, slipped the lethal end of it into my pocket. The barrel had been cut from an automobile aerial, most of which are perfectly chambered for .22's. Detroit ingenuity. I found a lamp switch and shed a little light on the subject.

I was in the living room. It was an ordinary middle-class furnished apartment. Grand Rapids had been nuts about it once. Nothing had been changed in it since the *Titanic* went down and wouldn't be until it came up again. Off to the left there was a closed door with a crack of light under it and that was the only element of the décor which interested me.

My welcoming committee was still chewing a corner of the carpet. He made a feeble effort to get to his feet when I closed the door to the hall. I caught him by the back of his collar and helped him along.

"No more," he said. "Damn, Jack, no more."

"Mr. Jack to you." I could have wheeled him around like a pushcart by latching onto the wrist again, but I decided it would be easier with the Luger. "This one's glued together nicer than yours," I told him. "How about you and me taking a stroll to that bedroom, huh, doll?"

He looked at me with glassy black eyes that were either out of focus from too many needles or else were naturally bleary. Anyhow they hadn't gotten their dim look from poring over books. He was a punk as I had thought, maybe a year or two past twenty, narrow-jawed with a lot of greasy black hair and a mustache like an eraser smudge. If the leather jacket was in hock he'd have it back as soon as he jimmied his next pay phone. He said nothing and his breath was still coming hard.

"Move," I told him.

He was no bigger than he had felt when I'd handled him in the darkness. He shuffled forward without much enthusiasm, protecting the wrist as if he thought I might not let him have his share when mealtime came around. When he got to the door he stopped again.

"You want the other one, too? You want it so you can't bat from either side of the plate?"

He opened it. I elbowed him in but he didn't go anxiously. He was hurting but he was also scared now. Nobody told me why. Bright Harry. I just had to look at the girl who would be Sally Kline.

She was a pretty girl. She was a redhead, with freckles and green eyes, and she had lovely high breasts. I could see clearly how lovely they were, because Junior hadn't bothered to cover them up when he'd come out to answer the door.

She was tied into a chair with her arms drawn back and locked behind it. There was a gag over her mouth that was probably her last matching nylon. She was wearing slacks the color of crème de menthe and she had on a yellow pullover blouse which Junior had ripped down the front and left hanging open. Her torn brassière was on the floor.

The cigarette Junior'd been puffing for something more than the simple joy of fine tobacco was still burning in an ashtray near her.

Junior's head was tilted around and he was looking at me now. He hadn't moved away from the muzzle of the Luger but you could see from the quiver in the line of his jaw that he guessed the latrine didn't quite pass inspection. You could also see from the way his shoulders were drawn up that he knew damned well he was about to get a scolding.

Now a Luger does not have a particularly heavy barrel, but you do the best you can. The front sight helps some. I laid his skull open to the bone with the first one and then I gave him two more, which made one for each of the dirty black burns on the upper curve of the girl's left breast. He was already going down when the second one landed. The third one was a knee in the neck to get him out of the way of the decent folk as he fell.

The girl's eyes were wide and she was still frightened. The knot in the stocking came apart quickly and her head drew up and back and she sucked in air. I untied the belt from around her wrists.

Her hands went to her face. For a minute she sat forward, breathing deeply. Then she began to sob.

Junior was going to nap until Mommy kissed him and brushed back his precious locks. I put the Luger away and went into the john. There were a couple of washcloths on a rack and I held one of them under the warm water, then wrung it out.

"Easy," I told her then. Her head was on the back rest of the chair now and her arms were limp at her sides. She was still inhaling deeply and her eyes were closed. I stood next to her and pressed the wet cloth across the upper part of her breast, cupping it there but not rubbing it. Most of the ash came away.

I went back and found some Unguentine. She sat there while I coated the burns with a heavy film. I lifted a torn half of her blouse and tried to drape it across her. I kept running out of material.

She'd stopped crying. She lifted the other half of the blouse herself, holding it and looking down, and then she dropped it again.

"I guess it doesn't much matter, does it?"

I showed her my best don't-you-fret-about-old-Uncle-Silas grin. "You feel all right?"

"You *are* Mr. Fannin?"

"Harry," I told her.

"I thought—"She looked at Junior, then shook her head. "The bell rang and I thought it was you. About fifteen minutes ago. I looked down and I didn't see anybody outside. I was just so darned scared by then that I—I went to the door and asked if it was you and he said yes. And then he put his gun against my stomach and I—" Her breath caught. "Oh, I'm so glad you came. I was—"

The butt end of Junior's smoke was still burning. I crushed it out, then went and sat on the bed.

"Will there be . . . will the scars last long?"

"A few months," I told her. A generous racketeer had let me smell a six-bit panatela along the cheekbone once. He had been going for the eye so I'd still consider myself the big winner if I was seeing a mark every time I shaved. But it had faded out.

"He put that gag on when I rang the bell?"

"Yes."

"You tell him what he was trying to find out before that?"

"I couldn't. I don't know where she is, Mr. Fannin. Harry. I tried to tell him I haven't seen her since the day before yesterday. But he wouldn't believe me. He kept standing there and puffing on that cigarette until it would glow and then he'd put his hand over my mouth so I couldn't scream and—"

I waited for her. She bit her lip, turning her head away. The flap of her blouse had fallen away again but she did not seem aware of it. Part of her had gotten a suntan someplace.

"I don't know *where* she is. That's why I called you. She told me she was going away with him and Duke, the one she's been seeing, and that was Tuesday and I—"

"You mean a friend of this one's?"

"Duke something, yes. And then when Eddie came in he said something about them getting split up—something about some kind of 'job,' I don't know what he meant—and—"

I had gone across and put my hand on her shoulder. "Sally, listen, can we start with the cast of characters maybe? Eddie is this throw rug on the floor here?"

"I'm sorry. Yes. It's Bogardus or something like that. And his friend's name is Duke. Duke Sabatini. Duke's the one Cathy was going out with. She brought them up here one night, it was about two weeks ago. I didn't like them and I told her so then, Mr. Fan—Harry. Duke is older, maybe Cathy's or my age, and he's handsome, but he still looks like one of those horrible kids you see all over. I wanted to hide my pocketbook while they were here. I told her she'd get into trouble hanging around with them but Cathy just laughed. You know how she is, never taking anything seriously, always running around after somebody new and—"

She had been looking at me. She didn't turn away. "I'm sorry."

"Tell it the way you want to."

"Have you—may I have a cigarette?"

I gave her one. Her hands trembled a little when she took the light. She took a long drag and then stared at the cigarette.

"I don't know what it is," she went on. "It's as if—well, as if she's sick in some ways. Lord knows, every girl who gets to be old enough starts sleeping around a little. But golly, you discriminate about it, you wait to see how it works out with someone, if it's going to be a good thing. Oh, sure, sometimes you get a little tight and you crawl into bed the first night, that can happen too, but you don't make a habit of it. You do it and then you hate yourself for it, and so you're all the more careful the next time, or at least most girls are that way. Lord knows we talk about it enough. But Cathy always just laughs. It's as if she has to have adventures all the time—new experiences, whatever you want to call them. She goes out to the places down here where the Village crowd hangs out, bars mostly, and—well, sometimes three or four nights a week she doesn't come home at all except to change to go to work in the morning. And then sometimes she stops. Sometimes she won't go out for two or three weeks, not once, just sitting here all evening and reading or something. Then it starts again. It isn't anything that shocks me—I don't mean it that way—but it seems like such a waste. I mean she's so bright and she can be so good to be with, I always think it's such a shame that she doesn't get married—

"I keep forgetting," she said then. "I suppose this is the same kind of thing that happened when she *was* married."

She had looked away awkwardly, but when she went on with it she was still off on the same side road. I was going to have to tell her pretty soon that it was a dead end.

"Gee, I've, well . . . I asked her about you a dozen times, but she won't ever say anything. She changes the subject every time, but I can see she's still in love with you. It's all over her face when she mentions your name. But if I ask her why you don't try it again or something she—"

"Sally, you were telling me about Junior here. And somebody named Duke."

"I'm sorry, Harry, I am. I guess it's just seeing you this way after knowing about you for so long, and being worried about Cathy. I suppose I sort of wish you and she would get together again. Probably I'm butting in, but Cathy's so good, basically, that if there was only someone who could understand her and try to help—"

"Sally—"

I had wanted to get the story first, and maybe get her out of there, too. Once upon a time I had also wanted to be Johnny Ringo or Wild Bill Hickok and ride a big white mare. Life is rough.

"Cathy's dead, Sally."

She didn't react, not for the first few seconds. She looked at me as if she hadn't heard what I'd said. The corners of her mouth twitched. Then her face melted and she began to shake.

"Oh, no! No!"

She started to bawl. I walked across the room and held her by the shoulder. It took a couple of minutes.

"What happened? Oh, it can't be true, it—"

I gave her the *Reader's Digest* version. There were tears on her face and she kept shaking her head. And then she jumped up and ran to where the guy named Eddie was lying. She had soft ballet slippers on. She kicked him eight or ten times in the small of the back. I supposed the kicks would have cracked an egg if he'd had one with him. She kept saying, "I told her not to go with them, I told her, I told her!"

It didn't last long. I was standing next to her when it finished and she turned and fell against me with her head on my chest. I held her until that finished also.

"Tell me now," I said. "Just let me know what you can and then I'll get you out of here for a day or two."

"Yes," she said raggedly. "All right." She found the chair again. I gave her another cigarette and took one myself.

"Whatever you can think of. Don't skip anything."

"There isn't much, I'm afraid." She was staring at the burns and her voice was tiny and mechanical. "I think I said they came up here with her one evening about two weeks ago. Cathy was with Duke. She didn't bring Eddie along as a date for me or anything, he was just with them. Anyhow I was going out. They were gone when I came back, but I told Cathy the next morning I didn't like them. They were—well, you can see what this one looks like. Maybe they think it's clever to talk that way, as if everybody owes them something. I couldn't understand what Cathy was doing with them. All she'd say was that she thought they were amusing. Amusing! And now she's . . ."

She dragged on her smoke. She was all right, however. "Anyhow I forgot about it after that, until the other night when she said she was going with them someplace for a day or two. She said she'd told the office that she had to leave town but that she'd be back yesterday. And then she said something about an experiment—that was the word she used—but she wouldn't tell me what. She kept smiling about it all evening, so that I thought maybe she was a little drunk, but she wasn't. I was upset about it, Harry. I tried to make her tell me, but the only other thing she'd say was something strange, about ethics. How she was going to prove to herself that nothing really mattered at all. I thought about it all the time she was gone. She'd gone away with boys other times, on weekends or things, but this time I kept imagining all sorts of things. And then when she wasn't back when I got home from work tonight I got scared. I had a date but I called home a couple of times to see if she was in. I came back early, deliberately, and when I did I noticed Eddie across the street. I didn't recognize him, not until he came up. The phone rang a few times too, and there was never anybody there. I guess he must have gone someplace and called. I thought about calling you right away but I didn't know whether you'd—Oh, dear Lord, maybe if I'd called you earlier it wouldn't have happened, maybe she'd still be—"

She came apart again. I left her alone with it this time, going into the john. There was a galvanized pail under the sink and I held it under a bathtub faucet until it was a third filled. There was a white blouse over a wire hanger on the shower nozzle. I'd known a girl once who was crazy about white blouses. I'd bought her this one.

Sally was watching me when I came out. Her eyes were raw.

"I'm going to wake up Lefty here," I said. "I'll wait until you put something on."

She looked down at herself as if she had forgotten about the ripped blouse. I supposed she had. "It doesn't hurt now," she said vaguely.

"I'd put some cotton over them, maybe. You won't need a doctor."

She had picked up the brassière from the floor. She walked past me to a dresser and took out a laundered shirt the shade of freshly minted pennies. She held the blouse and the brassière in her hand for a minute, staring at them with her back turned as if she wasn't sure just what they were for, and then she set them both down. I started to move toward her when her hands came around to the back of her slacks and jerked out the tails of the torn blouse she was wearing. The blouse dropped into a heap on the floor before I made it across so I stopped again. Her hands were little fists opening and closing at her sides when she turned around naked from the waist and stared at me.

"It's something, isn't it?" she said. "All the things you do, the way sex is the most important part of half of them. Cathy showed me your picture once or twice and I used to think, Lord, she cheated on a man like that, and if I had him and he was half the man she said he was I'd never let myself get out of his sight. I even used to have fantasies about it once in a while, how with somebody like you it *would* be one of those first night things but it would be one that would last. And then something like this happens and I sit here half undressed in front of you for twenty minutes and it doesn't mean anything at all, not one goddam thing because Cathy's dead and—"

Her mouth was twisted and her breasts rose once as a sob racked her body. There was a rip in the paper of my cigarette. I stood there wondering just what the hell you could do about that while she ran with her shirt and brassière into the bathroom and shut the door.

CHAPTER 6

The punk named Eddie Bogardus groaned almost sadly when I dumped the bucket on his head. Probably I'd busted in on the middle of his favorite Bach cantata. His greasy black curls fell into his eyes when he shook himself.

He came out of it but his co-ordination was all loused up. He started to reach for the back of his skull with his right hand, then fell forward again and clutched the break. He lay there with his teeth grinding. Finally he looked up at me.

"All right, Bogardus, let's have it."

"Bananas, Jack, I gotta get a doctor. You gotta get me to a doctor."

I sauntered over to Sally's chair and sat down. I got comfortable. I grinned at him.

"Look, now, look, it's all out o' shape. If I don't get to a—"

"We'll do it make-believe, Bogardus, how about that? You must be the ailing prince and I must be the royal physician. Won't that be fun?"

He didn't dig games much. He sucked in his breath with his lips drawn back and he didn't answer.

"Talk. All of it."

"Can I sit up?"

I nodded. He built himself up against the bed, working with the weight on his good arm, and then leaned there with his head back. Sweat had broken out on his boyish face with the effort. He breathed deeply three or four times, then let his head fall against his chest. He did not look at me.

"What did you want here, punk? Let's start there."

"The broad," he muttered grudgingly. "I dint mean to rough up the other one, the redhead. Honest, Jack. All I want is my split. I got a right to my split."

"What split? All right, you and Duke pulled something. What?"

He wet his lips. "You a cop?"

"I got the milk route here. Talk, punk."

He was studying me blankly. The next expression would be the one that was supposed to tell me he knew his rights. I leaned forward.

"Look, punk, you might have some luck. You might even last long enough to get your full growth."

"Okay, okay, I don't want no more."

"Your split of what?"

"We pulled a job yesterday. Big stuff. We—"

Sally came out and he let it hang there while he looked at her. She wasn't the same girl he'd had on that raw edge a while back. They never are when they can get five minutes in front of a mirror. She hadn't done much with the tired lines around her eyes, however. She looked at me as if she wanted to say something and then she changed her mind. I waited until she went to a chair.

"Whenever you feel up to it, Bogardus," I said then. "What kind of big stuff? What about the girl? You keep making me ask questions, I'll ask some hard ones."

"Okay, I tole ya. This shirt factory up in Troy. The payroll. They deliver from an armored car, half a month's loot on the first and the fifteenth. The broad was Duke's brainstorm, not mine. I knew she'd mess it up, but the minute Duke gets hot on a broad you can't make him see nothin'. She drove. I kept tellin' Duke she'd—"

"Bogardus, I'm slow. Even when my old man helps me with the homework it ain't right. Are you trying to tell me that Cathy Hawes drove the car while you and Sabatini pulled a heist on an armored truck?"

"Not on the tin truck, no. Not them bananas. You think we're nuts? Hell, we had it figured. They dump the loot at one-thirty on the button. There's only one guard from the factory, see? He comes out and gets it, and then the tin truck goes off again. The guard's got to bring it back upstairs in this freight elevator. Sometimes the elevator goes back up while he's pick-ing up the bag, see? There's always a minute, maybe two, but me an' Duke had it lined up even better. Duke's cousin works in the joint. He's the one who lined it up. He fixes it so he's on the second floor when the guard goes down, and then he pushes the button for the elevator to come back up. When he gets it on the second he presses for it to keep on going up and stop on all the floors. It's one of them self-service things and it's slow. By the time it goes up to six and the guard can get it back down, we got three, four extra minutes. We wait until after the truck pulls out and then we hit. Bananas, you think we'd mess with a tommy gun behind all that tin plate?"

"Come on, come on, the girl. What about Catherine Hawes?"

"She's in the car. We pull in about twenty-nine minutes after one, see? Duke's cousin has it down sharp. Duke's drivin' with the broad next to him and I'm in the back. Duke leaves the motor running and gets out and switches places with the broad. The truck comes by while we're makin' the switch. Hell, it don't look like nothin'. Anyhow they been deliverin' the same way for years, nothin's ever happened. We sit there for the min-ute and the guard comes out. He's an old guy. The guards on the truck don't even get out, just open up and hand it to him. He stands there gabbin', maybe another minute, and then the truck pulls out. That's when the broad drives up. The truck turns the corner a block away, so it's already gone when we hit the freight door. Duke an' me is out and runnin' while the old guy is still waitin' for the elevator. But then the fruity old jerk starts to give us trouble. There's this wooden loading platform that we got to jump on, and he hears us. He turned around the first damn thing, he's goin' for his gun. But there's no shootin'. We're right on him, see? Duke clobbers him and grabs the dough. It's supposed to be forty, forty-one grand, accordin' to what Duke's cousin tole us. And then the damned broad don't wait for me. Duke jumps down and makes the car and I fall. I tripped on a damned plank and went on my kisser, and when I look up the damned bananas are sprayin' gravel in my face and goin' off with the loot faster 'n hell."

He stopped. When he did I heard an alarm clock ticking. It was the first time I'd heard it. Observant Fannin, the astute private eye. I, eye. Ask me what the bedroom looked like and I'll tell you it had some walls.

I was trying to see her driving the car. For the experience. I looked at Sally Kline. She was staring at the Castro they'd squeezed in against a far wall. They could squeeze it out again.

"Tell me the rest," I said.

"There ain't no more. The bananas leave me to take the rap. But I get a break. Some dame in a Caddy is pulling up just as I start to run. She's still got her keys in her hand and I grab 'em and shove her the hell out of the way and take the Cad. Me an' Duke had this other car stashed, see? That was the thing, we'd switch cars and beat it out of town easy. But I donno the town so good and when I get to the place where the other heap is, Duke and the broad is already there an' gone. I kept the Cad as far as Albany and then dumped it and swiped a Imperial."

"What time did you get back here?"

"Five, maybe. I couldn't see pushin' it, not in a stolen heap."

"Then what?"

"What the hell you think? I start lookin' for the rat."

"Where?"

"Where he lives. The joints he hangs out. Here."

"Where?"

He gave me addresses. Nice addresses, if you were a pander or a two-bit hustler. You'd be sure to tuck a picture of your mother in your locket when you went down there.

"Where's he live?"

"This hotel on lower Bleecker. The Watling. But he ain't gonna show up there again. All right, I tole ya. How about a smoke now, Jack?"

I threw him one. He picked it up with his left hand and put it where you use those things and looked at me.

"You'll get a match when I get the rest of it."

"What else? Damn, I tole ya the whole thing."

"How did you get her into it? What did Duke have on her?"

"Have on her? Bananas. Don't make me laugh, will ya? He dint have nothin' on her, not on that one. The minute she got wise that we were onto somethin' she started squealin' she wanted in. Hell, you couldn't keep her out of it."

"Tell me."

"Tell ya what?"

"You want to Indian wrestle, Bogardus? I'll give you the edge, my left hand against your right."

"Okay, okay, just tell me what you wanna—"

"Where'd Duke meet her? How'd she get into it?"

I was leaning forward. I wasn't sure whether I was going to hit him on principle or just throw up. I could feel Sally watching.

"Harry?"

"Yeah?"

"Do you really want to hear it? Does it make any difference now?"

"Sure," Bogardus said, "why all the interest anyhow? What is she, your ex-piece or somethin'?"

It's nice when other people make your decisions for you. The back of my hand took him across the jaw and the cigarette shot out of his mouth like something researched by Wernher von Braun. He let out a yelp like an unpaid madam.

I was standing there. Maybe Sally was right, maybe there was no point in finding out how she'd gotten into it. Maybe there was no point in breathing. Sometimes you wonder. I went back to my chair.

Bogardus was being a stretcher case again. He was huddled over the wrist like a monkey trying to make time with a football.

"You keep grinding your teeth like that, I'll sharpen a file in there."

"Okay, okay. But it's just like I tole you. She's just nuts, is all." He took a deep breath and sat up. I showed him another Camel.

"We met her in this bar," he said wearily, "maybe three weeks ago. Yeah, that's all, maybe three weeks. Duke was half bagged and he shot off his mouth some. He's always talkin' anyhow. He starts braggin' about jobs we pulled. The broad's eyes all lit up, for hell's sake. Duke took her to the hotel and he saw her a lot o' times after that. He said she wanted to go along on it. We was gonna do it alone, just leavin' the motor on while we was inside, but he said she could push the wheel until we switched cars. I tole him she'd probably chicken out but he said she wouldn't. Duke drove up from here in the morning. We had the second car goin' up, the one we stashed to switch to later. That one was stole, too, but it was fixed up, you know? We got there about noontime, maybe, an' we met Duke's cousin on his lunch hour. We put the car in the place we were supposed to an' then he helped us swipe another one for the job. He had it all lined up. The broad was scared while we were waitin'. She was all white, like. We killed an hour in this lunchroom and she dint eat nothin'. I tole Duke he shouldn't ought to let her drive but he said she'd be okay when it got movin'. I guess maybe she was, I donno. She pulled in by the freight door okay, and she waited okay, even when the old geezer saw us comin'. I donno whether it was her idea to pull out without waitin' for me or whether Duke tole her to. I donno nothin' else. Damn, Jack, what else do you want me to tell you? She's just a broad, is all. Just a broad wants some kicks."

I gave him the cigarette and lit it. "What was the setup for last night? For when you got back to New York?"

"Nothin'. We were gonna come down here, to this joint. We figured we'd get here before this other broad—dame—got home. We were gonna split the take, me and Duke and a corner for his cousin. Then I was gonna blow. I dint have no special plans."

"Not split for the girl?"

"Let Duke worry. He brung her in on it, not me. But she dint want none anyhow. Like I'm tellin' ya, she comes in on it for laughs. Different, she says. Just to see what it feels like. How you gonna figure broads anyhow?"

"She supposed to go somewhere with Duke?"

"Who knows? Duke was tryin' to talk her into it but she wouldn't say. But anyhow, we figured we didn't have to leave

New York. Hell, Troy's a hundred-sixty, a hundred-seventy miles up. Once we got clear this was as good a place as any."

"What kind of heap is the doctored one?"

"Chevy sedan. Fifty-six. Dark green."

"You know the plates?"

He shrugged.

"You call here before you came up?"

"Two, three times, yeah. I wanna see who's answerin'."

I looked at Sally. "Three calls?"

"I think so, yes."

"You ever hear of Harry Fannin?"

"Just when this here broad said the name. That you?"

"Ain't it been a pleasure?"

Bogardus grunted. I sucked on a knuckle, wondering who'd phoned me that way. There'd been that one anonymous call just before Sally's. Cathy herself maybe, checking to see if I was there before she came over? Or Duke? Duke would know more about her background than this clown did. If they'd gotten split up he might have called, decided she hadn't gotten there yet, then parked himself along the street to wait. It would have been a fair bet for him if he hadn't been able to find her anywhere else.

I sat there staring at Bogardus. He still looked like exactly what he was, a poolhall rumdum whose head would shrink in a light rain, and the trouble with his story was that you could believe it. You could see her doing it, see her getting just fed up enough with her Keats-spouting Village boyfriends to think that Duke might be exciting. Exciting. And what will we do *after* we give syphilis to all the natives, Mr. Columbus?

"Duke Sabatini," I said.

"Yeah."

"I suppose he's another rugged ninety-seven-pound terror just like you. What's he look like?"

"Taller 'n me."

"I suppose he's got the same greasy hair you pretty bastards put up in curlers every night, too. I suppose he's—"

"I don't put up my—"

"Shut up, scum. What's his cousin's name?"

"Sabatini. Just like him. Freddie Sabatini."

"What's Duke's first name?"

"Angelo. Hey, look, this thing hurts bad, Jack. Ain't I gonna get a doctor?"

I told him what he could do with the wrist. I supposed Angelo Sabatini would be a hundred miles off already. With a murder rap on his neck a punk like this one would be sprinting fast enough to make Roger Bannister look like a hitchhiker. It was Duke all right. All that cash in the balance, a girl like Cathy who probably started feeling guilty or scared when it was over—anything could have set it off. I'd find out the details after the cops picked him up. The cops. Sure, they'd get him sooner or later, but I wasn't going to be in on it. Hell no, Fannin would be home reading witty lines out of his *Bartlett's Quotations* and waiting for some potted dame to climb the stairs and fall into his lap for the big romp in the hay. You could set fire to the end of the bed and Fannin wouldn't smell smoke until morning.

Sally had come across to where I was pacing. Her hand was on my arm.

"Harry—now let me be the one to tell *you* to take it easy."

I didn't say anything because anything I would have said would not have had more than four letters in it. I picked up the phone and dialed my home number. Dan got it on the first ring.

"You called Brannigan yet?"

"Just about to. You said an hour. You onto anything?"

"Looks open and shut. Don't ask me how, but she rode along on a payroll heist up in Troy yesterday with two punks. Guy named Bogardus I got wrapped up, another one named Sabatini. Sabatini's the one who killed her. They—"

"*Killed* her!" Bogardus was staring up at me from the floor, slack-jawed. I ignored him.

"Evidently she got scared," I said. "She'd probably told the guy what I did for a living, and then she was probably just innocent enough to think she could go to me and promise him she wouldn't mention any names."

Dan did not say anything. Bogardus was still gaping like a six-year-old watching three of them sneak up on James Arness at once.

"I'm going to ice this joker I've got down here," I said. "When the badges get there just tell them I'll have it when I come. I've got a couple of stops to make first."

"Right. You got any line on where this Sabatini might have ducked to?"

"He's got forty thousand in his glove compartment."

"Makes it tough."

"Yeah. I'll see you in an hour or so. But listen—" I gave him Sally's address. "Tell them to pick up Bogardus here. Brannigan can put through a call on it. I'll leave a key, same as up there."

I put back the phone and turned to Eddie Bogardus. He screwed up his face. "Damn, Jack, you sure you got it figured straight? Duke wouldn't of killed the broad, not her. He was nuts about her. He even wanted to marry her an' all."

"He'd have a sweet honeymoon doing twenty for armed robbery."

"He still wouldn't of killed her, even if she was gonna rat on us. Hell, for all he knew I might of got caught and ratted before that. He could of just run and hid out. He had the loot, dint he?"

"Did he?"

He thought about that, sitting there against the bed like

Newton under the tree. After a while you could see it fall on him. Cathy had somehow managed to wind up holding all the coin. Duke hadn't knifed her to keep her from talking. Repossessing the forty thousand had been a better reason.

I had turned to Sally. "You know an Adam Moss, 113th Street?"

She'd been sitting with her hands in her lap like the little lost girl at the station house. It took a minute, then she frowned. "Not at all. Is he involved in it somehow?"

"Cathy was driving his car. He must be somebody she went to before she came to me."

"Funny, it's not a name she's ever mentioned."

"I'll check it. You have someplace you can stay a day or two?"

"Golly, you don't think there's going to be anymore—"

"Just until the other one's picked up. There might be loose ends."

"I guess I could call one of the girls from the office—"

"Do that," I said. It was 5:34. "Meanwhile I'll take care of the southpaw here. On your feet, Gomez."

"What're you gonna do? I thought you tole that guy to send the cops down?"

He was still hanging onto that leg of lamb at the end of his sleeve. It was beginning to look overcooked. I took him by the elbow and nudged him into the chair.

"Hey now, bananas, you said you'd get me a doctor. I got to get a splint on this or somethin'. Damn, Jack, it's—"

"You'll get a splint," I told him. "You're sitting on it. There tape in the bathroom, Sally?"

She went for it. Bogardus was squirming.

"Put your wrist on that armrest."

"What? Hey, you ain't gonna—"

I frowned at him, so he put the arm down. He did it the

69

way you'd set down nitroglycerin during an earth tremor. He clamped his jaws tight against the yell when I took hold of it, changed his mind and opened it again. The yell didn't come because I snapped the bone into place just then. That Bach cantata came back instead. He could hum it for the cops when he woke up. I took the tape from Sally and told her to make her call.

"Tell her you'll explain later," I said. "And scribble down the name and number for me, will you? And your office number if you think you might go to work."

"I won't go in."

I taped Sleeping Beauty into the chair, then picked up the stocking he had used to gag Sally and bound it around his mouth. I didn't want him rousing up any neighbors and convincing them he was the victim of foul play before the wagon got there. The stocking had a run in it anyhow. Sally got her friend out of bed after a wait. She wrote the name Judy Paulson and the address and number on a sheet of yellow tablet paper. I chewed a cigarette while she threw some stuff into a blue leather bag which might have been manufactured to carry manhole covers.

I looked around the bedroom. Furnished apartments. Toss your gear into the closet, come in to use the sack after the last bar closes and there's no place else to go. Live in one sometime. See if the place ever shows anymore outward trace of your personality than an iron lung.

Sally put her hand on my wrist. "I guess I didn't say it before. I'm sorry, Harry."

"Let's go," I said. Bogardus was wheezing with his head on his chest. I double checked the tape and the gag and then we locked the door. We went down the quiet stairway and I left the key under the rubber in the lower hall. The street was as hushed as a sickroom. We walked the block and a half to Seventh and then up to the MG. We were not talking.

Her girlfriend lived off Gramercy Park and I drove her over there. The car didn't make anymore noise than four flatulent drunks in a YMCA shower. If Adam Moss turned out to be a nice guy maybe I'd buy him a muffler.

She did not get out when I parked. You could see a few streaks of gray in the sky and a bird was acting moronic about it in the park. We were just sitting there when the couple turned the corner. The man looked as if he would have been willing to quit hours before. He kept telling Evelyn it was time to go home.

"My neck, home," Evelyn said. "I'm going up to the church and scream bloody murder—"

Maybe she went. We were under a street lamp. "There's something else I didn't say," Sally Kline told me. "Thanks."

"For what?"

"Just for coming. Are you going up to see the police now?"

"Somebody's got to tell Cathy's mother and sister. I thought I'd get it over with."

"Oh, Lord, I'd forgotten all about them—" My hands were together on the wheel and she put one of hers over them. "Would you like me to come along, Harry? If it might make it easier I'd—"

"You get some sleep. I'll call you later."

"Will you?"

"Yes."

She was turned toward me. She leaned across and kissed me on the cheek like a sister. I never had a sister so I turned around and looked at her, and then we weren't related anymore. Why do people do those things? People do all sorts of things. I once had a client worth seven and one-half million dollars and she used to do her laundry in the toilet bowl. So we sat there stuck together like two halves of a boiled potato with the water burned out of the pot. After a while she got out. I watched her until the door buzzed and I saw her open it and go inside, and then I pulled out and headed up toward 72nd Street West.

I had thought about calling, but I hadn't spoken to Estelle in almost a year. She would know something was wrong the minute she recognized my voice. The decent thing was to go there.

I took Lexington all the way and then cut across. There were the beginnings of traffic now, and the sanitation trucks were out. I found a slot about a block from the building and walked over.

I pushed *Hawes,* which was 12-C. Cathy's mother was too deaf to hear the ring. There was another one of those broadcast systems in the center of the block of bells and I knew it would be Estelle who would call down.

It was a good minute and then her voice came clearly. The Russians weren't jamming this one yet.

"It's Harry Fannin, Estelle."

"Who?"

"Harry Fannin."

There was a silence. Finally the buzzer rang. I went in, crossed the long lobby with mirrors and potted stuff that I remembered and pressed for the elevator. It was a self-service job, silent as an anaconda slithering down a cypress, and it got there a lot more quickly than I wanted it to. Because I was wondering what Emily Post might have to say about just how you go barging in on someone at six o'clock in the morning to let her know that her kid sister had gotten caught up in an armed robbery and then had been murdered by a cheap hood named Duke Sabatini.

I was still wondering when I walked along the corridor on

the twelfth floor to the door marked *C* and pressed the bell. And then Estelle opened up and I didn't wonder anymore, at least not about part of it.

Because part of what I had been going to say was wrong. Duke Sabatini hadn't done it.

CHAPTER 7

Duke hadn't done it because he was here, and there could only be one reason why he'd come. He had to be looking for Cathy. So he didn't even know she was dead.

"In," he told me. He didn't say it precisely the way Eddie Bogardus had said it. Bogardus I'd tagged as an Edward G. Robinson fan, and this one was a trifle more suave—say the early Cagney sort. The gun was Cagney's kind also, a foot-long Army Colt which might have looked less likely to drag him to the floor if it had been mounted on a caisson. He was standing several feet back from the door, calmly pressing the thing into Estelle's ribs.

It was Duke all right. New York wouldn't be *that* lousy with random armed punks waiting behind entrances. Actually he was prettier than Cagney. Taller too, although the Vitalis alone gave him a three-inch edge. He had eyes the color of broomstraw.

We were standing there. "Remember that scene when he squashes the grapefruit in Mae Clarke's face?" I said. "Always got a boot out of old Jimmy. Or was it Jean Harlow's face?"

"Let's save the chatter, huh?"

"Well now, sure, if you didn't see the picture I guess we can't discuss it. Truth is I can't stay anyhow. I just dropped by to deliver some bananas."

He caught the reference and he scowled at me, so I scowled back. I was being rather silly. He knew I wasn't going anywhere.

"You want to step out of the way," I asked him finally, "or am I supposed to crawl through your legs?"

"Hard," he said. "First he's comic and now he's hard. Just ease in the door. There's room for six of your kind, Oliver."

Oliver, Jack. Different cast, same writers. Same old story-line too. Boys lose girl, so one of them checks out the roommate and the other one checks out the mother and sister. Two wrong endings on the same double feature. A girl like Cathy would go to a man when she got into trouble.

Sure. So what man?

I went in. I'd seen too many females messed up already that morning to want to make him really impatient. Estelle was trembling, next to him. She couldn't have looked much worse if vandals had trampled the chrysanthemums.

"That wall will do swell," he told me. "Let's turn around and get your hands up on it."

I did that too, standing next to a highboy. I could see a little of the other furniture and it was what I remembered, all very antiseptic and uncomfortable looking. Estelle's taste. There was a TV set in the corner. Just a little while and the three of us could catch Sunrise Semester.

Duke had closed the door. "On the couch," he told Estelle. "And get glued there."

I heard her going, then felt the .45 hook into the small of my back. I'd already made up my mind not to horse around with this one. Years ago I'd made up my mind. It's a cinch to be psychological, Fannin's one mental block, but any muzzle you can lose a fountain pen in is just too big.

But he really didn't make me that nervous. He'd be looking for information, not a murder rap.

He was frisking me, running me down with his left hand. "The gun's on my right hip," I told him. "If you're looking for the forty grand, I already blew that on chewing gum and soda."

"We'll get to that news later, Oliver." He jerked out the Luger and then my wallet. Then he found the barrel and trigger-assembly of Eddie's zip-gun.

That seemed to amuse him a little. He wheezed contemptuously through his nose and I heard the pieces fall against the seat of an upholstered chair. The .45 crowded my spine some more, so he was probably busy with my wallet. After a while that dropped to the floor.

"Big of you," I told him. I could see that he'd left the money in it. He wasn't interested in my paltry fifty or sixty bucks.

"Fannin," he said. "Cop, huh? Okay, cop, it's too early for you to be on it for any bonding company. So Bogardus spilled about the heist. What else do you know that's interesting? Let's have it."

He didn't know me from Little Black Sambo, which meant that Cathy had kept us private after all. I didn't feel so high-spirited anymore, knowing that. Under the circumstances I suddenly felt considerably like a slob.

"Spill, cop."

"Shove that rod against me one more time and you'll get one goddam lot of answers," I told him. "Back off and let me stop climbing this wall. What the hell do you need besides that howitzer to keep me in line? You want a tin whistle maybe?"

"A wit," he said. "A real genuine wit."

"Yeah, I know, the man who wrote *Snowbound* was wittier."

A little time passed. He grunted. He could turn colors before I'd explain it to him.

He decided to be accommodating. "Drop 'em," he said.

"Keep your feet right where they are when you come around. Anything fishy and this thing goes off."

I turned. He had backed out into the middle of the room. His gray sharkskin suit had shoulders as outsize as the cannon in his hand and the knot in his purple tie was big enough to moor something of Cunard's. Cathy's latest beau. So he hadn't killed her. So I still wasn't rushing off to ask permission to bunk with him next semester.

The .45 was centered on my intestines. "Okay," he said then. "All nice and relaxed, huh? Now where is she?"

I ignored him. He could throw that one at me all night and not get anything, not while Estelle was sitting there that way. She was wearing a drab blue robe and house slippers. Her hands were locked in her lap and her lips had no blood behind them. She was staring at me helplessly and I realized it was the first time I had ever seen her without glasses. Oddly enough it made her look better than I remembered.

"Where, cop?"

"Cathy hasn't got the money," I told him evenly. "You don't have to look for Cathy."

Estelle winced when I mentioned the name. Obviously I hadn't changed the subject by butting in on them. I changed it now.

"Where's your mother, Estelle?"

She looked across at me vaguely and her voice was strained. "She's in the hospital, Harry. She had an operation last weekend."

"Oh, my busted back," Duke said, "if that ain't touching. How was it? I sure hope everything came out okay?"

"She's all right," Estelle said distractedly.

"That's great. I'm real glad to hear that. You be sure and tell her how glad I am." He had not taken his eyes off me. "How many times I got to ask you, cop? What's your pitch in this?"

Estelle's breath was audible. She was staring at me now, probably wondering the same thing. I did not want her to be putting too much of it together.

"Damn it, where is she? Where's the broad?"

"What *broad?* You mean the *girl* Eddie says you're nuts about? The one you're supposed to marry?"

"Yeah, marry. That cheap double-crossing no-good skirt, I'd like to—"

I was pleased to hear how he felt about all that. I wanted a little information myself and that could be just the needle to get it for me. "I told you," I said. "Your girl hasn't got the money, Angelo."

"Can that. My old lady calls me Angelo. Her and the priest. Not you, Oliver."

I grinned at him. "What does Cathy call you?"

"Spit," he said.

"Always happens, doesn't it? Trust a dame and then turn your back for half an hour and she's—"

"Half an hour, hell. Ten damned minutes. Her and all that chatter about how she'd stick it out. And then all I do is go down for a deck of butts. Not even ten minutes, because the clock in the lobby says two-sharp when I go down and it ain't even two-ten when I come back. Faking like she's asleep and then—"

I kept grinning at him. I couldn't help myself. Another minute and he'd be letting me read his diary.

His face had changed. He wasn't sure what he'd told me but he realized he'd made a boo-boo. It wasn't much, actually, but it was all I had and I already loved it dearly. Two o'clock. And she'd gotten to my place around three-thirty. Time for one or two stops. Adam Moss? Who else?

Duke's lips had pulled back over his gums in a grimace of disgust. The Colt jerked up an inch or two in his hand. "Turn back to the wall, cop."

"What's the matter, Angelo? I thought you wanted me to answer some questions."

"Turn around, you phony bastard. Who you trying to con anyhow? Spit, Oliver, you ain't got anymore idea where she is than me. You come up here on what Bogardus told you and you find me so you figure it means she's got the dough. Bright boy, trying to con me into spilling something else. Well, you been told all you're getting, bright boy. You phony cops, for crying out loud. Eddie lets out about the loot and you come sniffing around for it like any two-bit chiseler smelling a free beer. Turn around, phony, right now, or I'll blast that fat smirk right off your kisser."

I took a last look at the gun. I was sure I could knock him off his feet after one shot. One. And Max Schmeling could have taken Joe Louis if he'd been awake after the first round. I knew I'd hate myself for it in the morning, but I turned around and memorized the wallpaper again.

I suppose it didn't matter much. He still wasn't going to do any shooting unless somebody drove him to it. All he wanted was time. Let him go looking for Cathy. The law would pick him up sooner or later on that Troy thing. Me, I wanted someone else.

"Higher, cop," he told me. He had moved up close. I knew well enough what was coming and I tried to set myself for it.

I heard Estelle suck in her breath and begin to whimper. I hoped he would be dumb enough to switch his grip to the business end of the gun first, but he was finished with being dumb for today. And then I said the hell with it anyhow. I waited until the last second, when the shadow of his arm was lifting along the wall.

I jerked my head aside and went for him.

CHAPTER 8

I was happy. Bach might have been meant for Eddie Bogardus alone, but I had my Wagner. *The Siegfried Idyll.* Far off, through drooping willow trees where gentle rain fell. A small wind was rising, and the rivers flowed. The rug beneath me was soft as new down, and softer daylight was breaking through the windows beyond, bathing me in its warm sweet radiance. I dreamed of fair women.

Innocent peace, melancholy contentment, what more could a man need? Let some other kid grow up to be president.

My wallet was lying three inches from my nose like a dead mouse.

A clock on a desk across the room said it had been less than fifteen minutes when I came out of it. I considered myself extremely clever to figure that out, since the clock was upside down. Curiously enough so was the rest of the furniture. I rolled slightly. Lazy clumps of dust ignored my intrusion along the floor boards.

I had caught it in the temple. Old devil-may-care Harry. *Go get 'im, Harry!* Ha.

I lay there throbbing like a bongo. Was I in the mood to encourage all that by moving? Did it matter, since I could

EPITAPH FOR A TRAMP

hardly move anyhow? I wondered if the publicity people at that nice Johnson & Johnson company had any idea how many dandy home uses people can find for their ordinary two-inch adhesive.

My hands were behind me somewhere. I tried them a little, delicately, so that only half of the hair on my wrists came out. I gave up on it. Quitter Fannin. Rapidly discouraged, beaten in a nonce.

In a trice?

I rolled over a little more and there was Estelle.

Poor Estelle. Somebody'd left her on the couch, tape on her ankles, tape on her toes. Hadn't clobbered her, though, used a gag instead. Still, pains a chap to see someone all taped up like that, you know?

We stared at each other like a pair of indecently dressed manikins in a Fifth Avenue window wishing all the people would go away.

After an undetermined period of time, roughly an eon, it struck me that I might hazard a small experiment. I opened my mouth.

No gag. If I tried harder I might even say a few well-chosen words.

"You okay, Estelle?"

She nodded, but her eyes were dull and empty. She was reacting badly. But then living with a widowed mother and teaching the third grade for fifteen years would do that. It was not the best conditioning for the rest of what I would have to tell her either.

"I don't suppose there's a knife around anywhere but in the kitchen? Anything sharp?"

No response. I wondered precisely how she was supposed to go about giving me directions anyhow. I wondered how my lame head would take to the idea if I started wriggling.

I tried it like a worm first, bracing my shoulders and shoving forward with my heels. Highly commendable. I managed all of about eight inches in the time it takes to roast a small hen. I grinned at Estelle and tried a roll instead.

That was better. I cut the hell out of my wrist, but I made it across to the kitchenette doorway in maybe ten flops. I stopped to let my head screw itself back into place.

I had to twist around and go back to the other method to get through the door. Estelle was watching me. "Keeps me in shape," I said. "The rolling Fannin gathers no moss."

I was being the lightheaded lad again. So lightheaded I hadn't realized it until I'd said it. Moss. Adam Moss. I snaked my way into the kitchen thinking that Mr. Moss was next on the agenda.

No, next was a blade. I was going to have some case getting to one if Estelle was a compulsive housekeeper. I was lucky. I saw the point of a fruit knife extending over the edge of the drain on the sink. I slithered over there.

The sink was just low enough. I swung up and around into something which approximated a sitting position, then wedged my hands under myself and lifted like an automobile jack until I was able to catch the point between my teeth. I let it drop to the linoleum.

The rest was a snap. It didn't take me more than fifteen minutes and I only cut myself four times.

I stopped for a second in the bathroom, throwing some water on my face and then gritting my teeth like Mike Hammer while I bathed the gashes in iodine. Coming out I glanced into the bedrooms. Duke had given the place a quick ransacking before he'd left.

Estelle sat up numbly when I cut her free. She rubbed her hands, not saying anything. I gave her a cigarette. She took the first couple of drags as if no one might make it back down into that caved-in mineshaft again.

"I suppose you understood part of all that?"

She nodded uncertainly.

"Estelle, Cathy got mixed up in something that I'm afraid— well, it isn't very pretty."

She looked at me. All I'd been doing was telling people about it. Dan and Helen Abraham, Sally Kline, now the sister. I could start a service to go with that drunk's suicide plan. Why leave a note when Smiling Fannin can break the news for you? I was glad her mother wasn't there.

"Cathy's dead, Estelle."

"She—"

I could actually feel her go rigid next to me. After the first gasp she didn't make another sound. Her eyes were wide and she was staring at me but nothing came out. A kick in the stomach might have brought on roughly the same initial reaction.

I put my hand on her arm when the sobbing began. It was broken and harsh. It was the sort of thing that comes without any tears. It was all inside, which is the rottenest kind.

"I'm sorry, Estelle—"

A while passed. Her cigarette was in a tray. Finally she fumbled in her pocket and came up with a handkerchief.

"How?" she said then. "Oh, Harry, did one of those men—?"

"Somebody. With a knife."

She gasped, clenching her fists. I stood there and watched the faint curl of smoke.

"Who? Why? Oh, God, why?"

"I don't know. Until I found him here I thought it was our boy with the cannon. He was . . . Cathy'd been involved in something with him. I don't think she understood how serious it was. It was armed robbery, Estelle. What Duke wanted was the money, which seems to be missing. That's what she was killed for. She'd been . . . well, running around a lot."

I didn't know how you were supposed to tell it to someone like Estelle. You can be doddering, bald and approaching senility and still feel awkward in front of an old-maid school teacher. She and Cathy had been only a dozen years apart, but when I'd been in the family I'd always thought of her more like an aunt than a sister-in-law. I had wondered more than once if she were a virgin.

She looked up at me from no more than two feet away, but her voice might have been coming from a shut closet. "Mother," she said. "Mother will—"

She made a choking pitiful sound deep in her throat, and then she was running toward the bathroom. The door closed and I could hear her sobbing behind it.

I stood there for a minute, feeling rotten, then I flicked on the TV without the sound. A morning-program MC gave me what was probably a very famous grin. I turned him off.

She was more composed when she came back. She had dried her eyes. She sat down, not close to me.

"Tell me, Harry," she said. "I . . . I want to know."

"It's nothing more than I've already said. Really, Estelle. She got involved with this fellow Duke somehow, and one thing led to another."

"No," she said. She was not looking at me. "I want to know about her, Harry. This . . . running around, you called it. That was it all the time, wasn't it? When you and she broke up?"

"Estelle, it's a messy story. She was your sister—you know as much about the kind of girl she was as I do."

"Yes," she said, "I know." She was chewing her lip. "That's why when I think about telling mother, or trying to hide it from her, I . . . Oh, Harry, I've been hiding things about Cathy from mother for so long. Oh, God, and now this! Now I'll have to hide this, too! Because I always did it. I always did it and I used to hate myself for it. Oh, Harry, it's such a terrible thing to say, but I've always thought of her as such a—"

She cut herself off but you could guess the word easily enough. Tramp would do. Someone like Estelle could not think of a girl like Cathy in any other way, and I supposed you could not criticize her too much. But now she was being hurt because of it.

She had started to cry again, and her body began to shake like a child's. I got up and walked across the room and stood by the windows. There was an air-conditioning unit in one of them but it was off. It was almost 6:30. Traffic was loosening up down below. In another couple of hours it would be something to hide from.

"But I know one of the reasons," she said behind me.

"What?"

She was not looking at me. "Why she was that way."

"I don't get you."

She still did not look up. "She must have told you about the time she was lost in the mountains up beyond Lake George. When she was six."

"Sure."

"She didn't get lost, Harry. Someone . . . a man . . . attacked her. Criminally."

"Oh, damn, Estelle."

"He . . . they sent him to jail for it. But that isn't the point. The point is that Catherine somehow forgot about it, Harry. Or she deliberately put it out of her mind. Sublimated it, that's the word. I heard her talk about it afterward a dozen times, and all she ever remembered was wandering in the woods and being cold. She talked about it like some marvelous childhood adventure she'd had, and the . . . the other part of it was out of her mind completely. I wanted to tell her about it but I never could.

I never could say anything. But that must have been part of it, I'm sure. She buried the memory of what happened because it was such a shock, but there was some kind of inverse reaction, as if she were unconsciously trying to prove to herself that it hadn't hurt her, or . . . I don't know. But she should have been under analysis. I did tell her that once, two or three years ago, but she merely laughed at me. Maybe I'm making too much of the whole thing, maybe it wouldn't have made any difference anyhow. But now she's . . ."

Estelle had been staring at the rug all the time she was telling it. It was not simply that she was upset. I had to wonder how a woman could grow to thirty-six or thirty-seven and still be embarrassed by something like that.

I didn't have much idea what the story was worth. Psychology was another one of those things I'd missed because of wind-sprints and signal practice at Ann Arbor. Not that it mattered much now anyhow. I went across to her.

Her head was still down. I put my fist under her chin. "Look, will you be all right? I have to check in with the law. I haven't seen them yet, Estelle."

She started to get up and I helped her. For a moment she stood there with my hand on her wrist. She started to say something and then her face twisted up again. After that I was holding her with her face on my shoulder.

"It'll be all right, Estelle."

We stood that way. She was breathing unevenly and I could feel her breasts rising beneath the robe. They were full and firm. It was probably a shoddy thing to consider at the moment, but I thought she very likely needed a man a lot more than she needed consolation. I squeezed her shoulders, waiting another minute, then I eased away.

"I better call them."

"Will you . . . I won't go to school today. I'll see mother

this morning, but I won't tell her. Harry, will you stop back later?"

"Sure."

I watched her shuffle into one of the bedrooms. She closed the door.

There was a phone on a stand and I dialed my number. Dan wouldn't be answering. It rang once and then the voice was Nate Brannigan out of Central Homicide.

"Fannin, Nate."

"Well," he said. "Well, now. Fannin, huh? Isn't that grand? Wait until I check my watch and see just how grand that is. Six forty-one. Putting the time of death at roughly three-thirty, that makes a lapse of three hours and eleven minutes. What the hell, let's call it three hours even. Nice of you to ring, Mr. Fannin. Would you like a little more time, maybe? Would you like to make it four hours? Five? I'd hate to inconvenience you."

I let him get all that out of his system.

"Well, Fannin?"

"I wasn't sure you were finished."

"I'm not. Not by a damned sight. But first I want to hear your end of it. Tell me a story, Fannin. Make it a good one. Where the damned hell you been? Where are you now?"

"I'm across on 72nd. You get that pick-up on Perry Street?"

"Yeah, yeah. Bogardus. I sent a car. They hauled him in twenty minutes ago, but I'm still waiting for a charge. You better have one, Fannin. You get me stuck with a false arrest to cover a fist fight you had with some wet-nosed kid and I'll—"

"You read a bulletin on a payroll job in Troy yesterday? Some shirt factory? Roughly forty thousand?"

"Not my department. He in on that?"

"Him and another couple, cousins named Sabatini. I had a session with one of them also, but I lost. He'll be poking around in some of the same places your boys will be working on the killing, looking for the girl. It slipped my mind to tell him she's dead."

"Dan gave me the background on you and the girl, Harry. Sorry about that."

"Thanks."

"She rigged in on the Troy thing?"

"That's pretty much it. She was with Sabatini until roughly two o'clock, then she scrammed. That would have been fine, except she took the money with her. She went someplace before she came to me, more likely two places. One of the guys she went to see had a second thought and followed her. I've been using the MG she came in. She—"

"Damn it, Fannin."

"I was in a hurry, Nate. But let me—"

"No, let me. Okay, so the guy stabs her out front and then grabs the money and guns off. And after that the girl gets back on her feet bleeding like a stuck pig and rings your bell and dances up the stairs, huh?"

"I know how it sounds. But either he thought she was dead or he lost his nerve. You can—"

"The girl didn't say anything?"

"Not about who killed her, no."

"But you talked?"

"A couple words, yeah."

"Fannin, you amaze me. How long have I known you—five, six years?"

"Come off it, will you, Nate? What gripe have you got except that I should have called sooner? What the hell would you have done in my position, got up a bridge game maybe? Let's play it without the weary cop sarcasm, huh? I'm not much in the mood."

"Fannin, I'll finish what I started to tell you. And like I say, if I didn't know you and you hadn't played it straight for five years I'd have had every badge in nine precincts out of bed and hunting for you two minutes after I got here—"

"Now listen—"

"*You* listen. All right, the girl comes up and dies on your doorstep. You used to be married to her, maybe that's good enough reason why she's there. But don't tell me you had a cozy little chat before she died and she didn't say word number one about who—"

"Damn it—"

"And don't hand me any fairy tale about somebody she went to see who followed her and took the money, don't give me that either. Don't give me anything. Just get yourself over here and make it fast. You get me? I don't know what you're trying to cover, or who—the girl's reputation probably—but I don't like to be suckered. I'll trust you on it for the fifteen minutes it'll take you to get across town and not four seconds longer. What the hell do you take me for anyhow?"

"Why, you old rummy. You old dim-witted country Irish jerk. Five years, huh? And just how many things have I handed you in that time? Every damned one of them crated up and slapped on your desk without a loose string anywhere. Which is a damned good thing because if there *was* a loose string you'd trip over it and fall on your fat face. And here I get one that I'm not even doing for money, see, no fee at all because sometimes I can get to be sentimental as hell, you know? And in three hours I've done half your legwork and found your motive and—"

"What motive, Fannin? What motive is that? You mean the forty-two thousand, three hundred and sixty-seven dollars and thirty-four cents?"

"You bet your tin badge I mean the—"

"Yeah? What's the matter, Fannin, you get hoarse all of a

sudden? You lose the voice from trying so hard to make your-self sound good?"

"All right, all right, let's have it. I thought the Troy heist wasn't your department?"

"Never said it was."

"Damn it, Brannigan, where'd you get the exact figure? Do I have to come over there and shake it out of you?"

"Why, hell, Harry, not at all. Like I say, it's all among friends. You just trot on over and I'll be more than happy to show you the cash. After all, we found it in your laundry bag, didn't we?"

CHAPTER 9

Brannigan didn't ask me how the money had gotten there. It was just as well. For the moment all I could think of was that I'd eaten my oatmeal every day that week without making a single naughty face, so maybe the Good Fairy had left it as a reward. I grunted something unsociable and said I'd be over fast. Brannigan said he'd bet on it.

Actually he would have lost. I had a stop to make first.

Estelle was still inside. I called so long through the door, took the eerie silent elevator down to the lobby and walked toward the MG. From across the street it looked as if some industrious member of the city's overworked traffic force had ticketed it.

It was only a handbill. *Men and women everywhere,* it said, *make sure today of the salvation of your souls. Are you living a spiritual life or a carnal life? Be saved now!* I tossed it into the glove compartment. Let Adam Moss worry about such things, if and when he got the car back. For myself I was more interested in my dirty drawers.

Obviously the killer had been inside after I'd left. Framing me to cover himself would be his only possible out if he thought Cathy had talked before she died.

He. Four hours on it and I came up with a personal pronoun. I wasn't even sure I had the right gender. Her, maybe. It.

I wondered if Moss was going to have any notions. I was going to find out just about then.

I went up Riverside Drive, cruising more slowly than Brannigan would have liked. My broken head would have liked it a lot slower than that. A morning haze was trying to overextend its visa along the Jersey shore across the Hudson, but the sun was cutting it quickly. It was going to be another scorcher.

Moss's address would fall somewhere between the Drive and upper Broadway. A new Caddy was pulling away just short of his corner and I nosed the MG in. There would have been room for a fleet of us.

Across the street a junior-grade Eddie Bogardus of perhaps fourteen was hacking away at the seat of a park bench with a knife of the sort they outlawed about five years back. He saw me watching him.

"Don't you know a mean cop you could practice on with that thing?"

"Drop dead twice," he told me indifferently.

The place I wanted was a rundown apartment building of six or seven stories, several doors up from the Drive. Moss's registration listed him for 3-G but there were no names on any of the bells and no letters either, merely numbers. The vestibule door was open and hooked back. Behind it a couple of unshaded 25-watt bulbs were trying unsuccessfully to make the long narrow lobby look like something other than the esophagus of a submerged whale.

Moss would not have a full apartment of his own. It was one of those buildings in which the original railroad flats had been broken up into separate singles, where they sold you one room for yourself and you got to use the john and the kitchen if the other half-dozen people along the corridor happened to oversleep that morning. The landlords got away with the deal because of all the tight-budgeted Columbia University kids from around the corner.

The hall marked *3* was around to the right in the rear on the main floor. It was exactly seven o'clock when I rang the bell near the outside door. I had to wait a full minute and then I drew a beautiful young Chinese girl with an armful of potted plant who wasn't interested in me at all except to let me hold the door.

"Moss?" I said after her.

"Last room on the right," she called over her shoulder. I stood there a moment, watching to see if she had on one of those slit skirts that Chinese girls always wear. I wondered why they always do that. Not that I had any complaints. This one had good legs and I watched them until she turned into the lobby.

The doors along the corridor were marked with peeling gilt letters. I found G and rapped twice. The door behind me opened while I was standing there and a face poked itself out. It was a woman's face, about forty years older and not too much longer than Seabiscuit's. The face stared at me, probably wondering if I'd brought the hay. I stared back. Finally the woman grunted and went away.

I rapped on Moss's door again, harder this time.

I heard bedsprings, then footsteps and what I judged to be unpleasant muttering. The bolt snapped from inside. "For crying out loud, what time is—?"

I looked at Adam Moss. He was a kid, eighteen or nineteen at most. He was husky and good-looking, with a mop of curly brown hair. He was wearing white boxer shorts and a pair of shoulders that the young Max Baer might have envied. He was patently annoyed.

"Moss?"

"Yeah. Who're you? I don't know you—"

I had my wallet in my hand and I flashed it. "You want to step back inside?"

He glanced at the card and then back at me, puzzled. "Police?"

And then his face brightened. Adam Moss grinned at me as if I'd just told him he'd earned his first varsity letter.

"Hey, that's great. That's sure what I call fast action!" He glanced at his watch. "Gee, not even five hours since I reported it. Where is it? You bring it back, officer? It wasn't wrecked, was it? Come in, come in!"

He was beaming. My one lead. My only lead. I sat down on the kid's rumpled bed and took a cigarette. I would have been happier with a cyanide inhaler but I'd left it in my other suit.

"You leave the keys in it, Moss?"

"Yeah. Like I told them when I called. I parked it around midnight, up on Broadway near 111th, and then I had a couple of beers with some of the guys from school in the West End bar. I guess it was around 2:15 or so when I realized I'd forgotten them. We ran down, but you could see it was gone even before we got to the place. Boy, I was pretty worried for a while. What a dumb stunt. My old man would have booted me one. He just bought it for me last month. Can I get dressed and get it now? Is it here or do I have to pick it up someplace?"

"You never ran into a girl named Catherine Hawes?"

"What? Who?"

"Hawes?"

"No, why? She the one who had the car? You didn't tell me—it isn't smashed up or anything, is it?"

"Runs like a top. I use your phone?"

"Yeah, sure." He gestured but I had already seen it. "Say, what do you mean, runs like a . . . you been driving it or something? What's all this about a girl?"

"You call the local precinct?"

"Of course," he said. He was eyeing me uncertainly.

I dialed Central and asked for 103rd Street. When I got the desk I said, "Hello, my name is Adam Moss, 113th Street. I called last night about 2:30 to report a stolen car. I wonder if you've gotten anything on it yet?"

He asked me the make and license number. I told him and he said to hang on.

Adam Moss was scowling at me. "Hey, what is all this?"

"Just checking."

"Checking what? Now you look here, friend—"

The desk sergeant came back on. "Nothing yet, Mr. Moss. It's pretty early, but the listing has gone out on it. We'll let you know if we find it."

"Thanks."

Adam Moss had his hands on his hips. "Relax," I told him. "The car's okay. I'm a P.I., not a regular officer." I showed him the card again and this time he stopped to read it. "There's no trouble, Moss, but you might have had some if you hadn't called in as soon as you did. A girl took it. She was in a hurry and she must have spotted the keys when she came out of one of the hotels up here. An hour and a half later she was killed."

"Say, now—"

"The police will be checking you sooner or later. You go back to that bar after you found out it was gone?"

"Yeah, sure, that's where I called from. The guys were with me. The bartender knows me too."

"You're all right then. The car's around the corner but I'll have to turn it over. They'll probably hold it for a day or two until they get you squared away."

"Well for crying out loud, my heap in a murder case. Isn't that something?"

I had opened the door. I took two singles out of my wallet and tossed them on his dresser. "Gas," I told him.

"Say, you don't have to do that. Thanks. Who's the girl, anyhow? She good looking?"

"Aren't they always?"

Seabiscuit opened the stall across the way again as soon as I started out. I turned and winked at her. She slammed the door and something fell inside the room.

Young Moss was grinning at me. *"Mishugganah,"* he said. He had a good smile and he was a nice healthy kid who had most likely never seen the inside of a squad room in his life. It would have been no trouble to hate him for it.

"See you, Mr. Fannin. Thanks again. Boy, wait'll I tell my old man."

I went along the corridor and out into the lobby. The Chinese girl was coming back. She had dumped her plant and was carrying a man's suit about Moss's size on a cleaner's hanger. I waited until she went past.

"Say, uh, just out of curiosity, you think maybe you could tell me why all Chinese girls wear dresses with—"

She had stopped and turned toward me. "Yes?"

"Never mind. I was being silly."

I was grinning at her and she looked at me vaguely. Then she smiled. "It's out of deference to old custom, obviously. Why, don't you approve?"

She had a voice like a small bell tinkling under water. I told her I approved in spades and she laughed. I went out of there wondering if Moss's old man knew about that personal valet service. In my day at school I'd had to room with a two-hundred-and-twenty-pound reserve fullback named Irving.

I took my time walking back to the Drive. I supposed I'd expected exactly what I'd gotten from Moss. I knew I'd expected it. I didn't have a gun. I'd walked in on two of them already that morning, and I wouldn't have rapped on the door to the vestry at St. John's Cathedral without the Luger if I'd seriously thought I might run into a third.

I cut through Central Park and made it across town in the MG without getting squashed by any of the large economy-size models. It was just 7:42 when I swung off Lexington toward my apartment building. I didn't go all the way down the block. I didn't go down the block at all. I jerked the car over to the side just after I made the turn and pulled in at a fire plug. I sat there for a minute, watching him.

Anybody could stare at the house. At least a dozen other people were doing it, either at the building itself or at the three squad cars parked out front. Most of them were clustered on the other side of the street but there were also two or three near the door, talking to the plain-clothes cop on duty who wouldn't be telling them anything but to move along. But the one I cared about was a good hundred yards up from the others, standing alone almost directly across from me.

He was wearing a brown tweed sports jacket that Brooks Brothers had never been ashamed of, and the lizard briefcase under his left arm would have gone for close to a hundred dollars in any shop on the same avenue. In the light of day the crewcut took ten years off his age, even with the gray at the temples. His tie was Countess Mara or Bronzini and every bit as sleek as the stained one he'd probably tossed under the bed a few minutes after I'd seen him that morning.

I was over there next to him before he noticed me, and then his head did an almost imperceptible nervous shudder before he turned fully. But if it should have been an ace of a hangover there wasn't any other sign of it.

"You selling many of those policies?"

"I beg your pardon?"

"It *is* insurance?"

97

"Why, yes, only I don't seem to recall—"

"Must have been at the lodge. I'll tell you though, I've been giving it a lot of thought. Maybe you're right. Fellow shouldn't go round with such inadequate coverage, certainly not a family man like myself. I'm afraid I've misplaced your card, but if you could spare another I'd—"

"Why certainly." I stood there while he slipped a calfskin wallet out of his jacket and fumbled in it. "Spragway," he was saying. "Ethan J." I'd already looked at him so I let him look at me while I read the card. It listed a Lexington Avenue agency address in one corner and a Park Avenue home address in the other. The home number would be only two or three blocks from where we were.

"I'm frightfully sorry, but I don't seem to recall your name at all." He had decided to frown slightly.

"Hobbes. Thomas Hobbes."

"How curious. Just like the philosopher."

"Doesn't bother me if he doesn't mind. Something going on down the block there?"

"Evidently. Well, yes, good to have seen you again, Hobbes. Afraid I've got to be running."

"You didn't notice anything when you passed here last night?"

"Last night?" Spragway frowned fully now. "Here? What makes you suggest that I—?"

"Come off it, mister. You were here all right, drunk as an owl. A little before four. I asked you if you noticed anything."

He got indignant. "My good man, if I happened to come down this street last night, or for that matter any night, it would be because I live only two blocks away—as you saw on my card and which, it strikes me now, is no business of yours. I am not accustomed to being called an alcoholic. Good day, Mr. Hobbes."

He turned on his heel and I let him go, the only insurance man in captivity who ever let a prospect slip by without taking an address and phone number. I supposed a respectable drunk would have a lot of practice deliberately not remembering people he'd met when he was boozed up. Even one whose eyes were perfectly clear four hours later and whose breath smelled of nothing stronger than Ipana.

I stood there sucking air through my teeth and thinking about nothing while he disappeared around the corner.

CHAPTER 10

The plainclothes dick in front of my building started toward me with an expression of bored annoyance when I eased the MG between two of the squad cars, all three of which were double parked. He reached the curb being so weary of the stupidity of the unenlightened masses that it was killing him.

"This look like a parking field, Mac?"

"I could have sworn."

"Move it! Move it!"

"How you going to watch it if I do that? It's evidence. I was even thinking maybe we ought to wrap it in tissue paper or something."

He grimaced sourly. "Funny man. They been biting their nails upstairs there, waiting for all the jokes. Let's see it, huh?"

I showed him the wallet. He glanced at it and then nodded.

They had cleaned up the blood, or probably they'd let the superintendent do it after they'd gotten their pictures. A well-clipped poodle was sniffing at the sawdust. He went off, limping a little in the left forepaw.

The door was wedged open with a folded tabloid. BERRA HITS TWO, YANKS . . . something or other, it said. When I turned at the top of the stairs I could see that the apartment door was open also. There was another detective in the hall, a gaunt, underfed younger specimen of the breed with a neck as long as a beer can.

"Fannin," I told him.

He turned to relay the name inside but he didn't get to say anything. Young cops rarely do. Brannigan came into the doorway, a beefy, red-faced, Sequoia-size man I'd once seen get jumped by a trio of longshoremen during a rackets case. He hadn't had time to get his gun unsheathed and so he'd used his fists. He'd left the three of them propped unconscious against a wall like so much garbage. His tie was pulled down now and he was looking at me in a way that was supposed to make me stand on one foot with my head hanging. He got over that in a minute, not saying anything. He jerked his thumb disgustedly and went in.

A hawk-nosed medical examiner I had met once or twice was just leaving. "I'll send the wagon," he told Brannigan. He had to step across the body to get out.

Someone had covered her with my raincoat, probably Dan. He was sitting near a window in his shirtsleeves, dark-eyed and unshaven and looking sleepy. He nodded, smoking.

There were dead flash bulbs in a couple of ashtrays and one or two drawers were open. Print powder was dusted around. The laundry bag was on the floor and the money was stacked up in piles of different denominations on the desk. Home. The place looked as inviting as the rumpus room at Buchenwald.

There was one other detective with Brannigan, a lieutenant named Coffey who was totally bald. The skin under his eyes was pouchy and discolored. Possibly too much night duty had done that, I didn't know. But it hadn't put the glaze of menacing resentment in his eyes that you saw the minute you looked at him. That would be part of the personality and it was probably why he was a cop. A grand cop, and I was glad he was there. If we had to use a rubber hose on anybody he'd have two in each pocket.

I said a single filthy word which no one paid any attention to. Finally I went in and walked around to the kitchen and stuck my fingers into five glasses and picked up the bottle of Jack Daniels I'd left out earlier. I carried the bottle and the glasses back into the living room. I poured myself about an inch of the sour mash and drank it straight. I poured myself one more, not drinking it, and left the bottle open. "Fannin's back," I said. "Party time."

Coffey took one. No one else did. I went across the room and pulled out a straight chair and sat down where I would not have to face her. Part of her was sticking out, like spillage from a dropped pocketbook.

Brannigan still had not said anything. He was giving me a minute. He had been on the force for twenty years but he could still drink his morning coffee without somebody's blood in it. I supposed I might as well get to it anyhow.

"Can somebody take it down? I don't much want to have to repeat it later."

"The kid can," he said. "Pete?"

The young flagpole came in from the hall. He already had his notebook out. Brannigan walked across and closed the door and came back. He sat down in the good chair, slumping forward and tilting his hat across his eyes. Dan was still by the window and the kid sat next to him.

"No questions until I'm done, huh? I know how to tell it."

"Tell it," Brannigan said.

I did. I gave it to them in detail. I skipped the things Cathy had said, knowing that Brannigan would ask me about that afterward anyhow, and I left out some of the things Estelle had told me, which were purely personal. I didn't mention Ethan

J. Spragway, but I wasn't sure why, except that the whole business was probably irrelevant. I didn't make any bones about the kind of life Cathy had been leading, or about why we'd split up. I suggested that it would be a good move to stake out the Perry Street apartment on the chance that Duke might nose around there during the day. I had been talking nineteen minutes when I finished.

"What did the girl say when she came through the door, Harry?"

"She was dying, Nate. She knew she was. She told me she was sorry about things."

"That all?"

"That's all."

Brannigan sat up and pushed his hat back. "Somebody followed her here from wherever she'd gone after two o'clock. He knifed her for forty-two thousand dollars. And then he came upstairs and made you a present of it."

I didn't answer him. "The rest will be pure speculation, Pete," he said. "You can cut it there." He jerked his tie lower across his shirt. "I hate to begin hot days with guesswork, Harry. But you might as well."

"No premeditation," I said.

"Meaning?"

"He was looking for the money, not trouble. Maybe he thought he could talk her out of going to anybody else about it, I don't know. Anyhow all he wanted was more conversation on the subject. And probably she had the stuff in her hand when she walked back to the guy's car. I don't know in what, but the guy'd seen it when she first went to him."

"Canvas sack." Brannigan motioned and I saw it on the floor at the side of the desk.

"All right, she's carrying that. He wants it, and bad, but this time she tells him to make his pile some other way. Maybe

103

this sets it off, maybe something else, but either way it's quick, so probably they'd had the start of an argument about it before. And then they're not arguing anymore. The guy grabs the sack but at the same time he sees that she's not dead. He panics, but he hasn't got the guts to stab her again. So what does he do?"

"You're telling it."

"Okay, I am. So he sees her get up and make the bell, and a minute later he hears the buzzer. He gets out of there like a shot."

"With the money?"

"Sure with the money. But he's probably not even shifted into third before it hits him. A fat lot of good it's going to do him to scram if she's lived long enough to talk. For all he knows she could have come up to borrow a Band-Aid. Hell, she may live to be ninety, and either way he's damned sure got to find out. He comes back and watches the place. I come out twice, and the second time I take off in the MG."

"And he comes over and walks in. Through the door you've conveniently forgotten to lock."

"Hell, Nate, I left the keys under the rubber for Dan."

Brannigan didn't say anything.

"So what else?" I said. "The minute he gets inside he knows he's done murder. He also knows that if she's talked you'll have him on it so fast it will make him nauseated. But if he plants the money here it's my word against his—and I'm the one with the dead horse in the bathtub."

"Fine," Brannigan said. He had taken out a cigar. "But if she hasn't talked he's throwing the money away."

"Wouldn't you? You going to take the odds that she didn't spill? Standing here with the body on the floor and me possibly on my way to the police at that very moment? You leave the coin, Nate. You leave it and you pray like hell at the same time that she didn't talk so you'll be out of it completely. You can't get a much better bargain for the price."

Coffey had gone to the bottle. "You've got the killer's impulses figured out pretty clearly for pure speculation, Fannin," he said sarcastically. "Any of this based on anything you know and haven't told us, maybe?"

I let the sarcasm ride. "It's based on what didn't happen."

"Namely?"

"Namely that the guy didn't come up and try to take me out myself while I was still here. A pro wouldn't take the chance that I could tag him for it. It's got to be somebody who didn't intend to do it to start with, and who chickened out fast after it happened."

"How do we know he saw her get up?" Coffey said. "Suppose she lay there a minute. Suppose the guy drove off and left her for dead?"

"Say what you mean. You mean there wasn't anybody out there at all."

"I didn't say that, Fannin."

I turned to Brannigan. "Look, Nate, if there's anybody else in it but me it's got to be my way. He sees her come in because he comes in himself. If the guy drives off like Coffey says then there's no point in putting him out there to start with, because it means I've got the dough all along. It kills the motive for anybody else. It means I knife her on my own doorstep and then come back up and wait while she crawls up after me. She'd do that. And I'd leave the loot stashed away with my sweat socks. I'm clever like that. Just like I'd have Dan call you. Hell, I'd call the papers, too. I'd print invitations. Come see Fannin electrocute himself. One wire in his ear and the other up his back. Free smoked mussels for everybody."

"Fannin, I didn't accuse you," Coffey said.

"Who the hell did you have in mind, W. C. Fields?"

"Look, Fannin—bug off. The body's in your apartment. The money's here. The victim's your ex-wife. So you come back three or four hours after you should have, tossing off some story on pure spec, and you get touchy if I question any part of it. Well, you can shove your touchiness, friend. You greasy private johns give me a swift pain anyhow. If I made a list of every time one of you meddlers make us take three weeks to do what we could have done in three hours the department wouldn't have enough paper to type it on. For my money you still got a lot of scrubbing to do before you stop smelling bad."

If Brannigan hadn't been there Coffey probably would have spit on the carpet. He sat there eyeing me like something in the gutter he'd stepped in on the way to work.

"Funny," I told him, "I've got a list, too. Not as significant as yours, Coffey, just something I think about when I run out of comic books. People who've given me kicks, added an extra dimension to my prosaic life. Guys like, say, Einstein, Gandhi, Adlai Stevenson, Toscanini, Willie Mays—people like that, you know? And you know something else? There ain't a cop on the list. Not one."

"You're funny as sick people, Fannin. Be funny, what I said still goes. Who the hell are you that I got to wear kid gloves? You somebody's favorite nephew all of a sudden? Chew nails, huh?"

It wouldn't get any pleasanter so I let it drop. His wife had to live with it, not me. Probably some of it was my own fault anyhow. They weren't setting any departmental records to get her off the floor over there. The room was still for a minute.

"You girls about finished?" Brannigan said.

Coffey grunted.

"Take a drink," I told him. Mine was on the floor near me and I picked it up and stared at it.

Brannigan made a clicking noise with his teeth. "All right,

it's as handy as we can establish for now." He turned to the stenographer. "Pete, get out that description on Sabatini first of all. And run a check on that Adam Moss, too; see if there's any file on him just in case. You might as well get started now. Call in on the way and put through the stake-out for that Perry Street address, my authority."

"Right, Captain."

"And take the money in. Report the recovery of it, but tell the insurance mob it's impounded indefinitely. They'll probably be on your neck in four minutes. And put through the pick-up on that cousin of Sabatini's in Troy."

"Yes, sir." I watched him load the satchel. He threw a half salute like a scarecrow flapping in a breeze and when Brannigan returned it he went out. Brannigan got up and walked into the kitchen. Water ran into a glass.

"So it all hinges on who she'd go to," he said when he came out. "Whose doorbell she'd push when she found herself in a jam. No family besides the mother and sister?"

"None."

"Then I suppose we check with the Kline girl first, get a list of everybody she can tie in with the deceased." He stared at Cathy for a minute, then at me. "It'd seem like there'd be a fair-sized list of names."

"And no-names."

"One-night stands?"

"Something like that."

He cursed once, chewing on the cigar. It wasn't burning. "You want to call the Kline girl?"

"I'm working with the department?"

"You don't think maybe it's about time?"

"Nuts," Coffey said.

"You got a problem, Art?"

"Damn it, yeah. There's nothing in the book says we got to

play potsie with some hot-shot peeper just because he used to be married to the dame."

"Report me," Brannigan said. "I haven't had a reprimand in fourteen years. The commissioner probably stays up nights worrying that I'm getting complacent. You going to make that call, Harry?"

"Right now," I said. I dug out the slip of paper with the Gramercy Park address and number. My hand was no more than six inches from the phone when it started to ring.

"Let me," Brannigan said. "If somebody's checking on what happened to his investment it might just relax him into a slip or two later on if he figures you're not running loose."

He lifted it as it started its third ring. He said, "Brannigan, Homicide," and then nothing else. All of us were close enough to hear the click and then the dead buzzing.

He stood there for a minute, holding the receiver and looking at the chewed end of his cigar. "Don't you just love a son of a bitch who'd tease like that?" he said then.

CHAPTER 11

Sally Kline said on the phone that there were only two or three people Cathy had seen with any regularity. One was a writer on Bank Street in the Village named Ned Sommers. Another was a photographer named Clyde Neva who had a live-in studio loft on East 10th Street. She said Neva was a pretty blatant homosexual.

"But gosh, Harry, I hope I don't sound as if I'm suggesting that either one of them might have—"

"It's just routine," I told her. "One of them might remember something, or know things you don't. Anymore?"

The only other one she could tag was an Arthur Leeds. She thought he was a musician and she gave me another Village address, on Jones Street this time. I told her to get some sleep.

Coffey had been checking the addresses in my directory when I repeated the names. "No women, huh?" Brannigan said.

"There wouldn't be."

"This Kline girl. She came home at eleven, was there all night until she called you?"

"For crying out loud, Nate—"

"Just asking. She'll have to make a statement anyhow, this

109

afternoon will be good enough. I'll see her then." He took the phone and dialed headquarters about something. I went into the bedroom and dug out a .38 Police Special and a shoulder holster to replace the empty Luger sheath. Dan followed me in.

"I got all the time in the world if you want anything," he said quietly.

"I'll call you."

"Be at the office. Don't strain it, huh, fella?"

I stood there a minute after he went out. I took out Ethan J. Spragway's card and looked at it. Spragway spelled backward was Yawgarps. I stuck the card in a drawer. The sour-faced plainclothesman from outside was just coming up when I went back out front.

"The wagon will be here any minute, Waterman," Brannigan told him. "Stick around after it leaves. You'll be called about relief. And take that MG when you go in. Give him the keys, will you, Harry?"

I tossed them over. Waterman dropped them. He bent to pick them up with the same sick-of-it-all expression that he probably had when he made love to his wife. Brannigan had turned to Coffey.

"All right," he said, "Fannin and I will check out those three intimates, but first we'll take a look around that Perry Street place, give it a run-through for address books, mail, all the rest. I want that Moss kid seen again, and I want his alibi authenticated. Pete'll know pretty quick if there's any local sheet on him. I also want to know if Bogardus is still telling the same story he told this morning. After that you can start checking the hotels up near where that MG was parked on Broadway. I want all of them for three blocks in every direction. A clerk just might remember Sabatini going out for smokes and the girl ducking out five minutes later. Maybe she said something, asked a question, looked scared. You can pick up a partner first, anybody who's unassigned. If it looks like you're going to have to waste a day waking up off-duty clerks call in for an extra team. Keep Pete posted on the desk every hour or so." Coffey grunted in acknowledgment. Maybe in disgust, it was an ambiguous sort of sound. He was leaning against the wall near the door, sucking a flat toothpick.

"You got any questions or are you just learning to like it here?"

"Nuts," Coffey said. He started for the door, threw Brannigan a salute which could just as easily have been translated into an obscene gesture as anything it was supposed to mean, and went out. The toothpick lay on the carpet where he'd been standing.

I looked at Brannigan. He was still working the unlighted cigar and he did not say anything.

"What the hell is all that?" I asked him. "You guys give him white mice to play with when he wants them, too?"

"Tell you later," he muttered. "Let's go, huh?"

I stood there a minute after he was gone, then I knelt next to the door and lifted the raincoat away. Woodsmoke would have had more color than her face. Waterman was watching me. I went downstairs.

The stenographer had taken one of the cars. Coffey was just pulling out in the second one and Brannigan was waiting at the third, one without insignia. "Counting Waterman it looks like three vehicles for four men," I said when I got in. "Evidently the whole department's gone soft."

Brannigan looked at me, made a face, then finally got rid of the decimated cigar. "Guys who came with Coffey and Pete have been checking out every apartment on this block for an hour and a half," he said almost indifferently, "trying to rouse up somebody who might have had insomnia and been staring out a window when the deed was done. I've once in a while been known to give a legitimate P.I. his head, Harry, but I don't particularly sit on my butt and read Ralph Waldo Emerson while I'm letting him run. Four other officers are out pulling hack drivers out of bed to see if any of them noticed that red MG on the streets last night, or any red MG, and where, and every patrolman who was on duty is being asked the same thing. We've already talked to everybody in your building, and it may also interest you to know that your office has been pulled apart and put back together again, just in case you might be working on something that could have tied in with this, or for that matter to see if you'd had any communication from the deceased lately which you might not want to mention. Also I used your phone to call and check the figures on that Troy heist. You can bill us on it, I suppose. You got anymore questions or are you beginning to like it here, too?"

"The Perry Street apartment's in the block between Fourth and Bleecker," I told him.

He'd had the car idling. He grinned at me, shifted and swung out. He went across to Second Avenue and straight down. He drove like most cops, treating the general run of working men's cars like moving targets. Once or twice he gave me a nudge and I opened the siren for him. If I'd been in a better mood I would have watched the street corners for familiar faces to wave to.

"You were going to tell me about Coffey," I said after a while. "What the hell, he walks around as if he knows where the department hides the bodies."

He stopped the shenanigans with the car when I asked him that, punching his tongue into the side of his cheek for a minute before he answered. "Coffey's all right," he said then. "His wife and kid were killed in an auto smash up near Poughkeepsie about two months ago. Son of a bitch driving the other car was drunk as a calf and walked away without a bruise. They booked him on vehicular manslaughter but I don't suppose that helps Coffey much."

"He's going to work it off, you think?"

"Either that or he'll walk in on some trigger-happy junkie one afternoon and not get his own gun out in time, and who's going to know whether he was really trying or not? I talked it over with the day chief. At least he still gets things done. He's thorough."

"He would be," I said meaninglessly. I sat there remembering how I'd needled him.

We cruised through the Village slowly. Brannigan cut west on Charles Street, so that we could come back along Perry with the one-way traffic. "I want to roll by once," he told me. "Perry's left-side parking only, so the stake-out will be on my side. I'll tell him to give us a horn signal if anything comes up while we're inside." He glanced at his watch. "Not that anything will, though. Sabatini's had more than three hours since he slugged you. He was probably down here long before I had a chance to put anybody on it."

"He'll be back," I said.

"You got reasons?"

"Two. He still doesn't know she's dead. Also he won't be expecting badges. He thinks I'm in it alone. I'm the same kind of grifter he is."

We had made the turn from Hudson Street and I could see Sally's building up ahead. I pointed it out but Brannigan was more interested in locating his stake-out. He was moving on little more than half a horsepower. "Ought to be along in here. Yeah, the Ford. Joe Turner. Now what the silly hell's he got his motor running for?"

We stopped next to the Ford. The detective named Turner was being busy with a day-old *Journal* but he had spotted us before we came alongside. He gave Brannigan a nod instead of a salute, showed me a sallow, pock-marked face I had seen in a squad room once or twice and was talking before Brannigan could say anything.

"You're just on it, Capt'n. Green Chevy sedan, '56. The guy driving checks out perfect with the Sabatini make. He's cruised by twice, circling the block and looking at the house. I was going to wait until I catch him in the mirror again and then pull out easy—let it look as if I'm giving up the parking space but then block him when he gets in close. The street's narrow enough."

"How long's it take him to make it around?"

"Four, five minutes. He's about due. You want to pull up the block so I can have room to—"

"Too late," I said.

Turner and Brannigan looked. "That's it," Turner said. The green car had just made the turn a block and a half away.

"I'll fake a stall up ahead," Brannigan said quickly. "Pull out behind him, Joe. We'll box him."

Brannigan accelerated slowly, watching the rear-view mirror. Sabatini was coming on in a crawl. We crept past five or six parked cars, then came to a hydrant area. Brannigan swung left and into it, then backed out again. Sabatini wouldn't see the hydrant. Nate was being just another incompetent driver, misjudging the size of a parking slot.

Sabatini kept on coming. One more ridiculous maneuver and we were angled across the middle of the road like beginners flunking the test. Brannigan cut the ignition then. "Wait for Turner," he muttered. He bent forward and began to aggravate the starter noisily.

I was slumped low and out of Duke's line of vision. He had held up about fifteen yards behind us, probably ready to start leaning on his horn. And then Turner pulled out to barricade the street behind him.

"Now," Brannigan said.

Duke's car was facing us like the stem on a letter "T." Brannigan was on the side closest to him. He threw open his door and swung out fast. I had to go out the opposite side and chase around the rear of our car. Brannigan's hand was in his jacket before I was moving.

"Police, Sabatini! Get out of there with your hands high!"

But Duke wasn't buying. His eyes shot to the rear and he saw Turner running toward him. His gears clattered and the Chevy leaped forward with a roar like something being abused in a wind tunnel.

It lurched wildly. There was no room in the street for it to get by. So Duke decided to take the sidewalk. Brannigan let out a yell and heaved himself aside and I saw him go sprawling into the gutter.

I was coming around from behind our car on the dead run, between it and the curb—just where Duke was aiming the Chevy. I snatched at the post of a no-parking sign to stop myself. My .38 was in my right hand so I snatched with my left. I swung up and around like a kid on a maypole. And then the streamer broke and the playground came up and whacked me in the shoulder.

I heard Turner's Special fire twice, still from behind Duke somewhere, but somehow I didn't seem to care. Not really. All I cared about were the four thousand dollars in the First National City Bank it had taken me thirty-one years to accumulate. I lay on the sidewalk, feeling very sad and wishing I'd had the sense to blow some of the money on a little fun in my youth, while the Chevy rocked along the concrete directly at me.

CHAPTER 12

I rolled. I squirmed. I even slud, like in "He slud into third base," from the collected writings of Jerome Herman (Dizzy) Dean.

There was a barred window at ground level in the building nearest me. I was over there and hugging the bars like a frenzied chimpanzee who can't reach the peanuts when the car screamed in my ear and jerked around at a lopsided angle back into the street.

Turner sprinted after it. He stopped, fired five more times. The fifth one was the click of his hammer striking an empty shell.

"Son of a—"

I got back on my feet fast. The rear window of Duke's car was shattered and half torn away, which stopped him as much as water stops a trout. He was a hundred yards off before Brannigan heaved himself into our car. I grabbed up my gun from where it had slithered away and threw myself into the back just as Nate ground gears and started up.

I yanked myself to my knees, clutching the top of the front seat. Brannigan was cursing like an upstaged heroine. We were still angled across the roadway and so he took the curb himself when he swung around. Turner yelled once from somewhere near us.

We were a full block behind the Chevy before we accelerated past the first corner. Brannigan had it down to the floor, muttering between clenched teeth. "Trying to run us down like—"

He didn't finish. Tires screeched up ahead. The signal on Seventh Avenue was red and there was a heavy stream of vehicles crossing the intersection. I saw four cars swerve at once as Duke tried to force the Chevy into the line of traffic.

The screeching stopped. A big, Winesap-colored Olds was cutting sharply away as Duke wheeled to the right. There was a fraction of a second of absolute stillness, as expectant as if Mitropoulos had just lifted his baton.

Duke slammed into the Olds. The right rear end of the larger car tilted up like an elephant raising one leg at a tree-trunk, hung there, then rocked back. There was another dull crashing sound as a panel truck marked *Flowers Say It Better* skidded into the back of the Olds.

We were still moving. A Mercury convertible swung hard to the right and into Perry to avoid the pile-up. It jammed the intersection and blocked us off. Brannigan braked frantically and we shrieked along the curb.

Duke had already bounded out the righthand door of the Chevy. He was running without looking back, making a long diagonal down and across Seventh.

People shouted. I was no more than thirty yards behind him, already out into the street myself and hearing Brannigan pounding after me, when Duke reached the opposite sidewalk. There was a line of store fronts ahead of him and then a gas station on a corner where another small street cut into Seventh at an angle.

"Stop or I'll shoot, Sabatini!"

That was Brannigan. The big Army Colt was pumping with the movement of Duke's arm as he ran but he didn't turn. I threw myself out of the line of fire, breaking toward a string of parked cars on my left. I was halfway there when the single sharp report of Nate's revolver exploded behind me.

Brannigan was good. There was only one shot. Duke's left leg was striding forward when he buckled on it like a ballet dancer with a sudden cramp. He seemed to waver for a fraction of a second, waving his arms like a stricken man on the edge of an abyss. A woman's scream was lost in an almost gentle tinkling of glass as he finally made up his mind to spin to the left and tumble through a plate glass window.

I got over there. It was an antique shop and there was a lot of junk on display. Furniture mostly. A couple of tall, stiff-backed old chairs which looked almost as good as new because nobody for a dozen generations had been quite tired enough to sit on them. Two or three nervous-looking little tables on legs carved so delicately they would probably collapse under the weight of an empty shot glass. A set of yellowing bone china which Pocahontas had gotten as a shower gift from the girls at the wigwam. Henry Wadsworth Longfellow's favorite bronze candlesticks, the ones he wrote *Hiawatha* by the glow of.

Duke Sabatini was on his back in the middle of it all, writhing in his own blood with his neck against the base of an enormous maroon ottoman. About eight inches to the left of his head a neatly hand-lettered sign had fallen. It said: A MINIMUM DEPOSIT WILL SECURE ANY OBJECT IN THIS WINDOW.

A plump, Slavic-looking woman had come rushing out of the store. She gasped and then stood there with her mouth open, staring at me and then at Brannigan as he puffed toward us. "What?" she said. "How—?" The woman had a kerchief around her head and for some absurd reason she made me think of Nikita Khrushchev at the housework.

People were swarming after us now that the gunplay was obviously done with. Brannigan still had his Special in his hand, however. Duke's automatic was at rest in a scarred silver serving tray.

"—Lord, did you see that—"

"—Shooting a man just because he caused an accident—"

"—Cops—"

"—Woman in the Olds isn't even hurt—"

Brannigan said nothing. He jammed the revolver back into his shoulder holster and stepped past me purposefully. Turner was just getting there, red-faced as if he had run all the way, as Nate grabbed Duke by the lapels and hoisted him up effortlessly from the broken glass and the debris. I didn't offer to help him. It would have been like asking Bronco Nagurski if he was sure he could lift a football with all that heavy air in it. Turner and I followed as he eased into the shop and then set Duke down gently on a low overstuffed chair just inside the door.

Duke was in a semi-conscious daze. His jaw hung loose and his eyes were blank. He was bleeding badly.

There was the sound of a siren, evidently headed for the smash-up from nearby, probably from the Charles Street station. The run had started my head throbbing again where Duke had skulled me a few hours before.

"Turner, get back up to the corner and grab the first team that shows up," Brannigan snapped. "Radio for another car on the accident. And get an ambulance."

Turner went off. I shut the door after him. Mrs. People's Chairman was still gaping. "My window. What happened? Is he—?"

"Law," Brannigan told her. "Get some wet cloth, cotton, anything. Hurry up about it."

"Wet—Oh, yes, right away." She stood there another minute, staring at the widening stain of blood soaking into the upholstery along Duke's shoulder. Her eyes went hopelessly toward the smashed window. I supposed you couldn't blame her for being somewhat concerned. Finally she went off.

Brannigan was picking splinters of glass out of Duke's clothing. Duke was slumped low in the chair and his mouth was working now. "Mother," I thought he said. He looked like something the Mau-Mau had left behind as a warning. I reached over, found my Luger in his jacket, smelled it. He hadn't been experimenting on anybody with it. I put it away.

"Damn it," Brannigan said then. "Oh, damn it. What the hell did he think I'd do, let him try a stunt like that and then romp off like it was a high-school picnic or something?"

"He'll live."

"I caught him in the thigh. You saw that."

"Sure."

"I thought the silly son of a bitch would just go down."

"It was just a freak."

"These punk kids. These damned punk kids."

There was another siren. We were standing in the middle of enough lamps to illuminate Minneapolis. The woman came back from the rear, hesitated, then bent forward and began to bathe Duke's forehead with a damp handkerchief. She smelled remotely like a wet spaniel.

Turner got back. Two uniformed cops were with him. "Second car's there now," he reported. "There was a woman driving the Olds. Got banged up a little but she looks okay. We called for two wagons just in case."

"You tell them to get the first one down here?"

"Yes."

Brannigan gestured toward Duke. "Keep a man on him at the hospital and report in as soon as you're squared away. All of it goes on the Hawes sheet. Resist of arrest will be enough for now."

"Right," Turner said.

Brannigan stared at Duke for another minute, then turned and walked past us. Thirty or forty people were milling around out front, gawking, and one of the patrolmen was trying to force them back. Brannigan shouldered through them.

I started to follow him. "That's the one who shot him," a thin-faced busybody was saying after Brannigan. "That big guy."

"What'd it do, make you stain your bloomers, Mac?" Turner snarled behind me. "Go the hell home and change, huh?"

I walked up. Brannigan was talking to a sergeant behind the Olds. There was a hospital one short block up the street and I could see two ambulances camped outside. Angels of mercy in a bureaucracy. They could have had one of those things parked on the slope at Golgotha and they wouldn't have used it without official authorization. Brannigan gestured and after a second the sergeant ran over. There was another dick directing traffic around the tie-up.

There wasn't much damage. The right rear fender of the Olds was crushed back like the lecherous grin of a toothless old man, and the wheel was badly out of line. Duke's front fender was crumpled also, but then he'd wanted to smash it against my head anyhow. There were three neat punctures in the metal just below his back window from Turner's shooting. I didn't see the woman who'd been driving the Olds.

Flowers Say It Better had backed off into Perry. A lanky young Negro unfolded himself from the curb near it, tossed away a smoke and came over to me.

"Can you take my name and tag and let me cruise out of

here?" he wanted to know. "I've got a mess of orchids in there for a party who's going to be right upset if he gets buried without them."

I nodded toward Brannigan. "Better see the boss."

"Don't you gotta always?" he said wearily. He sauntered over that way.

I went over and leaned against Brannigan's car, waiting. It was getting hot. The ambulances finally started up, swinging through a stoplight and letting their sirens growl halfheartedly as they came. My suit was filthy where I'd rolled in it keeping out of the way of the Chevy.

I dragged on a Camel, watching a Village fag come by. Not just another amateur, this one was a classic, a prototype. He was wearing purple pants about four sizes too small, desert boots with tiny bells on the ends of the laces, a tailored blouse. He had a single gold earring in his left ear, none in the right. He was leading an expensive Siamese cat on a pink ribbon that matched his blouse. The cat had the same tiny bells on its collar. I supposed the cat was that way, too.

Brannigan came over after another two or three minutes. "You got a cigarette?" he asked me.

I gave him one. He was looking across at the antique shop and his face was flushed slightly. Two young boys in dungarees were staring at him.

"There's blood on your shirt, mister."

Brannigan grunted. He had a stain along his tie. He closed his jacket but there was another one along his lapel, shaped like a Dali watch.

"You all cleared?"

"That son of a bitch," he said. "That crummy punk. I should have put one into the middle of his spinal column, trying to cut us down that way. And instead I feel my guts flop over when I see him go through that window. Twenty-three years on this job and I still . . . Damn it, Fannin, did that slut of an ex-wife of yours have running hot water up the street here or is it another one of those half-assed Greenwich Village bohemian joints where I'll have to wash off this mess in the toilet? You got a match for this thing?"

I gave him a folder, ignoring all that. "Listen," I told him, "I haven't eaten since about Mother's Day. You want to sit with a cup of coffee while I grab a bite before we run through the apartment?"

"Hell, what time is it?"

"Twenty to ten."

"And it was three-thirty when she got knifed."

"Close enough."

"Six hours and ten minutes. And what have we got?" He handed me back the matches. "I'll tell you what we've got. We haven't got a pot."

"Let's eat, huh?"

"What the hell," Brannigan said. "What the hell."

We walked down Seventh. After about two blocks we found a place that looked all right. It was grand. They had imitation Aztec carvings on the orange-and-green-striped walls and they gave us underdone eggs and yesterday's coffee. We might have stayed all day, but a sign over the register said that occupancy by more than thirty-eight people was dangerous and unlawful and we would have hated for them to get into trouble on our account. Thirty-seven other customers might have dropped in at any moment.

CHAPTER 13

We went back to Perry Street. Bogardus was long gone, but otherwise the place was the same. The dishes and silver were all Woolworth's pride, the upholstery smelled vaguely of insecticide and old sin, and there were seven different water-color views of the same flower pot on the wall, all executed by that color-blind old lady who turns them out for every furnished apartment in the world. Anything Brannigan and I wanted would be tucked away in drawers or stashed in closets. We washed up before we got to it, and then we gave it almost an hour.

We would have been better off using the time to do push-ups. The only item we discovered even remotely connected with crime was a hardcover copy of a Raymond Chandler novel and that had my name in it, dated from eighteen months before. Nothing was hidden under the rug, inside the toilet tank, behind the Shredded Wheat. Nothing slipped out of the pages of the books we flipped except a newspaper recipe for braised squab, and the only notation on any of the recent sheets of the desk calendar was a week-old scribble reminding Cathy to replace something called "Love that Pink." There were snapshots in one of Sally's drawers, mostly beach stuff, and we

124

found an expensive set of blown-up portraits of Cathy stamped on the reverse with the signature of Clyde Neva, the photographer on Tenth Street Sally had mentioned. A book called *Under the Volcano* was the property of Ned Sommers, and two or three re-issue Bix Beiderbecke records had *A. Leeds* scrawled on their jackets, completing Sally's list. There were no unusual deposits or withdrawals in either girl's bank accounts. There were bills, receipts, ticket stubs, circulars, theater programs, canceled checks, folksy letters from Sally's family in Maine, soap coupons, match folders from a dozen Village bars. The only address book had Sally's initials on the cover and nothing in it which interested us. A small scrap of ruled paper in a cracked vase had a phone number penciled on it and when we had run out of other ideas I dialed the number. A syrupy, old-maidish voice said:

"Hello there, we have a message for you. The gift of God is eternal life through Jesus Christ our Lord. Thank you for calling and please give our number to a friend. This is a recorded response. Hello there, we have a message for you. The gift of God is—"

I passed Brannigan the receiver. He listened a minute, hung it up and then stood there picking his teeth with a discolored thumbnail. If the glad tidings had made his day any brighter he was doing his best to hide it. "The Black Knight of Germany," he said after a little.

"I'm listening."

"Nothing. Nothing at all. I was just remembering a game we used to play on the barn roof, being air aces after the first war. Me and two other kids. The names we always used were von Richthofen, Eddie Rickenbacker and Georges Guynemer. They always stick together in my mind, always in the same order."

"Too early for me. Tom Mix, Buck Jones and Ken Maynard, maybe. Which one do you want to see first?"

125

"That Ned Sommers I suppose. Bank Street's only two blocks up."

I called Sally before we went out, telling her that Duke had been roped and that she could come home. She had been asleep. It occurred to me that I could probably use some sack time myself, but it had not caught up with me yet. We left the key under the rubber again.

It was pushing eleven o'clock and the asphalt was already the texture of secondhand chewing gum. They had cleared out the intersection up at Seventh. Brannigan drove the half-block to Fourth Street and turned north.

"You expect to get anything out of these guys?" I asked him.

"Who knows? Some background, anyhow. We'll take it all back to the office later and sort it out with everything else that comes in. Hell, it's all routine, you know how it goes."

"I suppose," I said.

The address we had for Ned Sommers was a beat-up old brownstone with an entrance below street level. Four chipped slate steps went down past a battered regiment of empty trash cans into a tile alcove. It said *Sommers—1-R*, on one of the bells, but the front door was unlatched and we went in without ringing. Uncarpeted steps went up again along the lefthand wall but 1-R would probably be back under them. The hallway smelled like a sanatorium for cats with kidney disorders. We found the door where we expected it to be and Brannigan knocked.

It took a minute, and then the door did not open.

"Who is it?"

"Ned Sommers?"

"Who *is* it?"

"Sommers?"

It could go on that way until one of them got laryngitis

before Brannigan would say "Police." More than one accommodating flatfoot has gotten his wife's name on the department's relief list for needy widows by doing that. He just stood there waiting calmly. Finally we got a crack big enough to pass mail through.

"Ned Sommers?"

He peered out at us, furrowing his forehead. He was a sallow-faced man of about twenty-eight, lean almost to the point of being undernourished. I judged him to be close to six-feet-even but he would not have gone in as more than a welterweight. He had wavy black hair which he had gotten cut for his grade school graduation and not since, pale brown eyes and a nose which had been flattened once. It was a nose which might have made another man look belligerent. It only made Sommers look like someone who ought to have known better. He was wearing cord slacks and nothing else, and if he had been dressed there would have been a library card in his shirt pocket.

"I'm Sommers," he said finally.

One of his hands was on the inside knob and his other was on the door jamb. Brannigan identified himself then, flashing his shield. "We'd like to ask you some questions."

Sommers continued to frown at us. "Questions about what? I'm pretty busy."

We were standing there. Sommers had glanced behind himself, pursing his lips. He turned back. "Let me get a shirt on. I'll come out."

"Step away from the door," Brannigan told him.

"Oh, now look, a man has a right to privacy in his own—"

He moved aside. He had to, since Brannigan was already on his way in. The expression on his face suggested that he would have liked nothing better than to bop one of us with a choice volume of the *Cambridge History of English Literature*. I could see the full set on the wall behind him, along with what looked like

127

every other juicy bit of bedtime reading from *The Nicomachean Ethics* to *The Coming Forth by Day of Osiris Jones.* I couldn't see the woman, but she would be behind the door someplace.

She wasn't quite, but only because the bed wasn't there. It was along the far wall to our left. She was sitting up in it with the sheets drawn around her shoulders. I supposed she might have ducked into another room if that hadn't been the only room there was.

One room. It seemed hardly adequate for Sommers's creative pursuits. The books went from floor to ceiling along two walls. There were enormous piles of what must have been every issue of the *New York Times* since Harper's Ferry and Sommers appeared to be reading all of them simultaneously. There were copies of *Time* with pictures of Neville Chamberlain and John Nance Garner on the covers. There were a hundred different photographs tacked on the two empty walls, and every one of them was of Ernest Hemingway.

The girl's clothes were scattered among the debris as if she'd been caught in a cyclone without enough safety pins.

She was staring at us, still as cut stone. An adder being held by the back of the jaws would have had the same expression in its eyes. She was a Negro and as beautiful a girl as I had ever seen.

Brannigan turned to Sommers, red-necked. "Out front," he said. "And make it quick." He turned around and went out without looking at me.

We waited at the foot of the steps below the sidewalk. Across the way a sign in an unwashed store window said: *Sonny Tom Laundry Will Moving at Monday for Corner Fourth Street Downflight.* Brannigan had taken out a cigar and stripped it but did not light up.

Sommers got there in a minute. He had pulled on a yellow sports shirt and thonged leather sandals and he was smoking.

He glanced at me, dismissed me as a mere adjutant, then waited expressionlessly for Brannigan.

Brannigan was above him on the steps. "I suppose you were here all night?"

"Most if it, yes."

"What time did you get in?"

"Three-thirty, perhaps four. Why?"

"Any other people with you before that?"

"Yes. Two or three young writers who come to me for advice and—"

"Where?"

"The White Horse Tavern, then a coffee shop down on Macdougal. Exactly what is all this, anyhow?"

"There any gap between the time you left the others and came here?"

"No, none at all. They walked me up, in fact. These other fellows haven't been published yet, so it's sort of an obligation to let them hang around as much as they—"

"Okay, okay, you're a famous writer and the disciples cluster around like flies. We get the general drift, Sommers. The girl with you all evening long?"

Sommers's face had darkened. He didn't answer.

"I asked you if the girl was around all night."

"Yes. Now look, I don't think I have to answer any of this. If I don't get an explanation I—"

"When's the last time you saw Catherine Hawes?"

He frowned slightly. "Cathy? A week or so ago. No, more than that. It was a Sunday, so it's almost two weeks."

"Tell us about her."

"Now just what is that supposed to mean?" He glanced at me then back to Brannigan. "She isn't in some kind of trouble—?"

"What kind of trouble would she be in, Sommers?"

"Well, how would I know? Look, what's the point in giving me a hard time? Ask me a sensible question and I'll give you a decent answer, huh?"

Brannigan bit off the end of his cigar, turning to spit. "Tell us about her, Sommers. What she does, what she thinks."

"Oh, come on, will you? If you'd let me know what it's about maybe I could—"

"You're the writer. So write. Give us a paragraph about Catherine Hawes."

Sommers shrugged wearily. He studied his cigarette, dragged on it, flipped it out toward the gutter. He would have liked more of an audience but he gave it to us anyhow. "Catherine Hawes," he said. "About twenty-five, exceptionally pretty. Bright too, but without much intellect. Neurotic, divorced, essentially uninhibited. Just enough sensitivity and awareness so that she can't be satisfied with the ordinary middle-class existence—husband, family, that sort of thing—but not enough creativity or drive to find anything to take its place. She drifts, goes off the deep end sometimes, generally out of sheer boredom—drinks too much, looks for new kicks. There are a lot of girls like her. They shouldn't go to college to start with. They get just enough ideas about art and rebellion to get restless. But most of them settle down eventually, wind up at cocktail parties in the country club and forget they ever knew the difference. They play golf. Cathy probably will too, sooner or later."

"You said she *was* married."

"She cheated. It broke up."

"She a nympho?"

"I wouldn't put it that way. She was knocking around a lot before the marriage. People get used to that. It's not the sexual satisfaction so much as the excitement of somebody new. Hell, even I was the same way. I was married a couple of times myself, out of this same Village milieu. It was good enough while it lasted—I didn't *need* other women, no—but the idea is always there. You get the urge, you follow through. Anyhow it's an important experience for a writer. You've got to—"

"Edifying," Brannigan cut in. "Who would she go to if she got into a jam? Who is she closest to?"

Sommers shrugged again. "Look, I don't really know. The girl she lives with, perhaps. Sally Kline. Maybe she'd come to me. How about it now—what kind of trouble?"

"You sure you haven't seen her in a week and a half?"

"Positive."

"She come around here often?"

"Once a week, perhaps. A writer has to discipline his use of time. In any event there's nothing steady about it, if that's what you mean."

"I gathered that inside," Brannigan said.

"Now look, if that's a crack—"

"Probably it was. Skip it. I don't read books myself so I wouldn't know what it takes to write them."

Sommers chewed his lip, not knowing whether he could afford to get angry or not. We stood there. Two young girls passed us on the street, chattering. "That illiterate," one of them said. "All he did was say hello and then keep shoving me into corners—"

I was taking a Camel. "I bum one of those?" Sommers asked. "I left mine in back."

I gave him one and lit it. He nodded, hardly looking at me. He hadn't really seen me since we'd gotten there, which I supposed explained why he liked Hemingway so much. Hemingway never sees anybody either.

"I don't know what else to say without knowing what it's all about," he told Brannigan.

"That's good enough for now," Brannigan decided. "You'll hear from the department again." He had started up the stairs.

When he did get the urge to read, it patently wasn't going to be something of Sommers's.

"Well, for crying out loud," Sommers said after us, "this is some deal. You come around asking all kinds of personal questions and then you—"

"You can go back in," Brannigan said, stopping. "Your sweetheart's probably getting edgy in there."

"That's none of your damned business!" Sommers had made up his mind to get sore after all. "Police. Try to be decent and what does it get you? Thanks a lot, mister."

"You're welcome. You've been a cooperative, helpful citizen. And now you can blow."

"The hell with you," Sommers said abruptly. "Sure, I've been cooperative. And I didn't have to answer a damned one of your questions. You guys give me a royal pain. A bunch of tough, cynical, uncreative clods, what the hell do you know? What I do in my apartment is my own concern and I don't need any comments from your end. I'm a writer and a good one, and if you want to know I spent four years in jail. Sure, lift an eyebrow when I tell you. Go back and look it up, it's all there. I stole eleven thousand dollars when I was eighteen. Eighteen! You guys wouldn't have had the imagination to swipe apples! Well, I did my time and I don't owe you anything, see?"

I wondered precisely what had brought all that on. Brannigan was at the top of the steps, looking at his cigar. "Nobody said you owed us anything, Sommers," he said quietly.

"Yeah, well, I don't have to make any explanations about my private life either. What I do to make myself a better writer is my business. You slobs wouldn't know an experience if it hit you in the face."

He made a point of deliberately flinging away the cigarette I'd just given him. That was quite an approach he had toward his profession at that. I could almost visualize him at work, writing stirring exhortations in his notebook: *Very important! Every Tuesday and Thursday, nine to eleven, be sure to have an experience!* The vestibule door slammed after him when he whirled and went inside.

Brannigan was already walking. "Writer," he said. "If that self-centered phony is a writer then I'm—I'm—"

"Marcel Proust," I said. "Ducky Medwick. What the hell, you didn't have to needle him that way."

"Greenwich Village," he grunted. He did not say anything else until we had gotten into the car. Then he said, "And the next one is a queer. That Neva, the photographer. And I suppose the one after that—what's his name? That Arthur Leeds—will be a hermaphrodite. Why don't you go the hell home and catch up on some sleep? They'll have the body out of there by now."

"You're a comfort," I said.

"I get that way."

He cut down Seventh before turning east on Tenth Street and we passed the antique shop. The smashed window was already being boarded up. "I suppose there'll be a suit against the city for that," he said then. "And probably one on the accident. Causing Sabatini to flee at excess speed, some such malarkey. Maybe it isn't Greenwich Village after all. Maybe it's just people who make me sick."

He was still laboring the unlit cigar. We passed the rear of the Women's House of Detention and that gave him a few more ideas. "And right in there is where she would have wound up if she hadn't gotten knifed. In with the whores and the junkies and the lovely little seventeen-year-old mothers who get drunk and bash their kids' heads against the wall for crying too much. Sweating out an arraignment for driving the car on the Troy heist. Because she was bored. Because she was too sensitive to be satisfied with the middle-class way of life—is that what the bastard said it was?"

"Why don't you shut it off, Nate? I'm the one who ought to be disgusted."

"Are you? You don't much seem to be. Buster Keaton I got to ride with. Just how do you feel about all this anyhow?"

"Go to hell," I told him. "As a favor, huh? Just for me?"

CHAPTER 14

Clyde Neva's address turned out to be a six-story warehouse structure on a block taken up almost completely by the sides of large apartment buildings which fronted on other streets. The place had two entrances. One of them was a gigantic sliding-gate affair for trucks. That one was boarded up. The other one was small and newly painted, the color of a stale whisky sour. A neatly polished metal plaque in the center of it said:

Neva Portraits—Loft

The smaller door opened into a narrow stairwell with concrete fire steps and a metal handrail leading upward. There was another plaque just inside which said simply *Neva,* and still another on the first landing, this time with an arrow pointing upward. Underneath the third plaque someone had scrawled in lipstick: *Oh, Clyde, if I come up all that way I'll just never, never come down.* The fire doors from the unused warehouse were barred on each landing.

The stairwell was sweltering. There was one final *Neva* at the top, in case someone hadn't been paying attention, and a bell that you worked by a chain. Brannigan worked it and we heard it tinkle somewhere inside. I crushed out a cigarette, sweating.

Clyde Neva called out to us as he started to open the door, saying, "But darling, you're *so-ooo* early," and then he got a look at us and said, "But it *isn't* you either, is it? I don't know you, do I? But then that's always *so-ooo* exciting! Do come in, do!"

"Can it," Brannigan said.

"I *beg* your pardon?"

"Can the swish talk, we're not buying. You Clyde Neva?"

He looked at us, pouting. He had the sort of face that was meant to pout, the kind that would have looked charming in the mirror over a lady's dressing table while its owner plucked her eyebrows, if its owner had been a *her*. So it had probably looked sickening when its owner had plucked *his*. He was wearing rouge, and you could have hitchhiked to Rochester and back in the time he'd spent on his hair. Each tiny blond curl had been twisted into place separately, in a way which made his head look as if someone had doused it with mucilage and then dumped the contents of a bait can over it. He was wearing an orange turtleneck sweater, and the buttermilk-colored things he thought were pants were so tight that he had probably had to put them on with Vaseline.

"I said are you Neva?"

"But *naa*-tur-a-lly. Surely you didn't miss the darling signs?"

Brannigan had wanted to know what I felt. I could have told him now. Just tag along, Harry, come meet all the jolly sorts she'd shared her Ju-Jubes with in the past dozen months. I felt an incipient nausea just looking at this one.

We'd gone in. Neva had the full floor, and most of it was one stadium-size room with windows along the rear and a skylight in the roof. The place might have been the ballroom in a sorority house for unmatriculated screwballs on party night.

Instead of chairs there were pillows scattered everywhere, all of them violet and all about the size of recumbent hippopotami. Most of the wall space was taken up with weird, leering African masks, and there were Chinese lanterns hanging from the ceiling like Yuletide at the Mao Tse Tung's. A broad platform raised the level of the floor about ten inches in a far corner, and in the middle of the platform, draped in pink, was the largest bed I had ever seen. It would have accommodated the starting five from the Harlem Globetrotters and probably two or three substitutes. They could have practiced in it if they didn't feel like sleeping. A white picket fence ran around the outside edge of the platform, and in the center of the fence was a little red gate. A lantern hung on the gatepost. A sign said: *Neva.*

The photographic equipment stood by itself in another corner, near a door marked: *Dark Room—For Pictures, Silly.* There was another door near that one with a large half moon carved into the paneling.

Neva was reading Brannigan's shield and being remotely concerned. "But, *dears*," he was saying, "what can you want with little old *me?*"

I took a cigarette. I was running out of them.

"Neva, I've got some questions and I want some answers," Brannigan told him. "Straight answers without the phony affectations. Save that for the misfits you think you have to impress. You got some clean young boy who'll give you an alibi for last night?"

"Have I got—oh, *come* there, must you be so crude, Mr. Brannigan? And you haven't even been polite. The *least* you might do is introduce me to your *hand*-some friend."

He looked at me with a sly, simpering sort of grin that was supposed to be clever and quaint and superior all at once. It made his face about as appealing as the back end of a dachshund. I went over to a window and stood there, which was the

137

only thing I could think to do to keep from drop-kicking him through the skylight.

"Neva, I asked you about last night."

"Well, of *course* I was with someone, darling. Isn't *everyone?*"

Brannigan had meant it about not being on the market for the gay talk. Neva finally got the clue when he found himself being hoisted by the front of the sweater and dumped onto one of the huge purple pillows. He let out a gigglish little squeal, like a goosed hyena.

"You *needn't* be so aggressive! Please, my analyst says my psyche is very delicate. I just *mustn't* get upset!"

"I bet. And your analyst can lick my old man any day of the week." Brannigan was towering over him. "I won't say it a second time, Neva. Anymore of that 'darling' routine and you'll do your answering down at headquarters under lights that'll make that mascara of yours run down into your socks."

Neva was pouting again. He got to his feet with a gesture like petals opening, then stood there posing with his hands limp in front of him. He nodded grudgingly.

"Who were you with last night?"

"A chap named Anton Quayles. We were developing—"

"Here?"

"—pictures. Here, yes."

"What time did he leave?"

"About nine o'clock this morning. We were *working* quite late."

"He going to admit that?"

"If you're as offensive with him as you've been with me, I'm certain he'll have no choice."

"Never mind the editorial comment either. You have any other visitors?"

"Would you?"

"Damn it, Neva—"

"No, no other visitors. We were *quite* alone."

"When's the last time you saw Catherine Hawes?"

"Catherine—" Neva pursed his lips. His hands were still raised limply, as if he'd just finished an exhausting concerto at an invisible Steinway, but he seemed suddenly conscious of the gesture. He opened his mouth to say something, then thought better of it.

"When, Neva?"

"I—well, it's been weeks, we—"

Brannigan had him by the sweater again, jerking him forward. Neva squirmed, trying to draw away. He kept running his tongue over his lips, and now his eyes were darting from Brannigan's to mine and then back. I went over there.

"What about her, Neva?"

"I—they *weren't* pornography," he gasped then. "They were art. Anyhow I didn't send any of them through the mail so there's no charge that can be—"

"Son of a—" Brannigan flung him aside like something unclean. Neva went to his knees. He snatched at one of the pillows, hugging it to himself and cowering behind it. He had begun to whimper like a setter pup with its first dose of worms.

"There was only one set. Only one, honestly. That's all I ever printed. And I never took any others. You can ask anyone. I'm a very serious portrait photographer. Some of my young men's faces have won awards in—"

"Get 'em, Neva."

"But I—"

"Get them!"

Neva swallowed once, getting to his feet, then scampered across the room toward a filing cabinet with a series of mincing, tight-cheeked little steps. A high-jumper with hemorrhoids would have moved just about the same way. Brannigan had glanced at me. I ground my cigarette into the floor with my heel.

Neva was rummaging through a top drawer. He was mumbling.

"Talk up, damn it," Brannigan said.

"I merely tried to say that it wasn't my idea, not at all. We were—well, it was after a party and she was tipsy, and the boys she was with were tipsy too, and I—"

"*Boys* she was with—"

Brannigan took three strides toward the cabinet. "Get the grease off your fingers and hand them over here, Neva!"

"Yes, yes, I—" Neva scurried back toward us, white-faced. He held out a manila folder awkwardly.

I was staring at the palm of my right hand when Brannigan opened it. He did not say anything. He looked at the picture on the top of the pile long enough to flush and then he dropped his hand without looking at any of the others.

"Let's see them, Nate."

He handed them over. They were about what I expected. Neva was not even much of a photographer. I had seen better at stag parties in college.

I looked through all of them. Cathy's eyes were squinting against the light as if she'd been hopped up on marijuana when they were taken, but I did not bother to mention it. I handed them back without saying anything at all.

They would have made splendid illustrations for a book I had just begun thinking about writing. I was calling it *Fannin Grows Up.*

"Get the negatives, Neva."

Neva brought out a smaller folder. Brannigan lifted out one negative, held it to the light, put it back. There was a sink on a wall behind us and he went over there. He tore the prints into pieces, then crumpled the negatives on top of them.

"There anymore of these? Anyplace?"

"No, honestly, none at all. Just the single set."

Brannigan dropped a match into the sink, standing there while the pile flared up. There was a quick stench from the negatives.

He turned back after a minute, talking quietly now. "Neva, if I didn't want to keep the girl's name out of a mess like this on top of everything else I'd take you in so fast your jeans would unravel. I'll forget I ever saw those things, or for that matter you. Especially you. But I'll give you fair warning. If I ever hear your name once in connection with anything that comes through the department, I'll have a vice squad cop on your neck twenty-five hours a day and thirty on Sundays. I'll have you hauled in and booked if you so much as shake hands with a business acquaintance on the street. You got that straight?"

Neva nodded. He was not the same frivolous lad who'd greeted us at the door a few minutes before. But then I had to wonder just who was.

"You pig," Brannigan said. "You slimy, ugly, perverted son of a bitch. You—ah, the hell with it. You've been told. Get even a parking citation from here on out and you'll see whether or not I'm just making conversation."

He turned and looked at me, then went out. He went down the concrete stairs quickly and I didn't rush to keep up with him. I was only a short way down when Neva called after me. I stopped and looked back.

"About Catherine," he said hesitantly. "You didn't say. Is anything the matter? I—"

"You know Ned Sommers?"

"Slightly, yes. The writer."

"You could call him," I said. "He'll probably be interested, too. She's dead."

I couldn't have told anybody why I'd bothered. I didn't wait for his reaction. Brannigan was already in the car when I got down. The street was like a stokehold and my shirt was clinging to me.

"That was some dame, Fannin," he said when I got in. "I never did congratulate you on getting divorced, did I?"

He didn't expect an answer so I didn't make one. He jerked away from the curb and then swung down into the lower east side of the Village before heading across toward Jones Street. I did not say anything all the way over. I kept seeing the photos of Cathy in my mind, and when I tried to get rid of them the only thing that came instead was an image of her on the floor in my doorway. It made the ride fun. I had such a swell choice of things to think about.

The Arthur Leeds address was another brownstone. Brannigan parked across from it and then sat there for a minute without opening the door. "Forget it, huh?" he said. "Rubbing you, I mean. Hell, you didn't know how far she'd gone."

"No, I didn't."

He made a sucking sound between his lips, leaning forward on the wheel. "I still don't get it, you know. You. God knows, you've been around. And yet you stayed married to her for damned near a year."

I didn't answer him. He went on talking without looking at me.

"Promiscuous as a mink. And judging from the evidence, about as discriminating as a hungry hound in the town dump. You've got ten or a dozen buddies doing time who'd like to have fooled you that long."

I still didn't answer him. I took a cigarette and pulled on it deeply, watching the smoke break against the windshield.

"All right," he said, "so it's none of my business. You want to go in?"

I nodded, opening the door. I hadn't answered him because

I didn't have any answers. I'd spent a year trying to get rid of what I'd felt about Cathy and then this morning had brought it all back. It was still rotten, thinking that things might have been different for her if she'd had some help, and I had to feel guilty about that. But I was not feeling much of anything else now. Brannigan was probably right that it would be something you would figure out sitting at a desk or using a phone, and even that did not bother me the way it would have six or eight hours before.

We were walking across. "Soon as we see this one we'll check Coffey out," he was telling me.

Leeds was listed for 3-B and it was another one we didn't have to ring. Some misguided soul had hooked back the outside door in the hope that it might let a little cool air in. Maybe there was cool air on Annapurna or Orizaba. I dragged myself up the two rickety flights like an old-age pensioner. We found the door we wanted at the end of a corridor and Brannigan rapped on it.

That was when I noticed that the heat was getting to Brannigan also. He was sweating badly and his face was flushed. We heard a voice say, "Get that, will you, Henry," and then when Henry opened the door and said, "Who intrudes?," Brannigan did not ask for Leeds the way he had asked for Sommers or Neva. He had his wallet in his hand and he lifted it with a tired gesture and said, "Police."

The man in the doorway did almost nothing. He squinted out at us behind thick glasses as if he had not heard us correctly, and then he turned to repeat the word over his shoulder. "Police, dads?" he said curiously.

He didn't get an answer. There were about six quick footsteps and then there was the sound of a chair clattering to the floor. A second after that a window went up, hard, jarring the weights inside its molding. The man in the doorway had blocked us unintentionally, but I had a hunch the elbow I planted in his liver would remind him to be less careless in the future. I saw the second man's back as he cleared the window ledge, which was about twenty feet away in the far wall of a rear room, and then he was out of sight and rattling down a fire escape.

Twenty feet. A man with my stride, or Brannigan's, can cover the distance from a standstill in approximately a second. We both started to, but neither of us quite made the window. Because the second hadn't fully elapsed when the sound began, and when it came we were both rooted like snow-heavy birches, bent forward and frozen.

It was a man's scream. I had heard one exactly like it a dozen years before in North Africa. Press me and I could tell you the date, the name of the crossroads, exactly what I'd been doing when it happened. The G.I. had been sleeping off a binge on the edge of a ditch. When they'd backed the tank off him you could have peeled up what was left of his legs to wrap your holiday mailing.

Brannigan looked out first. He said, "Oh, God, oh, my God," and a priest giving final rites would have had a voice just as hushed. After that he choked and was fighting to keep himself from vomiting and you could hardly blame him for that.

The man had gone down one flight of the fire escape toward the narrow yard below and then had changed his mind. There was an alley behind the building which faced on the next block and he had decided to go over there. There was a spiked fence between the yard and the alley, with its spikes sticking up about a foot above the crossbar which held them in place. The spikes were about an inch thick at the bar, tapering sharply to four-sided points from there upward. Evidently the man had climbed the railing at the second landing and tried to jump it.

Whoever he was, athletics obviously hadn't been his long suit. Half of him had gotten across.

He was hanging face-downward with his arms and trunk over the far side and his legs toward us. The spikes were set closely enough together so that he had caught three of them in the bowels. They were sticking up through the back of his pants like dirty fingers through a moth-eaten scarf.

The shoelace he had tripped over was still swinging loose.

CHAPTER 15

I climbed out. Brannigan was turning back to the man called Henry as I went, but Henry was not leaving. He wanted a look, too.

He got it as I was climbing down. From the way it tore him up, I gathered that the lad on the fence would be a grief he'd find hard to sustain. "Man," I heard him say, "like shishkebob!"

I got down there. "Any point in an ambulance?" Brannigan said.

"Hearse, Nate."

The deceased had been about thirty-five and a redhead, but you could not tell much from his face about anything else. He had bitten a deep gash into his tongue, which was hanging out like an empty mitten, and his eyes were bulging.

I stood there for a minute. He was impaled at just about the level of my shoulders and he did not look heavy. He would have leaked, however.

I glanced up. "You want me to?"

Brannigan's face was drawn. The other man was still gaping. He was small and thin-faced and maybe forty, and his lenses looked thick enough to double as casters. "Leave him," Brannigan said finally. "Wait a second."

He moved away from the window. There was already a fly or two at the man I supposed had been Arthur Leeds. I doubted that he was the boy who had killed Cathy, since he would not have been just waiting around for us that way, so I shooed the flies off.

Brannigan came back. He had a balled-up tan bedspread in his hands and he tossed it down to me. He was right enough about that. There were only eight or ten windows looking out that way, but sooner or later someone's favorite aunt was going to open one of them to sprinkle the geraniums. Some of them should have shot up when he'd screamed. Probably there was a quiz show on.

I billowed out the spread and threw it over him, then ripped it across some of the spikes so that it would not slip off. I left him like that.

The other man was slumped in a straight chair when I came up. He was wearing a red and gray plaid jacket that some peddler's stout horse was happier for the lack of, and a black string tie which disappeared into the top of his pants. That left all of four inches of the tie showing, since the pants ended under his armpits somewhere. He had taken off his glasses and was holding them, and it seemed to have finally gotten through to him. His face was the color of soggy oatmeal.

Brannigan was standing over him with his hands on his hips. "Leeds, man, oh, yes," the man was muttering. "Arthur indeed. Like wow, what a fadeout!"

"Damn it," Brannigan said, "what was it all about? What made him run?"

"Sugar, man, you're the flatfoot. I just spin tunes, you know? Like I mean, you ought to know what he bugged out for."

Brannigan hit him. He brought the back of his hand across the man's jaw from right to left and the man sucked in his breath with a sound like a punctured accordion. He scrambled backward, losing the chair. It started to go over and he caught it with one hand, dancing behind it and waving his glasses hysterically. "Don't, man!" he screeched. "Like don't! Sugar, it ain't none of mine! Like I couldn't whistle note-one of that tune, that's for real, except that he just now told me. I just ambled over to spin some lyrics, you know? Like right there—there's my notebook on the piano, see? Oh, yes, oh, yes, Henry Henshaw, like it's got my name on the cover. Like I wouldn't even blow my mother-in-law's coin for that stuff, you dig me? I ain't been hooked for lo, these ten years. I—"

His voice trailed off as Brannigan stood up. Brannigan's jaw was set and his lips were tight. He grunted disgustedly. "What did he have? Had Narcotics been on to him?"

"The real goods, oh, yes. Far out. The mighty H, like. He announced they had been bugging him bad. They picked him up two weeks ago but he was clean. But like he was terrified, man. He just got in this new horn full. That cat on the fence, you know? I mean not me. All this is just what he mentioned in passing. True, dad, that's straight. I don't lay a hand on hide nor hair, you know? Like I don't even want to hear any of that chatter, not Henry Hiram Henshaw!"

"He push it?"

"I'm weak on details, man. Like he's in the middle someplace, kind of a transfer point, you take my meaning? Like some cat dumps it into his pocket and another cat lifts it out again. He gets maybe two bills a week for this inconvenience, like it's better than they leave it in a locker in Grand Central. He—"

"Where is it? Where's he keep it?"

"In yon head. Like that's what he informed me. You dig how calm and cool I'm telling you, don't you, man? Like I mean, sugar, why ought I not? I'm just here to spin a tune, oh, yes, oh, yes. If I just happen to be coincidentally cognizant of the fact that the cat stashes his nasty old heroin under the sink, like, that saves labor all around, does it not? *Doesn't* it?"

Brannigan did not answer him. He nodded to me and I went into the latrine and felt around on the underside of the sink. It was taped into place but it pulled away easily. It was a carton about the size of two packs of Pall Malls end to end, maybe a little more thick. I brought it out.

Brannigan's mouth was still set. The carton was sealed with transparent tape and he tore it open. He glanced inside.

Henshaw giggled, clutching the back of his chair. "Like you want to be sure of the contents," he said, "you sniff it. Ha! Like you could be the coolest cat in coptown, man. Hahahaha!"

Brannigan walked across the room and set the carton on top of the piano. It was a fairly new upright, probably the only item in the apartment which did not come with the rent. Everything else had that same twenty-seven-tenants-and-still-holding-its-own look of the stuff in Sally's place.

When Brannigan turned back he was taking out a set of cuffs. Henshaw had just gotten seated again. He jerked himself upright with his knees drawn up and his heels clutching the front edge of the seat. "Hey, man, like ain't I been coming on real cooperative like? True now? Am I to be a victim of circumstance? I, Henshaw, innocent bystander? Like I've got my rights—"

Brannigan ignored him. He yanked Henshaw's left wrist toward him and clicked the bracelet into place, then locked the other ring around a narrow steam-heat pipe which ran up to the ceiling next to the chair.

"Like help, now," Henshaw kept protesting. "For crying out loud, dad, I want a lawyer. I want ten lawyers. I want my agent. You can't bug me like this, I'm—"

Brannigan took him by the lapels. "Shut up," he said. He did not raise his voice. "Just shut up and don't say another word. If

149

you're clear you'll get off and that will be the end of it. But in the meantime you're going to sit here until I straighten this thing out and you're not going to be any bother. You're not going to talk unless you're spoken to. You're going to be seen and not heard. You're not even going to breathe too heavily. You got that?"

Henshaw gulped helplessly. He glanced toward me but I did not have anything for him. He opened his mouth, had a second thought, said nothing. He stared at the cuffs as glumly as a stripteaser confronting a low thermometer.

Brannigan had picked up a phone across the room. He dialed a number. When he got it he said, "This is Nate Brannigan, Central. Give me somebody big in Narcotics, will you? Somebody who knows what's current. Charley Peakes, maybe. . . . Sullivan'll do. Thanks."

He looked back to Henshaw while he was waiting. "Where was Leeds last night?"

"We were blowing, your majesty, sir," Henshaw said bitterly. "This joint over on Second Street. We're there four nights a week, you know?"

"How late?"

"We retired early, your highness. One A.M., your kingship. We had another session scheduled for *après* that, but Leedsie wasn't coming on too cool. Sir. Like he was all shook up on this police bit, *comprenez vous?* He kept flatting. What occurs if I got to go to the head here? I am like sometimes prone to have complications with my kidneys. They—"

Brannigan had gotten his connection. "Brannigan, Sully. Fine. Listen, an Arthur Leeds, Jones Street—there be a reason why he'd take a dive out a window rather than talk to two cops at the front door?"

The Narcotics man had a gravel voice and I caught a few random words as he talked. He went on for a minute or two and Brannigan frowned once or twice. "Yeah," he said finally, "working on something else entirely. Just walked in on it. Yeah, dead. No, that's all right, Sully, I'll call. But I've got what reads like eight or ten thousand dollars' worth of the stuff sitting on a piano here, so you can send a pick-up on that. I've got a pal of his cuffed to a pipe also, name of Henshaw. Might be a delivery, I'm not sure, but I'll leave him for your boys at the same time. No, never mind, I'll get a precinct wagon for the body. Right. You want to give me a switch? Thanks. See you in church, Sully."

He turned back to me while he was waiting for his transfer. "They've been sweating him out for months," he said, "trying to get a make on his contacts. Some bonehead rookie picked him up by mistake two weeks ago and they figured the whole thing was shot. If Henshaw here isn't their boy it's dead now completely. Leeds was a heavy traffic point."

"Me!" Henshaw screamed. He clattered his cuffs. "Hey, now, man, like I declared, I was just here to spin a—"

Brannigan got his other call. "Brannigan, Central," he said. He gave the Jones Street address. "Corpse impaled on a fence, accident while fleeing interrogation. Central operation. A wagon, one car. No, nothing else, it's a Narcotics mix. They're on the way. Right, I'll be here. Yes."

He hung up and glanced my way again. "Twice," he said. "Twice in one morning. That punk through the shop window and now this. Damn it."

I didn't say anything. He stood there a minute, staring at nothing, and then he dialed once more. He was looking rotten. "Brannigan," he said. "Get me Pete Weller in my office."

I sat down across from Henshaw and took a cigarette. It was my last one.

"Me, Pete," Brannigan said. "What's with the Hawes sheet? Coffey make that hotel check? Yeah, I expected as much. You match up the Bogardus story with what came out of Troy? Right. What about the run-down on Fannin's block? That too, huh? Hospital report on Sabatini? Well, that's something, at least. What's on red MG's? Oh, sweet damn. No, give it to me now, just read them down so I can see if any of the locations sound interesting—"

He listened expressionlessly to something for several minutes. "Hell," he said finally. "All right, yeah, tell him to keep checking in. No, all looks like a big bust. Yeah. Stick on it. So long."

He put the phone back and looked at me. "Last Monday I had three different tips on the same horse," he said somberly. "Three. Thirty bucks I put down, money the wife doesn't even know I've got. You know where the horse comes in? I should have known what kind of week it was going to be."

"All of it?"

"All of it. Coffey couldn't get a tumble at any of the hotels. About sixty different overnights and any names in the bunch could have been Sabatini and the girl. The plainclothesmen I had checking your street for possible witnesses got nothing at all, a couple of people might have heard tires screech around three-thirty but nobody bothered to look out of any windows. Sabatini's all right, but his version of the story pairs up with the other punk's—no variations, no loose ends to make anything of. All we've got are red MG's. You know how many of them? Forty-one, for hell's sake. Twenty-eight cops and thirteen hack drivers saw vehicles of that description on the streets last night, but not one of them had any reason to pay attention to plate numbers. Forty-one, all the way from the Cloisters down to the Battery and back, all between roughly two and three-thirty in the morning. Every shoe clerk and his brother drives a red MG, for crying out loud. And not one of the locations fits with anything we know so far—none here or at Neva's or at Sommers's. Nobody even saw it parked out in front of your place. Damn it to hell. We're nowhere, Harry. Except at a nice rosy dead end."

He walked across the room and parked himself heavily on a studio couch, then took out a cigar and looked at it. When he did, Henshaw began to giggle.

Brannigan heaved the cigar at him. The small man ducked, but he reached out deftly with his free hand at the same time and snatched the cigar out of the air. He righted himself and flipped it into his mouth, wrapper and all, and sat there grinning smugly.

Dead end—except that we'd forgotten to wind up one small aspect of the interrogation. Henshaw had the cigar tilted up at a rakish angle, watching me merrily as I walked across.

"Okay," I told him, "so like it's a canary. So swallow it or spit it out. What did Leeds do after one o'clock?"

He wiggled the cigar. He tittered. He slapped his knee. "The Hawes *sheet*," he chortled. "Oh, I dig that, oh, yes, oh, yes! That's what the man said, is it not? The Hawes sheet? What a far-out place to get high! Who needs a measly fix when the Hawes sheets lie awaiting!"

And then Henry Hiram Henshaw abruptly stopped paying any attention to me at all. I took him by the shirt front and he dropped the cigar, but he did not seem to notice. I shook him but all he did was turn his head. He shuddered, and then two wet tears trickled out from under the hubcaps he wore for glasses.

"Ah," he said softly then, "alas, poor Leedsie. Last night the Hawes sheets, this morning the cold, cold shaft."

CHAPTER 16

I was at a window which faced the street. Everything was bright and sharply etched in the sun, and I watched a woman come out of one of the brownstones across the way, smartly dressed in a conservative aqua summer suit and leading a small boy by the hand. The boy was blond as snow, six or seven at most, and they made a lovely picture together. At the bottom of the steps the boy stopped and said something and the woman gave him a belt across the ear which would have felled a first-growth spruce. I turned back to Henshaw.

Brannigan was standing over him. It left me cold. Leeds, the thing on the fence, anonymous as a side of cheap beef. I'd wanted a live one. I'd wanted one with a face I could put a fist into. I wanted a cigarette also, but I didn't have any. I chewed on a match.

"All of it," Brannigan was saying. "In plain, simple, ordinary American English, Henshaw. When did you see the Hawes girl here?"

"Okay, dads, okay. But give a cat room, stand back, you're fogging my spectacles. I'll reconstruct, I'll come on strong in all details. But like allow me room to stroll my thoughts, huh, man?"

154

Brannigan took a deep breath. "From the beginning, Henshaw. The name of the joint on Second Street. Everything from the time you left there."

"I'm recalling, man. The handle on the house is indisputable. I mean unless they sold out shop this morning, like. Handleman's Happy Hour. They even got my picture out front—under glass, you know? The Bird blew there once, man. Charley Parker in the flesh. You cats dig jazz, incidentally? Or am I cast awash on an alien shore, like?"

"You'll be awash someplace if you don't get to it," Brannigan said. "You finished a performance at one o'clock. Leeds was nervous about the heroin so you canceled the next show. Then what? Where'd you go? Who was with you?"

"Awash, I am awash at that. So I will feed it to you straight, like, sans rhythm, sans melody, sans life! Ah, lackaday!" Henshaw sighed dejectedly. Brannigan took a quick step toward him and the small man made a protective gesture with his free hand. "No, man, like no! All, I'll tell all. One, yes, one o'clock. Here, man, we lit out for here. To this very pad."

"Just you and Leeds?"

"You dig me, your highness."

"Damn it, and then what?"

"Bliss, man, bliss. An exclusive cutting of a new Charley Mills disc. Private, unreleased, for our own hip ears alone. Man, if that Mills ain't the coolest with the longhair stuff, if that cat ain't the sole last living genius in Greenwich Village, I'm—"

"Henshaw, you want me to hook that bracelet higher up on that pipe? You want to tell this hanging by your wrist from the ceiling?"

"Well, man, man, ain't I coming on? Am I obfuscating, like? Like you requested, in detail. In detail, I, H. H. Henshaw, and the late lamented A. Leeds, repaired from the pad known as Handleman's Happy Hour to this here pad known as where we are now in session, solo and by ourselves, to soothe our savage breasts by paying profound heed to a rendition of something *très* cool, *très* far out, by that yet unrecognized master, C. Mills. We listened and then I kid you not, we listened anew. And then the chick made an entrance."

"Catherine Hawes?"

"Well now, dads, get with it, huh? Who else? Edna St. Vincent Millay? Bess Truman? The siblings Brontë, maybe? The Hawes chick, man. But, yes, oh, yes."

"What time?"

"Give or take a chorus, the little hand was at the two and the big hand was breathing down the neck of the four. Like two-eighteen, maybe."

Brannigan was sitting across from him. He stared at his right fist, then covered it with his other hand. "And?" he said patiently.

"And Henshaw departed. I mean, sugar, man, like I could share a cat's coin, or borrow his pad, or even, when my straits are dire, might I sip the last ounce of Grade A in the big white box. But a cat's mouse, never! Anyhow he told me to fly. The chick was coming on real queer, like maybe she put butane in her syringe by mistake, and I am not one to mix unnecessarily in troubles. I debouched."

Brannigan glanced at me. "No needle marks," he said. "She wasn't on anything." He turned back to Henshaw. "Could she have been just scared?"

Henshaw shrugged, gesturing. The cuffs rattled when he did. "I write them like I see them, dads. He was an old man, like, and he got hung up looking for big fish down there in the Gulf Stream, you know? But like he wasn't hooking them, and so he dreamed of Joe DiMaggio. You read that book? Man, she *could* have been scared. She could have had hepatitis like, too. If I'd been cognizant of the fact that I'd be contending for a Nobel

Prize like this, I'd have done a biopsy and penned a report in pure iambic, you dig me?"

"All right, all right. What did she say when she got here? What next?"

"Like who listened? Like she whispered to him a minute, and then she gave him a gander at something she had in this reticule. That's a sack, Jack. And then Leedsie gives me the nod. I'm all bugged up for home-fried potatoes anyhow, had the things on my mind all day. Like you know how you get bugged that way sometimes, man? So I amble up the square to Kirker's and get me a double order. Which is when I espy the chick again. When I'm satiated with home-fries, that is. I'm strolling home, back past this pad here again, when I see the chick make for her heap like Leedsie blew the wrong riff, you know? Those forty-one *rouge* MG's you cats are all shook up over, she had one of those. That heap came on like Louis himself, I josh you not. You get all forty-one of those fiddles jamming together on one block sans mufflers that way, you couldn't dig that sound with a shovel."

"Damn it, Henshaw, what in hell are you talking about? You had two orders of French-fries and then you saw the Hawes girl beat it out of here in the MG?"

"*Home*-fries, man, like *h-o-m-e*-fries!"

"She still have the sack with her?"

"Pressed to her bosom like it wouldn't grow tooth number-one for lo, these many months yet."

"What about Leeds? You see Leeds again?"

"Man, how can I blow this tune if you keep standing on the score? Like sure, I saw Leeds again. But, man, I ain't *come* to that part yet. Chapter three, book sixty-four, verse nineteen, brought to you by Welch's Grape Juice. You know? Like I say, first she blasts off in this MG bomb. I'm maybe five pads up the block, and I'm debating. If Leedsie flubbed the dub with the chick, maybe we can dig that Mills record one more time. I'm still giving the matter considerable ratiocination when he bounces out the front door like some cat set fire to the joint and who's got the gauze, you know? He's got his Dodge across the road and zoom, he's off like a tall bird. And I am alone in the still night."

"He go in the same direction she did?"

"There were stars above, man. I paused to dig the stars. I saw no more."

Brannigan was looking across at me with his tongue pressed into his cheek. He stood up, put his hands into his pockets, paced two strides, took them out again. "Arthur Leeds," he said then.

"Two-twenty," I said. "Make it two-thirty after Henshaw here had his meal. Even two-forty. It wouldn't take her that long to get to my place, Nate."

Brannigan grunted, turning toward Henshaw. "What time is it now?" he asked him.

"I dig the big hand approaching nine and the small hand touching one."

"You ain't got a watch?"

"Don't need one, man. Infallible sense of rhythm. It ticks off in my head, like."

I looked at my wrist. "Thirty minutes off," I told Brannigan. "It's a quarter after."

"Sure. Hell, this loony probably loses a week every time he misses a fix. What the devil, say she got here about three. You're not positive it was three-thirty when she got to your place. Call it three-twenty. She comes here, asks him for help, gets turned down. He changes his mind, follows her . . . well, why bother? We've been through all that."

"Wouldn't convict him in court," I said meaninglessly. "Not without a later witness."

"If I had him alive to take to court, I'd have a confession."

"I suppose," I said. I didn't know why I was questioning it. Henshaw wouldn't have known the right time if they'd roped him to one of the hands of the clock on the city hall tower. I was simply feeling let down, maybe cheated a little. It was a trifle tough to feel vengeful toward what was left of Arthur Leeds.

The apartment didn't tell me anything about him either. He had a lot of records, good hi-fi equipment off in a corner. He subscribed to half a dozen music magazines. He was reading a paperback called *Sidewalk Caesar* by someone named Donald Honig. That morning's *Tribune* was folded back to Red Smith.

I turned to Henshaw. "What about today?" I asked him. "Leeds say anything about last night?"

"Never asked, dad. Man's chicks are his castle."

"He act like he had something on his mind?"

"Dad, you cats just don't pay heed. Like I pronounced previously, he was all dismembered over that H. If that cat acted anymore shook up, you could have traded him in for a new Waring blender and got coin thrown in on the deal."

"How did you know Catherine Hawes?"

"Her?" He shrugged. "She pops up, man. Like she's here, like she's there, *comprenez?* How do I know my old lady? Who remembers? How do I know God? Like I mean, that cat is around, too. I believed in him the other day, for true. Last Tuesday. Great, man, great!"

Brannigan cracked his knuckles disgustedly. "You satisfied?"

I nodded.

"Police routine," he said. "Meet every nitwit in town. You want an answer to anything, you go to the nuts. I got a couple calls to make, Harry. You going to knock off now?"

"Might as well get some sleep," I said. I knew I had to see Estelle first. I also wanted to see Sally Kline, to get some background on Leeds. I wanted to make the son of a bitch come to life a little.

Brannigan was at the phone. "You going to want anything else from me?" I asked him.

"This morning's statement will probably do. Take it slow, fellow. And next time call a cop who doesn't spend all his time at a desk, huh? I'm a menace when I get out on the street, for crying out loud."

"See you, Nate. Thanks."

"Right, Harry."

I went out, still feeling anti-climactic. Probably part of it was the temperature. I was just beyond the door when Henshaw started to giggle obscenely behind me. "Hey, man," he said, "how about that? When the chicks ask me where Leedsie is I got to inform them, that cat is hung up. You dig that? *Hung up? Hung up?*"

He was laughing like a jackass but I stopped hearing him before I got to the second landing. I picked up *Vesti la Giubba* down there instead. Someone was bellowing it in an off-register Haig and Haig tenor behind a door that had been left open against the heat. The man had a swell audience out back in the yard, but apparently he didn't know it yet.

Caruso's girlfriend didn't know it either. Or probably it was only his wife. "Can I get dressed now, Herb," I heard her call out, "or do you want to use me first?"

Life was going on. You couldn't be sure exactly why.

CHAPTER 17

I felt groggy in the hack on the way uptown. I'd been fighting sleep more than I suspected. With all of it finished now I had abruptly sagged to half mast.

Estelle asked who it was through the speaker and a second later I got the buzz and went in. She was waiting in the doorway as I came down the corridor.

She tried a smile but she didn't have the tools for it, not today. There were lines around her mouth like cracks in pale china, and her eyes were dull. "I'm so glad you could come," she said.

"Just got clear," I told her.

"You look dreadful, Harry. I guess you haven't been to bed at all, have you?"

"Going now. We just wrapped it up, Estelle."

She looked at me vaguely, not quite understanding. She was wearing a white linen blouse with ruffles at the collar like Benjamin Franklin, and the plain gray jacket which matched her skirt was across the back of one of the sterile, antiseptic living-room chairs. I supposed the furniture would get sat in by relatives in a day or two and then not again until the next funeral in the family.

The air-conditioning was on and I walked over to the machine. Estelle had closed the door and was standing near it, watching me with a curious frown.

"Someone named Arthur Leeds," I said. "A musician in Greenwich Village. Cathy went to him when she ran off with the money. He followed her up to my place."

"You mean—" She swallowed, then clasped her hand over her mouth and whirled toward the wall. She started to sob, biting her fist.

"It's over now, Estelle. Completely over. Leeds is dead. He had an accident running from us. And you don't have to worry about our friend Duke anymore either. He was picked up also."

She stood there with her back turned. I walked over to her and put my hand on her shoulder. "It's okay, Estelle. Listen, what about your mother? Did you see her?"

She nodded, not looking at me. "Yes," she said distantly. "But I didn't . . . I didn't say anything."

"Is she all right otherwise?"

"Yes. But, oh, Harry, it's all so . . ." She shuddered again, then held her breath for a long moment. Finally she turned back toward me, wiping her eyes and trying the same unsuccessful smile. "I'm sorry. Can I . . . I'm afraid we haven't got anything but Scotch. Will that be all right?"

"Fine. But then I better scram."

She poured the drink at a cabinet. She put in the Scotch first and then had to go into the kitchen for ice. Estelle was the sort who would do it that way.

I dropped myself onto the couch. After a minute she came out and sat down a little away from me. She had not made a drink for herself. She kept her hands in her lap, like something someone had asked her to keep an eye on for a while.

The drink would have been just right for a teetotaling

Lilliputian. I sipped it without saying anything. It survived for three or four seconds.

"You never heard Cathy mention this Leeds, Estelle?"

She shook her head, looking as if she were thinking of something else altogether. Probably she was. I put the glass down on a coffee table. When I looked back she had begun to cry again.

"Harry, I'm so . . . must you go, Harry?"

"God, I've got to. I feel like an unplugged lamp. On top of that my head's been throbbing like six other guys'."

She was facing me. She reached up hesitantly, touching my temple with her fingertips, and I could feel it when she did. "He hit you so hard, I . . ." She winced, drawing her hand away. "It's gotten all black and blue."

"Another Scotch might help," I said. "I could stick around that long."

"Oh, I—of course." She got up, started to reach for the glass, changed her mind and brought over the bottle instead. "Forgive me. I never do know how much. There hasn't really been any whisky in the house since you and Cathy stopped visiting. We—"

She broke up again. I poured a second drink.

"Harry . . . would you sleep here? I'm so alone. If I could just be able to know you're here, in the next room. I know I haven't any right to ask, you've done so much already. But it would be such a comfort. You could use my bedroom. I can make it dark enough. And I can turn on the air-conditioner in there also, it would be—"

"Oh, look, I even took a roll in the gutter since I was here last, Estelle. I've got to get a shower and—"

"The bathroom is right next to my room, Harry. I can shut the corridor door until you're finished." She touched my arm. "Harry, I'm so shaky and upset. Just for now—for the afternoon. I'll wake you whenever you like. Just so I can know I'm not here by myself . . ."

Her voice tripped over a sob and she lowered her head. "Sure," I told her then. "What's a private cop for if he's not around when you need him?"

She jumped up, having a little more luck with the smile this time. I supposed it did not make a hell of a lot of difference. A bed was a bed, and the way I was feeling the tailgate of a rolling truck would have done the trick.

"I'll fix it," she was saying. "I'll get clean sheets."

"Hell, you don't have to—"

"It's no bother. Here." She was at a closet in the hallway, and she held out a folded bath towel. "I'll have the bedroom ready when you come out. I'll be back out here, so you can just go through the hall. And here—here are some hangers."

"Good enough," I said. "Look, it's a little after two. Suppose you wake me about five, maybe just before."

"You're certain? So early?"

"Be enough."

"All right. I'm sure I'll feel better by then. I appreciate this, Harry. I do."

"Don't be silly."

Accommodating old Harry. I took the gear and went into the john. I loafed under the spray for a good ten minutes, then toweled off and hung my clothes behind the door. I was still making like two-gun Doc Holliday, with both the .38 and the Luger, and I tucked them away in a corner with my shoes. I wrapped the towel around my middle and poked my head out.

"Okay to go through?"

"Yes, Harry. And thank you."

"Right, Estelle."

I ducked across the hall. There was a tiny crack of sunlight breaking through a lower corner of the blind when I closed the door after myself, but otherwise the room was gloomy, with that odd, cathedral sort of light you get when you draw heavy shades in the daytime. The sheets were crisp and fresh and I melted into them. I rolled over on my right side, jammed a fist into the pillow to give it some substance, and corked off about as quickly as I had when Duke Sabatini had mistaken my skull for a high inside fast ball.

You asleep, Harry? I asked myself sometime thereafter.

Sure, I'm asleep, I told myself.

How come she's here then? I wanted to know.

How come who's here?

Me, silly, she said.

It was a dame I'd known once. She'd floated into my arms out of nowhere. I'd thought she was dead. You never know. Was only undressed.

I AM dead, Harry, she said. *Isn't that absurd? I played cops and robbers because I was bored and now I'm dead.*

Go away, huh?

She wouldn't. She said, *You should have helped me, Harry. I told you to help me a year ago and you didn't, and now look what I went and did.*

She was chilly as wet oysters. I was doing my damnedest not to touch her, but she wouldn't be put off. *Hold me, Harry,* she insisted. *Don't twist away. Everybody holds me, why not you? Anyhow it's only a silly old dream.*

Some dream. I could hear the bedroom air-conditioning as clearly as I could hear her rustling in the sheets.

"Hold me, Harry," she said. "Oh, my God, hold me!"

I did not know how long it had been. It might have been two minutes or two hours. I could still see the crack of light through the blind but I could not tell how much it had shifted. I had been asleep deeply enough so that I had not heard her come in. It had been the touch of her flesh that woke me.

Her thighs were pressed tight along my own and her face was against my shoulder. She was staring up at me.

"Estelle, for crying out loud—"

My hand had fallen over the curve of her hip and onto her thigh. Maybe I was still dreaming after all. If I hadn't known better I would have sworn the body was Cathy's. Everything about its touch was exactly as I remembered it.

"Harry," she said. "Harry, I need you. I need you so much, so desperately. Hold me, Harry. Oh, God, hold me!"

No dream, Fannin. All very real, oh, yes, oh, yes. But did Fannin dig all this? Fannin was rather confused. He had had a bellyful of lunatic junkies, simpering fags, sour writers, greasy gun-punks. Now he had the frustrated old maid sister. The end of a perfect day.

Her arms had come around my neck, clutching at me, and I could feel the swell of her breasts. Her thighs were heaving. I hadn't moved.

So talk then, Fannin. Try art maybe, or literature. Try the last quartets of Ludwig von Beethoven. Try your all-time favorite football players. Maybe you can get her distracted and nostalgic over Jay Berwanger, Ace Parker, George Gipp, Whizzer White, Jim Dieckleman, John Kimbrough.

Sure.

"Harry," she said again. She said it like a cry from down a well, like a wail from a cell in the deathhouse, like a moan from an overturned car in a ditch. Her mouth was chewing my face and her legs were thrashing. Poor goddam Estelle. So you're tired, Fannin. So Thomas Hobbes says the life of man in a state of nature is solitary, poor, nasty, brutish and short. Win one for Hobbes. You can do it, Fannin. Win one for all the loyal alumni, for all our far-flung boys in service, for all those sweet white-haired old ladies who told us they'll never get off those sickbeds again if we lose, for—

"—Harry!"

It was a high, arching, lazy, end-over-end punt. It hung there, floating, almost suspended. Slowly, very slowly, it drifted down, and I waited for it between the goalposts. Five defense men swam up in front of me as I tucked in the ball and began my return. It was like running under water, and they never touched me.

After the game Knute Rockne himself came down into the locker room to pat me on top of the head.

"Harry," she said. "Oh, Harry, I've wanted you so, needed you so. Don't leave me, don't go away. Don't even move now, don't move."

Her face was turned. There was still sweat. And then she was crying.

"Harry." Her voice was ragged against the pillow. "I was so frightened. When you didn't call me back after this morning, I was so worried. I was afraid they . . . afraid . . ."

"Estelle?"

"—Afraid they might arrest you when they found the money in your apartment, might think you killed her and—"

She winced, gasping in pain. She had to, because I'd grabbed her so tightly by the shoulders that I felt bone.

My face was no more than four inches above her own. I could feel her hot breath, see the sudden fierce panic in her eyes. My voice belonged to somebody else who was trying to scream with gravel in his throat, and I was the only one in the room who could hear him.

You never told this woman about the money in your pad, Fannin, the voice roared.

CHAPTER 18

I sat there on the edge of the bed and stared at the floor in the unreal light. There were Luckies on a telephone table and I took one. The match flared and died. The smoke turned to steel wool in my mouth.

So Henshaw's batty clock had been right. She had had time to make another stop. Probably Leeds had not even found out what direction she'd taken when he tried to go after her.

"Here," I said. "She came here."

Estelle did not answer and I turned to look at her. The sheet was twisted low across her thighs and her hands lay motionless at either side of her, upturned and curled like dead things in the wake of plague. Her face was turned so that only the plane of her cheek was there. The line of her breasts was lovely, as beautiful as Cathy's had ever been.

"And it probably didn't have anything to do with the money then either," I said.

"No."

"Tell me, Estelle."

"Yes."

I heard the sheets whisper and when I looked again she was sitting with her knees drawn up. Her arms were clasped around her calves and her head was pressed forward, and a Modigliani or a Gauguin could have done something remarkable with her. She sat that way for a long time and when she finally lifted her face she kept it straight ahead, not looking at me. Her voice was muted and hard to hear.

"Two-thirty," she said, "perhaps a quarter to three. She was . . . I thought she was drunk. She told me about the robbery, things about Troy and running away from a man—it was difficult to follow. Perhaps I was too sleepy, too annoyed to want to understand. She hadn't been here in weeks, hadn't even been to see mother in the hospital. I told her to take back the money to whomever she'd gotten it from and to stop acting like a child. . . .

"She took the phone and dialed a number, then she hung up without saying anything and ran out. That was when I saw it in her face, I think, whatever it was that made me realize she really was in trouble. I wanted to make her explain it more carefully. My summer coat was in the front closet and I pulled it on over my pajamas. I took my pocketbook and ran to the elevator. . . .

"I had to wait for it. There was a small foreign car pulling out across the way when I got down, one of those MG's, and I saw that Catherine was driving it. I called out but she didn't hear me. My Plymouth was right out front. I got in and followed her. . . ."

"You didn't see anyone else? A red-haired man in a Dodge?"

"No."

"Go on, Estelle."

"Yes." She had not moved. "I thought I could pull up next to her, but she was driving too fast. She didn't stop for lights. I didn't either, after the first one. When she got over to 68th I remembered that your apartment was there. I realized it was probably you she'd called. I thought she would be all right with you. I was going to turn around and go back home. I . . ."

Her voice broke. I butted my smoke in the tray, not saying anything. Her eyes were deeply shadowed in the dimness. After a while she went on.

"I don't know why I stopped. I remember she made her tires screech. I parked behind her and I opened the door to get out, then I changed my mind. I don't think she'd been aware of me at all, she was in such a peculiar state, but she did look around when I closed the door. She turned back and came over to me. . . .

"My hands were actually shaking, I had been so unnerved by it all. I opened the door again, almost just to have something to do with them. I asked her what was the matter. . . .

"She had stopped next to the door, and she was smiling at me. She said . . . she said, 'Oh, I don't need you anymore, Estelle. I'm going up to see a man, he'll help me. The kind of man *you* wouldn't know anything about. The kind *you* couldn't get in your life.' And then she laughed. . . .

"She laughed. I don't think she meant to be cruel, she was simply upset. But to say that to me, after all those years . . ."

Estelle stopped. She sat there. I waited. "Nineteen," she said then. "I was nineteen when our father died, and Catherine was seven. Even then mother was deaf, capable of almost nothing. All those years when Catherine was a child I supported us. I brought her up. I never asked her to be grateful. But what time did I have for anything else—for men? What man would have married me anyhow, with two other people to support?

"No, I couldn't get a man. She was right. *She* was the one who could. She was sixteen when it started. I tried to talk to her but she wouldn't listen. Six years it went on, seven, I don't know how long. She was a slut, there was no other word for it. She had abortions. Not one, two. The first time when she was eighteen. Conceived children without even being sure whose they were and then had them torn out of her while I who was never going to have them, who would have given my life to have one, had to watch while she . . .

"She came to me for the money. Both times. I went with her to the doctor, hid it from mother. She always came to me, but only when it was something like that, only when it was dreadful and . . .

"And then she married you. You. And I was so glad for her, so glad, because that should have been the end of it. My God, what else could she ask but a man like you? And then when she threw you away, went back to being a tramp . . .

"And then to say that to me this morning, whether she meant it or not, to throw it up to me that she could still go back to you whenever she wanted, that even after the way she had been unfaithful she could still have you, while I who had no one, no one . . .

"There was a fruit knife wrapped in tissue paper on the front seat. I'd bought it the day before and forgotten to bring it upstairs. She was standing there, laughing, and I could hear the mockery of it, and I remembered so many things, so many. . . . And then the knife was in my hand and there was blood on it and . . . and . . ."

"Estelle—"

She sobbed once, making no other move. Her voice was still flat, almost emotionless, and I knew there had to be something she was leaving out. I did not say anything. I told myself to let her finish it first.

"I saw her kneeling there. I threw the knife on the floor. I tried to lean out toward her and I couldn't, I . . .

"And then she got up. She . . . Oh, God! She stumbled across the sidewalk and she almost fell and I still could not do anything. And then I saw her go into the hall. . . .

"The money was on the curb. I don't know why I picked it up. And then I was driving, running away. . . .

"But I stopped again. I was on Third Avenue. I sat there, shaking. I had to go back. . . .

"I didn't know what I was doing. I left the car and walked as far as the tailor shop on your corner and I stood in the doorway. And then you came down and the drunk was there and I was going to scream. I couldn't make a sound. I could only stand there, even after you went back inside, not knowing whether she was alive or . . .

"You came out again and drove away. I saw you leave the key and I ran across. I went upstairs and I saw her and I . . . I . . .

"I vomited in the bathroom. I flushed it three times. I remember that, three times, to make sure it was clean. I was going to wait for you but I couldn't, not with Catherine on the floor, not knowing I was the one who . . .

"I had the sack of money with me all the while. I put it in the laundry bag. I didn't think anyone would find it there, not right away. I thought I was going to be sick again but I wasn't. I ran out. . . .

"I put the key back under the mat. I walked slowly, I remember that, too. The knife was still in the car. I drove home and brought it upstairs and washed it. I didn't know if she had told you who had done it, I thought perhaps you had been here looking for me while I was still out, still . . . And then when that Duke came I thought it was you at the bell, I didn't even ask who it was, and then a minute later you were here and I could see that you didn't know, and . . . and . . ."

Estelle suddenly had her face in her hands. Her body shook violently. She threw herself face-down against the pillows.

I sat there. The soft light reminded me of places I'd been under dense high firs. If I hadn't been looking at her, the sobbing could have been the sounds of scavengers in the brush, chipmunks foraging.

"Why?" I said then. "Not just because she said something about a man you couldn't get, Estelle. Not just for that."

The sobs died slowly. She lay still. "Why, Estelle?"

Her face was still buried. She lifted it slightly, not toward me. "Yes," she said. "For that and . . . and . . ."

"What, Estelle? What?"

I was watching her. She pressed her head back against her raised shoulders with her weight on her forearms, holding it there. Her eyes were squeezed shut. Finally her head dropped again.

"This morning," she said. "I told you what happened to Catherine when she was six, what . . . what a man did to her. The man who attacked her was . . . his name was Robert Bell. He was twenty. My father was still alive, and Robert was staying with us for a weekend at the cottage we had rented. He was my fiancé, my . . .

"We were going to be married that autumn. And he did *that*. We were sleeping together. I was giving myself to him because I loved him, because I thought that was the way it should be. And he raped Catherine. She was six years old—six!—and he chose her over me. All right, yes, there was something the matter with him, he was obviously ill, but how do you think I felt? He had come into my bed that very night after my parents were asleep and then the next morning in the woods he . . .

"It was hideous when it happened, hideous! Catherine wandered off and it was three days before they found her. It was terrible for her, yes. But what about me? Everyone was frantic when the doctor told us what had happened, but no one paid any attention to me at all, no one stopped to understand how I felt, to care. . . .

"My father almost went out of his mind. His heart was bad to start with, and that was one of the things that killed him, I'm sure of it. The first night, after Robert confessed, when she was still in the hospital, we were in the waiting room. I was crying and so was mother. And then all of a sudden father was screaming at me, almost insanely. He told me it was my fault for going with Robert. He said . . . he said, 'You! You can't even get yourself an ordinary man like everyone else! No, the only man you can find is a degenerate, a pervert!' They had to put him to bed. I almost killed myself the same night. He never fully recovered, he . . .

"And then *she* forgot! Catherine forgot! While all my life I've had to live with the memory of it! And all my life I tried to give myself to her, because maybe it *was* my fault in part, maybe I was responsible. I cared for her, cried over what she was, what she had become . . . and then this morning when she said that to me, said almost the same thing my father had said, that I couldn't get a man, I . . .

"I just lost all sense, all reason, I . . ."

She was clutching the edge of the bed, sprawled across it at an angle near me. Her arms were rigid and her jaws were clamped tight. It was a long moment before her muscles loosened. She drew in her breath deeply.

"But even with that," she said then, "even with that, my God, do you think I wanted to do what I did? Do you think I *meant* to do it? Can you imagine how I feel, what I've gone through since it happened? I almost started to tell you this morning when I mentioned what happened with Robert Bell but I couldn't, I was afraid. And then later I even called your apartment but the police officer answered and I couldn't even ask if you were there. And then when you came in before and said that you believed someone else had done it, and that the person was dead, I thought no one would ever know, I thought I wouldn't

174

have to say anything at all. Because I . . . Oh, God, I didn't mean to kill her, I didn't! But when she said that to me about going to you, to *you* . . ."

Her voice dropped again. "You," she repeated. It was almost a whisper. "Yes, Harry, you were a part of it. Not just the contempt I thought I heard in Catherine's voice, not just the fact that she could get any man she wanted, but that she could still get you. From the first time I saw you I've thought about you, I've died a thousand times since you and she separated, hoping that through some impossible chance, some miracle, you and I might, that you and I . . . And then after all that happened she was going back to you, was telling me that you'd take her, and . . ."

She looked up at me then. Her face was like something sketched in charcoal on coarse gray paper and then abandoned in the rain. A shudder ran through her.

"All those years without anyone, all those years. Do you have any idea what it was? Can you know? There hasn't been anyone, not anyone else in all that time. After Robert Bell I couldn't, not for years, and then there wasn't any chance. Do I have to tell you how I once let myself get picked up by a soldier and let him take me into an alleyway—into an alley, Harry, in that filth, that stench—just to see if I were still capable of being a woman, if I could feel anything at all! And then just now with you, Harry, *with you!* Can you have any idea what that was for me? Can you? Even lying here with all the horror in my mind, all the horror! Oh, my God, I did it, yes, I killed Catherine! Call the police, do what you must! But hold me first, Harry! Hold me again! Harry, please, again, again!"

She had flung herself toward me. Her arms leaped around my neck and she was tearing at me, trying to drag me across herself with all the fierce, dead weight of her sick agony. Her breath was coming in wild sobs and her voice was choked and pleading. *"Harry, yes, tell them, do! But not now! Please, oh, God, later! Stay with me now! Don't leave me yet, Harry, don't!"*

Her head snapped upward viciously when I jerked away. For a moment she hung there, poised on her knees at the bed's edge with her arms outstretched and her breasts lifted like some doomed heathen priestess waiting in the twilight to be sacrificed. Then she collapsed in a heap, whimpering.

I stood there biting the knuckles of my right hand until I tasted blood.

I went into the bathroom and got dressed. When I came out again she was lying on her back with her face turned away. She hardly seeemed to be breathing at all, and the sheet was twisted and crushed about her loins. It might have been the remnant of a shroud in a violated grave.

The tiny shaft of sunlight through the blind had shifted a little, and my watch said 3:29. I stood there by the bed, staring down at her and not saying anything, and I waited the minute.

The phone felt as cold as a new Colt automatic in my hand. I put it to my head and dialed Brannigan.

EPiTAPH FOR A
DEAD BEAT

"They are very Christlike."
Jack Kerouac

"They are scum."
Somerset Maugham

CHAPTER 1

It is a small, not quite square office behind a smaller reception room on the fourth floor of a Paleozoic brick building on Lexington Avenue. Most of the furnishings have been out of style since Lucky Strikes were green, and in professions where they rate you by such things even the dullest girl in the typing pool would pick a more likely doorway to straighten her seams in. But it contains, such as they are, the tools of my trade as a private cop, and I have been spending the better part of five days a week in the place for seven years.

Probably it is a trivial complaint, but I will always have to wonder why nobody ever seems to need my services until I am out of there for the night.

So I was home undressed when the telephone rang, of course. It was after eleven, and I'd been reading on the couch. *Lolita,* a sad story about a twelve-year-old girl who couldn't find anyone her own age to play with.

"—This is Mrs. Skelly. Is this Mr. Fannin? The detective?"

A stranger. Not young, not wealthy, not educated. Probably gray and tarnished, and wearing something cut from shapeless cotton she would call a house dress. There would be a cameo pin.

"This is Harry Fannin."

"Mr. Lubitch said to call you—the lawyer. You'll have to bring a gun. It's about my uncle. There's so much cash, you see, and—"

"You want me to shoot your uncle for some cash?"

"I beg your—"

There was a pause. "You said there was something Ben Lubitch thought I might be able to help you with, ma'am?"

"Well—"

"I do have a gun—and proper permits. If you need one at this hour I suppose it's got to do with something you want guarded. Until the banks open?"

"Well, yes, as a matter of fact. It's Mr. Casey, who just passed on. The poor man was eighty-one, with the railroad for forty-four years. Mr. Lubitch says he's sure it will all come to us."

"You've found money?"

"In coffee cans, in the closet. Almost four thousand dollars. Mr. Lubitch says you charge sixty dollars a day, but it will be worth it to ease my mind. Especially since he said you would come home and sleep with me, and—"

"Madame?"

"What? Well, really, I certainly didn't mean—"

"Any old soft chair will do fine, Mrs. Skelly. If you'll tell me where you are—"

She told me. Grudgingly, but it was me or Jesse James. He'd obviously had an eye on those coffee cans for weeks.

I could have been more enthusiastic. I also could have stopped dreaming that the midnight disturbance, just once, would be a cry of distress from Ava, from Lauren, even from Tallulah. The place was about as far west as you can go in Greenwich Village without driving off a pier, and I said it would take me thirty minutes to get there.

I had to park a block away, on Hudson Street. The building

wasn't quite yet a tenement, although they were already getting interesting effects from the lobby. It was part tile, part chewing gum. The apartment I wanted was 6-B and there wasn't any elevator.

I made six, puffing, then saw the envelope tacked into the door frame from the length of a dismal corridor away. I put the paper currency into my pocket and scowled at the penciled note:

Dear Mr. Fannin:

I forgot about the police station around the corner. Thank you for your trouble, but the man said I could leave the money in the safe. If you guarded it until 9:30 A.M. that would be ten hours, which is $6 per hour. This $3 is for the time you said it would take to get here.

Yours truly,
(Mrs.) Kate Skelly

P.S. Really it would only be 9 A.M. since I would go to the bank as soon as they opened.

I had a smoke before I went down. I wondered if she expected me to leave her a receipt.

It was a nice night, warm for September. On other streets the gears of giant trucks were grinding mournfully, suffering their own version of life's small abuses, and back on Hudson I patted the Chevy on a fender in sympathy. Fifty yards away a sign which was not entirely unfamiliar said *Vinnie's Place, Beer on Tap,* in buzzing red neon. I tried, but I couldn't think of anyone who would be waiting up for me with a candle in the window. I went in.

It was a mistake, although I could not have known that then. All I had in mind were a few inconsequential drinks.

I thought I could afford it. I'd just picked up all that easy money.

CHAPTER 2

Vinnie's was a bleak, untinseled cavern about as long as a throw from first base to third, with a bar at the left hand wall and six or seven tables at the right. It had been a sensible longshoreman's hangout in its day, but since the war the bohemians had been driving out the laboring folk. They had even made something of a shrine out of it, which can happen in the Village. Someone like Edith Sitwell stops a cab one night and trots inside to visit the ladies' room, and for some people the world is never the same again.

Ten or a dozen stags were scattered along the rail, most of them dressed as if the *Kon-Tiki* had just discharged passengers at the curb. I found a slot near the back, wondering why my barber hadn't heard about the strike. Next to me a tall redhead was talking intently to another man I could not see.

"—So like the cat was my best friend, you know? So he sacks out on the sofa for two weeks, and then I can see my wife is giving him the burning glance. So I move out, you know? As long as the cat doesn't swipe any of my books when he heads back to Frisco—"

"—Touching, man. Like brotherhood."

A handsome tanned athlete in an open blue button-down set aside a fishing lure with all the care of a museum director situating a mobile, then asked me what it would be. I told him Old Crow and he had to move a paperback called *The Way Some People Die* to get at the bottle. That made two of us who didn't belong. I swung around and leaned on one forearm, to get a look at the only girl in there.

She was worth looking at. She was a blonde, with high cheekbones and a delicate face that would not have been out of place on *Harper's Bazaar*. It would not have been a calamity on *Playboy* either, since there was nothing high-fashion about the rest of her. She was wearing jeans and a man's faded denim work shirt, and after the third button the shirt fell like the sheer drop off a precipice.

She was at a table with two men. One of the men was very young. He had on a tweed jacket with leather patches at the elbows, and he was toying with an unlit pipe. The other one's back was to me. That one had the same patches on the sleeves of his black turtleneck sweater, and a spiral notebook was jutting out from the hip pocket of his Levis. I got the impression that neither of them would have been chagrined if I got the impression they were writers.

One of them said something and the girl laughed. It was a soft rich furry laugh, like cashmere, and it was wasted in September. In January you could have wrapped it around yourself to keep warm in. Some guy probably did. It made me sad, because the girl reminded me of someone I had been in love with once who died, named Carole Lombard.

I kept staring at her, being ridiculous. She was drinking beer from a bottle, lifting her head and tilting her chair against the wall as a man might. The way she did it would have made it acceptable at a D.A.R. meeting.

She was still sitting back, holding the bottle between her lifted knees, when the front door slammed inward against a table with a sound like a gunshot.

A man had come in on the dead run. He halted himself just past the entrance, hanging forward in a half crouch like a defensive left end posing for stills. For an instant only his eyes moved. It did not take him long to spot the girl.

He sucked in his breath and began to draw himself up. He wasn't anybody's left end. He went to five and a half feet, no more. He had on G.I. slacks, and there was nothing under his seersucker jacket except a T-shirt. The T-shirt had possibly been clean earlier in the month. Barley-colored hair lay flat above his pink, fleshy face, which apparently he was trying to make look menacing.

He needed coaching. He looked as menacing as Rumpelstiltskin.

"You slut," he said hoarsely. He was either out of breath or somewhat drunk. I had the sensation I could smell sweat from fifteen feet away. "She learned it from you, didn't she? Where is she, Fern?"

I looked back at the girl. Whatever it was, she wasn't buying. She wasn't even in the shop. She lifted the bottle deliberately, gazing at him the way she might gaze at a rain she knew she did not have to go out into.

The man wanted more response than that. He lunged forward, stopping about three feet from her table. That put him into profile for me. His features were babyish, and he had almost no eyebrows, which gave him an exceptional amount of forehead. He could have been thirty, in spite of the outraged seven or eight he was being at the moment. He'd fastened his hands to his hips. In a minute he would stamp his foot.

"Damn it, where is she? Who is she running with tonight?"

Neither of the men at the table had made a move. The young one dug out a tobacco pouch and did some busy rooting around in it.

"Why don't you take it easy, Ephraim?" the second one said.

"Why don't you chew axle grease?" Ephraim told him. He was leaning between the two men now, gripping the sides of the table top. "Where is she, Fern? I've been ringing the bell over there half the night. You're the one who gives her all the crummy ideas. Or is she chasing around with that other tramp friend of yours?"

Near me the redhead with the exalted sense of brotherly love coughed meaninglessly once. The girl's eyes were meeting Ephraim's evenly. Very slowly she set down the beer. She spoke softly, but what she said was not meant to be cherished by Ephraim alone.

"I don't really believe them myself, Eph, so why don't you make a formal denial of the stories? You don't spend *all* your afternoons watching little girls on the swings in the park?"

He slapped her. It was not a hard slap, since he was off balance, and she hardly jerked her head. Next to her the lad with the pipe jerked his own just about as much. Then he got to his feet. He did it with all the drawling indolence of James Stewart in the scene when the Bad Guy is about to learn he's been making sport of the wrong townspeople. I was bourgeois enough to watch for the shoulder to drop before the punch. I had forgotten where I was. His pal in the sweater joined him and the two of them walked away from the table.

They didn't leave. They merely strolled to the front end of the bar. They shook their heads gravely as they went. It was all extremely unfortunate, but it really did not concern them. Assuredly everyone would understand their position.

"I asked you a question, Fern—"

No one else in the place had moved. The girl's hands were drawn into fists and her eyes were smarting. Ephraim was still glaring when I took the couple of steps that got me over there.

"Got a match, *hombre?*" I tried to give it more of the John Wayne touch.

He grunted, not seeing me. "Beat it, huh?"

"All I want is a match—"

He turned. He had thick lips and protruding teeth. He might have been going to bite me, but the eight inches he had to raise his eyes changed his mind. "Well, for Chrissakes—"

He stabbed a hand into his jacket and came up with a folder. He shoved it at me, starting to turn back.

"Say, thanks. How about a cigarette now?"

His jaw dropped. "How about a fist in the mouth instead?"

"Aww," I said. "A fist or a slap?"

He got red. His corneas were slightly glassy. He could have been junked up, but even so he wasn't about to fight me. He grimaced, then whirled and started out. Halfway across the room he paused long enough to point a nicotine-stained finger at the girl, being ominous once more. "You can tell Josie she'll get the same thing—"

"Grrr," I said.

"Agh—" He swung a hand in a gesture of contempt. "Tourists!"

I laughed, a little foolishly. The door banged after him. Those two stalwart young Balzacs were watching me, but they turned when I glanced that way.

The marks of the slap had begun to show on the girl's cheek. She was staring at the table, sitting rigidly.

"Buy you a refill?"

She looked at me for the first time, biting her lip. I realized that she had no make-up on except lipstick. Her eyes were incredibly blue, and also remote. Or maybe just uninterested. She was a beautiful girl and she appreciated the assistance, but no thanks.

I was wrong. It took a minute but then she smiled. It was quite a smile. Two-Gun Ephraim lay face down in the dust, the streets were safe for womenfolk, law had come to the Pecos.

"I'll be heartbroken if the chivalry was just to pick me up?"

"Not me, ma'am. Now I saddle my trusty roan and ride off into the sunset."

"Inscrutable and alone—" She laughed.

"I like the quick recovery," I told her.

"I make an even better one when I'm removed from the battlefield. I don't think I want another drink, but you can take me home if you would?"

"Sure."

She stood, then nodded toward the rear. "Half a second—" Her voice was husky, and it hung around after she'd walked away from under it.

There was talk again, and the young bartender came across to pick up her bottle. I'd half suspected he'd left for the evening. "You were real good in there," I told him. "You keep things running smoothly."

He bent to wipe the table with a rag. "Be a hero. I can get the skirts without it."

I put my hand on his wrist. Gently, but he stopped wiping. We considered each other.

"So hit me," he said. "Six bits a week they withhold, workman's compensation."

I let him go. He went away whistling.

There's that about Greenwich Village. Nobody ever takes a poke at you, but you're never quite sure who's winning.

CHAPTER 3

She'd been forcing it. She smiled when we went out, but the power lines were down again. I told her my name and she said that her own was Fern Hoerner, but she would have given it to a kitchenware salesman in the same tone.

She turned south, walking glumly with her hands thrust into her pockets. I indicated the Chevy when we came abreast of it.

"We don't really need it," she said. "It's only Grove Street."

She shuffled along, kicking out with a tennis shoe once or twice and scuffing it on the concrete. I took her arm when we crossed Hudson. There was no traffic, and the few neighborhood stores were closed. The usual imposing American intellects were going slowly blind in the glare of television screens behind random windows.

"Do you live down this way, Harry? I've never seen you in Vinnie's before."

"Up off Third Avenue. You don't have to make conversation if you're feeling rotten."

"I'm sorry. I guess it was a little embarrassing at that." She shook her head. "Although I'm acting childish. I was pretty nasty myself, as I recall."

"Hell—"

"Maybe, but it was just poor old Ephraim. That's Ephraim Turk—his mother told him he was a poet."

"But mother died."

She managed a laugh. "But now I'm being bitchy all over again. I'm no judge of verse, really—sometimes I can't tell William Butler Yeats from Woodbine Willie. All I've ever done is fiction myself."

She said it matter-of-factly, not seeming to notice when I glanced at her. "Can I ask," I said, "or is that the touchy question?"

"It's okay to ask. You damned well better—" The smile was warming up again. "I've done a novel. In fact it's coming out next week."

I frowned. She stopped walking when I did. I kept on frowning when I put my hands on her shoulders.

"You've done a novel," I said.

She nodded uncertainly.

"It's coming out next week."

"Um-hum."

"You're at least twenty-three years old."

"Twenty-four."

"I'm going home," I said.

Her eyes were bright. I lifted a hand and let it drop, slapping air. "Greenwich Village—"

"You don't really have to be impressed, Harry," she decided then. "Sometimes I think the book isn't much good at all. I get the feeling they just want my picture on the dust jacket."

"I'll take a dozen."

"That's what they're counting on. Not that it isn't a reputable publisher—which could be another reason why Ephraim isn't too happy with me these days. The only place he sees his name in print is on his phone bill."

189

"I gathered he was a little anxious about some girl named Josie?"

"Ephraim would be anxious about what color the grass will come up next April." We had turned at Grove and were headed toward Seventh Avenue. "Although it's a funny story, actually. It couldn't have happened with anybody except Josie—Josie Welch, the girl I live with. She's as pretty as a picture, but she's probably the most scatterbrained kid in town. It's Zen—that started it all."

"Sin?"

"Zen. Zen Buddhism, you must know about it—?"

"I hear there's a lot of it going around."

She threw back her gleaming head. "That's as good a comment as any. Damn, but I hate these fads—you can't turn around without hearing words like *satori* and *atman* and Lord knows what else, all of it mixed up with undergraduate profundity and stale beer—"

"It sounds pretty subtle for a girl like this one—"

"Oh, it is. But somebody gave her a lecture on it one night. Some intense young man, no doubt. Josie's always getting lectured, it's a way she has of being seduced."

"Zen Bedism—"

"Oww—" She winced. "But you don't know how right you are. It was all she talked about for a week or two, and then last Sunday I came in about midnight and there were she and Ephraim, sitting on opposite ends of the couch with their legs crossed and their arms folded, both of them stark naked and staring into space. You learn not to be surprised by much of anything Josie does, but this was a little extreme. I thought they were probably high at first, but then Josie admitted just that—they were supposed to be practicing Zen, trying to lose all awareness of their physical natures and achieve a state of absolute spirituality. I asked her when the practice session ended and the game began, but she wouldn't say another word. The pair of them were still contemplating eternity when I went to bed."

"Zen Nudism—"

"Clown—"

"And Josie achieved Nirvana while Ephraim didn't—which explains all his anxieties—"

"Not quite. The next morning Ephraim was coming out of her bedroom when I was leaving for the library. I do free-lance reading for film people, incidentally, screening books that might make movie properties—not so much, now that I've gotten my advance on the novel. If I have any luck I'll be quitting altogether. Anyhow, I let it pass, as I do with most of Josie's sundry indiscretions. But that evening Ephraim showed up again. You'd have to know Josie to appreciate this, but the minute he made the first hint of a pass at her she hauled off and socked him. She told him flatly that she wouldn't go to bed with him if he were the last man on earth—"

"Huh?"

"That was Ephraim's reaction, likewise. He asked her where she thought she'd gone the night before, but Josie said she'd had nothing to do with what happened. Even if she'd consented in so many words, it hadn't been her real self. She'd been with-drawn from the external world, and her mind hadn't had any-thing to do with her body. All this in dead seriousness, mind you. It broke me up so much I had to get out of there. And Ephraim's been chasing her ever since."

"Waiting for her to come back to earth."

"Literally. But that's what I mean about him. All right, she wants to pretend it never happened—so anyone else would leave her to her little self-deception and forget about it. But not Eph. You'd think she'd suddenly spurned him after ten years of wedded bliss."

"He seemed to want to blame you for something or other."

"Sure he would. He followed me around like a puppy for months. It wouldn't occur to him that a girl just might not be interested—if he thinks she's intimate with anyone else he has to convince himself she's a tramp he never really wanted to start with. And now after last weekend Josie's obviously a tramp also, only in this case it's my influence. Sometimes it does make me a little sore—"

We had stopped walking and were standing below the steps to a three-story brownstone, just off Seventh. It was lighted over there, and cars were passing, but you could have held hearing examinations where we were. I took a smoke, offering her one, and she said no.

"I haven't shut up since we left Vinnie's, have I?"

"Most of it about some girl named Josie—"

"Chattering like an imbecile, just so I can hide how I really—" Her voice caught. She was standing two steps up, against the stone balustrade, and she turned away. "Oh, damn him, anyhow. Just because you live in the Village they think they can treat you like—"

The delayed let-down startled me. "Hey," I said.

She nodded, compressing her lips. I went up. "Listen—that joker isn't worth three wasted thoughts in thirteen years—"

"Oh, I know it, I just—"

"Anyhow he's gone. He's off writing sonnets to a dirty sock. Ain't nobody here but Shane, ma'am—"

She smiled. She didn't make anything of it when I kissed her. I had a hand on the rail at each side of her, and only our lips met. It was just light testing, like the first warm drop from an infant's bottle you touch to your wrist.

"That wasn't me," I told her. "I've attained other-worldliness, complete withdrawal—"

"You're a Tibetan monk—" She came up with two keys on a tiny chain. "Do they let you drink coffee—I mean in those monasteries?"

"You show them your Diners' Club card—"

She grimaced, going to the door. It was an old paneled wood affair, under an arch, and I pushed it in after she'd worked the key. She skipped lightly up one carpeted flight and led me along a corridor to the front. "Josie must be off somewhere if Ephraim said he rang," she said quietly. "She goes uptown a lot. If she'd been home she would have let him in to torment him some more."

I waited while she used the second key on a door marked *3*, then followed her into a large living room. A low couch on tubular legs faced us from the far wall, and there were leather sling chairs in corners. There was an expensive hi-fi arrangement, and wrought-iron racks were jammed with records and books. Tan drapes covered the windows overlooking the street. There was no rug but the floor was inlaid of hard dark wood squares and highly polished.

Fern grinned at me. "I'll bet you wanted something devastatingly bohemian—"

"Orange crates, driftwood, sprawling Beatniks—"

"The furniture's mine. I was married once, it's what I got to keep as a souvenir. In the bedrooms also—" She gestured toward two doors in the wall at my left. "Left one's me, right one's Josie. You go to the john through the kitchen, but don't ask me to explain whose concept that was. Do you take it black, Harry?"

"Swell."

She waved me toward a chair, then slipped through a doorway near the couch. I heard water run. After a minute an inner door closed, which would be that jerry-built latrine.

I was just standing there. The door to Fern's bedroom was open about half a foot. The door to her roommate's was closed. So I picked the roommate's.

I don't know why I do those things. Maybe I do those things because I'm a cop. Maybe I'm a cop because I do those things.

Mother was right. I should have been a poet. There was no future in the business I was in, no future at all.

There was a small lamp burning on a table in there. It hadn't shown with the door closed. I took a single deep breath and then I backed out. I drew the door after me as carefully as if there had been unstrung pearls balanced on its top.

"Nosy," Fern Hoerner said.

She was at the kitchen door, holding a bag of sugar. Common household granulated sugar. She was going to drop it in a minute.

"That Josie. There's one door in here to the pantry and one to the bathroom. So I just found this on a shelf in the medicine cabinet. Sometimes I think that girl doesn't know her own name."

"Josie Welch," I said.

"Actually it's Josephine."

"Josephine, yes—"

She frowned. "Aren't you being strange, Harry? What's so important about her name?"

I wanted to think of a way to tell her. There wasn't any way. The girl looked as delicate as old dreams, and I despised what it would do to her face. I felt like a man about to slash a Leonardo with a dull blade.

"Someone will have to identify the body," I said.

CHAPTER 4

I had been right about the sugar. The package twisted in her hands and began to empty itself in a thin, fluid stream, like time spilling. It whispered as it built itself into a mound at her feet.

She never saw it, gaping at me. I hadn't moved. Heifetz could have strung a bow on the tendons at the back of my calves.

It was not the first time I had found a corpse. But I generally have some vague professional notion when there might be one around. Like the vague notion a steel worker has that one of those high girders might be slippery. It's the same fall. You just don't expect to take it off a trolley on the way home from work.

The bag was crushed and empty when I finally got across. She had not made a sound.

"She's been shot, Fern—"

"But—" She shivered once, looking past me toward the bedroom. "But I— Oh, dear God, are you sure? How could—?"

"The police will ask you to go in. If you'd rather do it before they come—"

She turned a little wildly, pressing a hand across her mouth.

195

Very probably the police would be more comfort than a total stranger, which was a status I had just reverted to. She finally nodded, however.

I took her arm. The shade on the one lamp in there was orange, and it threw an unnatural cast over everything, like wildfire beyond thin curtains. The girl lay across the bed with one arm flung upward and her cheek turned against it. Her long thin legs were bent over the side, and her feet touched the floor. She had slippers on. The strap on the left shoulder of her red brassière was severed, and the brassière had slipped toward her throat, exposing that one small breast.

Her face was to the light. She could not have been more than twenty, but somehow there was no innocence about her. The face was small-boned, and she had been pretty. She was fragile, but the way Bardot is fragile. The small blackened stain at her heart was hardly visible.

Fern had come only one step into the room. Her fingers were digging into my forearm.

"Get yourself a drink, Fern—"

"I—"

She broke away, running jerkily toward the kitchen. I did not follow her.

The girl had been killed instantly. The wound was from a .25 at best, more likely a .22, and a single shot from that kind of bore would have to be perfect to kill at all. There was a faint smear of blood on the girl's palm, where it had touched the hole in what must have been sheer reflex.

I pressed my hand against the inside of her thigh. There was no stiffness, although the skin seemed cold. That could have been an illusion. I guessed it was an hour. It might have been three.

I let out my breath. There was nothing which did not belong in a bedroom. A freshly laundered brassière, white this time, lay on the floor between a dresser and the bed. She had been changing, so the other one had evidently ripped of itself, not in any struggle. A window near the bed was lifted two inches. There was a fire escape in the blackness beyond it.

A lot of clothes in the closet, just as many cocktail and semi-formal things as casual items. A girl who had not made a career out of Greenwich Village. A girl who had had a friend intimate enough to change a brassière in front of. Or had she answered the door and then come back in here alone? None of this was any of my business.

I had touched both doorknobs before, so I touched them again, going back out.

Fern was watching me grimly from the couch. She was clutching a tumbler of whisky in both hands. She was not crying, but her face was the color of cooled ashes. I looked into her room also.

It was the same size as the other, set up almost the same way. The window was not open. Nothing seemed to have been disturbed.

"Would she have had anything in there worth taking, Fern?"

She frowned, not understanding.

"It could have been a prowler, although I doubt it."

"Could have been—Oh God, who? Why? I—"

I had been waiting for it. She broke apart like a bridge collapsing, in slow motion, letting herself fall to the side with her face in her hands. I could hear the coffee perking and I went in and turned it off. I used up another minute or two brushing the sugar against the base of a cabinet. I found a glass on a draining rack and brought it out. She had a bottle of Four Roses on a table at the end of the couch.

I hadn't been right about her face. Even torn up that way she was lovely.

"You're being so calm, Harry. And I don't know anything about you at all, do I?"

"I'm a detective, Fern. Private."

"You're—" She looked up in alarm. "I don't understand. I mean, you being here and—"

"The police won't particularly like the idea either. It was just chance that I was in Vinnie's."

"Oh, God, it's so—" She bit hard on a knuckle, fighting it. The phone was on a small stand near the windows. It wasn't going to go away.

"I better call them now, Fern."

She said nothing. I dialed. My name, the address, the apartment number. It would have taken longer to order a rib roast.

It was 12:53. I let myself slide into one of the sling chairs. "They'll be a while," I said. "If you want to talk instead of just sitting—"

She stared at me absently.

"Did you know her long, Fern?"

"About a year." Her voice was ragged. "She's lived here for five months."

"That when that marriage you mentioned broke up?"

"That was before. Do you—may I have a cigarette?"

I went across and gave her a Camel. It trembled between her lips.

"You don't have any ideas?"

"There just isn't anybody, any reason—"

"Ephraim?"

"But you heard him yourself. He said he was looking for her and she didn't answer the bell—"

"So did fifteen other people hear him. He could have kept all that private over there. He might have wanted the edge on an alibi."

"But Ephraim—he's such an ineffectual sort of boy. He's

198

frustrated, I guess, and maybe deep down he knows he's not much of a writer, but I just can't—"

"There was another girl he mentioned. When he was asking where Josie might be—"

She picked up her glass, sighing, then replaced it. "Dana O'Dea—"

"A good friend of Josie's?"

"She was. Until—" She let it trail off.

"You'll have to tell the cops, Fern."

She nodded. "They had a fight. At a party, just a few nights ago. Both she and Josie had a crush on Pete Peters, the novelist. He's—well, just part of the gang down here. I told you before how I met Ephraim coming out of Josie's room that morning. I've met Pete coming out a dozen mornings. But the thing is, if I were Dana's roommate I would have seen Pete over there also—" She paused, and her arms dropped between her thighs. "I guess Josie and Dana were both kidding themselves, thinking Pete was playing it straight. But then something came up at the party, somebody made a crack, and Dana blew her top. She was drunk, I guess, but she called Josie every name in the book, and then she told Pete to take her home. Pete said no, but it was curious, somehow. He didn't say he wouldn't go with Dana—I'm almost certain he said he *had* to stay. In fact I was tempted to ask Josie later if—"

"She might have been pregnant?"

"I don't know, Harry, I—"

I was scowling. "Ephraim's interest doesn't make much sense if everyone knew Josie was going with this Peters—"

"You saw Ephraim—he's a little crazy. He told Josie the other night he wanted to marry her. I think he felt—well, I got the idea he wanted to do it deliberately, knowing she might have another man's child. As if it might add some simulated sort of tragic stature to his life, like Byron's limp or something—"

"You said she went uptown a lot. Anybody special she saw?"

"Connie, yes."

"Connie?"

"I don't know his last name. She's never said anything about him, nothing at all. He just calls, two or three nights a week, and if Josie isn't busy she goes up. Oh, God, I mean *went* up. It was always odd, I guess probably he's a married man—"

She turned aside. I waited again.

"The cops will have one other set of questions, Fern—"

Her breasts rose and fell sharply in profile.

"I got to Vinnie's Place about ten to twelve," I said. "They'll want to know what time you got there."

"I saw you come in," she said distantly. "I couldn't have been there more than fifteen or twenty minutes. Gregory and Allen might know, those two boys I was sitting with."

"Before that?"

"I went to see that old Humphrey Bogart film. *Casablanca.* Over on Sixth Avenue. I guess I went about eight-thirty."

"Alone?"

The cigarette lifted in a gesture of futility. "I just wish that were all that was on my mind."

I watched her. Her hands were across her knees. Smoke trailed up from one of them, disappearing against the sheen of her hair.

"That bullet—it was from a twenty-two, wasn't it?"

"It looked like it."

"It will be. I owned one. A Colt Huntsman that someone gave me once."

"Owned?"

"It was stolen out of my dresser. Two weeks ago. I didn't report it, because we'd had a party that weekend and I thought some poet had probably pawned it for a meal. But now—"

The siren cut her off, whining once like a troubled animal outside. She was looking down desolately and she drew in her breath, holding it. And then she did something that twisted my stomach into a sick knot.

I got over there as fast as I could, but not fast enough. She hadn't said a word, moving only the hand which held the cigarette. I was standing over her when she let the dead butt drop to the floor.

"Fern," I said. "Oh, Christ—"

She got up, shaking. I stared at her lifted wrist. The doorbell rang with a single authoritative blast.

The foul odor of singed flesh followed me when I went to the buzzer.

CHAPTER 5

The cop who caught it was a lean, long-necked, wide-shouldered sergeant named DiMaggio. He had a face roughly the shape and color of a clumsily peeled Idaho potato, and he had a jaw like the end of a cigarette carton.

He was strictly business. He let us tell him that we had come in together and found the body, and then he spent twelve or fourteen minutes supervising his lab men. After that he spent twenty more with Fern in her bedroom. There was another detective with him, an amiable, laconic redhead named Toomey.

Fern stayed inside when they came out. Toomey rejoined the technicians and DiMaggio indicated the kitchen with a nod. I followed him. He hoisted one flat hip over the edge of the sink, then swung the door shut with the toe of a shoe big enough to row.

"You have something with your name on it?" he asked me.

I gave him my wallet, open to my state license. He stared at the ticket for a lot more time than it would take to read it. Then he let out his breath, with all the weary resignation of a plumber finding a coat hanger in a drain.

"A private detective," he said without inflection. He handed the wallet back. "Must be an exciting line of work. Thrills, adventure—"

He wasn't smiling. I didn't say anything.

"Anything exciting happen to you lately, Mr. Fannin?"

I supposed I was expected to lend myself to the routine. "I had a real scary one two weeks ago," I said.

"What would that have been, Mr. Fannin?"

"A dognaping," I said.

"Oh?"

"The owner decided to pay the ransom. I had to meet the dognaper in a dark street in Flatbush at four o'clock in the morning."

He nodded thoughtfully. "Things work out without trouble?"

"The dog bit me."

That changed his expression the way drops of syrup change the expression on a buckwheat cake, no more. He took a cigarette.

"What are you working on now, Mr. Fannin?"

DiMaggio. Toomey had called him Joe, which people would do. On his birth certificate it probably said Melvin.

"I was in a bar on Hudson Street," I told him mechanically. "Vinnie's Place. Before midnight tonight I'd never seen Fern Hoerner in my life. Somebody insulted her and I walked her home. She was in here and I happened to look into that bedroom. Before approximately twelve forty-five I'd never seen the Welch girl either. Anything else I can tell you would be hearsay, based on conversation with Miss Hoerner. Except for what went on in the bar—that involved Josie Welch also."

"Tell it."

I went into detail about Ephraim Turk, then summarized what Fern had said about background. When I finished he leaned there chewing on it. He was an obvious kind of cop and there would be an obvious question for him to ask. He had already asked it once.

"What are you working on, Fannin?"

I didn't answer.

"You simply happened to be in Vinnie's. You weren't there because you were trying to make contact with Miss Hoerner for some reason—or to get into this apartment?"

"Oh, now look, just because I've got this license—"

"Just because. I want to know what you're working on, Fannin. I think I want to know right about now."

I sat there for another minute. He had too many preconceived notions and too much sheer habit to take any story of mine on faith. "Would Captain Nate Brannigan be on duty up at Central Homicide tonight?" I asked him.

He stared at me. "Exactly what does that mean?"

"It means I went in there for a drink. All the rest was just luck."

He cracked a knuckle the size of a walnut, not looking at me.

"I had a security case," I told him then. "Woman named Skelly found some cash. She decided to leave it in the precinct safe instead."

"You could have mentioned this before, you know."

"We got off the road."

"So we did." He finally made up his mind to smile, although it was still an effort. "You know Brannigan pretty well?"

"Four, five years."

He went to the door. "What the hell—it didn't look very kosher."

"I figured it wouldn't."

"Yeah. You'll have to see a stenographer later. Stick around if you want."

"Thanks."

Toomey was alone in the living room. "Watch your language in front of the man, Floyd," DiMaggio told him. "He's a P.I. with connections."

"I'm genuflecting," Toomey said.

"Ah, I guess he's not pushing it." DiMaggio went back into the second bedroom. The lab men had left and someone else was in with the body, probably the M.E. Toomey went to the bottle.

"What's his real first name?" I asked.

"Who, Joe?"

"Yes."

"Joe."

"Joe?"

"So there's two of them. You know something makes it illegal?"

I let it pass, getting a new drink for myself. Toomey sat down in one of the sling chairs and scratched an ankle.

People wandered in and out. It was only 1:47 when they came for the body, which meant it was a quiet night at the morgue. Maybe the juvenile delinquents had declared a truce for Tuesdays. Fern's door remained shut while they were getting the stretcher out.

DiMaggio was on the couch. "You see that bankbook in there?" he asked me.

"I didn't dig around."

He punched his tongue into his cheek. "Pretty queer. According to Miss Hoerner the girl was nineteen—came here after high school in Kansas City two years back. So first we get regular weekly deposits, checks, which would be a salary from somewhere—" He flipped pages in a notebook. "Yeah, here. Fifty-eight bucks and change. But then for the last eleven, twelve months the girl'd been putting away between one and three hundred a week—"

Toomey whistled. DiMaggio nodded and went on. "Spend-ing a fair bit, but the income is regular enough—all deposits in cash, and never more than an even hundred at one time." He grunted. "And no visible means whatsoever—at least none since Miss Hoerner met her. The girl claimed a relative was supporting her—"

"Uncle Aga Khan," Toomey said.

DiMaggio looked from him to me. "The uptown chum?" I said. "This Connie?"

"There's an address book, but nobody with the name. I think I'm ready to lay about eight to five she was on call."

"Age nineteen," Toomey said. "You suppose Vice Squad will have a make on the guy?"

"I want the other end of the odds on that one. Hell, there's a high-class pimp working out of every other nightclub these days. But anyhow, one other thing. Like I say, all deposits are fairly consistent—and then two months ago there's a fat one. July tenth. One thousand, eight hundred and fifty-two bills—again cash."

"Daily double at Belmont," Toomey said.

DiMaggio did not smile. "Miss Hoerner says she knows nothing about the uptown pitch—she'd rather read this Con-nie as a married cheater. There's no lead to him—no letters, not even an uptown match folder. The girl was neat as a squir-rel. Almost too neat, as if she had something to hide. And just incidentally we've got no family address either. We'll have to contact Kansas City and see what they can file."

He dropped the notebook into a side pocket of his jacket. After a minute he lifted his face toward me, squinting. "Ephraim Turk—a runt of a guy with a face like a sponge? A writer?"

"Close enough."

"For Chrissakes, sure, that son of a bitch has a shoplift-ing record. Six, eight months ago—somebody had a party, reported some stones missing. One of those rich hens who thinks it's quaint to let a pack of poets with greasy hands paw the draperies. We checked the guest list and this Turk's background came out—he'd done a suspended on the coast someplace. San Francisco. We never did find the gems. Yeah, yeah, Turk left the party with friends and slept in someone else's apartment. It gave him an out, since he didn't have time or opportunity to get rid of the haul."

"I remember," Toomey said. "But didn't we decide it was too big a job for him?"

"Swiping Miss Hoerner's twenty-two wouldn't be," Di-Maggio said.

"I just thought of something," I said.

DiMaggio raised his cardboard jaw an eighth of an inch.

"It doesn't have to mean much," I said. "Turk didn't have his fight with the Welch girl until just recently. The gun was taken two weeks ago."

DiMaggio traced his tongue across the tips of his teeth. "Okay, it's a point. Still, we run him in the same time we run in these others. This Dana O'Dea, the girl Welch had the fight with at that party. And this Pete Peters—Peter J. Peters, Miss Hoerner says. Although we'll need the pregnancy report to bring him into it—"

"Me, I like the uptown bird," Toomey said.

"I'll let you fly up and find him for us," DiMaggio said. He glanced toward Fern's door, then puckered his lips.

"Hell," I said.

"She has to be automatically suspect."

"Me too," I said.

"Okay, you too." DiMaggio got to his feet. He fished around in his breast pocket and came up with a small white card. "You and Miss Hoerner can see the steno anytime—in the morning, if she doesn't feel up to it now. Tell her, will you? Meanwhile, here—it's got my home number on it. In case you just *happen* to be in some more bars and run into something before we wrap it up."

I took the card. Only a rare cop would have one. It said:

Giovanni Boccaccio DiMaggio
Detective Sergeant

Toomey laughed nasally, heading out.

CHAPTER 6

Once, long ago, a girl had let me kiss her on a darkened stone stairway on a quiet street. Now she was letting me hold her hand, but she wasn't the same girl, and my hand was any old hand. She would have held Iago's, if he was the guy she happened to have to go to the station house with.

We had the statements to make. That sent us back past Vinnie's and around a corner, then up a flight of worn concrete steps between two concrete pillars with green globes at their tops. And then we were in another country.

Cop Country. As bleak as picked bones, as dismal as the floor of the sea. DiMaggio had been and gone, and a young patrolman took down what we had to say in shorthand he had probably learned in hope of a promotion. He was no more than twenty-five, and a promotion was the only thing he would ever hope for in life. He had a face which had already seen everything twice, and had been bored the first time.

Cop Country. As cheerful as a leg in traction, as inviting as a secondhand toothbrush. Other cops came and went while we sat on a bench waiting to sign the typed copies. Cops with faces like wet gray sand, cops with eyes like whorls in hardened wax. One of them passed us carrying what might have been an undershirt. "He still bleeding?" I heard somebody ask him. "You need boots in the squad room," he said.

Cop Country. It was pushing three o'clock when we got out. It hadn't taken long. It had only seemed that way. It always will.

That corner of the Village was even more quiet than before. We had not spoken fifty words in an hour, but I stopped her when we came back past the Chevy. She was still wearing that work shirt, and there was a Band-Aid on her wrist.

"Listen—you don't want to spend the night home alone. Is there some girl you can call? I'll drop you anywhere you say."

She stared at the pavement, animated by all the spontaneous gaiety of Joan of Arc on her way to the stake. "I don't want to call anybody, Harry. Not to have to tell them about it, not tonight."

"I know. Play it again, Sam." I opened the door at the curb. "Come on," I told her.

We got in. Halfway uptown she said, "Damn, oh damn," and then nothing else. I lived on 68th and used a garage on Third, but there was an empty slot a few doors down from the apartment on the side which would be legal in the morning. I locked the car and we went up the one flight.

I had two and a half rooms. I'd gotten the place as a sublet five years before and the original tenant had never come back. He'd sold me the furniture by mail after a year, most of it battered and masculine, and then a girl named Cathy had added a few things in the ten months she'd used my name. Fern saw that. I'd turned on a Japanese lantern and she fingered its shade, not looking at me. "A woman bought this," she said.

"Yes."

"A mess?"

"A mess."

She slouched to the front windows. The blinds were separated and she stood with her back toward me in the shadows.

There was nothing to look at out there. Her hair glinted, high-lighted by a streetlamp down below.

"I guess I know without asking," she said. "Are they always so rotten? God, but mine was."

I didn't say anything, but I did not care if she talked. I could not think of many things she could do or say that I would mind. I might have wished it were another night, when she would not be so vulnerable, but there was nothing I could do about that.

"I was twenty when I married him," she said. "He was a writer, older than I was. I thought he was a good one, too, and I had all the proud dreams about giving up my own absurd ambition so he could fulfill himself. I quit college and got a job so he could stay home and work. Selfless, dedicated little Fern. It took me two years to discover that he hadn't done two full months' writing in all that time. When he wasn't in the bars all day he had women in. In the apartment I was paying rent for—"

She let it die, standing there. She did not expect an answer. After a while I crossed behind her and went into the bedroom. I put on another small light.

She followed me. She was toying with the adhesive.

"That hurting?"

"Not at all. It's almost strange."

I punched her lightly on the cheek. "It's just chance, but a maid comes in on Tuesdays. Everything's fresh. Towels and stuff in the closet in the john. I'll throw a sheet on the couch."

"Breakfast in bed in the morning?"

"Go ahead, be merry. I know how you feel."

"No, you don't—"

The way she said it stopped me. I had been headed toward the closet. She was staring at me, and her hand was at the lamp. The light snapped off.

211

I went across. The girl had hit me hard, but it was still the same bad night. I put a hand on her sleeve. She was shaking.

"Oh, God, does it make me terrible if I want—if I need—?"

I kissed her so hard that my mouth ached. I had to, once at least. Then I picked her up with one arm behind her knees and the other at her shoulders. I put her down on the bed.

I touched her hair. "Get some sleep, Fern."

She didn't say anything. Something caught in her throat, but it was only a sob. I went out of there.

It was easy. Like walking out of the Kimberly mines with nothing in your pockets. I tried to remember when I had held a girl as breathtaking. It had been the week before they knifed Julius Caesar. It was when they were starting the Pyramids. I got myself a drink. I managed not to spill too much of it.

I needed a pillow and a couple of sheets. I waited fifteen or twenty minutes, until I was sure she would be asleep. I couldn't come out of there a second time if she wasn't. Martin Luther couldn't have.

She had not gotten undressed. She was breathing softly. I untied the tennis shoes, hardly touching them, and eased them off.

"Do I get a bedtime story also?"

"Oh, hell. Oh, sweet hell."

She laughed, reaching toward me. "I'm all right now, Harry."

"You're all right now," I said. "That's fine. I mean I'm glad. You're sure you're all right now—"

"I think you're a little crazy."

"Yes. I may well be. Yes, indeed. And you're being a great help. You're all right now—"

"Oh, heavens, come here. Will you come here—"

We weren't in another country anymore.

CHAPTER 7

She was gone when I woke up. I'd never heard her.

I hadn't heard the alarm either, and it was after nine. There wasn't any note. She'd disappeared without a trace, like Cinderella.

Cinderella would have forgotten a slipper. Three or four meager hours of sleep had left me just groggy enough. I actually caught myself searching around for one of those tennis shoes.

I got to the office by ten, but it was a meaningless achievement. The waiting room was as barren as Pompeii.

I looked her up and dialed the Grove Street number. I didn't get an answer.

It made the afternoon papers. Not much space, no photo. Police were questioning several unnamed suspects. The body had been discovered by a Miss Fern Hoerner, roommate of the deceased, along with a private investigator named Henry Fannin. I tried her again at four.

I supposed the daylight had made it easier for her to go to a girlfriend's. I also supposed I might come up with a client if I sat there patiently again tomorrow. I locked the office and went home.

DiMaggio was easy. I caught him at nine-thirty. "We found the gun," he told me. "In our sneak thief's apartment. I had a hunch."

"Turk?"

"Yeah, the first place we looked. It's Miss Hoerner's—it was registered. No prints—he'd wiped it clean—but Ballistics fired it and the slug matched. He claims it's a plant, of course—says he never saw it before. But we also found a neighbor who heard him pounding on the door over there about two hours before you called in. Made enough of a racket so that she took a peek down the stairway, and she's willing to make a positive identification. She says she heard him threaten the Welch girl with bodily harm if she wouldn't open up."

"She hear the shot?"

"No. She says he quieted down, either he was let in or else he went away and came back. Turk is screaming about an alibi, says a friend was with him all evening, but the friend hasn't shown. We'll get a confession sooner or later."

"You make it sound easy."

"They usually are, Fannin. You should know that."

"The others get themselves clear?"

"We're not really interested in them. For the record, that girl Dana O'Dea was too blotto to have handled that kind of shooting. Toomey practically had to carry her in to the station when he picked her up. Which is nice work—she's quite a looker."

"Peter J. Peters?"

"Never questioned him. The girl wasn't pregnant, which eliminates his interest. He's the friend Turk claims he was with. It's up to Turk to produce him, if he really is an alibi—which I doubt. The neighbor says she didn't see anybody else in the hall. It looks pretty cut and dried."

"I'd hate to think a man was stupid enough to leave a murder gun under his nightshirt."

"In a coat pocket. Hell, we got over there before three o'clock. He probably planned to dump it later."

"You look into this uptown joker—Connie?"

"Vice Squad can't make him for us. Miss Hoerner could be right about him being a married man. I'm not going to worry about it—it'll be Turk. You know this Village gang, they're all psycho. We'll get our confession and then instead of a lawyer he'll bring in a head doctor to prove it was his mother he was really mad at."

"She loved him."

"Huh?"

"Nothing, nothing. Thanks for all the dope."

"See you around. I spoke to your friend Captain Brannigan, by the way. I'll mention your name, somebody needs something that isn't strictly departmental."

"I'll appreciate it."

I watched the last few innings of the Yankee game. Jimmy Piersall beat them with a double in the eleventh and it wound up after midnight. Her girlfriend had an extra bed. She was sleeping over.

DiMaggio would be right about the Village. Artists, social exiles—there was always a lot of sensitivity on the loose down there, a lot of overplayed emotion. Even on the chance that it wasn't Ephraim it would still be something simple. I did not have any investment in it.

She didn't answer Thursday morning either. There was a girl I had charmed, all right. She was probably locked in a phone booth somewhere, still telling them all about it back home.

I sat some more. The detective profession was on the skids. I hadn't had a paying customer in eight or ten days.

Maybe it was all in my mind, but the whole building seemed remarkably quiet. Nobody came, nobody went. Only Fannin, who paid the rent.

Percy Bysshe Fánnin, the Shelley of the Sherlocks. The Keats of the Keyhole. Me and Ephraim.

So she'd needed a shoulder to dig her nails into, and mine had been closest. So there was another shoulder someplace with her name stenciled on it. So there hadn't been any reason to mention it.

I couldn't remember a week so hushed since the Giants went west.

I tried her one more time that evening. I tried another girl after her, and I got an excuse and a promise. I had a substantial file of both items. I didn't want to see the other girl anyhow.

I was a fool. I sat there again Friday. Nobody wrote me any letters except the University of Michigan Alumni Association, looking for contributions. I sent them what I had left of Mrs. Skelly's largess. Nobody dialed my number, even by mistake. I stared at the back of the door to the reception room.

HARRY FANNIN, PRIVATE

Apropos of nothing at all, I wondered whatever became of Wrong Way Corrigan.

It was something to do. I wondered whatever became of Schoolboy Rowe. For that matter, whatever became of Doyle Nave, who beat Duke with that pass in the '39 Rose Bowl game? Whatever became of Jean Hersholt?

Oh, sure—poor old Jean Hersholt. So then whatever became of Sonny Tufts? *Sonny Tufts?* Whatever became of Lucius Beebe? Who the hell *was* Lucius Beebe? Whatever became of Sir Stafford Cripps?

So it's my office, I damned well guess I can use it for what I please.

HARRY FANNIN, PRIVATE

I decided I better get out of there. It was ten to five. I shut the drawer I'd been occupied with. Since I was leaving I had to take my foot out of it anyway.

I was lifting my jacket off the hook when the buzzer rang, meaning that someone had opened the outer door. It could have been another tenant from along the corridor, wanting a little group therapy. Someone like that would just look in.

Nobody did, so I went over and looked out.

There was a man in the reception room. I stared at him.

I decided I was going nuts altogether.

CHAPTER 8

He said his name was Ulysses S. Grant.

I didn't argue. For at least fifteen seconds all I could do was gape. He was possibly the tallest man I had ever seen. He also might have been the filthiest.

He reached seven feet at the least. He was as gaunt as he would have to be, and there was no way to guess his age, partly because of his sunken cheeks and his oddly dull eyes, and partly because of his beard. The eyes were a shade of gray I had never seen before, almost opaque, like damp cardboard. The beard was scraggly and needed trimming, preferably with garden shears. It and his hair were the color of rotting straw. So were his teeth.

He had on a raincoat. I thought it was a raincoat. Someone had been wearing it to change truck transmissions in. The coat was torn in a few places also, but no more than five or six.

He was grinning at me, but I wasn't the man he wanted. He wanted someone at the Bowery Mission, maybe the basketball coach.

"Grant," I said finally. "Like in Appomattox."

He had a smudged, dog-eared card to prove it. Just the name, nothing else. Cards were the rage that season. I was thinking of having some done up myself. Also just my name. Wolfgang Amadeus Mozart.

"A whim of my father's," he said. "His own name was Thaddeus." He had a voice about four reaches below baritone. "You are Mr. Fannin?"

"There is that possibility," I said. I nodded, but I could not take my eyes off that coat. It was streaked, splotched, spilled on. Even a lazy research chemist could have had a field day, taking samples from it. In some remote future era it was going to drive an archaeologist insane.

It bothered Ulysses S. Grant not at all. "I've grown fond of it," he told me idly. He brushed at something on a sleeve, soot from the Chicago fire. "One of these days I suppose I ought to drop it off to be cleaned."

"I think so," I said. "But not an established firm. Maybe you can find a new shop, one that just opened."

"I'm afraid I don't understand. Why a firm which—"

"Someone just starting out in the business," I told him. "Trying to make a reputation."

He laughed. Not a laugh in any ordinary sense. It came honking up out of his throat like a flight of geese out of a marsh. Of course it would. Friday afternoon, and diligent Fannin had to hang around, wondering whatever became of Jeeter Lester. I trudged back into the office and sat down.

I waved him into a chair. Trying to ignore him would have been like trying to ignore Kanchenjunga.

He had opened the raincoat. That didn't make the day any brighter. Grandma Moses wiped her paint brushes on rags cleaner than the shirt he had on under there. I leaned forward on my arms, pushing a stray pencil back and forth across the blotter.

He was still clucking. "Trying to make a reputation, indeed!

Excellent. Oswald told me to be prepared for your irreverent sense of humor."

"Oswald did," I said aimlessly.

"Oswald Fosburgh, yes. It was he who recommended you."

I was sure of it then. I was a sick man, sicker than I knew. O. J. Fosburgh, attorney at law. His Park Avenue office was not much more plush than the Four Seasons. I picked up the pencil and tossed it into the tray.

"Oswald J. Fosburgh," I said. "You and he share the same locker at the Harvard Club."

"Hunk!" said Ulysses S. Grant. It was only one goose this time, caught on the wing by a load of twelve-gauge shot. He slapped himself on the knee. "Indeed, indeed! Ozzie also informed me that you were not particularly subtle. What you mean, of course, is that you cannot conceive of any connection between myself and someone of the stature of O. J. Fosburgh."

I shrugged. "Okay," I said. "You're an eccentric millionaire."

Ulysses S. Grant pursed his lips. Slowly he began to nod his head. Then he beamed at me.

I had been reaching for a cigarette. I stopped. I put my hands flat on the desk top.

"No," I said.

"Yes," he said.

I heaved a sigh. Ulysses S. Grant heaved one in sympathy.

"Millions?" I said.

"Actually only thirteen," he said cheerfully. "And not the principal, merely the interest. To tell the truth it's all relatively new. Thirteen is what remained after taxes. My father—"

"Old Thaddeus—"

"The same. Yes. He passed away a year or so ago. I was the sole heir. Coffee, I believe it was. South America."

He believed it was coffee. I had my head in my hands. I hoped I had a handkerchief. I thought I might weep.

"I'd like someone located, Mr. Fannin. A daughter, by a marriage long since dissolved. I believe the girl is living in Greenwich Village."

He flicked away some ashes with an unwashed finger which appeared to have enough joints to bend into a square knot. He was studying me with those odd eyes and he missed the standing ashtray by a foot. I was surprised he hadn't dropped them into a cuff.

"You appear curiously indifferent, Mr. Fannin?"

"No, no," I said. "Just a little relieved, maybe."

"Relieved? I'm sorry, I don't see—"

"Nothing." I was reaching for the phone directory. "No, I guess I don't mind looking for people. I just thought it might be some sort of dull security job. I've had a little bad luck with them lately."

"Security? But I still—"

"All that coffee. I thought maybe you had it piled up in the breakfast nook and wanted a watchman."

More geese went honking southward. Geese, ganders, goslings. I wondered what it would take to offend the man. I dialed the number I wanted and waited.

"You remember an old American League outfielder named Goose Goslin?" I asked idiotically.

"I don't know baseball," he said. "Why?"

"Nothing. I was just wondering whatever became of him."

I got my party. "Harry Fannin calling," I said. "Can I reach Mr. Fosburgh at this hour?"

The girl asked me to please hold on. Grant raised a bushy eyebrow at the mention of the name.

"Be sneaky if I waited until you were gone," I told him.

Fosburgh came on. "Fannin," he said, "how's the lad?"

"I'm not quite sure."

He chortled into the wire. "I should have phoned, but I thought you might find him amusing. It's all strictly on the up and up, you know. Thaddeus Grant was one of my first clients, left a considerable sum in trust for Ulysses last autumn. Surprising in a way, since they hadn't seen each other in twenty years. On the other hand he'd been supporting Ulysses all that time. Anything in particular I can help you with?"

"Not at the moment, Mr. Fosburgh, no."

"He's there with you, eh?"

"Yes."

"I see." He laughed. "Actually I can probably anticipate your key question. Old Grant sent him two hundred dollars a month for all those years. I imagine Ulysses got used to living as a bohemian and hasn't quite gotten around to changing."

"Literally."

"Indeed, yes. Although you shouldn't underestimate him. He's a bright fellow—could have been a writer, perhaps even a lawyer. But that two hundred started coming in during the depression and for some reason it seemed unnecessary for him to do anymore than live off it. I don't imagine I'm abusing any confidences here, since he'll be a client of yours also. He drinks, of course, but at the same time he's read more books than you or I have heard of. He's forty-six—tallest man in captivity, isn't he? I hope you can help him out, Fannin. He'd like to find that girl, assist her in whatever way he can."

"We haven't gotten to that yet."

"Oh. Well, I can't say I blame you for checking first. I'll admit quite frankly he has been something of an embarrassment at times. Bill my office when you've wound it up, eh?"

"Sure. Thanks."

"Not at all. Don't hesitate to give me a ring if I can aid you."

We said something pleasant to each other and hung up. Ulysses S. Grant had been waiting patiently, picking his nose behind a red bandana he could have been carrying since Madrid fell. He was still being amused.

"I hope you're reassured?"

My hand was draped across the phone. I lifted the hand, frowned at it, dropped it again. I looked around the office.

I decided it was a pretty shoddy place. I supposed I was fond of it, but only in small ways, and only in spite of some of the people who'd sat in that chair Grant was in at the moment. Hoodlums, junkies, crooked cops, racketeers, at least one murderer. I'd taken them as they came because they were part of the business, and even the conventional, ordinary customers had always made me a little blue—people with problems, a lot of them piecing out my retainer in crumpled bills I'd known they had hoped to buy some small joy with, instead of the grief which had brought them there. Very few of either kind ever came in with as good a guarantee behind them as O. J. Fosburgh.

So I sat there scowling another minute and then I stood up.

"I'm sorry," I said. "I'm afraid I can't help you. It's after hours, but most other agencies have answering services."

"I'm afraid I don't—"

"I'm busy."

"But you gave the impression—"

He let it trail off uncertainly when I went around the desk and took my jacket down again.

"The coat I could get used to, Mr. Grant," I said then. "Maybe it's almost got a certain style. It would look cavalier as hell over a Brooks Brothers suit. But not on top of—"

I bit down on it. I knew it wasn't the man or the man's shirt. Maybe it wasn't even a girl with a Band-Aid on her wrist who wasn't answering her telephone that week. I didn't know what it was. I just wanted to be away from there, and now.

I was at the door. He hadn't gotten sore. Obviously he wasn't the type. He was just leaning forward with his head bent and his arms triangulated backward against the arms of the chair, like Ichabod Crane on a slow horse.

"I'd like to lock up, Grant."

"Mr. Fannin, I can hardly see—"

"Can't see what? Okay, it's none of my business, but damn it, if you'd look in a mirror once you'd—"

"I mean I can hardly see *you,* sir."

"Huh?"

He was standing, not facing me. "My sight is approximately eighty percent deficient," he said distantly. "I have glasses for what reading I do, glasses plus a four-inch magnifying lens. But I believe I appear freakish enough without making my eyes look like a pair of enormous bugs, so I rarely wear the glasses in public. Very few people are aware of the condition, I've even hidden it from Fosburgh. But it has hardly seemed important for me to notice whether my clothes are particularly fashionable, or for that matter clean. When a man has not been able to recognize a beautiful woman as such since his late twenties, he can lose interest in certain of the more trivial amenities. I'm sorry if I've offended your sense of good taste, Mr. Fannin."

The door swung into place behind me. The man's eyes were closed. He was tilted forward with one bony hand lifted, and I could not decide whether he looked more like John Carradine in the role of a tattered preacher, or a parody of Don Quixote, or a dead tree.

I went back and sat down, of course.

CHAPTER 9

His marriage had lasted seven years. He did not tell me in so many words why it had broken up, although he implied that his wife had been something of a tramp.

At the time of the divorce their daughter was six. The girl, named Audrey, went with the mother. Elizabeth Muller Grant asked for no alimony, and Grant assumed she had met another man. She did not marry again, however.

Grant did not question this, asking only to be allowed to visit the child regularly. He also did not question the fact that, two years later, Elizabeth Muller gave birth to a second daughter, not his, who was quickly sent out for adoption. The woman herself was living well, and his own child appeared to lack nothing.

He did not see the girl as frequently as he had intended. Explaining this, Grant said that his vision had taken a severe turn for the worse in that period, and, fearing total blindness, he had begun to keep to himself. Too, the girl had been enrolled in an out-of-state boarding school and was rarely home. The visits had become entirely unrewarding when they died of their own inertia in 1950, when Audrey was fourteen.

Ten years later, and two months before he appeared in my

office, Grant happened upon the newspaper obituary of an Elizabeth Muller of Manhattan. It listed as her only survivor a daughter, Miss Audrey Grant, also of New York. Funeral services at a midtown chapel were announced for the following day.

Ulysses Grant evidently lived in considerable disorder. He read the death notice only because, having misplaced his magnifying glass, he found it resting on that page of an opened *Times*. It did not occur to him to check the date on the paper. When he arrived at the mortuary at the specified hour he learned that the funeral of Elizabeth Muller had been held nine days before.

The mortician was able to furnish Grant with two addresses. The first, Elizabeth Muller's, led him to an expensive furnished apartment in the East Fifties. There he was told that the personal effects of the deceased had been removed by her daughter almost a week before. The second address was that of a residence hotel in Greenwich Village, where Audrey Grant had rented a single room for several years. She had left no forwarding address when she moved out three days before Grant asked for her.

Grant took about fifteen minutes to tell me all this, gesturing now and then with a hand like a hungry skeleton's. When he finished he reached into an inside pocket for a billfold fat enough to have his lunch in it. He searched around and came up with a folded white envelope, then did not pass it across. A muscle in his throat might have been working slightly beneath that parched beard.

"This was early in the summer?" I asked him.

"In early July, yes."

"And you haven't done anything about it since?"

The hand lifted. "I went to both of those addresses on the first day," he said. "That night I had second thoughts. The girl

226

knows she has a father. I've lived in the same apartment all her life. She could have—"

He turned away. There were traffic noises below the window, remote but savage. It was moving up on six o'clock.

"But now something's come up to change your mind again?"

"I hadn't quite changed my mind to start with, Mr. Fannin. Not about wanting to see the girl, or to help her if she needs it. Let us merely say—well, that I held the matter in abeyance. About a month ago I asked Fosburgh to look into the question of my ex-wife's finances. It was something to be discreet about, since it was no business of mine, but evidently there was no will. I assumed Elizabeth had—"

He studied the linoleum. I waited for him.

"Men would have supported her," he went on. "She was handsome enough to have lived well in concubinage. She might have left some small amount of cash—it would have been like her to keep money lying about her apartment. And she would have told Audrey about it, I'm sure. The superintendent at the building said that two young women had been there frequently during her illness. It was cancer, I believe—"

"One of the two girls was definitely Audrey?"

"The superintendent knew her by name."

"Any assumptions about the second one?"

"If you mean it might have been Elizabeth's other child, yes, I've thought of the possibility. In any event the second girl would be of no concern to me." He realized he was still holding that envelope. "This arrived today, special delivery as you can see."

The envelope was plain bond, addressed to Grant in a south-paw scrawl, with no return address. It had been postmarked at nine that morning in a Village sub-station. It contained two newspaper clippings.

One of them was a two-column photograph of three men and a girl seated at a table. I recognized one of the men before I read the caption:

> BEATNIK TO READ: As part of the new trend in night-club entertainment, the Blue Soldier in Greenwich Village has announced a series of poetry recitations by noted writers of the Beat Generation. Featured this weekend and next will be Peter J. Peters, novelist and poet, left. Also shown are poet Ephraim Turk, painter Ivan Klobb, and Beatchick Audrey Grant.

The shot had been clipped from the top of a page in the *Post* and the date had been left above it. It had appeared exactly a week ago. Audrey Grant was a brunette and could have been reasonably attractive. Peter J. Peters had a neatly trimmed beard. Ivan Klobb, who looked old enough to know better, had a sloppy one.

The news story I had not seen, but only because I don't read the *Journal*. It was one day old:

BEATNIK WRITER
HELD IN MURDER

It said nothing that DiMaggio had not told me on the phone, except that Turk had been officially booked on suspicion. They were still calling me Henry. I frowned at the two pieces, not really thinking about anything.

"No idea who they came from?"

Grant shrugged.

"Fosburgh told you he knew me when he saw them?"

"He phoned the police first, since your name was incorrectly reported. Then it seemed only logical to come here."

I nodded. "I know a little about the murder, Mr. Grant. Until now it hasn't been any of my business. It probably still isn't."

"I don't quite follow you."

"There doesn't have to be any connection between your daughter and the killing—except insofar as it's already been made. Someone could simply be using it as an incidental, to point out to a man worth thirteen million dollars that his little girl is pretty chummy with the riffraff."

"A crank, you mean?"

"You run into any before?"

"Nothing of any consequence. The usual absurd requests."

"You want me to try and find out who sent the stuff?"

Grant had wet his lips. He stood up. "I don't care about the clippings, Mr. Fannin. If it seems necessary to investigate their origin in finding my daughter you may do so." He shook his head. "I have told you a lot about myself, sir. It has not been pleasant for me, nor, I'm sure, especially interesting for you. I would like to speak to Audrey. Merely once. If she desires no further communication I will not trespass in her life again. You may tell her so."

"I will," I said. "Before the end of the weekend."

"It will be that simple?"

"I've met some of these people. I might be able to find her at that bar tonight—the Blue Soldier—or there's a chance I can do it on the phone. After all, she's not missing in the usual sense."

He nodded thoughtfully. I had come around the desk, but we did not shake hands. "I'll call you as soon as I get something," I told him.

"Yes. Thank you." He turned to the door, stopped a minute, then went out without adding anything.

He'd run out of geese. Talking about his troubles had even given him a shabby sort of dignity. I supposed loneliness could do that, even if money couldn't.

Philosophical Fannin. I went back to the desk, got out a

manila folder, slipped the clippings and the envelope into it. I scribbled *William Tecumseh Sherman* on the folder and stuck it away. I locked the office and left.

A block away I passed a haberdashery which wasn't yet closed. I caught Grant out of the corner of my eye, towering over a neat little clerk like a sequoia over a sightseer. The clerk was busily showing him something that might have been a shirt.

CHAPTER 10

Behind the long dark bar in the Blue Soldier a bald Neanderthal type with a six-ply neck put down a wetly chewed cigar to take my order. It was a few minutes after nine. The man was about fifty-five. His shirt was white-on-white with a monogrammed Z over the pocket, his cufflinks were two more outsized Z's, and his figured silk tie was as wide as the business end of a shovel where it disappeared into his white smock. There would be another initial on the belt buckle down under there. The man himself would have driven a booze truck during prohibition, would have taken some small independent chances in the petty rackets in the thirties, would have made his pile from black-market peddling during the war. Now he owned a chromed, gaudy tourist trap on lower Sixth Avenue, and within five minutes of the start of any conversation he would say something about being legitimate.

I could have been wrong. He was chewing the cigar again before he poured my bourbon. "No poetry reading tonight?" I asked him.

The man stopped pouring. He stared at me. I could not read his expression, but it was considerably like the one I might have gotten from certain good folk if I'd said something nasty about General MacArthur.

"Poets," he said. "Beatniks. God almighty."

He turned, started to walk away, stopped, snorted, came back. He put his elbows on the bar and leaned forward until his face was no more than three inches from my own. When he spoke again I had to strain my ears to hear him.

"In answer to your question, friend—no, there ain't no goddam poetry reading."

"You're going to drop ashes in my drink," I said just as quietly. "Forgive me. I'm sorry I brought it up."

He backed away with a grimace. "I get something in your drink, you'll get another drink. Drinks I got."

"But no poetry readings."

The man braced himself with both hands gripping the inner rim of the bar. "You really want to know? You're not just making what you think would be friendly conversation?"

"I'd like to know."

"You'll stop me if I get violent? Sort of put your hand on my arm? I've got a touch of blood pressure."

"Sure."

He nodded gravely. He gestured toward my right with a stubby thumb. There were about twenty tables over that way, half of them occupied, and there was an empty bandstand.

"Nice little spot I got here, ain't it? Brings in a good living, sends the kids to college—all strictly on the up and up, you know?"

I smiled pleasantly.

"No headaches at all. No high-priced entertainment—just a little dance music—steady clientele. So what happens? I get one of these uptown agents dropping in, *hocking* me, I should have these readings. Me, I donno from nothing—poetry's out of my line—but be tells me out on the Coast they're buying it like maybe it's Equanil. Culture, he tells me. Three hundred bucks and I can own a poet for the weekend. A beard the guy's got. Big son of a bitch, too, looks like he could wrestle Antonio Rocca better than writing poems. You follow me?"

"Peter J. Peters," I said.

"Yeah." He grunted. "So last Friday it goes on. I even bring my wife in, she goes for that sort of thing. First show at eleven, and by nine you can't get a seat in the joint. Three, maybe four times as many customers as I ever had at one time before."

"This is bad?"

He set the cigar down carefully on the edge of a glass tray. "Beer," he said. "They wanted beer."

I didn't say anything.

"One," he said. "One to a customer. Sometimes one to a table." His nostrils quivered slightly. "This is the part where I tend to get upset. You'll watch me, huh?"

I put my hand on his arm reassuringly.

"Six, maybe seven at a table usually holds four, see? So a waiter goes over. Maybe one guy orders. The other six don't want nothing. Or maybe they say not yet. The waiter goes back, the six still don't want. And the first guy doesn't reorder, he's still nursing the first one. You ever see a guy nurse one beer for three hours? Regular customers I got can't get in, and six fully grown people are watching one guy nurse one beer for three hours. Characters talking all kinds of big words when what it adds up to, they can't hold a job. Intellectuals. There's even a table I got to replace, they carved things in. 'Middle class morality is primeval.' You want to tell me what the hell that means? A hundred and fifty people, and you know what I take in? I got more in the register since six o'clock tonight. Beatniks. The same slobs been hanging around the Village twenty years, this year they got a name. One more goddam poet or Beatnik son of a bitch sticks his nose in that door, I'm gonna—"

I squeezed his wrist. He stopped. "Yeah, yeah. Thanks."

"You tell it with admirable restraint."

"It's a week, it gets easier. What's your interest anyhow? You look like a man works for a living."

"One of them owes me money."

"The Russians should owe it to you, better. God almighty."

I put some cash on the bar. He pushed it back toward me.

"You'll remember it, you could come back," he said. "A customer wears a tie, a customer's got socks under his shoes—I'm just starting to see he's worth being nice to."

He was lost in thought when I went out of there. There was a cast of stolid, painful determination over his face. Like the look of a man learning to live with disgrace in the family.

CHAPTER 11

I tried Fern Hoerner from a booth in a drugstore. I might as well have tried Eisenhower when he was caught up in crisis on the back nine at Burning Tree.

The Chevy was in a lot around the corner. I left it there, walked a block east to Washington Square, then cut through the park toward Thompson Street. It's still a nice park, one of the last in New York you can pass after dark without having a homicidal sixteen-year-old step on your spine. I didn't even mind the prim queens in tight jeans mincing along the pathways, although I was happier with the Italians on the tenement stairs on Thompson. Old women in black with seamed faces, and old men who had hopefully named their sons after Garibaldi or Marco Polo or Boccaccio and were content with a cop or two in the family. I went up a flight of chipped slate steps into a building that only a successful bombing could have improved, climbed two more sagging flights inside, then knocked on a door I had knocked on once or twice before.

After a minute the door opened an inch. A pouchy-faced woman with red eyes and hair like an abandoned floor mop gave me the best she would ever have to offer: "Yeah?"

"Oh, I'm just fine, thank you, Mrs. Henshaw. Nice of you to ask. Is Hiram at home, by chance?"

"Job?"

"Not work, no. I'm just that old sleuth, remember?"

"Agh—"

She jerked the door inward as graciously as an animal hater letting the cat in, then clomped off on a pair of wooden shower mules, trailing gin fumes and the hem of a ratty housecoat. "Hiram!" she bellowed. She slammed another door against loud television noise and disappeared.

The man I wanted came out after a minute, pulling on a jacket the color of cranberry sauce. I supposed it went well enough with his maroon and gray checked pants. He smiled at me from behind a pair of glasses as thick as hockey pucks.

"Well, man," he said, "good to see, good to see. Fearless Fannin, the ideal of all us red-blooded American youth. Welcome to the humble pad, like."

He was a jazz musician in his forties, roughly the size of a sparrow with stunted growth and about as nearsighted as a bat at noon. He'd gone through Dixieland and Bop and, when he could get work, into a sort of reactionary's Progressive, and he'd spent more man-hours in Greenwich Village saloons than any relic since Maxwell Bodenheim. He was too old to be a Beatnik, and even the language he spoke was dead at least a dozen years, but he resurrected it with a flavor I liked, mostly unconscious. If Audrey Grant lived in the vicinity he would not only know her address, but also her mascara shade, her garter-belt size, and where she bought her Stopette.

"I thought you'd be out soothing the savage breast," I told him.

"Oh, man, don't bring up the subject, huh? That sax of mine is practically atrophied from lack of use. Last I looked there was rust on the reed. I haven't seen a taxable dollar since Morgenthau stopped signing them."

He gripped my hand, then went across to a piano bench

against a smeared wall. There wasn't any piano, but that would not mean anything in there. Everything else in the room had come in on the tide after the *Lusitania* went down.

"I've got a small fin not going anywhere, Hiram. A girl named—"

"Man, man!" He gestured excitedly, putting a finger to his lips. He cocked an ear toward the back of the apartment. "Like, shhh—"

I grinned, waiting. Finally he nodded. "Pianissimo on the do-re-me, huh? That witch could hear a dime drop in a deep well. A fin for a chick named—?"

"Audrey Grant. You know where she sleeps?"

He chuckled. "You phrase that question ambiguously. If you mean whereabouts does the damsel have a pad she can call her own, sure. If you want to know where she is prone to rest her bones of an evening, I trust you've got an hour or two."

"Easy mark?"

"Every doll to her own debauch. Leave us just say she is wont to wander."

"What's the mailing address?"

"East Tenth." He gave me a number. "This an event sinister, Harry? I would sleep poorly if I thought I was fingering a frail."

"Nothing important, Hiram. Just family business."

"Tame, tame. You anxious to make contact *pronto?*"

"Wouldn't hurt."

"Well, there's this brawl. A cat named Don McGruder just sold a slim volume of verse and is howling. Audrey Grant swings with that crowd, so McGruder's is where you'd latch on."

"A guy need an invitation?"

"To a pad in Crazytown? Man, you just sort of *go*, you know? But if you're shy, I could clutch your clammy little hand. For, say, another thin fin?"

"The wife won't care if you scram?"

He made a face, standing. "So who inquires? Like it's peaceful coexistence, *comprenez?*"

I dug out a ten. His eyes went to the rear again, and then the bill jumped out of my hand and into his breast pocket like something unbaited from a mouse trap. "Man, I appreciate that, I truly do. Hell of a thing, but I must be blowing flat lately. I wouldn't touch your *gelt* if I could get work, Harry."

"Sure."

He had one hand on the doorknob. "Hey, now tromp my tenor, I plumb forgot. I hear tell you were the lucky winner who helped Fern Hoerner strip the cellophane off Josie Welch that dreadful day—"

"Just chance. I ran into her in a bar."

"Yeah, yeah, Vinnie's. That creepy Turk. Boy, them poets. Deep, man, deep. I wouldn't have thought Ephraim could swat flies. Curious. Indeed, curious."

"Something on your mind, Hiram?"

He nodded absently, pacing back to the bench. "Like sit a second," he said. I watched him pop a filter cigarette into his mouth and chew on it as if it were a cigar. "Probably it's idle scratch," he decided. "Just dust on the needle, you dig me? But a small thought's been bugging me. I know beans about pistolas, but a bird would have to have a keen eye to commit the big deed with a twenty-two, *n'est pas?*"

"Or else a lot of luck."

"Yeah, curious. Curious." He sucked on the cigarette. "So the minute I became cognizant of the gory details, Lucien Vaulking hove into mind. He was my age, but one of them screwball athlete types, you know? Always rupturing himself with a football over in the Square, making bets with the young cats like how many push-ups they could do, all that boff. But the thing that bugs me, he was flipped over guns. He even got hauled in by the fuzz one time for practicing on a roof. But good, man, good—"

He laughed abruptly. "Except here's the hitch. Loosh bought the box about a year ago. Had a ticker attack, trying to chin himself at a party. Poor old Loosh." He studied his cigarette, then looked across again. "But like I say, it's still weird. I mean Josie Welch, and now you put me on about the Grant chick. Loosh was the local thigh man, had a hand under every skirt. But the chicks who were current when he copped out were these very two. I mean simultaneous-current, you dig me? Neither of the wenches bunked with him steady, but the pair of them would be pattering about his pad together on many a cozy night. On many a frosty morn. According to community folk tale, it was a real squooshy *ménage-à-trois*."

I took a cigarette of my own. "I don't get what's on your mind, Hiram."

"Man, like I don't either. Just chatter, you know? But Ephraim bugs in here also. This Lucien was a writer. He scribbled two novels, both pretty hip—anyhow none of this sloppy Beat boff that's all mushy chorus and no melody. The word was out that he was probably compounding something real far out when he died, because it had been nigh on to half a decade since he'd last spoke for publication, but there weren't any pages. Like the manuscript had blown away. Probably he'd just dried up—what I mean, down here most of the cats dry up before they get wet, *comprenez?* Anyhow, Ephraim had a case on him, hero worship. Like if Loosh came into a bar, say, Ephraim had to scoot over and dust off a stool for him. And then when Loosh played the last note Eph started chasing both the chicks. Like he was trying to make it with the pair of them because Lucien did. Identification with the master, like—"

"Trying to beat him, even—"

"Indeed, indeed. Except what's the moral? Just that Eph finally flipped enough to lay out poor Josie. Writers, man. Too much brain work. It gets real hot inside the skull, you know?"

I didn't see what point he had. I decided he didn't have any at all. "A guy named Pete Peters," I asked him. "I hear he saw a lot of Josie Welch also."

Henshaw shrugged. "Like saying a cat goes to a house of ill fame two, three times a week. Those beds are swinging when the cat is not there, too."

"Who's a painter named Ivan Klobb?"

"A cool specimen. He's got a showing in some far-out uptown gallery next week. I mean you take a look, you know whether it's a sunset or a commode. *Mucho* nudes. Josie Welch used to hold still for him sometimes. So does your Audrey Grant, although mostly he works with a real built body named Dana O'Dea. Sure, I forgot—this O'Dea rooms with the chick you're looking for. If Audrey Grant isn't swinging at this ball tonight, Dana probably will be. You can't count on the Grant chick—she comes, she goes. A traveler. Like I've spied her making for home at maybe eleven bells in the morning."

"Out all night, you mean?"

"Indeed, but not down here among the peasants. Up where the tall money flows, the nightclub circuit."

"She goes up—" I cut it off. I took a slow breath, staring at him.

"Have I like served up something with a bone in it, dads?"

I didn't answer. I was looking for Audrey Grant because her father wanted to chat about the family estates. It was supposed to be an innocent matter, and maybe it still was. Maybe the girl had friends uptown. Maybe not one of them was somebody named Connie.

"Let's check that party, Hiram," I told him.

CHAPTER 12

It was just after ten when we got to the McGruder place. Henshaw had taken me five blocks west along Christopher Street, then through an iron gate and down a hand-truck ramp into a cluttered alley. Light came from a turning in the rear, where it gleamed on a dozen battered trash cans. There were sounds of a cool horn that could have been Miles Davis as we went back, and there was talk. The air was rank.

The light was from an unshaded bulb over a doorway in the right-hand building. Four plank steps led down into a low room which at a glance looked wide enough to store obsolete bombers in. There was only one light inside, another naked bulb hanging from a cord socket looped over a water pipe in a far corner, and it could not have been more than forty watts. The walls of the room were whitewashed concrete, and there were no windows. There were at least fifty people standing around in clusters. A long table thrown together from sawhorses and boards stood off to the left, crowded with drink-making paraphernalia, and there was a phonograph on another table in the corner which got the light. The only other furniture seemed to be half a dozen auditorium chairs, lost in all that floor space.

"Tut's other tomb, like," Henshaw said. "McGruder claims

he digs his doom better in the depths. He communes with the dark night of his soul."

"He'll commune with pneumonia if he lives here in the winter."

Henshaw gestured toward the rear. "There's a lone radiator out yonder. He hibernates in one room when it frosts up."

There were doorways in the far wall, leading into what looked like a maze of corridors. The corridors were illuminated by kerosene lamps with red chimneys instead of electricity. Except for a section where heating equipment would have to be, McGruder evidently had the full basement to himself. I could think of about ten housing-authority violations his landlord could have been cited for, but I wasn't particularly trying.

"We just help ourselves to that booze?"

"Like the butler is indisposed, you know?"

We had started over that way when a tall, narrow-shouldered man in a pink-and-white-striped polo shirt waved a limp hand in Henshaw's direction, peered at me, then detatched himself from a group and pranced toward us. He was in his late twenties, and so thin that a June breeze would have bent him double. That lifted hand flopped around near his shoulder like a drooping epaulet all the way across. "Hiram, dear," he twittered. He stroked about fourteen excess inches of beer-colored hair out of his gay blue eyes, not looking at Henshaw at all. "I'm so glad. I was certain you would have a previous engagement."

"If you mean work, man, I'm applying to the sanitation department Tuesday. Meet a cat. Don McGruder, Harry Fannin."

He didn't curtsey, which was a small boon. The hand fluttered hither and yon some more, then finally got down to where mine was.

"Delighted, Harry. You're new blood. I simply adore new blood."

"Like you could save it, Don," Henshaw grunted. "Harry goes for dames. It's kind of a fad."

McGruder pouted. "A shame," he said wistfully. I got my hand back, not without a caress. "You're more than welcome anyway, dear," he decided. "We try our best to get along with the minority groups. Have a ball, won't you?" He tweaked Henshaw's ear, gave me an exaggerated wink and flitted off, as harmless as a falling leaf.

"Poets," Henshaw said. "I forgot to clue you about that."

I shrugged. An extremely young girl with wild black hair and a shape like an ironing board was pouring herself a Canadian Club at the makeshift bar. Most of the rest of the stuff appeared to be unadvertised house brands, so I waited for the bottle. On the floor to my right a hulking Negro in a fluorescent white shirt was slumped against the wall with a set of bongo drums between his sprawled knees and a dreamy expression on his face. A girl in a dress that might have been cut from old gunny sacks was hunkering next to him.

Just beyond them a man in a leather jacket and knee-length laced boots was fishing around in an army knapsack. The knapsack seemed to be filled with equal quantities of canned goods and paperback books.

"—You have to read the *Lankavatara Sutra*," someone said loudly behind me. "It's the only way to get in—"

"—James Jones?" someone else said. "*James Jones!* You can't *mean* it?"

Ironing Board finished with the bottle and passed it to me. You could have buried bones in the dirt under her fingernails. "Is it true?" she said. "Are they really coming tonight?"

"Who?" I said.

"Corso and Ginsberg."

"Who are Corso and Ginsberg?"

"Who are Corso and—" She gaped at me as if I'd just heaved

a rock through a cathedral window. "Why, only the two greatest poets since, since—"

"The greatest ever?"

She went off shaking her head. "—Herman Wouk?" a voice said. "*Herman Wouk!* You don't *really*—" I poured a healthy belt of the Canadian. I expected I might need it.

Henshaw was filling a tumbler with red wine from a gallon jug. "You see the Grant girl?" I asked him.

He squinted, looking around. "Her roommate." He gestured toward the far corner. "That chick I mentioned—Dana O'Dea."

There was only one girl over that way. She had short, coal-black hair, and she was wearing a tight shoulderless sheath dress. In better light the dress might have been the color of a burning barn, but its color didn't matter anymore than color matters on a Rolls Royce. At sixty miles an hour its loudest noise would have been from seams stretching in the appropriate places. I could understand why a painter would make use of her. She was as voluptuous as overripe fruit.

She looked drunk. She was doing a solo shuffle to the music, rocking a pair of hips like two cruisers in a heavy sea. A man coming out of one of the corridors snatched at the back of her dress as he passed. She let out a high-pitched squeal, scampering away.

"She's worth looking at, isn't she?" a husky voice said next to me then. It was a voice I knew, one that sounded like fog whispering. It didn't really sound that way. That was just a metaphor my blurry little brain had come up with in a hectic moment between all those clients in the last three days.

"Hi," she said. She was wearing tan slacks and a powder-blue blouse which was slashed deeply between her breasts. The blouse had a high collar up under that yellow hair, and the only make-up she had on was lipstick. There was a faint touch of the same shade on a pillow slip I hadn't gotten around to changing.

"You're that girl whose phone must be out of order."

"Oh, Harry, you must think I'm dreadful, but that morning, I—" She glanced past me, but Henshaw was talking to someone. No one else was at the bar. "I was going to leave you a note, Harry, but there just didn't seem to be anything to say that wouldn't sound banal. I'm sorry—"

"No harm done."

"I've been uptown almost every minute since. About the book. It's been a good thing, actually. It's kept my mind off Josie."

"Sure."

"Although I guess I have to admit it's also kind of exciting. It looks as if there's going to be a movie sale, a big one."

I was glad she was going to have a movie sale. That would make her rich and famous. She would be able to afford an answering service to take her incoming messages, like when Sam Goldwyn called. There was still a square of adhesive on her wrist.

"We're being awfully uncommunicative," she said.

"I haven't meant to be, Fern."

"You did call, didn't you?"

"Once or twice."

"I'll be less busy next week, Harry."

"Sure."

"Please? I haven't meant to make it seem so casual. It wasn't— well, they weren't the most romantic circumstances—"

"That's true."

"What's true?" somebody asked. A man Henshaw's age with a beard like a devastated wheat field had come up in back of us. He was wearing a paint-stained sweatshirt and he had strong features behind the stubble, sharper than they had appeared in Grant's clipping. An expensive unlit briar hung inverted in one corner of his small mouth, and he took it out to kiss Fern on the cheek.

"Ravishing," he said.

"Hello, Ivan. Ivan Klobb, Harry Fannin."

Klobb gave me a firm right hand. "Fannin? The chap who was with Fern on that unfortunate evening?"

"I'd hate to have it make me a celebrity."

"You're a private detective, the newspapers said."

I nodded. He did also. I didn't like him. There was something bland about his expression, almost vicious. After a moment he took Fern's arm. "Indeed, yes. Well, look, you two, I hope you'll pardon the intrusion, but if you're not discussing something earth-shaking, I'd like to speak with you, Fern. A personal matter—five minutes, no more." She glanced at me uncertainly. "I'll bring you back, old girl, if it's worrying you. You don't mind, my good man, do you?"

I minded the phony English accent more than anything else, although I had decided what it was about him that grated. Without the beard he would have had a face just like those I remembered from old newsreels of Bund meetings in the days of Fritz Kuhn, when he himself would have been a susceptible twenty.

"You won't be leaving, Harry?" Fern asked me.

"I'll see you later."

"Do, please." Her hand touched my wrist. I watched them walk off toward one of the rear doors.

Henshaw had disappeared, I hoped in search of Audrey Grant. I took a drink of the whisky I had been carting around and made a face. Evidently McGruder had had some empty bottles stored away. What he had poured into the one with the Canadian Club label had not been Canadian. I turned back to the bar and added water to the glass.

"—James Gould Cozzens?" someone moaned. "*James Gould Cozzens!* You're *mad*—"

A record ended with a screech and someone started to monkey with the machine. Near me the Negro tapped a brief staccato on the bongos in the break. Before I looked he was lolling back against the wall, as if it had all been reflex.

"Go ahead, Rosie, take off on it!" someone yelled.

The man made an indifferent gesture. "I thought maybe Donnie wanted to read us some bright new words now," he muttered.

People turned toward Don McGruder, but he dismissed them with a flutter of that pale palm. "Later, dears, later. Play some of those old Bird Parkers like a sweet lad, why don't you, Nicky?"

The boy at the phonograph began to dig through a stack of records. Behind me two others were raving. "—Hitch-hiked all the way? Well, man, I hope you read *On the Road*—"

"—Now how could I read when I'm on the road? I mean, I've got my duffle in one hand and I'm using the other to thumb with, so how could I hold a book?"

A new record started. I saw Dana O'Dea's red sheath disappear into a cluster of five or six men, several of whom had run out of razor blades as long ago as Klobb had. One of them might have been Pete Peters. I had been trying to spot him out of curiosity, but I was a bust as a beard watcher.

Even water hadn't helped McGruder's whisky. I checked the stock more carefully and came up with a fifth of Old Crow on which the seal had not been broken. I was looking around for something to cut it with when I heard a sharp metallic twang, like that of a small spring being released, just off to my right.

A gleaming switchblade flipped past my arm and gouged itself into the bar. It shivered to a stop no more than two inches from my hand.

"Try that on your bottle, hot shot," a voice said. "And consider yourself lucky you didn't get it in the ribs about three nights ago."

I let out my breath. Ephraim Turk was not quite grinning at me.

CHAPTER 13

———

I pulled out the knife, staring at him. I didn't say a word.

He showed me several large teeth. "Scared you, huh?"

I couldn't think of anything to say to that either. I was still holding the bottle, so I let him watch me run the blade around its neck. Then I flipped the knife over in my palm, hefting it. Its lethal end could have pinned my hand to the table with about five inches of steel to spare.

He smelled unsubtly of sweat. He had a clean white basque shirt on, but the jacket over it was the same seersucker he'd worn the other night. The jacket looked as if he'd been sleeping in it ever since. A few more jolly little tricks with the knife and someone would bury him in it.

"That was neat," I told him finally. "You develop the skill with practice, or did it just come to you during one of those naked Zen sessions on the living-room couch?"

"Hell," he said. He flushed. "But I suppose that slut would shoot off her mouth at that, wouldn't she?"

I pressed the point of the blade back into the wood, snapping it shut. "If you mean Fern Hoerner, maybe you ought to call her by name."

"Sure. Okay, so you got friendly—I didn't know. So I'm even sorry. Hell, you don't think I was especially happy about that mess over at Vinnie's? I don't usually go around slapping females."

"Or shooting them, evidently."

He gave me a wry grimace. "You're funny. They let me out this afternoon. How about the knife, huh?"

He lifted a hand, but I shook my head.

"Okay, so keep the thing. I just found it back there in the hall five minutes ago anyhow. It might be McGruder's."

"He shaves with it."

The little man shrugged, then stepped past me. I poked a Camel into my mouth and watched him pour himself a glass of white wine. I realized I wasn't really surprised to see him. A record stopped with another screech, this time sounding like chalk going the wrong way on a blackboard. Ephraim winced.

"You were with her when she found Josie?" he said then.

I nodded. He was being pleasant enough, but there was something almost spinsterish about his manner. In spite of his baby face he made me think of things that get shriveled up, like prunes. "How come they let you scram?" I asked him.

"I had an alibi. They finally got around to believing it."

"What about that gun?"

"Aw, hell—" He screwed up his enormous forehead in disgust. "People know about my record. Every damned time something gets stolen around here I get put down for it. Just because I got arrested for shoplifting in California once. You know what I hooked? Six cans of smoked oysters and a slab of Bel Paese cheese. I was trying to write a blank verse epic on Sacco and Vanzetti and I was practically starving. Boy, I began to feel like Sacco and Vanzetti myself over there this week. You know who they were?"

"Vaguely. Somebody planted the gun after the killing—picking you because it would look convincing?"

"I'll plant something on him quick enough, when they find out who. Sacco and Vanzetti were two Italians up in New England in the—"

"A lot of people know about the smoked fish?"

"Oysters are animals, not fish. Sure, that's the trouble. I gave the fuzz at least twenty names."

"Just names wouldn't convince them."

"I told you. I had an alibi. A guy was with me—he even walked me to Vinnie's, just before I ran into you."

"Somebody named Peters—"

He started to answer, then stopped. "—Somerset Maugham?" a voice wailed. *"Somerset Maugham!"*

"Evidently it took your pal a while to show up," I said.

He was considering me. "He got drunk that night," he said after a minute. "He didn't hear about anything until today."

"I thought the upstairs neighbor said you were alone over there?"

"Pete was down on the landing. The human eye isn't constructed to see around corners." He grinned suddenly. "You're asking as many questions as they did."

I didn't smile back. "I just realized I know more than they do," I told him.

He had been drinking. He lowered the glass, then reached to the table and set it down. "Just what is that supposed to mean, huh?"

"Nobody walked you as far as Vinnie's," I said without emphasis. "Maybe I didn't make it clear to the police, but you came in there on the dead run. It doesn't prove anything about the killing—just that for one reason or another both you and Peters are lying."

"Why, you son of a—"

His face got livid. June Allyson could have made herself look more ferocious with a minimum of effort, and I was a little sorry I had badgered him. I had simply been thinking out loud, and there wasn't any real reason for it.

"So run the hell back and tell them," he snarled then. "Don't you think they checked the story? What's it your business anyhow, you—"

I didn't answer him. I was chewing on a knuckle awkwardly when someone tapped me on the shoulder. I started to turn, thinking that it was probably Henshaw.

It was Mount Everest.

It fell on me.

CHAPTER 14

I caught it flush on the jaw. I staggered back three or four drunken steps, flailing my arms, but that was only for effect. I crashed down like something miscalculated at Cape Canaveral.

A thousand lights came on. They kept bursting like expanding stars. I was the only one seeing them.

All by myself on the floor of a seedy Greenwich Village basement, and I was forging ahead of whole nations in the race for outer space.

I had a remote idea that the party had come to an abrupt halt. "Well, for crying out loud!" someone screamed. "I saw that, Pete Peters! Why, that man wasn't even looking at you, you brute!"

Good old Donnie McGruder, just the ally I needed. I couldn't make him out in the mists. All I could see was a bearded monster nine feet tall, with forearms like hams and shoulders like a yoke.

Nobody had told me Peters was nine feet tall. That worried me. I closed my eyes tightly and shook my head before I let myself look at him again.

253

So it was only six feet. So I'd still never get up there without help.

I didn't want to get up anyhow. Let somebody else go climb mountains just because they're there. I didn't have any spirit of adventure. I didn't have any pride either. I just sat, sucking in air.

"You've got some damned nerve," McGruder was sputtering. "Now just what was that all about?"

"Aw, he was bugging Ephraim," Peters said. "Giving the poor kid a hard time. After Ephraim spends two days in jail, for gosh sakes."

"That's still no reason to sneak up behind a man and hit him," McGruder said. "Especially you, you big ape. Why, you might have killed him."

It was me they were talking about. That was nice. Even Ephraim was interested. "He had it coming," he contributed brightly. He was dancing around as gaily as a doll on a string. "He's that private detective who found Josie the other night. What's he butting in down here for anyhow? Maybe that will teach him to stay where he belongs, the carpetbagger."

"That's not the point," Peters said. He had a remarkably soft voice for a big man, a voice like marshmallows toasting. Soft and gooey, like my head. But that was nice too. I found comfort in his marshmallowy tones.

I got myself lifted to one knee, with all the cosmic temerity of a creature emerging from a Darwinian swamp.

"Nobody should bother Ephraim," Peters went on. "Two days in jail is enough. Ephraim suffered. Do you people have any concept of how he suffered? It makes him—why, it makes him holy."

"So get him a tin cup, like," somebody put in. Good old Henshaw also. "He can go beg alms."

"It isn't something to joke about," Peters told him. "You

people don't comprehend the alchemy of it. Being in jail does something to a man's soul. Something ultimate."

"It makes him a saint," I said then. "I'm sorry, I didn't know I was intruding upon a religious awakening. Fact is, I must have come to the wrong party altogether. I was looking for the protest meeting about Sacco and Vanzetti. Whatever became of Sacco and—oh, sure, poor old Sacco and Vanzetti—"

People were looking at me strangely. It didn't mean a thing. They were just disturbed by the sound of my scrambled brains. They kept sloshing around in the pan when I got to my feet. I hadn't known I was going to say a word.

"What were we talking about?" I said. "Oh, yeah, oysters. I always thought they were fish myself. Actually I like toasted marshmallows better. No I don't either. Ha! Come to think about it—you know what, about toasted marshmallows?"

"Say, listen, fellow—are you all right?"

That was Peters. He was watching me with genuine concern. I laughed in his face, swaying like a lunatic. I hadn't known I was going to laugh either.

"Listen, there are beds out back, maybe you better—"

"No, no, first ask me—what about toasted marsh-mallows—"

"Sure," Peters said. "Sure. You take it easy now, fellow." He glanced past me, nodding anxiously to someone. "You want me to ask you about toasted marshmallows. Sure. What about toasted marshmallows, fellow?"

I grinned at him. "They make me nauseated," I said. Then I hit him dead in the middle of that beard with as hard a left hand as I had ever thrown in my life.

Somebody gasped, but it wasn't Peters. His head jerked, but for a second his body hardly moved at all. Then he went over like a felled oak.

A girl decided to shriek. Peters took two or three ringsiders with him, going back. One of them was Ephraim. I didn't break up about it. The girl I'd spoken to before with the unmowed black hair and the figure like an ironing board was another one. She wound up sitting spraddle-legged with her mouth open and Peter's head in the lap of her black skirt. She had on black stockings that ended just below her bony knees.

A man snickered. "The ultimate, man," a woman added profoundly.

I was still pulling in air a little desperately. I waited another moment, watching until Peters came up groggily on one elbow. A fellow astronaut. His head dropped onto his chest and someone accommodatingly dumped the contents of a beer glass onto it. Ephraim was still sitting there also, staring at me in sullen outrage, as if I'd just maligned James Dean.

The mob had begun to chatter again and I pushed through them toward the bar. I didn't see Henshaw or Fern, but McGruder took me by the arm. He gave me a precious, shy smile, the fairy princess I'd just won in the lists.

"I'm sorry about that, Harry. Dreadfully sorry. You must think we're all beasts."

"Forget it. I hope it didn't bust up the party."

"Say now, say, *you* forget it. You're most welcome. If anyone should leave it's Pete. That—that—"

He was leading me toward a corner. I didn't have the strength to fight it.

"You *are* a private investigator, Harry?"

"I think somebody hung a sign on my back."

He didn't smile. In fact when I glanced at him I realized he had discarded almost all of his mannerisms. He was picking at a corner of his thin lower lip, and the serious expression made him look unexpectedly older.

"This is all very puzzling," he said after a minute. "If not to mention tragic. I knew poor Josie Welch quite well. She was so young that I was something of a—well, a big brother to the girl. She used to come to me with her problems."

I was working my jaw. "Any problems the cops would be interested in?"

"Oh, no, nothing like that at all. Just her bad childhood, general depression—psychological problems more than any other kind. She was raised on a farm in Kansas. The poor kid was attacked criminally by an uncle when she was no more than fourteen. It soured her on men pretty badly."

I grunted. "I hear she slept with enough of them. You should pardon the expression."

He still didn't grin. "She did chase around a lot," he said. "Too much. But she never found any satisfaction in it. I think it was a fairly obvious syndrome—a way she had of getting even."

"You're going to lose me," I told him.

"Oh, you know what I mean. Giving her body contemptuously, almost as if she wanted to watch men make fools of themselves."

That was worth another grunt. "You didn't know she was a call girl?"

McGruder's head jerked, it startled him that much. "You're joshing?"

"I might be. But the possibility existed when the cops started digging Tuesday night. I'd guess it's pretty high on their agenda now that Ephraim's out."

He was scowling. "She could be a bitter girl sometimes. I even used to think she was capable of—well, violence. But I never suspected she'd found that sort of outlet. All of this is why you're down here, I suppose?"

I started to shake my head, then clamped my teeth together. A great Georgia halfback named Frank Sinkwich once played a full season with his jaw broken. I wondered how it felt to be beyond human frailty. "I'm looking for Audrey Grant. Strictly a family interest."

McGruder lifted an eyebrow, then shrugged as if he were disappointed. "She's around somewhere. I'll try to find her, if you'd like."

"I'd appreciate it. Nothing personal, but I've had about enough of your party. And thanks."

"You already paid me by hitting Pete." He tittered suddenly. Just as suddenly he was the old McGruder again, the one that all of two or three people undoubtedly treasured. "The big butch used to be my husband. We had four months of sheer bliss together before he decided to go straight. He's been just impossible ever since!"

That white hand went limp again. I sighed, watching him use it to toss some of that drooping hair out of his eyes. Zen Fruitism. By the time he was ready to flutter away he wasn't even touching the floor.

They'd gotten Peters off the launching pad and into an aid station somewhere. Henshaw was at the bar and I headed back over. The girl Peters had fallen against was standing behind him. I took a second look and decided I might have been hit too hard at that.

It wasn't the same girl. I realized that the one Peters had crashed into had not been the Ginsberg-Corso rooter I'd seen before either. But all three of them had the same stringy black hair and scrawny figure, the same black jersey, the same black stockings. They could have been members of some new uniformed sect.

"Something called *The History of Rome Hanks*," I heard this one say. "The paperback title is *Dishonored Flesh*—"

Henshaw was grinning at me. "Slugger," he said. "What do you do with the right hand—save it for Guy Fawkes' Day?"

"I work out two or three times a week. It gives me an edge."

"Like a cleaver. You saw the chick, huh?"

"When? When I was on my back?"

Henshaw was drinking. "I thought maybe previous to that. I spied her back in the end corridor. It was a trifle queer, come to reconsider."

I had picked up the Old Crow. "Queer how?"

"Ephraim. I guess people haven't been made cognizant he's one of the populace again. The Grant chick ambled out of the head back there and sort of turned sallow when she spotted him, you know? Real shook up."

I had put down the bottle. "Then what?"

"Well, man, I was sort of more interested in your small brawl. She's still yonder, I presume. I saw Ivan Klobb back there, but whether or not they made words I cannot avow." He looked at me, puzzled, then whistled softly. "Hey, like I see some light. If Ephraim is out, some other cat is due to go in, no? You think the sight of him gave the Grant chick some ideas? Like maybe, since it ain't Eph, she's got a hunch who?"

I was staring at him.

"Although on third hand I could be blowing hysterical," he decided. "Missing the whole beat. The chick might have just had heartburn, you know?"

"A brunette," I said. "What was she wearing?"

"Man's T-shirt." Henshaw giggled obscenely. "I am not as observant as many, but the Grant chick in a man's T-shirt I would long remember. Like better men than I have left hearth and home for dream of what lies beyond yon distant hills, you dig me?"

He was smirking into his glass. I left him with it, heading back toward that corridor.

CHAPTER 15

The corridor was roughly the length of a bowling alley. There were four closed doors along its left-hand side, and evidently it turned at the rear. The dim rose glow of the kerosene lamp made it hard to be sure. The sudden proximity of Dana O'Dea made it harder to be interested.

She swam up in front of me just as I reached the doorway. I stopped, and not just because I remembered that she lived with Audrey Grant. That red dress had made her noticeable from a distance, but at close range she would have been noticeable in a diving rig.

She was a big girl. Her full breasts swelled up out of the sheath into a pair of fleshy shoulders as sensuous as heavy cream, and there was enough ripe womanhood in her bare arms alone to melt nonferrous metals. She had boldly painted lips and flashing dark eyes, and her hair was so brilliantly black that it looked almost wet. She was as luxuriously molded as the hull of a yacht.

She was also drunk as a tadpole.

She pulled up short a foot in front of me, swaying, and then she almost fell. She took a full breath. "Wow," she said.

"Wow," I told her. She swayed some more. Those milky

shoulders were unbelievable. I reached out with a finger and touched the dress where it turned beneath the fold of her arm.

She eyed me speculatively. "Excuse me," I said. "I just wanted to see if it was painted on."

She gave me a smile that could have paid her rent for a year. I grinned back at her. I would have liked to spend a year doing it.

"You know where your roommate is?"

"Audrey?" She frowned. "You know Audrey? Audrey know you? Who're you?"

Her voice was no thicker than bread pudding. She steadied herself with a hand on my sleeve, looking at me more intently.

"Audrey doesn't know you," she said. "You know something? I'm glad. Don't even care what your name is." She nodded profoundly. "Don't care 'tall. Like you anyhow. You know my name? My name's Dana 'Dea. You know something else? I'm drunk. Been drinking since three 'clock this afternoon. Home all alone. You 'magine that?"

"You could do better," I told her. "Why don't we find Audrey? The three of us can get drunk together."

"Sure. Find Audrey. Good old Au'rey. Swell idea." She turned back into the corridor, took two steps and then almost went over again. I caught her by the wrist, so she decided to play. She hung away from me, balanced on her heels, and let me take all her weight. She had a few more pounds of it than the boys in the fashion business would have allowed, but then the same guys would design a blanket roll without ever spending a night in the woods. She was as yielding as gelatin. I hauled her back onto a level keel, so then she tittered and poked a finger into my chest. "Nope," she said emphatically, "don't know you. Wish I did."

261

"Audrey, huh? Like a pal?"

"Abs'lutely."

She had slithered away from me once more when a girl with a face like a wedge of cheese stepped past us into the hall. She was a mousy, intellectual sort, hiding a concave chest behind a bulky yellow sweatshirt. She glanced at Dana, then paused, lifting an eyebrow. "My heavens, girl," she said.

"It's disgusting, isn't it?" Dana agreed. "Started drinking at three 'clock. You 'magine that?"

"I don't have to imagine," the girl said. "You're a mess."

That disheartened Dana briefly. "I am?" She glanced down into the pasteurized cleavage at the top of her dress. Then she looked back to the mousy girl, lifting her gaze to approximately the same anatomical vicinity. It wasn't being very fair. Several seconds passed. Then Dana snickered.

"Well, of all the—" The girl whirled and stomped off.

Dana sighed. "All I said was I was drunk. She didn't have to call me a mess. You think I'm a mess?"

"You're no mess," I said. She wasn't. She had too much raw sensuality to move sloppily. She just swelled and receded, like surf.

"I'm glad you say that," she told me. "Been drinking all day, you know?"

"Audrey," I said.

"Oh, sure, Audrey." She brightened up again, nodding toward the first closed door. She beckoned. "Shhh—"

I followed her over. She twisted the knob, then pushed in the door silently. The room was dark and I reached past her and fumbled for a switch. A muffled masculine voice changed my mind.

"Let's just leave it be, shall we?"

"Oops!" Dana fell against me. I could see the vague form of a bed in the gloom as I eased her out of the way.

I got the door almost back where it belonged, then stopped again. There were two pair of shoes on the floor, both at least size twelve.

"Not Audrey," Dana told me with assurance. "Not Audrey 'tall."

I closed it, then stood there shaking my head. It didn't rattle. There had been two motorcycle crash helmets inside also.

Dana was already lurching onward, undismayed. She turned and winked at me from the next door, then threw it inward gleefully. This time there was a light on. I followed her in, a little grimly.

Furniture was not one of McGruder's passions. The room contained a single uncovered cot set about a foot away from a side wall, a straight chair under a high barred window, a telephone on the floor. I supposed we would have to make the grand tour. I turned back, but Dana had slipped around me to the door.

She was being playful again. She pushed the door shut and leaned against it, peering up at me slyly from under her dark brows. That made her about as coy as Mae West. The girl would have been bringing out the eroticism in every man who had run into her since she was fifteen, and I had to wonder what she would be like when she was sober. I pressed a fist along her cheek, then gestured toward the outside.

"Uh-huh." She nodded sincerely. "Find Audrey. Li'l while. That's a promise."

"The faster we find her, the faster we get drunk."

"Drunk already. Started to get drunk at—"

"I know. Three o'clock. You were home all day."

"I tell you that?"

"I think so, yes."

She frowned. "You're not drunk 'tall, are you?"

"Things keep coming up. You know how it is."

263

"Shame," she said. "Guy like you." Her eyebrows had knit. Then suddenly she beamed. "Got it," she told me brightly. "Doesn't matter if you're drunk or not."

"I'm glad. You've got what?"

"Nope, doesn't matter 'tall. Got something better. Was going to save it, but it just makes me sick when I'm drunk myself."

I had a pretty good idea what she was talking about. I waited while she hunched those lush shoulders and reached into her bosom, showing me the top of her gleaming dark oblivious head. It was folded into a small tube of white tissue, and she had difficulty unwrapping it. Finally she held out the thin marijuana reefer.

I gave her my best rueful smile.

"You mean you don't *want* it?"

"Maybe later, huh? As soon as we find Audrey."

She was pouting. "Just don't understand. Don't understand 'tall. Not drunk. Won't accept generous'st offer I can make. What *do* you do for kicks, anyway?"

In her soused way she was seriously troubled. I had to grin at her.

It took a minute. Then her eyes lit up. She giggled absurdly.

"Well, crying out loud, why didn't you say so in the first place?"

I grinned some more. "We can go now, can't we?"

"Crying out loud. Never thought of it. How do you like that?" She pursed her lips. Then she nodded decisively. "Well, by golly, nobody's going to say Dana 'Dea's no sport. No, sir, nobody's going to say that. You just don't go 'way and I'll—"

This time she was a step ahead of me. She lurched downward, pawing at the hem of her skirt, and came up with two handfuls of it. There was no slip under there to hamper the friendly little impulse. She laughed in delight, crossing her

264

arms as she straightened, and then yanked upward. Her head disappeared in a twisted red tangle.

She got stuck, squirming like something trying to work its way out of a cocoon, and her voice came merrily out of the depths. "Well, where'd you go? Crying out loud, have to give a poor girl some help—"

She needed as much help as Lady Chatterley. She was stumbling toward the cot, bent from the hips. I was probably going to regret it on cold winter nights in the future. I knew I was. The girl had a pair of thighs that could have sent the Crusades wandering off down the wrong roadway. I gave her a swift whack where her bright orange girdle was stretched most memorably and sent her sprawling.

She let out a startled little cry, skidding across the mattress with her arms flung outward and her calves flailing. I headed for the door.

I stopped again. I wasn't sure why, except that the incident should have merited some inane comment or other, and she hadn't made any. She had scampered to her knees and was staring into the gap between the cot and the wall. The dress had unfurled a bit, but she was still going to catch half a cold. She turned toward me, grinning stupidly.

"Told you," she said. "Didn't I tell you? Didn't believe me. Said I'd find old Audrey."

I had taken out a cigarette. Dana frowned then, but not because I dropped it.

"Don't understand. Lots of swell beds around. Why would she sleep on the floor?" She shook her head. "And how do you suppose she went and got all bloody that way?" she said.

CHAPTER 16

She was down there, all right. Her skin was warm and pliant, but there was no trace of a pulse.

I hadn't expected one. The knife was still sticking out of her breast, like a pencil out of a sharpener.

I turned fast because of Dana. She was on her feet, beginning to get it. She was standing lopsidedly, missing a shoe. A minute earlier it would have made her fall on her face.

"Is she—is she—?"

"Yes."

Her eyes widened. Her mouth opened again but this time it made only some small gurgling sounds, like a clogged toilet. She spun, breaking for the door.

The dress was still knotted around her hips. I caught a fistful of it. Something tore when I jerked her back.

"Kiss me!" I told her.

She looked at me as if I were mad. I was mad as a loon, but I knew enough to keep her away from that mob out front. She was still gaping when I brought up a short right and tagged her on the point of her gorgeous chin.

I got an arm around her before she could fall. It was like carrying a Volkswagen, but I got her onto the mattress.

It left me light-headed. It also left me with a corpse on the floor and an unconscious girl on the bed. I had a remote idea that the situation called for some firm, decisive action.

So I raised Dana's hips and pulled her dress down.

Middle-class morality is primeval. There was a key in the door and I got myself over there to turn it. I came back and eased the cot farther from the wall. The body rolled onto its spine.

Audrey Grant. She had on that T-shirt that had made Henshaw rhapsodic. The blade had slashed through it just below the heart. A thin red stream had traced itself onto the waist of her green skirt, but it had not been a prolonged bleeding. It could not have taken her much more than six or eight seconds longer to die than it had taken Josie Welch.

I had told Ulysses Grant there did not have to be any connection between the two girls. Astute, discerning Fannin. I probably would have told Alexander Graham Bell he'd never make a connection either.

Audrey Grant. Why? I didn't know why. It was 11:18. Less than six hours ago Grant had been in my office. That was why.

Now what the hell did that mean, exactly? Nothing, nothing at all. Fannin was just raving, in lieu of thought. Worry about it tomorrow, Scarlett, when your brains stop palpitating.

She had been a pretty girl. She had been tall, but a daughter of Grant's would have to be. She was leggy, and she had almost too much bosom for her slight shoulders and long neck. There was a tiny gold chain around the neck, twisted now so that the locket lay on the outside of the shirt. I didn't open it. There would be a picture of Philo Vance inside, sticking his tongue out at me. I kept staring at the knife instead.

That did it. I had simply not been conditioned to come suddenly upon the violently dead. Even when my hand lifted to my pocket it didn't register immediately. The knife was an exact duplicate of the one I'd taken from Ephraim.

I didn't have any knife in my pocket.

So I'd lost it when I'd been hit. Any one of fifty people could have picked it up.

There was a deduction for you.

I'd talked to Henshaw right after the brawl. No, first to McGruder. Henshaw had said Ivan Klobb was back in the corridor. Had Fern still been with him? Where had Ephraim and Peters gone?

The next question has several parts, Mr. Fannin. Name all the National League batting champions from 1900 to the present, in chronological order, with their averages. You have thirty seconds in the isolation booth.

Zen Boothism. I went to the telephone. There was a book lying under it. *The Subterraneans,* by Jack Kerouac. I got Central, then the desk at the local precinct. The man said DiMaggio was out. He said Toomey was out also. "You'll have to do," I told him.

"Sure, and for what? Just who might this be?"

"My name is Kerouac. Max Kerouac. Take this down." I gave him McGruder's address. "It's a basement, entrance in the rear through an alley. Drinking going on. There'll be a key under the plank steps where you come in. The key is for the second bedroom door in the right-hand corridor. You got that?"

"That I have, but just what is it we're to do with it, Mr. Carraway? What is it we're to find in this locked room?"

"Well, the body. You want me to drag it out front and spoil the party?"

I hung it up. I dug out a pencil and a spiral notebook, tore off a sheet, wrote: *Sgt. DiMaggio knows me. Girl knocked out so would not scream. Will call here.* I signed the right name this time, then propped the note on an uncovered pillow next to Dana's head.

There was a small slash pocket on Dana's left hip. There was a folded five-dollar bill in the pocket, and there were two keys on a rubber band. I left the money.

She didn't move when I touched her. Young Molly Bloom. She was boozed up enough so that she would be snoring contentedly when the cops arrived. I resisted a moronic impulse to kiss her on one of those creamy shoulders. I decided I was still goofy.

There was no one in the corridor. I was locking the door again when I realized that there was no sound either, not from anywhere in the apartment. No talk, no music. That stopped me cold. One sporty suggestion from the right nitwit and the whole pack of them could have been in a caravan of stolen cars on their way to Denver.

They weren't. It took me a few seconds in the renewed dark, coming into the main room. Someone had draped a rag over the one bulb. They were sitting on the floor in a scattered half circle, evidently all of them.

There was a chair out in the center, with Don McGruder standing on it. He was holding some papers, but I did not know how he expected to read from them in that gloom. Unless his inner glow would help him. His poetic flame. Maybe that was why he had all his clothes off, so that the glow would not be obstructed. He was naked as a new-dropped giraffe.

His voice came in a whisper. "My latest creation," he said. "I hope it is worthy of its subject, which has so devastatingly moved us all. I call it, 'An Ode to Josie, Cruelly Shot'—"

There were some sighs. It was way over my head, but then I'd never attended a poetry recitation before. For all I knew Emily Dickinson had reached immortality the same way. I went quietly along the wall. McGruder started speaking:

"Alas, poor waif, at savage rest,
The deadly missile in thy breast—
What immoral hand or eye
Would scar thy soft virginity?—"

I stopped long enough to plant the key. Two people were talking in undertones beyond the overhanging light outside. One of them was another of those uniformed witches from that weird sect.

"So I asked her," the girl said, "how could I protest against social conformity if I wore what everyone else wears—"

This time my head did rattle, I was sure of it. Poor besotted sexy Dana, she was the only sane one in there. I would make it up to her one day. On a slow boat to Patagonia. Just thinking about it would sustain me.

Sure. I'd think about it the next time I treated a murder threat like a missing-persons case.

I told myself I couldn't have known the clippings Grant got were a threat. Okay, I told myself, so you couldn't have known. So it isn't your fault that the girl is dead, but dead she is. Got any ideas, Kerouac?

Yeah, I got some ideas. Shut up and let me think.

I didn't have time to think. The Chevy was still near the Blue Soldier, but the cab I grabbed at Bleecker Street got me across to East Tenth in five minutes. I found the address that Henshaw had given me for Dana and Audrey Grant, an ordinary brownstone but well enough kept up to be expensive. I read *O'Dea-Grant* next to a bell marked *2-A,* used one of Dana's keys on the outside door, climbed the one flight. The building was as quiet as a sunken ship.

I found 2-A. Dana's second key was new and badly filed. It took me two or three turns to drop the tumblers, and then I could not twist the key out of the lock again. My hand was still working at it after I'd pushed back the door and stepped in.

It was my right hand. I do everything with my right hand except deal poker. Even if I could get a gun out with my left I couldn't hit the Atlantic Ocean from Montauk Point.

Not that I had a gun to reach for anyhow. The woman inside did, naturally.

CHAPTER 17

It was more than just a gun. It was Italian-made, a Beretta Olympic. It had a barrel almost nine inches long, adjustable sights, a compensator at the muzzle. Two hundred dollars would buy it, but you would have to live close to the store if you expected to take a taxi home on your change.

It was a .22, which made it even more interesting. Not that I was in a position to do much about that at the moment. I gave my attention to the woman in back of it instead.

She demanded the attention anyway. She was a young thirty, and she had a head of incredibly wild orange hair which she had apparently not cut since pubescence. Her lipstick, her belt and her shoes matched the hair precisely, and everything else she had on was purple. Including the paint around her eyes, although the eyes themselves might have been green. It was not a cold night, but she was wearing one of those knitted coat sweaters. Its lowest buttons were closed at her knees. With the rest of it open and falling away from her she looked like some exotic hothouse hybrid, just about to blossom. She was as chic as next year's best buy for the man who has everything.

Her voice curled out from behind the Beretta as idly as a

wisp of smoke. "I think I'll ask you to step all the way inside, darling. You'll find that agreeable, won't you?"

"Surely," I said.

I went past her into the middle of a living room. The gun nosed firmly into the small of my back. I heard the door close. "I'm sorry, but this does seem necessary. I'm sure you'll be sensible enough not to move."

I watched the bobbing of that rampant hair out of the corner of my eye while she frisked me. When she was satisfied that she was the only one who had thought to bring any artillery she backed off. She took my wallet with her.

"It can't be robbery," I said. "You forgot your mask."

"And my bathing cap." She laughed. "I'll be happier if you'll sit now, darling. On the couch, if you please—"

I went across. The place was just another furnished apartment, melancholy as a hand-me-down bathrobe. Overstuffed furniture, a threadbare maroon rug, listing floorlamps. A paperback book lay on the couch near me. By Lucien Vaulking, the dead writer Henshaw had connected with both girls who were now also dead.

My gift-wrapped redhead had perched herself on the arm of a chair near the door. Good calves, even though the stockings were tinted purple also.

She'd opened the wallet and was considering it, resting the Beretta along her thigh. After some seconds she considered me instead. Then she closed the wallet and tossed it across.

"Fannin," she said casually. "That would make you the chap who found Josie the other evening. We read the first name as Henry."

"The press is so dreadfully irresponsible these days."

No smile. "How curious. And now you appear at Audrey's. You *will* tell me why?"

"Nope."

"I *could* make it difficult. There happens to be a considerable amount of money involved in this operation. I'm not down here for social purposes—surely you realize that?"

"I do now. Does Connie step out from behind the arras, or do we toddle off somewhere to meet him?"

She had small bright teeth. "Perhaps we'll have to see him at that. Unless you wish to change your mind and tell me what you wanted with Audrey?"

I leered at her.

She lifted an eyebrow. "I rather doubt that. Meaning no offense, darling, but I don't quite believe you could meet the going rate." She stood, almost wearily. "You'll pardon me if I'm so quickly bored—but then it's not really being scintillating, is it? You don't intend to answer my questions?"

I looked at her pleasantly. After a minute she reached below the chair and lifted a bulky black pocketbook, moving with all the graceful indifference of a lynx in a forest full of chipmunks. The pocketbook rested against her hip when she adjusted the strap across her right shoulder.

"The gun will be inside," she said easily, "not obstructed in the least. I have an Austin Healy three doors up. You will drive, of course. I'm certain we understand each other."

Cool, cool, like a Christmas window in Tiffany's. So I shrugged, getting to my feet as if I really thought she might shoot holes in my head if I didn't. Then I nodded in the general direction of her knees. "If we're joining the maharajah, love, you really ought to hitch up that slip—"

It was so corny I was going to blush when I wrote it in my diary come bedtime. The edge of my left hand caught her at the inside of the wrist when she glanced down, and the gun went skidding noisily toward the base of a chair. She choked off an unfeminine sound, then broke after it.

I grabbed her around the waist. It was a nice waist, trim and girlish. I liked it, so I didn't let go even when she jabbed a spiked heel into my shin. I hopped on one foot, lost my balance, went down on my seat. It hurt me more when the red-head went down on hers. My lap was under it.

"Tell me honestly—do you feel as silly as I do?"

"If you will *kindly* release me—"

I kept one hand near her while I stretched for the Beretta, but it wasn't necessary. Madame was really far too civilized for bodily contact sports. She was already busy with her seams when I checked the gun.

There were five long-rifle cartridges in the magazine, one in the chamber. The bore was clean. I ejected the sixth shell, pressed it into the clip, then dropped that part of the mechanism into my pocket. She'd lost her satchel and I poked my nose into that next.

The usual female junk, nothing anymore lethal than a charge-plate. I stuck the eviscerated gun inside. A card in a calfskin wallet told me I'd been boorish with a Mrs. Margaret Constantine, Sutton Place. Mrs. Constantine carried over seven hundred dollars in subway money.

I handed the purse to her. She'd slipped off her coat. Within a minute she was sitting with those violet legs crossed, doing something remarkably studied with a Parliament and a gold-plated Ronson.

"My turn now," I said. "We'll talk about Constantine, huh?"

She fanned away some smoke. "Will we?"

"Okay," I said. "I know. No cash to toss around on fun and games, my suit's last year's also, and on top of everything else you find it uncouth to roll on the rug. So I'll figure it out myself with my plebeian wit. Constantine would be a man called Connie. He does some kind of fancy pandering uptown—a thriving business because he even runs to part-time help. Josie Welch and Audrey Grant have been supernumeraries of a sort."

That got me nowhere, so I said, "You hear your husband called a pimp so often you don't even yawn."

This time she looked at me as if I were something extraneous she'd unearthed in the vinaigrette sauce. "May I ask how many young girls you've hired to undress in cheap hotel bedrooms in divorce cases, Mr. Fannin? That would be your line of work, wouldn't it?"

I let that go past. I was hefting the loaded magazine.

"The newspapers said that Josie was killed with a twenty-two," she said in a minute. "If you are by chance thinking that it might have been my gun, you can forget about it. I'm here for some information, nothing more. If you are also, it strikes me that we might make some manner of mutually satisfactory arrangement."

I didn't say anything to that either. Until I'd discovered who she was I'd thought the character named Connie would know something. But she would not have been waiting around if either of them had any idea what had happened to Audrey Grant.

There was a door off to the right of the couch. "Two bedrooms?" I asked her.

She nodded, curious.

"Which one's Audrey's?"

"Her clothes are in the one further back."

"Stick around," I said. I went over there and flicked on a light in a short hallway. Doors on the right side led to a kitchen and a bath. I opened the second bedroom and snapped another switch.

It was a place to sleep. A double bed, some maple stuff with drawers and legs. A clipped-out book-jacket photo of someone who was either D. H. Lawrence or a dissipated young Abe Lincoln tacked into a wall. I started on the dresser.

Margaret Constantine came into the doorway and leaned there, trailing smoke. "Aren't you being a bit brazen, darling?"

I was riffling a stack of blouses. "They're both at a party."

"Oh, yes, this absurd other life of Audrey's." She sat down on the bed. "I'm not sure I understand this, you know. But the simple fact is that Josie's murder could affect us quite adversely. You're not here because you think Audrey might be involved, by any chance?"

I grunted.

"I don't imagine you'll tell me what you're searching for?"

"Bank book," I said. "Try that bed table."

She shrugged, then leaned across. After a second she held out the blue cardboard envelope. "Isn't this quite against the law? Or no, you had a key, didn't you?"

I didn't answer her, scowling at the pass book. Audrey Grant was leaving an estate of $4,100, but that was not what I had wanted to know. What I cared about was that she had made a deposit of $1,852 on July tenth, the same day on which Josie Welch had put the identical sum into her own account at another bank.

Ulysses Grant had told me that Audrey would have gotten whatever cash was left by Elizabeth Muller Grant. She'd only gotten half. Unless I was way off base, the matching deposits meant that she'd split the inheritance with her half-sister, the child Elizabeth Muller had sent out for adoption at birth.

It tied in with what Grant had said about his estranged wife being visited by two girls, and it also tied in with what Don McGruder had told me about Josie Welch and her hard Kansas childhood. I'd remembered the date of Josie's deposit when Grant had mentioned that Elizabeth Muller died in early July, but it had taken a second killing to make me put two and two together. Except I still did not have the foggiest notion what any of it meant.

I put back the bank book, checking my watch. Margaret Constantine did not know it, but we would be having company any minute. I decided I'd rather talk to her husband before the police at that.

Mrs. Constantine did not know that either. She had been watching me, leaning backward with her weight against her arms. Now she lowered herself to her elbows, lifting one of her crossed legs slightly. That shoe slipped off and dangled from her toes.

There was an amused twinkle in her eyes. In another second she swung around and hoisted both legs, letting both shoes tumble to the floor. It was an obvious play, but she could even be obvious with style. She blew aside some of that fantastic hair when I leaned over her.

"Anything a girl can do to protect the family business, is that it?"

I was wrong. One of her hands shot upward and clamped itself around my neck, and she jerked herself toward me. "You said they were both at a party. If they won't be back, we—there's time—"

I was so wrong it startled me. Before I knew it her legs were actually thrashing. The dame was compulsive as a hare.

It didn't have to mean much, since a sweaty plumber could get the same offer from half of the authentic heiresses in town. But I'd been wondering for twenty minutes how deep that sophistication really ran. "Call me darling again," I told her.

"Oh, yes. Darling, darling—"

I pursed my lips, braced above her. "One more thing."

"What? Yes, anything—"

EPITAPH FOR A DEAD BEAT

"Did Constantine marry you right out of the racket, or did you get the retread job before you ran into him?"

"Did I get—?" It took a second or two. Then she sprang back onto her haunches like an animal. "Why, you lousy two-bit son of a—"

I laughed, straightening. "That's pretty much what I wanted to hear," I told her.

She spat something else in substantiation, snatching up her shoes. She didn't stop to put them on. No more composure, no more composure at all.

"If you'll fetch your fancy coat, ma'am," I called after her, "we can go see Connie now."

I glanced into the kitchen and the other bedroom on the way out, having a tardy thought about something. Probably it just indicated that she was a neurotic housekeeper, even drunk. But there was no trace of that bottle Dana O'Dea had been home alone with all afternoon.

Mrs. Constantine had fetched the coat. We were climbing into the Austin Healy, as amicably as two hounds after a one-bone meal, when a patrol wagon pulled up sharply and double-parked three or four car lengths behind us.

CHAPTER 18

We discussed philosophy and religion on the way to Sutton Place. When we passed 23rd Street I said, "What shall we talk about—Existentialism?" Ten blocks later I said, "How about the Dead Sea Scrolls? Surely you have an opinion about the Dead Sea Scrolls?" Mrs. Constantine found it all so stimulating she ran three stoplights getting home.

When she finally swerved over to the curb it was in front of a tree-sheltered riverside apartment building where the rents would be as high as any you could pay in New York, or in the world. She left the motor running for a dignified, elderly doorman who wished her good evening by name. I followed her under a canopy and through a richly mirrored lobby, then waited while she pressed for an elevator. The elevator made as much noise coming down as a wounded moth. Its operator was as old and courtly as the doorman. They were both retired bank presidents, supplementing their pensions. He took us up three flights, and then we stepped into a private foyer instead of a corridor.

That meant the Constantines had at least half a floor. Mrs. Constantine discarded her coat across the carved mahogany arm of a towering antique chair, then led me stiff-lipped through an ornate archway into a living room.

King Farouk would have a bigger one. It ran about seventy feet back to where you would see the water, and that whole wall was glass, partly obscured by ungathered drapes. There were tall ferns, and there was a lot of whatever kind of furniture it was. Only one small lamp was burning, and everything was luxurious and dark and furry, like vespers at a mink farm. She stopped in the middle of it all.

Her eyes were still giving off sparks, but I didn't grin. Maybe it was the sight of all that indulgence, but she wasn't funny anymore.

"My husband has a slight cold. If you'll wait, it will be a minute."

I nodded, watching that orange mane disappear through another arch. I supposed hubby would have a study in there. Sure. He'd be camped in a contour chair in front of a twenty-inch screen, with a nasal spray in one hand and a notebook full of Johns in the other. I went across to the windows. Dutiful Margaret would stroke his hot little forehead before she told him about the nasty mans out front. Poor darling, has it been a trying evening with the runny nose? Would baby like a hot toddy before he works out the girls' schedules for tomorrow night? I looked down at the black sweeping river, but it only made me choleric to think of the sort of people who could afford to run it through their back yards.

So all of a sudden I was getting righteous. I was a Puritan. So the lady was wrong, I didn't do divorce cases. So what? What business was it of mine where the Constantines got the dough to pay the ice man?

Anyhow, I already knew how Mrs. Constantine paid the ice man. There was a bar in a corner to my left, with a single bottle of Chivas Regal on its mosaic top, and I started over that way.

I hadn't gotten across when he came striding into the room behind me. He was bellowing.

"Harry Fannin! *Harry!* Why, you old son of a gun, no wonder I never made the connection. The goddam papers said Henry—"

I must have stared at him witlessly for the first second or two. He was my height, but he would have weighed in at close to sixty pounds more than I did. That meant he had put on at least thirty in the dozen years since I had seen him. Oliver Constantine, left tackle.

"Harry, you old renegade! Why, if I'd known you were in New York I would have looked you up years ago!" He was pumping my right hand with his own, which was the size of a catcher's mitt, and his left was crushing my shoulder. "The best damned halfback in that whole crop of sophomores. Why, by George, I remember one time in scrimmage you ran right over me. Took me out so hard I almost didn't start the Illinois game. Well, I'll be damned—"

I got rid of the hands, shaking my head. We weren't quite long lost brothers, since I'd never really said more than two hundred words to the man. "I never thought of it either," I told him. "You made second-string All-Conference that year."

"Ah!" He waved it aside. "Should have made first. I mopped up the field with that big Swede from Minnesota they picked." He lumbered around the bar. He had a face like a chunk of scarred sandstone under a quarter-inch blond crew cut, and he was wearing a dark blue dressing gown with an ascot. "Boy, those were the days, weren't they, fellow? What's your poison, Harry?"

I gestured toward the Scotch, watching him dully. He came up with an ice bucket and two old-fashioned glasses, and he poured two drinks. "Yes, sir, best sophomore on the club. Drink up, Harry. To old Michigan—" He tossed off the whisky, grinning at me. "Old Fannin himself, the boy who was going to make them forget Tom Harmon until that knee went sour. Well, hey, hey, you're not drinking—"

I chewed on the inside of my cheek, nodding. He had been a harmless buffoon at college, but I had had to respect him as an athlete. I remembered a game in which he had played almost sixty full minutes when he was injured badly enough to have been in the infirmary. I was also remembering that Josie Welch had been nineteen years old.

Cotton Mather Fannin. "I'll drink to Michigan," I said.

"Well, for crying out loud—" He had been looking at me in amazement. "Why, you old son of a gun, you don't like my business. You really don't! A private cop. A divorce-case peeper and he's got a moral streak—"

I shrugged. "I never had to pay for a woman."

"Ha! Now you're talking. Listen, fellow, listen—there's half a million paunchy old men in this town, fat slobs who never got a cheek pinched in their lives except by their fat wives. They dial the right number, all of a sudden they're free-wheeling down hill on a bright red scooter. Well, they're going to buy the scooter whether I supply it or somebody else does. I like it better when the scratch turns up in my pocket." He poured himself another drink, motioning me to the bottle. "Ha! Or am I talking too much, being too defensive? What the hell, Harry, what the hell—to Tom Harmon, eh, boy? Drink up. To old Ninety-Eight!"

I drank to Harmon, then shook loose a cigarette. "I'd like to bat the breeze, Connie—"

"Yeah, yeah, sure. Brother, this mess. That Josie was a nice kid. But listen, listen, Margaret says you came sprinting into Audrey's place like you were trying to get back into shape—"

"The Grant girl's dead also."

"Huh?"

I told him about it briefly. It was obviously news, and I decided it was a fair exchange for anything he could give me in turn. When I finished he blew his nose in a yellow silk handkerchief, turning away. I had not expected that, but I couldn't think of any valid reason why I shouldn't have. "You haven't got any idea what gives?" he asked me.

"There be any chance one of your customers got mixed up with the pair of them?"

"Nah, never happen. Hell, the girls know better than to give out their home addresses."

He threw down what was left of his second Scotch, then wiped his mouth with the back of one of those meaty hands. "Boy, this can fix me, but good. Even without a tie-in, all I need is one wrong cop getting wind of it being two of my stable." The hand reached to my sleeve abruptly. "Hey, fellow, you're not going to have to mention my name—"

I used up the rest of my whisky, not saying anything.

"Hey, now, Harry, we played on the same squad, remember? All right, you can't promise—hell, I know how you can get hung up with bulls—but you'll do your best, eh, fellow?"

"Let's leave it there, Connie. I'll see what comes up."

"Yeah. Yeah, sure—"

"Where do you get the girls?" I asked him. "Not the ones who hang around the clubs—kids like these two from downtown."

He was staring at the bottle, preoccupied. "Got a contact, painter named Klobb. I give him half a grand whenever one of them works out."

I made a face. "Your wife down there for some special reason tonight?"

"Just looking for Audrey. We couldn't get hold of her all week—the girl she lives with kept saying she was out."

"Mrs. Constantine always use a gun when she's herding up absentees?"

"Ah!" The grin came back. "Margaret gets her little kicks. How about that, by the way? A glue-footed old linebacker like me, coming up with that kind of class—pretty neat, eh?"

"Sure," I said. I put the Beretta's magazine on the bar. "Look, I guess I better scram. The cops are going to rack me up as it is. Also I ought to get in touch with the girl's father."

"Well, here, here—call him." He pointed out a white phone behind me. "No extra motion, that's my motto. Always was. Hell, you compare college linemen to the boys in the pro game someday. The pros don't make a move until they see where the play's going." He dropped a shoulder and lunged toward me. "Am I right or am I right?"

"I still remember," I told him. I did. He'd been able to hit like an irritated rhino. And I was thirty-two years old and still enough of a kid to daydream once in a while about the All-America halfbacks I'd worshiped when I was twelve or fourteen. I supposed I could quit all that now. I dug out Grant's number.

I let the phone ring eight or ten times before I put it back. It was 12:40, but O. J. Fosburgh had said the man was a drinker. Most likely he would have a corner in a neighborhood bar somewhere.

Constantine was working the bottle again. "Funny," he said. "Those two girls. I figured it was something personal with Josie, you know? I mean whatever it was between her and this Beatnik writer they booked. But here's Audrey too. Whatever the connection is, neither one of them will get their money now, poor kids."

I frowned at him. "Get what money?"

"Well, that's the thing. They quit on me, both of them. They'd never mentioned it before, but they told me they were distantly related and that they were coming into a lot of scratch. Like I say, I thought it was just one of those things with Josie, so we were still trying to talk Audrey into sticking. That's why Margaret was down there tonight, actually."

"This wasn't two months ago, in July?"

"When they mentioned the money? No—hell, it was only a week, ten days back."

I stood there. For a minute it did not make any sense at all. Then it started to. If Audrey Grant and her half-sister had talked about inheriting money, there was only one person I knew that it could be coming from.

I felt as cold as a Christian on the way to the Colosseum.

It must have showed on my face. "Well, listen, fellow, what is it?"

I was already headed toward the foyer. "Just an idea, Connie, but I've got to beat it. Thanks for the booze." I pressed for the elevator, hard.

He followed me. "Well, say, get in touch, will you? I don't mean just about this—hell, I know you won't throw my name around with the bulls. Some evening, why not? Strictly social—" He was mauling my hand again. "Old Fannin himself—"

The doors opened, and he stood there grinning at me until they closed again. We were bosom buddies and he knew I wouldn't mention his name to the cops. Either he was still the campus clown or he was a lot more shrewd than I understood.

It didn't matter at the moment, either way. Neither did my haste.

Whatever time I got there, Ulysses S. Grant was going to be just as dead.

CHAPTER 19

I stood in front of a door marked *5-D* at the end of a corridor which had last been mopped during the candidacy of Alf Landon. There were other doors behind me, all closed, but judging from the odors they would have opened onto three stables and a sty. The Nineties, just east of Broadway. The neighborhood had been more than decent when Grant had first moved in.

Ask a landlord about the rot and he would blame it on the influx of Puerto Ricans. He would be well informed about Puerto Ricans. You would probably have to go to a beach in the Caribbean to find him.

Fannin, the social critic. Try the door, Fannin.

It had taken a cab fifteen minutes to get me across town. I'd pressed a bell at random to get a buzz, since Grant's had not answered. I could still have been wrong, and there was still that local pub for him to be in. But if Audrey Grant and her half-sister had talked about expecting money this was the only place I knew that it could be coming from.

Try it, Fannin.

A notice for an undelivered telegram was sticking out under the door. I took out a handkerchief before I worked the knob.

I could have been wrong. I'm never wrong. Somewhere down the hall a baby began to cry and I closed the door behind us, against the sound.

A window was open, and in the brief draft a single feather stirred near my foot, then fell again. He'd bought that white shirt.

Another body. Describe it, Fannin. The bullet which took him on the cheek, shattering too much bone to be a .22 this time. The mess where it had emerged at the base of his skull, making it a .38 at least. The whole thing, like how many others? It didn't make me light-headed this time. I slumped against the wall and stared at my hands, not upset either, just tired.

There were more feathers. They were from an ordinary bedroom pillow which had been used to muffle the report. I wondered remotely if the feathers were goose down.

What else, Fannin? A smashed alarm clock on its back, its hands stopped at 5:47. That was a mistake, although a minor one. Grant had been in my office at 5:47. But he had still been dead three or four hours longer than his daughter, which seemed to be the point the killer had hoped to suggest. He was cold as oceans.

There was a phone. I used the handkerchief again, dialing Western Union. A woman with seaweed in her mouth repeated Grant's name and address and then said: "'For information about your daughter try a man named Constantine. Can be located through Morals Squad.' The message is signed, 'A Friend.'" I thanked her.

I wasn't with it. I wasn't anywhere. Every seemingly logical thought in my head went just so far and then reversed itself like a buttonhook. If Josie and Audrey had anticipated an inheritance they had to have been involved in Grant's murder themselves. But then they would not have talked about it. Also they should not have been dead.

Button, button, who's got the button? Not Fannin, not now. I lifted the directory and fumbled pages until I found *McGruder, D., Christopher St.*

It rang twice. Grant was on the floor in back of me. His daughter was on the floor three feet from where it was ringing. My hand shook.

"Detective Toomey." A voice said.

"This is Fannin."

"Oh, brother—where are you?"

I gave him the street number. "I've got another one."

He whistled. "A couple more, you can start charging the department a commission."

"Yeah."

"But don't tell anybody I'm making with the jokes. You're lucky the sergeant's in the next room or you'd hear the steam through the wire. You better get yourself down here fast, chum."

"I just leave this for whoever wanders in?"

"Since when would that be a new trick for you? Hell, stay there, I guess. We might even do you the honor ourselves— we've accomplished about all we can in this madhouse anyhow."

He hung up. I felt like a crankcase full of sludge. I needed draining.

The place was cluttered. Everything was scarred, dilapidated. There were thousands of books. A console phonograph was fairly new, and there were at least two hundred records stacked near it. There was a complex radio mechanism, and there was a tape recorder.

The playthings of a man almost blind, who would have given special devotion to sound. There was no television set.

More books in cartons in the bedroom. The bed unmade, and a week's filthy laundry flung around the floor, looking like soggy flotsam on an unswept strand. An autographed photo of Eugene V. Debs framed on a wall.

A cockroach scuttled along the drain when I flipped the light in the kitchen. Thoreau's *Walden* was propped against a sugar bowl on the table, and something called *The Teachings of the Compassionate Buddha* was held open by a half loaf of black bread. A broken Chablis bottle lay on the window ledge.

Thirteen million dollars. The papers had played Josie's death as a Beatnik killing, and they would do the same with Audrey's. If the concept meant anything at all, Grant had been a Beatnik long before they invented the word. Ulysses, son of Thaddeus, by way of Harold Lloyd and Lemuel Gulliver. That classic raincoat was draped over a chair, trailing along the pitted linoleum, and I fingered it. There were even books in the bathroom.

Too many books. A lifetime full, and nothing else, nothing else at all. I found a cold can of Ballantine ale in the refrigerator and I nursed it, waiting for the badges.

CHAPTER 20

I got a pair of them, patrolmen, in about ten minutes. They were both younger than I was, and they took in the situation with all the sentiment of retired storm troopers. "You're Fanning?" one of them asked me.

I nodded. "They want you to wait here," he said. He noticed the beer. "Don'tcha know you're not supposed to touch anything?"

He was serious. He had a vacuous, inoffensive Nordic face that would never mean anything except exactly what it said. "I looked it over first," I told him. "The can was all misted up. I could see there were no prints on it."

He pondered that with all the efficacious ratiocination his ninety-two-point-four I.Q. would permit. "Well, I hope you're sure." He turned to his sidekick. "It looks under control, Eddie. You better wait in the heap."

Eddie shrugged, then wandered off apathetically. Santayana shut the door after him, taking a smoke. "Must have been quite a shock for a private citizen. Finding a deceased, I mean."

"It's been hours since the last one. I was beginning to think I was slipping."

"What? Oh, a joker."

"Makes it easier to take."

"Sure. Common psychology. Friend of yours, huh? Kind of a sloppy place he kept. All them goddam books, will you look?"

He stuck his face into the back, being curious, but he was just minding the store until some authority got there. I found myself a chair near the front windows.

The patrolman was on a second cigarette when the knock came. He butted the smoke fast and headed for the door, not quite making it. It was shoved inward so abruptly that it almost hit him.

DiMaggio had done the shoving. He stared at the body from the threshold for perhaps six seconds, then turned toward me. His blunt jaw was set squarely, and he had not stepped far enough inside for Toomey to get by. He held his breath. It was another ten seconds before he paid any attention to the patrolman.

"Stand by down below," he snapped then.

"I'll have to see some identification, sir. You're not in my precinct—"

DiMaggio was already past him. The patrolman glanced at Toomey hesitantly and Toomey flashed a badge. "The sergeant's had a long night, Mac. You know how they fall."

"Sure. Yes, sir. Just following regulations—"

"Can the goddam talk," DiMaggio said. "Get that door shut."

The patrolman pulled it after himself, glowering in my direction as he went. DiMaggio had taken a stance about four feet from my chair with his legs planted wide. "On your feet, Fannin," he said.

Toomey sauntered over. I sat there.

"Did you hear me, buster?"

"We got to it a lot faster the last time without the drama," I said.

DiMaggio was kneading his right fist with his left hand. "You got a gun?"

"Four. All home in a drawer next to the Three-in-One oil."

"Make sure." He spoke to Toomey without looking at him.

Toomey was at my side. "You'll have to get up—"

I did what he told me, chewing my lip. He ran me down quickly, then gestured.

"Put the cuffs on him," DiMaggio said.

Toomey's hand was still raised. "Oh, now look, Joe—"

DiMaggio came a step closer. His lips were bloodless. Toomey sighed almost inaudibly, finally reaching toward a hip.

I held out my wrists and the metal went on and locked, not tightly. Toomey didn't look at me. Just once I was going to meet two cops and the reasonable one was going to have the rank.

DiMaggio's eyes were as dark as wet tar. He was being as outraged as Captain Bligh when Clark Gable set him adrift in that dory. "You lied to me, Fannin."

I shook my head wearily. He ignored it.

"You used Captain Nate Brannigan's name and he okay'd you when I checked. So it isn't just a precinct sergeant the lie fixes you with."

This time I grunted. He didn't want answers anyhow.

"You found the Welch body and I let you convince me you weren't working on anything. The way I read it, the things you didn't see fit to tell the department Tuesday night might just have prevented the Grant girl's death and this one too, whoever this one is—"

"I didn't have a job Tuesday," I said.

293

"Don't lie to me a second time, Fannin. I don't like to be suckered."

Toomey had found something to contemplate on Grant's shoe, most likely a hole. "Why don't we find out what he's got to say first, Joe?"

DiMaggio kept measuring me. His forehead was slightly pocked. He flexed his fingers.

"Ten minutes, no more."

"I'll need closer to thirty."

"I'll know damned well when it stops meaning anything." He turned toward a chair. "You start at the beginning, Fannin, you got that?"

"Don't tell me how to tell it, DiMaggio."

He whirled back. I hadn't moved.

Toomey was still at the body. "Tallest man since Wilt the Stilt," he said idly.

"Maybe he'd rather tell it under the lights," DiMaggio said. "Maybe he thinks it's more romantic that way. Or maybe he thinks he'll get somebody else instead of me. Is that it, Fannin? You think because it involves two precincts the boys from Central will take over? Your buddy Captain Brannigan maybe? Well, I'll let you in on a departmental secret, how's that? Central's a little busy tonight, you understand? It so happens this case is mine—so I'm the baby you're going to have to chat with wherever we do it. And wherever we do it, I still think you're dirt."

"The corpse was named Ulysses S. Grant," I said quietly. "He hired me tonight to find his daughter, Audrey Grant."

"The corpse was named—why, you fatuous son of a bitch, if you think I've got time for a goddam joke—"

Toomey sprang across quickly, stopping him with a hand. "Hold it, Joe—" He flipped open the sandwich-sized wallet I'd seen when Grant was in my office. "Ulysses S. —— on his voter's registration."

EPITAPH FOR A DEAD BEAT

DiMaggio curled his lips, controlling himself. "The rest of it, Fannin."

"I was finished."

"What the hell—"

"I've identified my client and told you what kind of a job I was on. I didn't even have to say that much without a lawyer, not once you put these cuffs on. Although for the record I had a lot more in mind until about twelve seconds after you brought your bedside manner through that door."

He got around to it then. It was a hard enough punch but I was set for it as well as possible. I caught it along the upper jaw. I hit the cushions of Grant's couch, elbows first, then slid to the floor with the cuffs biting.

That fluttered a few feathers again. I supposed I could always report him for disturbing evidence before his technicians got there.

Toomey was between us, but DiMaggio had walked off. "Let that team take him in," he said tightly. "We got work to do here."

Toomey opened the door and held it for me, saying nothing. DiMaggio was standing over the body with his back turned. I stared at him for a minute and then went out.

That baby was screeching again, or still. I heard it through only one ear. Toomey rang for the elevator. "That was pretty dumb," he said.

I didn't answer him.

"So he called you a liar. It ain't such a highly illogical conclusion under the circumstances, you know. And you got to tell it anyhow, for Chrissake." The door slid open and he chuckled as we got in. "On the other hand I suppose all we can legally slam you for is leaving that stiff downtown, since you're right about not having to talk once we make you look like a suspect. If it turns out you're clean the sergeant will sweat all night,

wondering if you'll mention the incident to your friend Brannigan. The Commissioner's been pretty touchy about the rough
stuff lately. Poor old Joe."

"Yeah," I said. "Do me a favor, huh?"

"What's that?"

"These cuffs—wipe my nose if I cry."

CHAPTER 21

Someone had taped a newspaper photo of Marilyn Monroe behind the door of the interrogation room. One of her eyebrows was raised, and she was pouting, and she definitely had something in mind.

They'd taken my cuffs off, but for forty minutes she had been my only company. Now Toomey was straddling one of the room's two desks, and a severely combed civil service stenographer in a shapeless brown suit had just taken a chair near the far wall. It was 2:26. Behind the other desk a mountainous Laird Cregar type in shirtsleeves was considering me impersonally. His name was Vasella and he was a detective lieutenant. He had a chest like a tombstone.

His tone was completely neutral. "You're ready to make that statement now, I assume?"

I nodded.

"I've spoken to Nate Brannigan," he said, "and he's given me the same endorsement of you he gave Sergeant DiMaggio three days ago. He might be getting tired of it, which is neither here nor there." He sat down. "DiMaggio told me what went on uptown. He also told me that he'd been handling a separate homicide entirely before your call came in tonight and hadn't seen bed for thirty hours. I don't offer this as any sort of apology, but I don't like to work in bad air."

He did not wait for any comment on my part, turning to the stenographer. He gave her my name, my office address and my state license number, reading from a sheet he'd brought in, probably my statement about Josie Welch. "Nothing between your previous declaration and the time you were retained by this Ulysses Grant?" he asked me.

"Nothing."

"We'll start there, then. You've done this before."

I nodded again, taking a Camel, and then told it. I was able to forget Constantine's request for silence, since the telegram had taken me off the hook in that regard, although I did skip the matter of Margaret Constantine's exotic automatic. The whole thing took less than twenty minutes.

Neither Vasella nor Toomey had interrupted. Vasella had taken out a thick yellow copy pencil, which he clicked against his front teeth. "Turk is the keystone, of course," he said. "But I'd be more comfortable if Grant's money were all there was to it."

"Why Turk?" I said.

He looked toward Toomey, who was lounging against the doorjamb. "After that party quieted down over there," Toomey told me, "this swish who lives in the place, McGruder—he told us that Turk was married to Audrey Grant."

I frowned at him.

"Yeah, yeah, I know," Toomey said. "But according to McGruder it happened about six months back. There was a crew of them, they got one of these automobile bugs and wound up in Maryland. Just for laughs the girl and Turk woke up some J.P. and got spliced. Then she laughed in his face when he tried to claim his rights as a husband. McGruder says there wasn't much gossip about it because people felt sorry for Turk—evidently he's that kind of fool. We're checking it, but McGruder was sure the girl never did anything to cancel it out. The way these fruitcakes live down here—"

"You bring Turk in?" I asked him.

"Nah, that's the trouble. I suppose you did as well as you could at the party—just reporting the kill and then locking that room, I mean. In fact it was probably best that way, since we were able to surprise the whole mob." Toomey snorted. "Some screwball dame was standing on a chair in a bedsheet singing old labor songs, for Chrissake—'Join the Needle Workers' Union.' We got all the names and addresses, and we got statements from everybody who had anything to tell. But then, like I say, all of a sudden McGruder remembered this marriage bit—only Turk wasn't there. His name wasn't on the list, which means he'd ducked out before we showed up."

Vasella was toying with the pencil. "Turk was the one you booked on the Welch killing Tuesday. I thought he had a corroborated alibi."

"It has to be fishy under reconsideration, lieutenant," Toomey said. "This guy Peters didn't show up with his story until today—said he'd been on a bat. But here's the thing. Half a dozen people mentioned the brawl he had with Fannin over there tonight, but Peters wasn't on the list either. He must have scrammed the same time Turk did. DiMag put through an all-areas pick-up on the pair of them. We get Peters in here now, we'll find out he was just covering for the other guy. Turk could buy an awful lot of alibi for a share in that thirteen million he's due to inherit."

"A man would have to be little short of moronic to kill three people for a legacy when everything would point to him," Vasella said dubiously. "Or even to arrange for the killings. That knife—no one saw it after Fannin was hit?"

"It's McGruder's," Toomey said. "He said he always kept it in the latrine. But after Fannin it doesn't get mentioned."

Vasella shook his head. "All right, let's assume for the moment that Fannin's basic interpretations are correct. Audrey Grant and Josephine Welch are half-sisters. If Audrey Grant is going to inherit Grant's money and subsequently die herself, the Welch girl would have a strong claim on the estate. So she's disposed of first. Then Grant, and then Audrey Grant—the order leaves Turk clear title. But damn it—" He made a wet sound between his lips. "Grant is sent those clippings the day he's going to die. He contacts his lawyer about them and then he contacts a P.I.—but even if he hadn't done either of those things we'd still probably find the clips in his apartment. The man hadn't seen his daughter in ten years, and it's possible that no one would have connected the deaths—but this way we can't fail to. Except why would anyone want the connection made? If we didn't know the Grant girl had been worth all that money for the last four hours of her life we'd have no motive to hook Turk on. He could wait almost indefinitely to claim the legacy, or even claim it from somewhere he'd be nonextraditable—or try to."

"There's more than just Turk," I said. "Both of those girls told Constantine they were coming into money."

Vasella's hand lifted to slap the desk. "Which would appear to indicate they themselves knew Grant was going to die—"

"Where does that take us, now?" Toomey said. "It's as if the three of them were in it together—and then Turk crossed the two dames."

"No one talks about money someone is going to be murdered for," Vasella said. "It's too self-evident to mention. You don't think they could have been referring to some other money altogether?"

"Grant's dead," I said.

"So he is. Could this Constantine have been lying—repeating something which hadn't been said?"

I shrugged. "I don't get it, if he was. The only reason I went to Grant's was because of what he told me. Grant's money has to be the motive, one way or another."

"Something's missing, all right." Vasella reached to a phone. "This O. J. Fosburgh—you have any idea where he lives?"

"His office would probably have an all-night service."

He told his switchboard to put through the call, hanging up again. "There a collect-for-questioning on Constantine?" he asked Toomey.

"DiMag put it through as soon as we got the message on that telegram. Vice Squad finally admitted they'd heard of him, once we gave them the full name."

"Yeah, that telegram—wherever *that* fits in." Vasella puffed a cheek. "I think we better see that painter in here also, Floyd—Ivan Klobb. If he's able to provide girls for the racket there could be some sort of intimidation involved."

Toomey went out. The stenographer was still sitting, patient as a tin can on a shelf. Vasella nodded her out also. The phone rang before the door had closed after her.

Vasella identified himself and then apologized for the hour. There were pauses while he told Fosburgh about Grant's death. He verified my position, and after that there was considerable talk about Grant's financial situation. I sat there contemplating Marilyn again.

I decided she had a face that should have been given even more currency than it was. In fact currency was what it belonged on. They should have printed her picture on the one-dollar bill.

Toomey came back just as Vasella hung up. "No one gets it," Vasella said.

I dropped a cigarette into a dented brass spittoon, waiting.

"I mean no individuals. Grant was to receive all income the trust earned for the duration of his life, but the capital itself couldn't be touched. Now it gets distributed to charitable and educational organizations. All of it—there's absolutely no provision for any of Grant's own heirs."

"People wouldn't have to know that," Toomey said. "Or anyhow, look at the interest on thirteen million bucks. Even at an improbable three percent it's what?—roughly four hundred thousand a year. The guy lived like he was on relief. Take off three-fourths for taxes—Turk's still in line for a cool hundred grand—"

Vasella got to his feet heavily. "We'll get nowhere until we talk to these people," he said. "I want you to ride herd on those pick-ups, Floyd. Let's see some action."

He started for the door. "You want anymore from me?" I asked him.

He stopped. "You admit having had one of the murder weapons in your possession within a half hour of the first killing tonight," he said with no intonation. "You left that corpse and went almost directly to another, telling us it was only your professional sense of deduction which sent you there." He pressed his lips together. "Should I be able to think of anything else we might want you for? You can sign the statement if it's ready, or tomorrow if it isn't. Thank you for your cooperation."

He let me meet his gaze for another few seconds and then went out, a ponderous, not quite impassive man who did not like having rank pulled on him any better than DiMaggio did, but who would always be too efficient a cop to let it interfere with the way he thought he should do his job. Toomey gave me a parting wave and said, "Take it slow," but after two meetings Toomey would have found it hard to be unkindly disposed toward Attila the Hun. I made a mental note never to use

Brannigan's name again, short of finding myself on the wrong end of a hose.

I patted Marilyn on a cheek, following after them. I still liked the idea, although not on paper money at that, and not just her face. Molded on a coin, front and back side both.

I was being light-headed again after all, but I realized I was bushed. The statement wasn't ready. I took a cab to the lot near the Blue Soldier where the Chevy had been since nine o'clock.

I picked up a *Mirror* and checked the ball scores, but that only made me feel more stale. Ted Williams had gone hitless, and they'd had Stan the Man on the bench. The good people were getting old. A lot of them were already long dead, like John Garfield, Marcel Cerdan, Mel Ott. Fred Allen was dead too. Pretty soon I'd have no heroes left, unless I could teach myself to believe in Sal Mineo.

I left the car in the garage on Third, walked back the two blocks, climbed my one flight. The overhead bulb in the hall outside my door had burned out. They weren't making bulbs like they used to.

They weren't making private detectives like they used to either. I'd already turned the key before it occurred to me to find out who had wanted to make the next flight dark enough to hide on.

It was Peter J. Peters. He was sitting four steps up, as still as hewn rock, but I couldn't miss the gun in his hand.

I got the door open, grinning from ear to ear.

The gun was a Smith and Wesson military .38, but it might have been a musty volume of Spinoza he'd been browsing through. I went up quietly and worked it out of his fingers before I woke him.

CHAPTER 22

He hadn't been shooting anybody. There was so much rust in the bore that the weapon might have blown up in his face if he'd tried.

He was slumped against the wall. He started, opening his mouth and blinking. His lips looked pink and wet behind the beard. He saw the revolver and frowned.

"You intend to use this for the next round in our little competition?" I asked him.

"Oh, my gosh—"

I had no idea what that was supposed to mean, so I stood there while he shuddered a couple of times. I supposed he had been wearing the same Levis and turtleneck sweater before, but the view from McGruder's floor had not been remarkably vivid. He wasn't as big as I'd thought, but he was big enough. He was also handsome, although in a sallow sort of way.

"What's on your mind, Peters?"

"Oh, golly, I wish I knew—" He swallowed. "I had to talk to somebody. I saw Henshaw, and he said you were—listen, do you have something to drink, I—"

"Sure. I'm always good for refreshments. I'll open some beer and we'll nibble on the pistol, like with pretzels."

He looked at me blankly. For a minute I thought he was going to be another of those blissful nits you can't affront. His nostrils quivered. Then without any other sign he threw himself against the balustrade and began to sob like a baby.

That moved me. Two hundred pounds of blubbering Beatnik. He'd probably gone home and found a rejected manuscript in the mailbox.

He got to his feet, sniffling. I motioned him into the small dining area between the kitchen and the living room, then tossed the gun on the couch and dug out an open bottle of Jack Daniels. I poured two shots and sat down across from him at the table.

His shoulders were still twitching, and he was clutching an unclean white handkerchief. "Suppose we start with where you came by the firearm," I said.

"Oh, dear, I didn't mean for you to think—" He gulped the bourbon. "I work part-time as a security guard," he said then. "Night watchman jobs—it gives me a chance to write and make some money at the same time. I've never carried it before except to work, honestly, I—"

"Where'd you see Henshaw?"

"Late, after they let people leave the party. We'd been watching from down the block, Ephraim and I—"

I gestured. "Take it from scratch, huh?"

He nodded, sighing. "We left McGruder's after the fight. I felt—well, gauche. Lord only knows what possessed me, hitting you that way. I deserved the punch you gave me and more. I hope you'll—"

"Yeah. You beat it right away?"

"It was five minutes at most. I stopped to wash up first."

"Ephraim with you all the time?"

"He waited in the hall. But look, if you think he did it—that's the whole point. That's why I went to the police with that false alibi to start with—"

I stared at him carefully. His expression should have been grim, but it wasn't. He would have had the same look on his face if he'd been caught slipping a book under his coat at Brentano's.

"I guess it was a pretty dumb stunt?"

"If he's guilty you'll do time for it."

"Oh, gosh, I know. We were together a few hours Tuesday, not all night. But I know he didn't do it. Darn it, Ephraim is one of the most angelic people you'll ever meet. Why, he's almost saintly, he—"

"We went through all this before—"

"But it's true. Deep down he's so sensitive it hurts him to be alive. Why, he could no more have killed those two girls than—"

"They both treated him sensitively, from what I hear."

"Oh, I know all that. But Eph isn't like ordinary people. He's beautiful inside, priestly. Josie and Audrey were the only girls he's ever been intimate with. He knows the kind of unsanctified lives they led, but it still made them special to him. Loving them both in his tormented way has been a cross he bears, it—"

"All right, already—I've got a Gideon bible around someplace, he can autograph it. Skip Ephraim—was the rest of your story straight, at least? About being drunk all week?"

He lowered his eyes. "I wasn't drunk. I was with Audrey Grant."

That did get my attention. "That why you ran tonight?"

"I didn't run. Oh, darn it, we just left for a while. We were on our way back when we saw the police cars. And then when Henshaw told us what happened to Audrey—"

He refilled his glass, spilling some. He started to wipe the table absently with a sleeve, then remembered the handkerchief.

I had a vague thought. "When you went to the cops—did Audrey Grant know you were going to alibi Ephraim?"

"I didn't make up my mind myself until I was almost at the station."

"Henshaw noticed her just after she spotted Ephraim tonight—evidently she didn't seem to like the idea he'd been released. You remember if she mentioned anything during the week about having any other thoughts? I mean about it not being him to start with?"

"No." He frowned. "Audrey was painfully upset, and we tried to occupy ourselves with other things. That's why we went off together—she needed solace, spiritual consolation."

I sucked in air. "You read Corso and Ginsberg to each other—"

"Why, no, as a matter of fact we studied the exalted truths of Sakyamuni, about the suppression of anxiety, but why do you—?"

I lifted a hand. "Never mind," I managed. All this through that mouth full of starchy confections I'd come to love. "The girl was killed right after that scrap of ours," I told him in a minute. "Ephraim had time to do it, Peters, if you were alone in the john for a while."

"Look, please—I'd swear he didn't. Anyhow, I'm certain of it because of the way he reacted later. Oh, that poor martyred boy, if he—"

He stared at his palms. A little more and I'd be staring at them myself, watching for stigmata. "Something happened after you saw Henshaw?" I said.

"We went to this composer's studio—the place I'd been

with Audrey, in fact. It belongs to a friend of mine who's out of town. Then Ephraim suddenly got the idea that Dana O'Dea had done it. She was Audrey's roommate, she—"

"I know who she is."

"Oh?" He glanced at me, then nodded. "Dana had been angry at Josie Welch," he said. "Apparently Dana thought she had—well, that she had certain claims on me, and lately I'd been spending more time with Josie. On top of which Dana also knew about me being with Audrey this week. So Ephraim decided it was jealousy, that Dana—" He flushed. "I can't explain this too well, but Ephraim is capable of thinking a girl would kill two others because of me. He looks up to me, and he's made me into sort of an idol, as if—"

"The way it was with Lucien Vaulking—"

"You've been talking to people. Yes, the same way. But in any event I know he couldn't have been faking—he was even a little irrational. He said he was going to look for Dana. He ran out. I went over to Dana's myself, trying to find him, but there was a cop out front—that was Audrey's apartment too, of course." Peters bit on the handkerchief. "I guess the impact of everything suddenly panicked me. The next thing I knew I'd gone home and gotten my gun."

I had run out of cigarettes. I went over to a shelf and took down a fresh pack. He was watching me.

"You've played at being a fag, Peters," I said. "All right, maybe it didn't take. But maybe you're also fonder than you think about the idea of a frustrated little man following you around—"

He didn't flush this time. "I suppose McGruder told you about that. Look, that's all past—it's not influencing me in any way about Ephraim's innocence. Oh, gosh darn it, I don't expect people to comprehend how we live. Don McGruder is a poet, a fine one, with a clear, radiant vision. We were empathic to each other—we could communicate without even finishing sentences. So we talked gloriously night after night and it led to a homosexual affair—would I know more about the human heart if it hadn't happened? I'm trying to be alive in the fullest way I can. To be a writer I've got to experience all griefs and all joys, I've got to touch the inmost soul of man, to—"

"You've got to feel the throbbing pulse of the corner grocer, to contemplate the navel of the Chinaman who does your shirts. Oh, sweet damn, okay, you can take me to church some Sunday, we'll both be better for it. But not tonight, huh? Listen, is it an ecclesiastical secret, or do you think you just might get around to telling me what you wanted up here anyhow?"

He drew in his breath. "I might have known you'd be a square. The complacent, scoffing masses—dear God, a religious revelation could appear on their television screens and they'd phone for a repair man." He threw the handkerchief away from himself bitterly, like Billy Graham giving up on Las Vegas. "What I had hoped was that, since it's your profession, you'd come back downtown out of ordinary human compassion and help me find Ephraim before he gets into more difficulties. But I guess I can put it on a strictly business basis. Dedicated people like us don't have much money, but I can pay you off eventually."

"People like you—" I pulled a hand across my face. "Look, Peters, maybe you mean it. Maybe you're a serious writer and all this apocalyptic crap has some point—I wouldn't know. But I saw that mob down at McGruder's, and if there's any religious awakening underway somebody better get Congress to repeal the First Amendment. This is a murder case, not a fraternity bull session on salvation. If your chum Ephraim's as beatific as you claim, he won't get into anymore trouble—and if he killed those two girls he's already bought all he'll ever need. The gosh-awful truth is that it's pushing four o'clock in the morning and I don't much care. For that matter I don't much care about your offer of an installment payment plan either. I had my client for the weekend, except that somebody killed him."

"Him?" He had gotten up, gaping at me. "Somebody—you mean three people are—?"

"Yeah. It's been a long night, *padre.* You hit me, that wasn't too bad. But then a cop hit me and that I didn't like. I'm tired, my jaw aches, and I'm about due to lay me down to sleep. You can go to the cops or you can sack in here if you want, on the couch. I'd advise the former, especially since they already damned well know you lied about Tuesday night—"

"Huh?"

I didn't say anymore. The telephone was ringing and I went across to answer it.

I recognized the voice at a word in spite of its tone. "Harry," she gasped. "Thank God you're there! Something's happened, can—"

"Easy, Fern. What's—?"

"It's Dana O'Dea. She just came up the stairs and fell into the apartment looking like—well, as if a truck had hit her. He beat her terribly. I'm afraid he might have followed her, we—"

I cursed once, glancing at Peters. "You mean Ephraim?"

"Ephraim? No—I don't understand it too well, she's barely told me anything—but it was Ivan. Ivan Klobb, the painter. You remember, I introduced him to you—"

"You got the door locked?"

"Yes, but—"

"I'll be about twenty minutes, Fern. If anything happens before I get there call the police. I mean that."

"Oh, thank you, Harry—"

I hung it up and turned into the bedroom. Peters came into the doorway hesitantly. I yanked open the bottom drawer of the dresser, pushed aside some summer shirts, then settled for the first piece my hand touched, my Colt .357 Magnum. I checked the load, jammed the weapon into a clip holster and slapped that into my hip pocket. "Pick up that relic of your own," I said. "If you've got any sense at all you'll drop it in the first sewer you pass on the way to the precinct house."

"God," he said. "Oh, God! Listen, what's going on? Has something happened to Fern now too? Will you—?"

"No." I shoved past him, motioning toward his gun.

"Can I leave it here? Oh, golly, I guess I'll go down now after all. I won't stop home—"

"Come on."

I ushered him out of there and around the corner to the garage, walking hard and not talking. The late-shift attendant looked at me as if I were asking him to change the color on a battleship he'd just that minute finished painting, but for the pound of flesh I was paying they could shuffle the Chevy in and out ten times a night and like it. I broke half a dozen vehicle regulations going down, but all the traffic dicks were busy mooching coffee someplace. Peters sat mutely and meditated on his reflection in the windshield.

I dumped him in front of an all-night restaurant two blocks from Fern's, roughly the same distance from the station. He started to say something but I didn't wait. I would read all about it when they updated the Gospels. At the moment I was too busy speculating about an artist with an exhibition scheduled soon in an exclusive uptown gallery, and about a pair of dead prostitutes who had known enough about his spare-time occupation to have shut down the show before the canvases dried.

Most of it still did not make sense. But even an unenlightened sinner like myself could see where blackmail might have played hell with the revival meeting.

CHAPTER 23

Fern made me repeat my name twice through the door of the apartment before she opened up. She had on a pale blue bed jacket which fell just to her fingertips, and her face was wan.

I saw Dana beyond her shoulder, slumped on the low modern couch at the far wall. She was wrapped in an oversized yellow beach towel. There were raw, ridged welts, like parasitic worms, across her naked arms and along her thighs. A cigarette was burning in a tray on the end table near her, and her dark eyes studied me intently as she reached for it.

"It is you, isn't it? We never did get ourselves formally introduced."

I grinned at her. "You were pretty soused."

"You could be right—although I've got a hunch I was sober as a hen about two seconds before you gave me that smack." She puckered her bright lips wistfully. "Hell of a thing for a man to do. I seem to recall I'd been pretty darned accommodating, myself."

I laughed. "You're feeling all right?"

"Grand, grand." She touched her fingers to a swollen bruise at the side of her nose. "Half the pain was mental anyhow."

Fern was standing near me. "Do you think she needs a doctor, Harry? I didn't put anything on them except disinfectant—"

"I doubt it, not if the skin isn't broken." I went across to one of the sling chairs. "He didn't do that gaudy a job with his fists alone?"

"He decided I'd be more impressed by a leather strap. Come to think of it, I was impressed at that."

"You want to tell me about it, Dana?"

She nodded, reaching for her smoke again with one of those milky arms. Damaged as she was, the girl made you suspect that half the women in the world were grossly deficient in protein. Fern had taken a seat next to her, tucking her bare legs beneath her. She wasn't one of the afflicted.

"I don't come out lily white in the tale myself," Dana said. "But then I'm just about beyond salvaging as it is." She considered me thoughtfully. "That really was a honey of an exhibition I put on for you over there, wasn't it?"

"It was harmless enough."

"I'll bet. But thanks anyhow."

"You leave McGruder's with Klobb?"

"No, I didn't. I felt rotten when they let us go, and I walked around for a while. I ran into Ivan when I stopped for coffee, and we went down to his studio. It wasn't anything except company, someone to talk to. Although Ivan was pretty upset himself, for reasons most people don't know about." She glanced at Fern. "Did Josie ever tell you about a man named Constantine?"

Fern turned to me. "—Connie?"

"I found out tonight. The police hit it pretty close on Tuesday, Fern. Josie'd been taking calls."

"Taking—" She pressed her lips together. "I did begin to wonder about it, I suppose. It's just so darn hard to accept—"

"You're telling me," Dana said. "Audrey let me in on it a few

313

weeks ago. She was tight one night, feeling sorry for herself. Boy, it knocked me for a loop. We weren't that intimate—you know how you just share a place to save money. The fact is—well, I guess I didn't like her too much. I suppose everybody down here is always putting down everybody else, taking advantage of other people's weaknesses, but Audrey was worse, somehow. Bitchy. Oh, damn, what a thing to be saying. Anyhow, I'd always supposed she was seeing someone else's husband and had the sense to be discreet about it." She looked back across. "You know about Ivan introducing her and Josie to this Constantine—for a fee?"

I nodded, watching Fern lift a hand in puzzlement. "But he's such a successful painter. Sometimes I think he's the only real artist down here. Why would he—?"

"You go figure it." Dana butted her cigarette. "He didn't mention it tonight, of course—it obviously wasn't supposed to be known—but I was pretty certain that was what he was worried about. We had a couple drinks, and then he—" She made a face. "This is going to sound funny, considering the circumstances, but he decided to paint me. Ivan's odd. He's come looking for me more than once after midnight. So it wasn't anything extraordinary, and God knows I would rather have held still all night than go home by myself. I had some pot, one stick that—"

She frowned. "I tried to pass that off to you, didn't I?"

"We both could have used it."

"Be nice. Damn it all, sometimes I just—oh, what's the use? Anyhow, I smoked it—by myself, since Ivan was working. It did calm me down, even though all I could think about was Audrey under that cot. And I kept remembering the party tonight, too. Or maybe not just tonight, maybe it was all the damned parties all the nights—all the pompous philosophical excuses we make for acting like adolescents when none of us have anymore purpose than goldfish, how sleazy it all finally is—and anyhow all of a sudden I was taking a good look at myself and I guess it made me disgusted. And then I remembered what Audrey'd told me about the blood money Ivan had gotten, and—"

She confronted me squarely. "I told him I knew about it. I also told him he wasn't paying me enough to pose, and that I wanted fifty dollars an hour—retroactive for the last ten hours. Just like that I said if he didn't pay me I was going to the police—" She kept on facing me. "Which is what I mean about not being worth salvaging. Oh, damn, I—" She sobbed, turning aside. "Listen, Fern, have you got some sleeping pills, anything—?"

Fern's mouth was drawn. She got up forlornly. Dana closed her eyes and let her head fall against the wall. She sat that way without moving until Fern came back.

"It would be so darned easy if I could blame it on the marijuana," she said then. "At least I'm not going to say I didn't deserve what he gave me. He threw my clothes down the stairs and just about threw me after them. I don't know what it means, although when it started I was one mighty scared young extortionist. All I could think of was that Josie and Audrey might have threatened to expose him in the same way, and he'd—"

Fern's breath caught audibly. "You don't think—?"

"I don't know, I just don't know. What kind of people are capable of blackmail? If I was capable of the impulse myself, I think Audrey certainly would have been—and Josie too, for all that supposed innocence of hers. But my God, if they were blackmailing him and he killed them he would have had to kill me too. I couldn't prove anything the way they could have, but it still could have ruined his reputation—"

She shuddered once. Fern had set two capsules and a glass of water on the end table, and she brushed the pills into her hand. She swallowed them without water.

"What happens to us, Fern?" she said then. "What? All right, never mind all this, this is extreme, but just the way we live in general—how do we get so sick and miserable and self-destructive? I used to be a nice girl once, I swear it. I used to have clean, wholesome dates with well-meaning clods who actually brought me flowers once in a while. Dates. I haven't had one in any prearranged sense in so long that I've begun to feel like—like a public conveyance. A streetcar named Dana, flag her down in front of any saloon below Fourteenth Street and climb aboard. Do you know what I was going to do if Ivan was fool enough to come through with the money? I was going to pack up and get out of here, go to San Francisco maybe, anyplace—just to see if it's possible to start fresh. That isn't such a shameful motive for a blackmailer, is it? But do you know what I'm going to do now? I'm going up to see this man Constantine myself. Oh, yes. Except I'll have to wait until these bruises heal, won't I? They like their merchandise pure when they pay cash, don't they? Do you think it will take long? I'm really anxious, and—"

She had gotten a little hysterical, and Fern grabbed her by the shoulders. The towel fell away and for a second Dana's eyes darted nervously, but she caught hold of herself. She gulped in air, holding it.

"Come on, there," Fern said. "Everyone goes through this kind of thing one way or another, you know that—"

Dana let her chin collapse on her chest. "It's my night to play the fool. Forgive me, Fern, will you, I'm just—"

"Don't be silly—"

She made a half-hearted attempt to knot the towel back into place. "Aphrodite's fig leaf. Did Aphrodite have a fig leaf? I don't even know who Aphrodite was." She got to her feet, holding it where it had slipped around her hips again. "Cheap theatrics and a thirty-cent striptease to boot, to keep your mind off the bum acting. I better get to bed before I wind up howling Thomas Wolfe from the window ledge. Or aren't we supposed to like Wolfe anymore? That's one other damned thing—I keep forgetting who's hip and who isn't." She laughed a hollow, strained laugh. "Oh, good heavens, thanks, Fern, really—I'm sorry I'm such a pathological mess."

She headed toward the room which had belonged to Josie, moving stiffly. Fern glanced at me and then followed her. They spoke quietly, then Fern closed the door after her, turning back. She looked like a delicate mechanical doll that nobody'd remembered to wind.

"I meant to ask her where Klobb's studio is," I said.

"It's on Downing Street, but—Harry, you're not going over there with all this—"

"Just to look around, talk to him maybe—"

She had come toward me. "I'm sorry if I seemed cold before." Her voice was husky. "It was just so rotten Tuesday—not us together, you know that, but the way I sort of used you—"

"I'll call you, Fern."

"Do, Harry, please. I—" She trembled suddenly, then fell against me. I held her until the shivering stopped. Then I kissed her tightly once and went out.

It was still easy, like walking off a building. But I hadn't had too many dates in any prearranged sense myself lately. Maybe when this was over I'd have a few with a girl who'd be vulnerable until it was, and whose cheeks had been wet against my neck after I'd let her tell me she wasn't vulnerable three nights before.

The Chevy was on Seventh. I went down the few blocks with no other moving cars in sight. The number she'd given me was a warehouse, with a small private entrance at one side. A hand-lettered sign said, *Klobb-Penthouse,* which would mean a shed on the roof, nothing more. The door was not locked.

I went in, not being particularly quiet, not quite knowing what I had in mind. The stairwell was as empty as a tilted tomb, but if the police had only Klobb's home address and not this one he could still be around. There were six flights of reinforced concrete and then one last section of slatted metal, rising into a gable-like structure which would lead onto the roof. The door up there was open.

The studio sat thirty feet away, beyond a dozen or more random-shaped chimneys and flue pipes. It was built like a greenhouse. There were lights on, either a lot of them or just the brights a painter would use, but the glass panes were smeared and barely translucent. The roof of the warehouse itself was extremely still.

"Klobb?" I said.

A rag on a line flapped once. Maybe he was busy being creative over there, oiling that leather strap. There was a high sill to be stepped over in the doorway where I was, and I stepped over it.

That was when it came to me that I was never going to learn, not ever. This time it wasn't any slumbering Beatnik with a malfunctioning weapon some old uncle had brought home as a souvenir of the Meuse-Argonne. I was at least a full second too late reaching for the Magnum I'd concluded I would not need for Klobb alone. Something that could have been a fist lifted out of the shadows and slammed into the back of my neck. Something else that could have been a foot extended itself from nowhere and cracked across my shin. I went down like a defunct sputnik. I chewed tar.

"I used to think about it sometimes," a familiar voice said then. "No kidding, I really used to wonder—whatever became of that great soph halfback, Harry Fannin? I asked you to leave

318

my name out of it with the cops, fellow. I asked you politely as hell."

"Do you intend to chat all night, darling," said another voice I knew, "or are you going to get busy and dump him over the side?"

CHAPTER 24

I got up onto my elbows and knees, then hung there as limply as a sweaty leotard. Someone in rubber-soled desert boots stepped near me noiselessly. It was a task, but I lifted my head high enough to see the grain-colored beard that identified him as Ivan Klobb. I also saw the boxy black Colt .45 automatic in his right hand.

His other hand lifted the Magnum off my hip. "On your feet, fellow," I was told.

I managed it, a little shakily, watching Klobb pass the Colt to Constantine. That made a total of three pieces I was facing, since lovely Margaret was getting her kicks from the Beretta again. It made me feel dangerous, like Dan McGrew.

Constantine had shed his dressing gown for a dark blue serge suit. He had on a figured gray silk tie, and his collar looked too tight. It probably always did, around that tree stump he had for a neck.

"Damned glad you dropped in, fellow," he told me. "We would have looked you up one of these days, of course, but this saves trouble all around."

"I'm glad too," I said, but I was just making sounds. I'd

wanted to find out if I could. "I'd hate to put anybody out on my account."

"Sure. That's why you forgot to mention my name with the bulls, isn't it? My old buddy."

"You were in it before I saw them," I said.

"You won't write to the alumni magazine if I call you a liar, will you, fellow? The name Connie came up last Tuesday, yeah—I know because my Vice Squad connection tipped me. They played it dumb, and so far as they knew there was no Connie on the books. What did you think this was, Fannin? You think I'm playing sandlot ball?"

"Get to the point, Connie. You don't much care what I think."

"Sure, sure—I'll get to it. The point is that Vice Squad got another call a couple of hours ago—not about Connie this time, but Constantine. That much they couldn't fake. I might have spent my time in courses like outdoor cookery at Ann Arbor, fellow, but there's a little something besides oleomargarine between my ears. My old pal Fannin fixed things for me, didn't you, pal?"

"Let him send you a letter about it," Margaret said. "From the hospital." She was off to my right, leaning almost jauntily against a chimney. The glow from the studio left her half in shadow, and there was enough breeze to have flung some of that rampant hair into her face. Except for the Beretta she could have been soliciting over there.

Except for the Beretta. Constantine was still waiting for some sort of answer, and Klobb had moved behind me. I didn't like not seeing the third gun. I was fairly sure there was not going to be any shooting, not since they knew they were already tied into the case, but I still did not like it.

"There was another killing," I said finally. "Audrey Grant's father. Somebody sent him a telegram about the girl's whereabouts. Your name was in it."

Constantine frowned, watching me carefully. "Somebody who?"

"'A Friend'—no other signature."

He grimaced. "You find the telegram or did the bulls?"

"I got there first, if that's what you mean."

"If there was a telegram," Margaret said.

"That's not the point." Constantine did not look at her. "You could have ditched the thing if you saw it before the bulls, Fannin."

I shook my head. "Not after I unwrapped another dead one. I've got the matter of my own license to protect in these things."

"Your goddam license—" He spat across his shoulder. His thick lips were drawn back against his gums when he stepped toward me.

"Twenty-three girls. You get an expense-account convention in this town, it takes one phone call. Six years I've spent building up the reputation, until every big public relations man in the East knows I'm his man, and now some dollar-an-hour peeper spills the details in the wrong office. You know what this can do to my set-up? You got any idea what this can cost me?"

I didn't answer him. I could feel Klobb breathing behind my ear.

"I asked you if you know what this means to me, Fannin—"

Constantine poked me with the Colt so I nodded. "I know," I told him. "I'm sorry. You might have to go to work for a living."

He was going to satisfy those aggressions sooner or later anyhow. He hit me in the stomach with a fist like a runaway Greyhound bus and I doubled over, heaving sickly.

"Twenty-three girls. And if I have to lay low too long every damned one of them will be running for somebody else. All because of a punk halfback I used to punch holes for. Damn it to sweet hell—"

He was standing a foot in front of me when I got myself straightened up. He was pretty much oblivious to the cannon at his side, breathing hard and nurturing his hate, and it was a moment for heroics on my part. It was a swell moment, for noticing that Margaret would have had to tilt the Beretta about a sixteenth of an inch to take out my eye. I let him hit me in the stomach again.

He liked the way I folded in half. He liked the sounds I made, like cats being squashed. He liked the color of my face when I got it lifted. When I couldn't lift it anymore Klobb did it for me, jamming a knee into my back and using it for a fulcrum, and he liked that too.

When he quit, Klobb stepped back and I sank to my knees like something sticky being poured down a drain.

I vomited everything I'd had to eat since they took me off formula.

"The lad who was going to make them forget Tom Harmon." Constantine laughed, turning away. "Let's get out of here now, huh?"

"Half a moment," Margaret said. She might have been stifling a yawn. "I didn't mention it earlier because you said he was a friend, but he didn't just take the gun away from me at Audrey's. If I hadn't convinced the poor sap it would mean his life, I would have been raped on the floor."

"Well, now. Well, how about that, now?" Constantine was gripping the Colt by the snout when he turned back. Margaret was being careless with the Beretta also, and Klobb seemed to have wandered off. I couldn't be sure, but I was beyond caring. I threw myself at Constantine with every remnant of strength I could muster.

H. Fannin, realist of the old school, like Walter Mitty. The big man took a quick short step to the side, slammed a palm like a spade against my chest, yanked me to my feet, ran with me, and then slapped me against a wall like a trowel full of wet cement. He propped me into place with all the effort of Pancho Gonzales hoisting one for the serve, and then the checkered stock of his thirty-nine-ounce automatic mashed its way into my cheek like a fork through over-cooked potatoes. I saw constellations that Galileo never dreamed of, and after that I tasted blood and frustration and immeasurable sadness all at once, staring without belief at the one hand he was holding me with. The one hand. My head rolled, and he raked the gun across my face from the other side.

There was blood in my eyes also, but I thought I saw that resplendent orange hair bobbing in the vapors near me. My madonna of the rooftops. I even thought I saw a smile on those vengeful orange lips. "Darling," someone muttered. It was me, with all I had left. Words. "Audrey and her roommate aren't here. We've got time, darling, we've got time—"

Colors flashed, only some of them in my imagination. The Beretta jumped across Constantine's forearm and slashed down at my temple. He let her hit me twice more. Then he threw me aside like so much rank bedding, onto what might have been left of my face.

I kept on bleeding, which seemed a logical result of my activities. A pool of it grew under my nose, but it was only a small pool, like Tanganyika. There was quiet talk, but it did not interest me, not even as much as the latest article on Bing Crosby's sons. I'd be leaving such mundane things behind anyhow, as soon as they took action on my application to that monastery, the one that honored credit cards. I wasn't even going to write anymore letters to sportswriters about why they didn't elect Arky Vaughan to the Baseball Hall of Fame. Arky Vaughan, my all-time favorite shortstop who was long, long gone, who had drowned in a lake.

Someone stooped near me, and I saw those desert boots out of half an eye. I wondered remotely if he'd ever worn them in the desert. Zen Bootism. He was fumbling at my hip, and I had the curious sensation that he was shoving the Magnum back into my holster. He hadn't said a word since I'd come to call, not one. I'd hardly gotten a look at that incipient fascist face.

"I'm returning your pistol," he told me. "Solely in the hope that you might decide to blow your stinking brains out, old chap."

He stepped over me, and the roof door closed. Footsteps echoed in the stairwell, going away.

They'd left me, without a single chorus of "Auld Lang Syne."

CHAPTER 25

Someone had invented a magic time machine which gave men back their youth, and now in the machine Michigan's all-time football team was playing Notre Dame in a stadium on the moon. Tom Harmon was on the field, and Willie Heston and Germany Schultz were twenty again, and Harry Fannin was all in one piece. Quarterback Bennie Friedman called the signals for my wide sweep to the right, the ball was snapped back, and up ahead a hulking lineman named Oliver Constantine pulled out to lead my interference. The screams of a hundred thousand fans thundered in my ears. "Go, Fannin, go—"

I lifted my face out of the blood.

We went back into the huddle. Ducky Medwick was calling the plays now. Ducky Medwick hadn't gone to Michigan. On top of which he'd played baseball, not football. Did it matter? It was only a private fantasy anyhow. "Take it again, Harry, we'll go all the way this time—"

I dropped my face back into the blood.

They shipped me down to the junior varsity, and I couldn't make first string there either. I sat on the bench and glared at the players who beat me out, like Truman Capote, Liberace, Clifton Webb. I turned in my uniform.

This was ridiculous. Klobb's studio was less than ten yards away. What would have become of western civilization if a little travel had ever fazed Leif Ericson, say, or Linda Christian? Come on now, Orville, you can get that thing off the ground.

I crawled to the studio. It didn't take any longer than the voyage of the *Pequod*. I was carrying Moby Dick on my back and Moby was carrying Captain Ahab on his. Why the hell should I carry Ahab? All he had to complain about was a wooden leg, and I had a wooden head. Splintered. I dragged myself through the door, across a large room which reeked of turpentine, into a bathroom. Ahab, you hab, he hab. All God's chillun hab, except Harry.

I lay there, not wanting to get up and wondering why I'd thought of Ducky Medwick when I had football in mind. Oh, sure, because I'd seen him get smashed in the skull by a pitched ball when I was a kid. They'd carried him off the diamond and I'd cried because I thought he was dead. But he'd come back to play again.

There seems to be a moral there, Fannin, if you've got sufficient wit to find it.

I was staring at a bathtub. I got the faucets turned for the shower, and then I squirmed over the side, flopping. That was ridiculous too. Let's go, Ishmael, on your feet. The white whale was still on my shoulders so I hoisted him also, clinging to a towel rack.

I remembered the revolver Klobb had returned. And my wallet, with all those engraved pictures that ought to have been of Marilyn. I fished them out of my clothes and dropped them onto a mat. My ribs felt as if they were removable also, but I didn't experiment.

The roof of the john was glass, like the rest of the structure. Jolly. Nothing like a shower under the stars at five in the morning, especially in your best suit.

I sat down on the edge of the tub to let myself drain, like Katharine Hepburn after she fell into the pool in *Philadelphia Story*. Did Katharine Hepburn fall into a pool in *Philadelphia Story?* She should have, if she didn't. It was the first enjoyable vision I'd had since Dana dropped that towel.

I limped back into the other room, making squooshing sounds. A big place, a sloppy place, hardly anything to lean on at all. Paintings on stretchers, paints, rolls of canvas, cans of oil, drafting tools, brushes, filthy rags—and what I was looking for on a chest in a corner. A half-full bottle of gin. Sweet, medicinal, London dry gin. I'd have my cup of kindness yet.

The bottle wasn't any harder to lift than an anvil. Could Ducky Medwick have lifted it? Certainly Medwick could have lifted it. Here's to Medwick.

There was something on a wall near me that might have been a mirror. If it wasn't a mirror it was a portrait of someone who'd been buried at sea. Whichever it was, I hoped they didn't let in children who weren't accompanied by adults.

It was I, ah sadness, it was I—battered as a bull fiddle, bruised as a fig. There was still a trickle of blood from the deepest tear, where the recoil reducer on the Beretta had taken me. To think I'd given them back that magazine, or she wouldn't have been carrying it—this the unkindest cut of all. My cheeks were raw and swelling. I took another drink, a sorrowful drink, this time for Pistol Pete Reiser of the old Dodgers, who used to run head-first into concrete outfield walls.

There was alcohol in the john, and I bathed the gashes. They would have heard me in the Bronx if I'd had any sensation above my neck. I found gauze and patched the worst of the mess.

I could work my jaws. Maybe Pete Peters was right about that religious awakening in the air—maybe it was a time for miracles, maybe nothing was broken.

Maybe it was time for another drink. Was it? Of course it was. There was nothing else up there for me anyhow, except misery. To Ted Williams, who cracks bones and spits in the face of adversity.

I retrieved my wallet and the Magnum. I put them away, then reached a cigarette out of my shirt. It fell apart in my hands. I could have used a cigarette. Ah, well. I had a nip for Nile Kinnick of Iowa, a fine halfback who'd crashed in the war.

I wondered what Klobb would do about his showing next week. I cared. I had a drink for Leslie Howard, who'd also crashed, and for General Gordon whose head got hung on a spear. Poor Leslie Howard. I had one for Billie Holliday. They were small drinks but the feeling was what counted. I had a smaller one for Gunga Din, who was a better man than I was, which was decidedly not much of an achievement. I had half of one for Oliver Hazard Perry, just because I liked the name, and then I had the other half for Dred Scott. There were about six drinks left when I heard the noise.

I was near the studio door and I breast-stroked behind it. I could just see across to the roof doorway through the crack.

The door had been pushed toward me. A shadow hesitated along the wall. Maybe it was *the* Shadow. Who knew? The Shadow knows—heh, heh, heh. The weed of crime bears . . . or maybe it was someone from the Women's Christian Temperance Union. I took one more quick one for Lamont Cranston, just in case.

Never mind the stupid bottle, you cluck, a voice said. Don't you think maybe it's about time *you* got the jump on somebody? You've been bopped by a Beatnik, cuffed by a cop, pounded by a pander. . . .

I took the hint. No need to tell Mrs. Fannin's boy Harry anything a second time, no sir. I reached into my holster.

My son the detective. I'd put my wallet in the holster. I found the gun in the pocket where I keep my wallet on days when I wake up knowing my name.

The shadow advanced an inch or two. I tilted the revolver downward. Water dripped out of the barrel onto my shoe.

I supposed I could always throw it. Although I'd hand-loaded the cartridges myself, a little dampness was not going to make them defective. Never. Nothing defective about this detective. I suppressed a giggle.

But they were still well-sealed cartridges. Cartridges? Hmmm. I broke open the cylinder. Well—sincere old Ivan, he'd really meant for me to shoot myself.

There was still no activity over there. I was crouching now, like Pat Garrett in that room in Fort Sumner in 1881, waiting to lay out poor Billy the Kid. From 1881 to now was seventy-nine years. Billy the Kid had been twenty-one. If he were still alive he would be exactly one hundred years old. I hoped it was Billy the Kid. Most likely he would be sort of sickly, too.

The shadow finally spoke. Just a cautious whisper. "Ivan?"

I let him wait. I had a snort for Joe DiMaggio, the real one.

"You in there, Ivan?"

"Hrlggr," I said clearly.

Ephraim. Old son of a gun Ephraim, Bard of Beatville. The seersucker Swinburne. He stepped across the sill timidly, paused, then came toward the studio. On little cat feet, like Sandburg's fog, and as quiet as a Robert Frost snowfall. There was nothing lethal in his hands. No gun, no switchblade. Not even an Oscar Williams *Treasury of Mongolian Verse.*

"Ivan?"

"It's me," I said. "Geoffrey Chaucer."

"It's—?"

He drew up short, halfway over. For a minute he wavered on his toes, like a kid caught at the cookie jar. Like an architect of

330

epic odes, espying the esmoked oysters. Oysters were animals, not fish. I hoped they weren't neurotic about it.

"Het your gands up," I said.

"Huh?"

I stepped out and waved the gat at him, snarling like the desperate character I was. Dauntless Fannin, ominous as a crocheted doily.

"My God, what happened to—?"

"Ha! Don't ask," I said. "I've been suffering, young Turk. Little does the crass world know. Anguish, agony—just wait until I get it written. It's going to be the greatest spiritual exercise since *Peyton Place*. I've even had visions, all sorts of people I haven't thought of in—say, listen, do you have any idea whatever happened to Wallace Beery? It just struck me that I haven't seen him since—"

"What?"

He was shaking his head, frowning at the bottle. "Take a belt," I told him. "We'll drink to Sacco and Vanzetti."

He didn't want one. Very slowly he started to back away from me. I took a step after him. I stopped abruptly when my ribs took a step in the opposite direction.

"Don't leave, like," I told him. "Let's have a sermon or something."

"I don't have anything to say to you, Fannin."

"Sure you do. We'll parse sentences together. Do a textual exigesis of *The Cantos* of Jayne Mansfield. We'll talk of graves, of worms, and epitaphs, make dust our paper and with rainy eyes write sorrow on the bosom of the—hold it right there."

"You're flipped, you know that? You better get to a doctor."

He kept on backing off, a small, homely man, confused and frightened. So why didn't he stop when I waved the revolver?

"This is a Colt Three-Fifty-Seven, Ephraim. A Magnum. You know what a Magnum is? It could splatter your frail brains from here to Xanadu, cut you off before you finish your first sonnet sequence. Think of it, *The Efforts of Ephraim,* left undone—"

"I didn't kill them, Fannin. You know that—"

"Maybe. What the hell—not maybe, let's say probably. But we still have portentous matters to discuss—"

"Say, I'm serious about a doctor. You look terrible."

"I do not love thee, Doctor Fell—the reason why, I cannot tell." I laughed senselessly, cocking back the hammer on the gun. "Enough of idle literacy, Ezra. Leave us converse."

"You won't shoot me, Fannin."

"Won't I? Ha! I shoot poets just for practice. Bing—smack in the middle of the iambic pentameter—"

He stepped over the sill.

"Damn it," I said.

"People don't kill other people," he said.

"Sure they don't. How many of your ex-girlfriends are dead who were reading Dylan Thomas within the week? Listen, they shot Gandhi, didn't they? They shot Draja Mikhailovitch and Private Prewitt. They even shot Eddie Waitkus—you remember, that first baseman—"

"People are good, Fannin. People have beautiful souls."

"Come back here, Ephraim."

"You won't shoot."

"Come back," I said. The door closed. I started to laugh again, like a maniac. "Shane," I said. "Come back, Shane—"

I had one last fast one for Brandon deWilde before I followed him.

CHAPTER 26

I didn't run. The stairway was treacherous enough without my showing off. My chest was burning. When I reached the sidewalk a lamppost fell against my shoulder so I held it up for a minute, listening to it wheeze.

There was something under my feet at the curb. An abandoned canvas deck chair. If the fire in my ribs spread, I could be the boy who stood on the burning deck chair.

Ephraim was a block away, trotting toward Seventh Avenue. I made it across to the Chevy.

Was I in shape to handle a car? Don't bother me with foolish questions when I'm driving. Clutch in, brake off, starter down and we're rolling. Rolling? Hmmm . . .

I put the key in the ignition.

Come on, Ahab, get those lifeboats over the side, eh? I swung out sharply, reversed, then made a U-turn that put me facing the wrong way in a one-way street. Signs, signs, everyplace signs. But what did they mean in a *spiritual* sense, what did they say about man's true estate? Anyway there wasn't any traffic.

I saw him cut across Seventh on an angle, turning north. I tooled up there and then slowed again, nosing just far enough into the intersection to get a look. Peek-a-boo. Ha! He was a hundred yards off, turning east again.

I waited a few seconds and then followed him, cruising in low gear with no lights. He glanced across his shoulder once or twice, but only along the sidewalk. Old Ahab, I'd forgotten to drink to his hollow leg. My own wasn't hollow, but some things would have to wait.

I pulled up at each crossing, idling for as long as I could see that barley hair bouncing above the parked cars, then moving ahead. He made several turns, keeping to back streets except to cross Sixth, working steadily north and east. He had slowed to a walk.

When he hit Macdougal he cut south again. And then I lost him.

I gunned up fast. His head had been clearly visible and now it wasn't. I stopped, listening.

He'd evaporated like Marley's ghost.

Marley? Oh, sure, Marley was dead, dead as a doornail. A cliché, or had Dickens invented it? You're not that potted, Fannin. Poets don't just vanish.

Up? There were stairways rising to first floors, but the doors were all above the level of the cars. Not up.

Down? Hmmm, down. More stairs, leading into basements and storage cellars. Almost every one of the entrances was blocked by a chain. One of them was swinging slightly, almost imperceptibly. Come back, chain.

Was that sleuthing or wasn't it?

You down there, Jacob Marley? Don't try to kid me, Jacob. Not your old partner, not Ebenezer Scrooge.

Darkness. There would not be more than five or six steps, but I could not see the last of them. Hungry aardvarks might have been prowling in a pit at the bottom, wooly bears, boll weevils.

Did it frighten me? Nothing frightened me. People were good, people had beautiful souls. My baby-faced Byron had told me so. My bow-legged Baudelaire. I took out the gun I wasn't going to shoot any beautiful souls with.

I bent myself under the chain. My shoes squeaked.

Five steps, and then a flat concrete landing. A wooden door swung inward at the barest touch.

The mouth of an alley, very much like the one which had led to McGruder's. Darkness here also, but not absolute darkness. Back at the right an oblong shaft of light, spilling out of a window at ground level. A high brick façade unbroken along the left. Silence.

Marley? Bob Cratchit? Tiny Tim?

Humbug.

I went down on a wet knee at the window, bracing one arm against my ribs. Miss Fannin's gowns by Davy Jones, special effects by Oliver Constantine. The miseries of the hero in no way reflect the interests of the sponsor. The window was the type that hinges inward. It was propped open by a paperback book.

Dr. Zhivago? Dr. Spock? Wrong as always. Not even *The Metaphysical Speculations of Tuesday Weld.* Something called *Walk the Sacred Mountains,* by one Peter J. Peters. There was an l.p. record on the ledge beneath it, a session by Thelonious Monk.

I looked in. A small room, a bulb inverted from a cord in the ceiling. A black ceiling. Black, Ebenezer? Certainly black, saves on cleaning costs. Black walls also.

There was a cot opposite me, draped in a bleached sheet which hung to the floor. The only other inanimate object in there was a fluffy, snow-white rug, with two men and a woman sitting on it.

They were sitting cross-legged, like Burmese idols. The

woman was a spindling, horsey blonde I might have noticed at the party. One of the men I didn't know. The other was Don McGruder.

Dashing Don McGruder, mournful footnote from a psychiatrist's case book. Whatever the diagnosis was, it was catching. This time the other two didn't have any clothes on either.

God bless us, every one. For this I'd struggled out of a sickbed. But maybe I'd write a book now myself. By H. Fannin-Ebing.

There was an oriental water pipe in the middle of the rug, and they were passing its stem from mouth to mouth. I watched the blonde suck in smoke, then hold her breath. She had a bosom like a mine disaster. Even through the window the sweet stench of the marijuana was overpowering.

"They don't comprehend," the girl said. She slurred the words. "'Get married, Phyllis'—that's all I hear. What a drag. I love them, I really do, but they don't dig me, you know? They just weren't with it at all when I asked for the money for the abortion—"

"This isn't swinging me tonight," McGruder said. "It simply isn't. I'm not high in the least."

"Recite us some Kerouac then, Donnie. You do him so passionately. The part where he talks about how they make love in the temples of the East—"

"If you really want me to—"

She wanted him to. By the old Moulmein Pagoda, lookin' lazy to the sea, there's a Beatnik girl a-settin', and she's gettin' high on tea. I was sorry I couldn't stay, but I had a previous appointment.

I had an appointment with Fagin. We were going to teach a few middle-class youngsters some of the nicer subtleties of felonious assault.

I wondered if they would have a jazz band at that monastery

when I got there. If I stole the instruments, would that make me a felonious monk?

There was a turn farther back as I'd anticipated, but at the rear of the building I was in total darkness again. I found a door frame by touch. The door was open.

A hallway. Fifteen or twenty feet inside I saw a tiny wedge of light which would be the room I'd been watching. There could have been other doors in there.

I hesitated a minute, feeling dizzy. I couldn't hear them from across in that room. I pulled back the hammer on the revolver, making noise with it, then uncocked it again soundlessly.

"Ephraim?" I said softly. "That's that Magnum, Ephraim."

The place was as quiet as an unlit cigarette.

"I'm the ghost of Christmas yet to be, Ephraim. Speak to me, lad, unless you don't want to find anything in your stocking except worms and the bones of your feet."

"Damn your black heart, Fannin," he said.

There was a swishing sound after the words. Something flexible and hollow struck me behind the ear, not hard, and I danced away from it. That was fine, except that the abrupt movement sent a new pain through my chest, like tape ripping. I doubled up gasping and the thing hit me again.

It was nothing, maybe a length of rubber hose. On a normal working day I could have caught it between my teeth and chewed it into pieces. I hadn't had a normal day since they'd fired on Barbara Frietchie. Waves of murky nausea washed over me and I stumbled against a wall.

"Shoot," he said then. "Go ahead, shoot me—"

His voice was choked and theatrical. For a minute I had the batty notion that he was going to start reciting also, like McGruder. Then I thought I heard him, I could have sworn. "Shoot, if you must, this old gray head, but spare your country's flag," he said. . . .

Dementia, absolute dementia. He was sprinting, going away.

I let him run. I'd had it. I wasn't even ashamed.

I dragged myself out of there like a feeble old man whose favorite walking cane was sprouting leaves under the backyard porch, just out of reach. Come back, cane.

Sick, sick. I didn't stop to see how the literary tea was progressing, but I was perverse enough to slip the Peters novel off the ledge. Phyllis would find a husband one day, she'd be a steady fourth for bridge at the country club, a pillar. Me, I had gum on my sole.

It was almost an ultimate satirical indignity. The groaning gumshoe. There was a scrap of paper stuck there also.

It was a photo of a matronly, heavily made-up woman, torn from what looked like an inquiring photographer's column. The woman had practically fractured her jaw for the camera, getting it lifted to erase the lines in her neck. Next to the picture it said:

Mrs. Burner van Leason Fyfe, Cotillion chairman: "Of course there's still society in America. There just has to be. Why, what meaning would anything have without it?"

CHAPTER 27

There was a loose page in the Peters book. I stared at it without interest, leaning against a fender:

> *... digging it with Bennie and Jojo and those wild chicks
> (one of them an Arab, she had eyes like smothered stars)
> in the backseat of that brokendown Chrysler Bennie had
> driven to Tampico and back and sold for forty dollars in
> San Diego and spent the money on a two-week fix and then
> swiped it back again, and all night long Jojo talking about
> the Mahayana transcendence of our friend Wimpy, the poet
> who did not wash except on the coming of the new moon
> and who was the new culture hero of our time and who
> once said: "I dig Brahman and I dig The Bird but I do not
> dig housewives," which became a creed: and all the while
> (younger then and my jeans too tight; I'd borrowed them
> from a tranquil Taoist midget I'd met reading Lincoln
> Steffens in a public urinal in Times Square—ah, holy
> times, holy square!) pressing my hand against the knee of
> that swinging angel Arab lass and not minding the blood
> where I tore my skin against a broken spring in the seat, oh
> how I suffered, telling myself as soon as I make it with this*

*chick I will hop a freight and very religiously ride the rails
to Albuquerque to tell Herman (but first some detail here
about Herman, a raw maniac hipster kid who . . .*

That was all I needed. I wadded up the page and tossed it
in the general direction of a passing cat, then let myself ooze
wetly behind the wheel of the Chevy. I'd leaked water on the
floorboards, coming over. I supposed it wasn't any worse a
crime than leaking prose.

I wasn't sure I could make it uptown. Or maybe I just wanted
recognition for all my successful missions. I drove back to
Fern's.

It was almost six, and it got light in the few minutes I was in
the car. I leaned against the bell, feeling rotten about waking
her. After a minute I heard a window being lifted. I went down
a few steps, letting her get a look at me.

"It's Harry, Fern—"

"Harry, what—?"

She disappeared inside, and a second later the catch
released. I hauled myself up the one carpeted flight.

She was in the apartment doorway, wearing that short blue
jacket again. Her hair was tousled, and light from the stairwell
gleamed on her naked lovely legs. Her face slackened when she
saw my own. "Oh," she said. "Oh, Harry—"

"Don't take me out, coach."

She extended a hand, but it didn't look strong enough to
support me. I gave her what I could spare of a smile, then went
across to one of the leather sling chairs where my damp seat
wouldn't do any harm.

I sat for a minute with both arms crossed against my stomach, hearing the door close. When I raised my head she was
kneeling in front of me.

Her fingers traced across my forehead, near the patch of gauze. "It couldn't have been just Ivan—?"

"He led the cheering section."

"You look worse than Dana did. Does it hurt badly?"

"Only when I laugh."

"Oh, stop joking, it isn't something to—"

"I'm okay, Fern. I shouldn't have come. You've had enough for one night."

"You can quit that also." She had gotten up, considering me somberly.

"Have I ever told you how beautiful you are?" I asked her.

"Have I ever told you you're a little crazy? Yes, I think I did, the other night. There's coffee, Harry. I made some for Dana before, all I have to do is heat it—"

"Coffee would be swell."

She shook her head, then went into the kitchen. I worked myself out of the soggy jacket. Bloomingdale's better grade, eighty-seven bucks for the suit and I still owed them forty. Maybe the old Armenian tailor on my corner could salvage it. He was half blind from reading William Saroyan in the glare of his window all day, and he couldn't sew a straight seam, but his Negro presser was fair. The Negro read Karen Horney and Erich Fromm.

"It won't be a minute," Fern said from the doorway. "Listen, Harry, why don't—" She glanced toward the closed door to the second bedroom. "Good heavens, I'm not going to be coy. Dana will be asleep for hours with those pills. Get yourself inside and get undressed. There's a big quilted robe in the closet if you want a hot shower—" She smiled. "Or is that what you tried to take already? Maybe you ought to just jump right into bed, you big oaf. I'll bring the coffee."

I grinned at her. "If you touch me, I'll scream."

"Go on, now."

I left my jacket across one of the wings of the chair. A lamp on her bed table was burning, and the covers were flung aside. I gave my tie a yank, then growled at myself in a mirror over a dressing table. The wet knot was as tight as a wet knot.

There was a day-old *Times* in a magazine rack, and I spread it across the small bench before I sat. Maybe the raw-honed private cop would have more luck with his shoelaces. Not tonight, Napoleon. I bent forward about halfway, which was enough to make me dizzy again. Concussion, sure as shooting.

My elbow had nudged a book on the table. It was lying reverse side up. Fern's picture was on the glossy jacket.

"Advance copy," she said. She had come in carrying an enormous steaming white mug. "First one off the presses."

"I never met a famous author before."

She wrinkled her forehead, peering across her shoulder. "Who dat? Where he at?"

She looked wind-blown in the photo. The novel was called *Go Home, Little Children.* A sticker on the cover said that it was a book club selection.

She put the coffee near me. "Drink it before it gets cold. I thought I told you to get out of those wet things—"

"I would of, ma'am. 'Cepting I need a scissors for my tie."

"Oh, here, let me—"

She leaned down, working at it, and then stepped back and gave me an exaggerated scowl. "Maybe we'll need a scissors at that. Or a—" She drew in her breath. "Oh, damn me anyhow, I was almost going to make a joke about a knife, when poor Audrey—"

She pressed a hand across her mouth, looking away. I reached out and pulled her toward me. She came yieldingly, going to her knees again, and my hands slipped beneath that jacket. Her head fell against my chest.

She was not wearing anything under there. The soft flesh of her shoulders was still bed warm. I held her.

"It's as if it won't end," she said. "Three people dead. Dana's right, things get so terrible sometimes—"

Her face lifted. For a moment I didn't move. I didn't even breathe. The muscles in my jaw had gone tight, and something began to twist inside of me—into a hot sickening node, like fear or like horror.

It wasn't fear. The book thudded to the floor as I got to my feet.

"Three," I said. "Three people dead—"

"Well, yes, aren't—?"

"You couldn't have known about the third, Fern, unless—"

"What—?"

She was still on her knees. Highlights glinted in her silken hair. Her face was as delicately etched as a dream that only time itself was ever going to exorcise.

"Why?" I said. "Dear God, Fern—why did you kill them?"

CHAPTER 28

She got to her feet. Her face had no more color than dispersing smoke. *"Are you mad—?"*

"Am I? Maybe I am, because I can't conceive of any reason. Why, Fern—?"

I had taken a step forward. My shoe touched something and I glanced down. *Go Home, Little Children. A Novel by Fern Hoerner.* I stared at it like a man looking down from the rim of an abyss. *By Fern Hoerner.*

I saw it then, as clearly as fanatics see hell. I had to brace myself against the dressing table. "By Lucien Vaulking," my mouth said.

"What—?"

"Your husband, the writer who supposedly didn't write—that was his name, wasn't it? It has to be. There's no other answer, none—"

She didn't speak. Her eyes were wide.

"The author who died without leaving the novel everyone expected him to leave. You didn't write the book, did you, Fern? Lucien Vaulking did, and somehow you got hold of the manuscript. A manuscript you knew at a glance would sell to Hollywood for big money, since you were in the business. You—"

I had the rest of it. But I had to push the words up out of my throat like uncomprehending draftees out of a slit trench. "Josie and Audrey," I said. "The same two girls Vaulking had been seeing before he died. They must have found out—recognized the book—and threatened to expose you. Which has to mean that Audrey Grant's father was killed for no other reason than—"

"You *are* mad," she hissed. She let herself drop to the bed. "You have to be—utterly."

I groped for the cigarettes I didn't have. "Someone is, Fern. Someone who could kill those two girls to cover a theft, and then take a third life for no other reason than to throw suspicion in a different direction. Someone absolutely wanton, ruthless—"

"I—" Her hand moved, and light flashed on the patch of adhesive on her wrist. I sank to the bench.

"Christ. Someone who could even pretend to such terrible anguish that she would deliberately mutilate herself with a burning cigarette. All the acting you've done, every minute, so that I thought you were the only normal human being in this whole crew of psychopaths. My God, how sick you must be—"

Something changed in her face. Her lips parted, and then, incredibly, every trace of shock was gone from her expression. She dropped back onto one elbow, as casually indulgent as if I'd started to tell a joke she'd heard a dozen times before. "All this because I said three people were dead, which I shouldn't have known. You *will* go on?"

The unreality of the pose struck me like a blow. I stared at her. I didn't know whether I was physically ill or whether the whole thing had hit me too hard in a place I'd set myself up to be hurt, but I felt dazed. Three of them, over a manuscript, a novel. I had to force myself to realize how much money was involved. I was sweating from every pore.

"You would have been familiar with the background," I managed. "Josie would not have told many people about her illegitimacy, but her roommate would have known. You would have heard about Grant's wealth also, and you obviously knew about Ephraim's marriage—"

"I can admit all of that. And I was married to Lucien—it was never any secret. None of this means a thing."

I shook my head, thinking it out. "Blackmail," I said. "Josie and Audrey. Everything I've heard about the pair of them indicates they were capable of it. Not ordinary Village kids, but call girls, both of them bitter, opportunistic. Sure. They must have had proof that the book was Vaulking's. They told Oliver Constantine they were coming into money, and the logical assumption was that they meant Grant's—except that finally it didn't make any sense, not with the girls dead themselves. But they meant your money—from the movie sale, the book club. They couldn't very well admit to Constantine that they were leaving one dirty racket because they'd found an easier one, going from one rotten way of life to another, so they made up an excuse about an inheritance—probably the first idea that came to mind. So a story they contrived in all innocence helped you lead the police in the wrong direction—"

She said nothing, watching me. "Not that you needed the help," I went on, "since you'd already established a connection between Grant and his heirs by sending those clippings. Or no, you threw in that telegram also, didn't you? Just in case Ephraim didn't work out as a patsy, an investigation of Constantine would lead to Ivan Klobb. So he'd be the one the cops would have thought had been blackmailed—"

I let it trail off, feeling unsteady again. "Is this all?" she said.

I nodded. "Although some small items begin to fit now also. Like the twenty-two you said you got as a gift. Vaulking was a marksman. It isn't important, but it's a good bet he was the one who gave you the gun—which you planted at Ephraim's when you were supposed to be at that revival of *Casablanca*. You didn't go to the picture, Fern. After we made our statements that night, standing by the car—I said, 'Play it again, Sam.' It's ten years since I saw the film, and I don't even know if Bogart uses the line more than once, but I still remember it. You didn't react. At the time I chalked it up to your being upset. And sure, one other triviality. Tonight at the party—why was I there? You didn't ask. You knew the minute you saw me—that Grant had contacted me because of my name being in the paper. I suppose you did have a minute of panic Tuesday when you found out the sucker you'd picked to hold your hand was a private cop. Jesus, I can just see it. If I hadn't poked my face into that bedroom you would have found a pretense to look in yourself, of course, but what was next on the schedule? A coquettish little scream, a demure faint—?"

There was a minute. "I hope you're going to notice just a few of the flaws in all this," she said then. "Audrey and Josie were blackmailing me. And yet Audrey didn't suspect me in the least when Josie was killed."

"She did suspect you—tonight, when she saw that Ephraim was out. The gun in his apartment fooled her first, sure, like it fooled the cops. But she got scared the minute she spotted him at McGruder's. She knew the police didn't have anything on him. Then you knifed her about three minutes later—"

I had leaned against the table, and my ribs contracted sharply. "I suppose you would have killed her sooner," I said, "if she hadn't run off with Peters for the few days. But you were probably fairly sure they'd show up at the party. What weapon did you have for that one, Fern—I mean before you picked up the knife? The same gun you shot Grant with earlier?"

She ignored the question, toying with the top button of her

jacket. I could have made more sense out of her reaction if she'd shaved her head and danced on a chandelier. "I killed Ulysses Grant to make Ephraim's inheritance look like a motive," she said. "But suppose Ephraim hadn't gotten out of jail before tonight's deaths—who would be the murderer then?"

"The cops thought of that. Thirteen million would buy a lot of partner—they would have worked like hell to bring Peters into it."

She wet her lips. "And you've concluded all of this on the basis of something I said which I wasn't supposed to know. Suppose Dana had made the same slip—could you have built a case against her the same way?"

I must have been staring at her stupidly. "Damn it, Fern, what kind of dumb irrelevancy is that? You made the slip, not Dana. It's going to send you up for life at the least—can't you comprehend the fact?"

"Is it? What a shame—just when we were beginning to get along with each other, too." She came off the bed. I hadn't believed she could do anything with her face which might distort its beauty, but her lips twisted into a snarl that was more than ugly. "So I couldn't have known about the third killing," she said.

I didn't answer her, but only because the dizziness came back. I had to shut my eyes, fighting a sudden mounting nausea.

"I couldn't have known," she repeated. "Well, maybe you ought to ask Pete Peters if I couldn't have, mister. Or wake Dana—she was here when we heard."

My head was swimming. "Heard—?"

"Yes, heard. Pete called here, damn you, just a minute before you came down—after you'd dropped him off. *He* brought up the third killing—which *you'd* just told him about."

I forced myself off the bench. The room was murky as a

steambath, and I could hardly hear her. "My lover man. I think you better scram, Fannin, before I really do get sore—"

I reached toward her, but I grabbed only mist. I hit the open door with a shoulder, stumbling, before blackness swirled over me like a shroud.

CHAPTER 29

I was back in the magic time machine again. I was a small boy in a white bed in an antiseptic hospital room. I lay with my head buried against an arm, spurning the complicated, pernicious adult world about me.

"Little Harry is just shy," a voice said. "There's someone to visit you, Harry, come to cheer you up. It's that baseball player whose photo you've tacked on the wall. It's Mr. Medwick."

"*Ducky* Medwick?" I said. "Ducky—is it *really* you? Will you hit a home run for me today? Will you hit one off Carl Hubbell?"

But Hubbell wasn't pitching. Someone named Bowman was. *Bowman?* I remembered too late. Medwick was already at the plate and the ball was rocketing toward him, faster than I could see. My heart stopped in anticipation of the hideous, ringing carom. When I dared to look again the great idol of all my boyhood lay pinioned on his back with his arms outstretched, like a man crucified to earth. He didn't move, he didn't move at all.

The machine went out of focus, and a nurse was hovering near me. "No," I cried, "never mind me, take care of Ducky first—" She was a beautiful nurse, although I was seeing her through a smog. Her hair was the color of golden silk.

"You did it," I told her.

"You still think so. In spite of my so-called slip not being a slip at all. You poor tenacious sap."

"I saw you," I said.

"What?"

"You beaned him. You beaned the only man who ever led the National League three consecutive times in runs-batted-in."

"More delirium—"

"Shoot," I said. "Shoot if you must."

"Poor Harry. What are you jabbering about?"

Who knew? I thought it might help if I got my eyes open, but it didn't. All I could see was bedroom floor. My entire body was drenched with perspiration. I was weak as a watered cobweb.

A hand pushed something under my nose. "Here—see if you can drink the coffee before it gets cold."

I tried to lift myself. I couldn't.

"Drink it, Harry."

"Drink it yourself. Drown in it."

"Oh, now don't tell me you're angry? At little old me?" She tittered. "Just because I upset all your clever deductions? Would it make you feel better if I confessed, Harry? I think perhaps I will. It might be fun to talk about it."

She thought perhaps she'd confess. Because it might be fun. Somebody in that room was as batty as Lady Macbeth, but I didn't have time to figure who. I was too preoccupied with the blur in front of my face. Out, damned spot.

"You're right about it being Lucien's book, of course. Shall I tell you the details, Harry?"

I shuddered. Audio-hallucination, without doubt. Maybe if I concentrated hard enough on something it would all go away.

Famous dates. 1066, the Battle of Hastings. 1215, the Magna Carta. 1649, Charles the First lost his head. If you can keep your head when all those about you are losing theirs . . .

"—He'd fiddled with the manuscript for five years. That son of a bitch, treating me like dirt, running around with tramps who weren't worth my little finger—but that's beside the point. The book is good, all right. He always liked to get my judgment on things—he thought I had a fair ear, and I was also familiar with what he was trying to bring off. He gave me the final hand-written draft to read on a Thursday, and the next night he died. Showing off at a party, doing chin-ups to impress a couple of simpering girls as if he'd been fourteen instead of forty. Nobody knew I had the script—"

—1620, the Pilgrims. 1773, the Boston Tea Party. Tea? 1588, Spanish Armada . . .

"—Josie and Audrey were the only two I was worried about. He never let anyone see anything that wasn't finished, but he'd been playing his he-man games with the pair of them for six months or so, and there was a chance they might have gotten a look. Audrey was over here one day after I had galley proofs and I left the first sheet in the living room deliberately, as a test. She did recognize it, and of course she told Josie. Josie herself wouldn't have recognized *The Scarlet Letter* if her name was Hester. Audrey said that she had three pages of manuscript in Lucien's handwriting hidden away—part of an earlier draft he'd given her as a souvenir. They told me they wanted ninety percent of everything I made."

I forced my head up then. She was sitting with her legs crossed. Her face was flushed, and her eyes were gleaming, not looking at me. She wasn't Mrs. Macbeth, but that didn't keep the thing from being creepy. She was talking almost mechanically.

"They made it so absurdly easy. They told me they had the

three sheets in a safe-deposit box." She grunted. "I found them in Josie's closet Tuesday afternoon. They'd put them in the obvious place, thinking I'd never look. Like all stupid people they thought everyone else was stupid too. A hundred thousand dollars from Hollywood alone, not to mention the reputation that goes with it, and they thought I'd crawl, let them hold the lie over my head for as long as they lived. Fools—"

She wasn't conscious of me at all now. I could feel the Magnum on my hip when I shifted my weight. Her hands were in her lap, empty. That made things even weirder.

"You weren't quite sure why Audrey didn't suspect me when Josie died. She did, of course, although she couldn't be sure until she learned if I'd located the three pages. So she 'dropped in' yesterday. She brought Pete with her, although he had no idea what was going on. I knew damned well she wanted a look at that closet, so I let her have one. I made a pretense about needing something from the drugstore, and even asked Pete to walk me down so she could be alone in the place. Except by then I'd substituted three pages on matching paper in my own handwriting—close to Lucien's but unquestionably mine. I didn't know exactly when or where to kill her yet, you understand. She stole the pages—meaning she didn't notice the substitution. They'll most likely turn up in her apartment—absolutely meaningless. That was enough to convince her that I wasn't involved. I did have some luck with the timing on some things, but then everything was in my favor to start with—the degenerate way these people live, all the sordid relationships, Ephraim and his mockery of a marriage—God, how weary I'd gotten of all that. But I'm out of it now, you see. I'll be somebody—a rich somebody."

"With a number over your breast pocket," I said. "You'll be able to buy cigarettes and soap for everybody else in death row."

"Well, the man is recovering." She came back from wherever she'd been. "He's his ironic old self again. How droll."

I used all my hands on the bed, getting to my knees. She watched me indifferently. After a minute she smiled.

"You're not really one of the stupid ones, Fannin—you're just stubborn. Why do you think I've told you all of this? You'll go to the police, of course—"

I didn't answer, busy breathing.

"You will, all right. It's really quite amusing—except for one thing."

"I know," I said. "But you tell me anyhow."

"You're dopey. You staggered up here looking like somebody Noah left off the passenger list, and you collapsed on my floor. Tell them I did it. You won't even be able to explain what gave you the idea to start with, it's based on such a false premise." She laughed, rising gracefully in a little half-pirouette. Then she cocked an eyebrow toward the bed. "There truly isn't any point in rushing about it, you know. I've got a hunch your immediate future would be considerably less frustrating if you spent it sleeping. Shucks, I might even fondle you where it hurts."

I made it the rest of the way up, staring at her. I was gritting my teeth so hard I could hear them. "Three," I said. "One a man nearly blind you didn't even know."

"Two cheap whores and a filthy, odorous wretch who tried to put his hands on me when I walked in claiming to be a friend of Audrey's. An overwhelming loss to the world."

"You found the three sheets and killed the girls anyhow, because even without the proof they could still talk and cause doubt. You killed Grant only to cover your trail. Why did you bother? Why, if you were going to tell me all of this?"

"Oh, but I hadn't *intended* to tell you anything, you see. This was just impulse—"

"Just—" I swallowed. "My God, I thought people like

Ephraim and Peters were in bad shape. Harmless phonies who simply haven't outgrown their adolescence. But you—"

"What about me, Harry? You were getting stuck on me, to tell the truth, weren't you? Say that you weren't, especially after Tuesday night. When I wept on your manly chest, Harry—remember when I cried?"

"I'll get over it, Fern. I'll spend a night in a cesspool."

"Heck, that's a pretty flimsy parting line. Too bad you're not one of those Mickey Spillane detectives—you could shoot me in the belly and be done with it. But that would be murder, wouldn't it? I mean, since after all, you can't prove a thing."

She laughed again, slipping the robe off her shoulders. She glided to the bed, naked as a reptile. "You *will* excuse me then, but I do have to get my rest—a girl ought to look her best for the reporters. Yes, my little confession—just an impulse, but what a brilliant one. I wonder how many copies it will sell—a million, do you think? Surely, at least a million."

The light snapped off, and I heard sheets rustling, with sounds like nuts being shelled. "Drop in again, why don't you—sometime when you're feeling a little more friendly. I might even autograph a copy for you—'To helpless Harry, who had no proof.'"

I did shoot her—*through her twisted, malevolent brain, with every bullet in the Magnum, savoring each separate recoil as it jarred my arm to the shoulder*—but only in my imagination, only in my imagination.

"Good night, lover," she said.

CHAPTER 30

There was a Benzedrine inhaler in the bathroom. I crushed the gummy substance out of the tube with my heel, then chewed on the stuff as long as I could stand the taste. Dana was torpid from the barbiturates, and I had all the capacity for exertion of an anemic amoeba, but I wasn't going to leave her in that apartment.

It took a glass of water in her face to get her into a sitting position, and she kept mumbling something incoherent about San Francisco while I yanked the red sheath over her head. We went down into the street like walking wounded, but nobody asked us how the rest of our boys were doing at the front. She was out cold again the minute she hit the car.

I double-parked and left her for the five minutes it took to get some response from Joey Pringle, a hophead musician who lived on the third floor of my building. Between the pair of us we carted her up the one flight. Pringle didn't ask what was going on either, but only because at 7 A.M. he'd be operating on two hours' sleep at best, all of it induced intravenously.

I showered, worked myself into fresh clothes, then reheated yesterday's coffee and forced down two cups. After that I got Dana stripped again and between the sheets. I did it with all the jaded worldliness of an aging gynecologist. I made the precinct house just as Lieutenant Vasella was finishing his night's tour.

If I sounded as inane to him as I did to myself, he didn't show it. It took the two patrolmen still posted at Audrey Grant's apartment exactly sixteen minutes to locate the three manuscript pages under the base of a lamp. Their existence proved nothing about Fern's guilt, but at least suggested that my story wasn't sheer fantasy. The downtown lab had no sizable samples of either Fern's or Lucien Vaulking's handwriting with which to compare them, but within thirty minutes more Vasella was informed that the writing had been done long after Vaulking's death, in fact most likely within the last seventy-two hours.

A car was dispatched to my office with instructions for finding my Grant file under *S,* like in General Sherman, which I actually should have been asked to turn over earlier. Central Identification had Fern's prints on record, because of secretarial work she had once done for an insurance firm which registered all employees, but we learned quickly that they matched none of those on the newspaper clippings or the envelope in which Grant had received them. What prints there were belonged to Grant himself, his lawyer Fosburgh, two mail clerks, a letter carrier and me.

The original message form for Grant's telegram had been picked up at a midtown Western Union office, but this also bore no prints of any interest. It had been filled out laboriously in left-handed block printing by a right-handed person, and the line requiring identification of the sender listed the name R. E. Lee. The civil service intellect. No clerk had been alert enough to take a second glance at someone who had appended that signature to a communication addressed to one U. S. Grant.

The knife which killed Audrey Grant had been handled with cloth, and there was nothing which could establish Fern's presence in the death room. The same was true at Grant's. A check of the Hudson River near his apartment was already underway in an attempt to turn up the third murder weapon— a .38—and sewers in his neighborhood were being dredged also.

I learned most of this before ten o'clock, by which time the amphetamine and lack of sleep had me flighty. Vasella brought in an M.E. to look me over and the man decided I had a fracture of one rib, the obvious contusions but no damaged bones in my face, and only a lingering trace of my concussion. He taped me up and Vasella told me to get some rest.

Dana was still drugged. She tossed for half a minute when I woke her, then did a double take about the unfamiliar bedroom. She closed her eyes again, turning away with a moan. "Oh, heavenly damn," she said. "Dana, you done did it again."

She did another confused shudder when she got a look at my face. "You didn't done it either," I told her. She stared at me while I gave her the shortest condensation which would make sense, sitting up with a blanket around her bruised shoulders. I asked her if she could think of anything which might help, but she could only shake her head.

"Boy, I guess I owe you some thanks for getting me out of there. Leave it to perceptive O'Dea to pick the right girl to run to in an emergency."

"How are you feeling?"

She fingered one of the welts on her arm. "Delicate to the touch, hung over and still woozy from those pills—otherwise downright jovial." She glanced toward her clothes, then smiled. "I suppose it would be sort of superfluous to ask you to leave the room while I get dressed, wouldn't it?"

"Hell, there's no need to scram—the couch is okay for me."

"Oh, stop. You look like you fell under a tractor."

I grinned. "I'll tell you what. They strapped about sixty yards of adhesive around my middle—I'm as safe as Don McGruder, if you want to take a chance on moving over half a foot."

She lifted an eyebrow impishly. "Like old folks—cohabitation for companionship alone?"

"At least give it some dignity. Like wounded tigers, sulking—"

The clock on the dresser said twelve when I woke up. I had the bed to myself, but I saw the red dress still draped over the chair. I was stiff as Nebuchadnezzar's femur. My robe wasn't behind the door so I limped out front in my shorts and found her wearing it, reading something in my big chair.

"You're a good-looking girl," I told her. "You were pretty drunk at that party."

"I'm a shopworn Greenwich Village slut with acute dislocation of all functioning parts," she said. "I'm twenty-six. I fell in love with a guy when I was nineteen, the way it only happens once—a beautiful goddam scatterbrained hunk of test pilot who got himself disintegrated over some salt flats exactly one year to the day after we were married. Sex was the first thing I tried, then dope. I haven't quite abandoned either, but I guess I prefer Scotch. Although it's funny—I found where you cache the booze a good two hours ago, and I haven't had a drop. Did Fern really kill them, Harry?"

"Yes."

"I'll make you some breakfast, or whatever you call it at midnight. Bacon and eggs?"

"Four eggs. We did sulk at that, didn't we?"

"You kissed me once—on the ear. And then you started muttering. Oh, sure, I meant to ask you about that. You were insisting that somebody named Bowman had hit you in the head with a baseball. Do you often have delusions of grandeur—I mean mixing yourself up with Ducky Medwick?"

"For crying out loud, how would you know who—?"

Her eyes sparkled. "Older brothers. The louts used to beat it into me. Who do you want, the old St. Louis Gas House Gang? Durocher, Medwick, Dean, Rip Collins, Pepper Martin—"

"Marry me," I said. "Or at least bring your fielder's glove and move in for a month or two."

"You might just get me to think about it, if you were looking at me instead of the telephone. Call them, for heaven's sake."

I got Vasella, and since I asked he told me he'd slept in the office. "We decided to bring her in," he said. "About seven o'clock. She denies everything, of course. We checked Peters on that slip—he did tell her about the third killing."

I swore. "She booked?"

"We'd need a good deal more than we have. It's an odd one, all right—the girl couldn't be more sure of herself. We allowed her a phone call after a couple of hours, but do you think she contacted a lawyer? She called her publisher. He's been pacing halls here ever since, trying to make up his mind."

"I don't get you—"

"Evidently the book is in the process of being shipped all over the country to go on sale in a few days, with her name on the cover. They don't know whether to back her or not. He's anxious to hear things from you directly. Oh, yeah, just incidentally, our friend Ephraim Turk finally appeared—walked in on us twenty minutes ago. Considerate of him, we feel."

I said I'd be down, then ate and got dressed. Dana had to tuck in my shirt. I told her I'd meant it about sticking around, especially if she didn't want to spend time alone in the place she'd shared with Audrey. She said she'd stay the rest of the night.

I saw the publisher. He was five-feet-two at most, forty-five at least, shoulderless, pleatless, impeccable. He carried a severely rolled British umbrella, an alligator attaché case, a Burberry.

He was what all good little status-seekers get to be when they grow up.

"I just don't know," he said. "I'm shocked at the implications. On top of which I was supposed to have dinner this evening with Papa and I had to cancel—"

"Huh?" I said.

"I had copies of the novel rushed to a number of critics by special messenger the moment we heard, along with samples of Lucien Vaulking's work for comparison, but no one seems to want to make an unequivocal judgment about authorship. Lionel and VanWyck and Cleanth have phoned saying they have to have more time, and I haven't yet heard from Edmund. Edmund is in Connecticut, of course—"

"Of course—"

"It's like Shakespeare and Bacon, isn't it? I wonder what Bennett would do in such a situation. Perhaps I'll call him—"

He wandered away to call Bennett. He finally decided to call his lawyers also, three or four of them. A soft-spoken, darkly shaven young man named Dunn from the District Attorney's office had been brought in, and I told the story again for his benefit. I was going to get it by heart, like *Galia omnia divisa est.* At 1:10 my friend Nate Brannigan appeared from Central Homicide, big and beefy and sinewed like an ox, assuming responsibility probably because no one else could verify my reliability. "What are we doing about long-range background," he wanted to know. "Her relationship with this man Vaulking—how much did she see him after the divorce? Can we establish that he'd been writing?"

Floyd Toomey was handling that end of the investigation. He kept looking at me as if he hoped I might disappear into an open manhole. "We've dug up four neighbors from when they lived together, captain," he said. "Two of them claim he worked a lot, all the time."

"Would seem to indicate there should have been a script," Brannigan said.

"The other two say he never worked at all," Toomey went on stonily. "Old ladies. Both of them swear he kissed his wife good-by when she went to work in the morning, then used to crawl back into the sack. Had female visitors three or four times a week. They're both sure Vaulking is roasting in hell—I'm quoting here—while his wife suffered and was a dear."

A cop from technical detail came in. They had shut off the plumbing in Fern's apartment and drained the pipes. No burned papers, no trace of anything that could have been the original sheets in Vaulking's handwriting. The search for the gun which had killed Grant was also getting nowhere.

I told it one last time at two o'clock, and this time they had me throw it at Fern. She'd gotten that beauty rest, and after it she'd wriggled into a tight black jersey blouse and a tweed skirt that clung to her hips like the primer coating on an Alfa-Romeo. "You deny having made the confession Mr. Fannin claims you made?" Brannigan asked her.

"Wouldn't you?" she said.

"These pages of your manuscript at Audrey Grant's—how would Fannin have known about them if you hadn't told him?"

"Gracious me, how should I know how he knew? Certainly there can't be any harm in copying out passages of one's book as a memento for a dear friend? Does someone have a cigarette, please?"

She crossed her legs, waiting. The publisher went over, offering her a Pall Mall.

"Actually there *is* one thing I might mention," she decided then. "Embarrassing as it is, it seems pertinent. I spent a certain portion of Tuesday evening in Mr. Fannin's apartment—after we discovered Josie's body. It wasn't really a very successful arrangement. I hadn't thought of it before, but I imagine the fact that I repudiated Mr. Fannin's subsequent advances—once I ceased to be vulnerable—might well have some bearing on this curious behavior of his."

"You spent—" A gleam had come into the publisher's eyes. "Where is the press room, please? I should like to announce our position."

There weren't any reporters, whatever his position was. The police had issued no statement except that unnamed suspects were being questioned, and legally Fern was a material witness only. "We'd like to keep it that way for now," Vasella said reasonably.

"I'm sorry—but I've quite made up my mind. The public must be informed. This girl is innocent. Plagiarism indeed—the whole idea is preposterous—"

"Thank you, Ernest," Fern told him.

"You poor girl, not at all. I can only hope you'll learn to forgive me for having permitted myself any doubt—"

She dismissed his chagrin with a gesture, and he turned to motion one of his lawyers to the door. "Phone them," he said. "All the local papers, the wire services. Yes, don't forget the wire services—"

Brannigan kicked a drawer shut with a noise like a truck backfiring, walking out. He couldn't prevent the calls, and once Fern's identity was made known the department would have to commit itself about booking her. Every tendon in his thick neck was visible when the publisher stopped him in the doorway.

"You'll make arrangements for her release now, naturally? The entire situation is unthinkable, subjecting one of our most talented writers to this indignity—"

Brannigan brushed the man's hand from his sleeve as if it were something with eight legs and a sting. "Get me a writ," he said. "Until then I'd suggest you offer no more advice about police procedure."

"Well, I certainly shall, if this is to be your attitude." The publisher waved off another member of his portable bar association to wake up a judge or two. "Call Learned," he said.

"This man Fannin thinks he is some kind of Sampson," he told reporters thirty minutes later, "out to betray Delilah. A Delilah whose favors he demanded when she was too stricken with remorse to protest—" He glared at me for emphasis, presumably the way he would glare at some untutored wretch of an editor who'd rejected Bishop Sheen and Jim Bishop on the same afternoon. "But the Philistines shall rise up and slay him," he went on. "Fern Hoerner's brilliant novel will be on the best-seller lists within the week, and her thousands of readers will vindicate her. As will millions of other fair-minded Americans when they applaud the film for which negotiations are already underway. Indeed, I'm having lunch with Marlon this Tuesday—"

"Marlon who?" a reporter said.

They tried to corner me when he'd run dry, but Dunn from the D.A.'s office told them they would have to wait. They popped bulbs anyhow, wanting to know who had chewed up my face, and I was just sore enough to say a pimp named Oliver Constantine and to toss in the address. They began yelling for shots of Fern and the publisher insisted that they get them. Brannigan blew up then and restricted everybody to the outer lobby, then locked himself in an office with Vasella, Dunn and two of the publisher's lawyers. That left me eating Camels in a corridor, inconsequential as a raindrop in the Irrawaddy.

I was hunting for a drinking fountain up a flight when I ran into Ephraim. The police no longer had any interest in him and he was on his way out, looking whipped. He'd put on a suit before he'd turned himself in, cheap cord off the basement racks in a lower-grade shop and far from new. "I'm sorry I tried to hit you last night," he said clumsily.

"Forget it. Poets are out of my league anyhow."

He didn't smile. "Fern did it—there's no question?"

"A question of proof."

"Will they prove it?"

"If they don't come up with anything besides my version they'll never get into court to try."

"What happens then?"

I nodded toward the street. "Cocktails with the bookish set. A week from now she'll be telling Katherine Anne all the clever little things Vladimir said to Tennessee, between canapés."

That made twice he didn't smile, but I decided it wasn't particularly hilarious. "She won't go to any cocktail parties," he said.

I looked at him with care. "If that means you know some-thing, now's the time to spill it, Ephraim."

The expression on his face was reflective, gloomy, without much meaning. "I don't know anything," he said.

He scuffed away, plunging his hands into his pockets. I scowled after him, then got my drink and went back down-stairs myself.

The conference had broken up and they were letting the publisher play in the schoolyard again, which could only mean one thing. Nothing had developed which had given me any reason not to expect it. He was chatting with Dunn and one of his attorneys, and he broke away from them beaming like a gimcrack Cary Grant when he spotted her.

"Fern, I'll escort you home—"

She was coming out from the rear with Vasella. "Thank you again, Ernest, sincerely. You've been great—"

"Nothing, nothing—"

"Are there martinis tomorrow, did you say—?"

"Everyone will be there—J. D., E. B., W. H., E. E.—"

They went by arm in arm, clucking, like a couple of celibate hens who'd just got word about the new rooster. I was a handful of yesterday's feed they didn't glance at in passing.

She had a second thought when she reached the head of the steps. She stopped, said something to the publisher, and then came back.

"I really must say thanks, Harry, since it's worked out so beautifully." She was cooing. "After all, it *was* you who put the idea into my head. A mock confession to three murders I didn't commit—perfectly safe, and probably the greatest publicity idea in the history of literature."

"God almighty—"

"You don't think it's possible, do you? In spite of how ripe you were?" She laughed. "Oh, Harry, if you could only have seen the outrage in your face—you were so shocked you even gave these people a more convincing story than I gave you. Ah, well, not that it matters what you believe, not that it matters in the least—"

Bulbs began to flash in the stairwell. A nerve was jumping in my cheek as I watched her walk out of there.

CHAPTER 31

I didn't tell them. I didn't say a word. Vasella had gone into the interrogation room, and he and Brannigan were pacing with all the pent frustration of castrated steers when I looked in. Brannigan snorted once and told me to go back to bed.

The Chevy was on Hudson Street. I sat in it for a while, mumbling.

She'd made up the whole story. That was all I would have needed to mention. Pardon me, fellas, tee-hee-hee, but now she says she was just playing. So she could sell her book, you know? You know? I'm really sorry if I've put anybody to any trouble. . . .

The girl was as nutty as a two-headed gnu.

Even thinking about it was absurd. There wasn't anyone else in it. I could run it up and down the flagpole all day, she'd still be the only one to salute.

Okay, Ebenezer. But what have you got to show proof-wise, like?

Let the cops prove it. Me, I'd had enough. I was going back to sleep like the captain said.

Sure I was. So I drove up Hudson two blocks and then

parked again. The image in my rear-view mirror was leering at me. I leered back.

This was ridiculous. She did it.

The image kept on leering. It was a dark, amorphous blur, like an inkblot. What do you think you see in the blot, Mr. Fannin?

Fern killed them.

Of course she did. There, now, that's a good lad. Tell me, when did you first start to get this sensation that people were taunting you? Do you often feel inadequate, left out? Do you find total strangers smirking behind their hands when you walk into a room?

She did it, damn it.

It was 4:19 when I parked in front of a hydrant four doors down from her building. There was a faint mist from the river. The angle was bad, but I could see the glow of a lamp behind her blinds. She probably had a wax statuette of somebody named Harry up there and was huddled over it in a trance, jabbing it with long sharp pins.

Who do it, voodoo it? Something moved in the shadow of an alley across the street and I went over.

"Rotten detail?"

Toomey grunted. "Got to watch her, I suppose. Not that it'll lead to anything."

"The publisher with her?"

"Blalock? Yeah."

"Blalock?"

"Ernest B. Blalock—Junior. I thought you and him got to be pals."

"I keep telling him to call me by my first name."

"Those things take time. You look bushed."

"I'm past knowing."

"Just feel restless, huh?"

"Unfulfilled. Or does that make me sound like a Beatnik?"

"I know what you mean. They sure can't dump it on a jury with just your word against hers, in spite of your honest face." He chuckled. "I supposed you'll get sued for that, too."

"Sued for what, too?"

"You missed the cheery news, huh? They're going to slap papers on you for libel, slander, defamation of character—whatever his lawyers can think of. It'll make the tabloids for six weeks straight, with pictures of the Hoerner babe looking sexier every day. Hell, I might even buy that book myself."

I reached for a cigarette. "What's my face got to do with it?"

"When those newspaper guys asked you what door you walked into—I just meant that Constantine might sue you also. If nothing comes of his end he might feel kind of sore that you called him a dirty name for publication. Although on the other hand I suppose you could prove a few things about him—"

"And his Vice Squad contacts who claimed they didn't have any file on him last Tuesday." I was fumbling in a pocket. "You got a match?"

"They covered for the guy, huh? Yeah, here—"

He flicked a lighter, and my hand went toward his wrist. I never touched him.

"Jesus!" he said. "Oh, Jesus—"

We both broke into the gutter at the same time. I did not have a gun, but Toomey's service revolver was in his hand before we had gone three strides. The roar of the gunshots was still reverberating.

They had been incredibly close together, muffled so that they had sounded almost like a single explosion. My brain told me it had counted four but I couldn't be sure. We bolted around opposite ends of a parked Buick, getting across.

I was ahead of him on the stone steps. I yanked at the door handle once. Toomey pushed me aside, grabbing my arm for balance and slamming a foot against the lock. It gave with a splintering sound and I went through and then doubled over, clamping my jaws against the searing pain in my chest. I stumbled up the one flight after him and around to the front.

The door to the apartment held against his shoulder. He braced himself against the banister opposite it, then vaulted forward and took it with both heels. It rocketed inward.

I stopped dead, and my insides turned to stone.

Ernest Blalock was standing at the far side of the room. He was in his shirtsleeves. The shirt was white, but no whiter than his face. His stare was fixed on the low couch next to him.

She was sprawled hideously. Her head was twisted downward, and her golden hair was trailing along the floor. A trickle of blood had seeped out of her mouth, still gleaming, but I did not have to get over there to know that it would coagulate in a minute. Her eyes were gaping in their sockets.

She was still wearing the tweed skirt, but she'd taken off her blouse and put on that short blue jacket. The jacket was open. The flesh below her black brassière was so severely charred that the gun had to have been held flush against her. There had been five shots, not four. I could have covered the entire tight grouping with a poker chip.

There were voices in the hall, and I got the door closed somehow. I was vaguely aware of Toomey racing in and out of Fern's bedroom, and then into the one with the fire escape which had belonged to Josie Welch. He cursed once, reappearing, and I watched him take Blalock by the arm. "Tell it," he snapped.

Blalock shuddered. His look was glazed. He buckled against the wall when Toomey swung him around.

"Damn it—"

"That—that—Ephraim Turk. We were in the kitchen. He—"

Toomey motioned toward the second bedroom. "He go that way?"

Blalock forced a nod. "Oh, dear God. He literally dragged her around by the hair, he—"

Toomey was already on his way to the phone, jamming the revolver back onto his hip. He dialed rapidly. "Toomey, Lou—get me the lieutenant, fast. Or Captain Brannigan if he's still on it—"

Blalock had taken a faltering step toward him. He spun suddenly, plunging into the kitchen. "Sure, dead," I heard Toomey say. "Looks like a forty-five. What the hell, he had half an hour to swipe one someplace, he's had the habit. Right here, yes sir—"

He hung it up. I was looking at her again, smelling the burned powder and the burned flesh. I could hear Blalock being sick. Toomey frowned at me.

"Hey, fellow, not you too?"

"Too much," I said. "I better get some air—"

"Yeah, yeah, I can see how you'd feel. It would be your word alone he'd killed her on, wouldn't it?"

I didn't answer him. I couldn't. I went back outside on legs that did not want to do anything but fold in half.

CHAPTER 32

There were people on the stairway to the next floor, all of them in bathrobes. "Say, did we hear—?"

"Police matter," I managed, and then I heard Toomey telling them something behind me. I went down and through the smashed lower door, wincing at every step. I took hold of the concrete rail with both hands and hung there, swaying.

My word he'd killed her on. Sensitive, saintly little Ephraim. She won't go to any cocktail parties. I should have known, dear Christ I should have known.

Audrey Grant and Josie Welch. Call girls, tramps who'd had nothing for him but scorn. One of them had married him as the most brutal kind of joke, the other had given herself to him once and then pretended it never happened. But Pete Peters had been right. In his warped life they had been the only two women who mattered, and I'd told him that Fern had murdered them both.

I'd told him. I'd been so sure, so damned sure. And so convincing that thirty minutes after he'd talked to me he'd not only gotten the gun but had already used five of the six bullets it probably held, and now he'd be . . . now . . . I heard the first distant wail of a siren in the darkness as I started to run.

Commerce Street, I'd seen the address in the paper. It took me three minutes to get over there, no more, sprinting through the wet mist with both hands clasped against my side. The building was ancient, brick, and its glass vestibule door was open. *E. Turk, 3-F.* I lurched up the two flights. I stopped, gasping, just steps shy of the landing, fighting vertigo and pain and a dozen other things I could not have named.

"—Listen, listen, we ought to wait for the police—"

"—But time is passing, suppose he needs—"

"—Who's this coming now? They couldn't have gotten here so quick—"

Faces turned from a closed door as I dragged myself up the rest of the way. They might have been faces reflected in muddied water, for all I saw them. I staggered through the cluster to the knob. The apartment wasn't locked.

"Hey, who're you? You ain't supposed to—"

I turned my head. I must have looked like Raskolnikov on his way to get rid of the ax. I must have looked like Yorick when they dug him up. No one made anymore protest. I pulled the door after me.

There was only one room. It was close, disordered, filthy. He was on a narrow disheveled bed, on his back. One of his shoes was off, and there was a rip in the heel of his blue sock. The gun was still in his hand, although it had jerked out of his mouth at the recoil. A Ruger Blackhawk.

People don't kill other people. People are good, people have beautiful souls. There had been about forty books on two metal shelves above an unpainted wood table. It didn't seem that he would have had time, but he'd gotten his hands on each of them, rending bindings and shredding pages as if he'd decided that literature had been the cause of all his troubles. In a way, maybe it had been. The debris was scattered around the bare floor, except for a single page which lay near his shoulder. It could have been there by chance, but it was corny enough for the fanciful son of a gun to have meant it. It shook me, because of the foolishness I'd been quoting to myself before he'd hit me in that alley last night:

> ... It is a far, far better thing that I do, than I have ever
> done; it is a far, far better rest that I go to, than I have
> ever known.

Two cops were pressing up the stairs when I came out. One of them was Sergeant DiMaggio.

"I guess you better go back over, Fannin."

I nodded. An elderly man touched my sleeve as I started down, lifting a leathery, concerned face. "He was an author, that boy. I don't know if he was any good or not. He's dead, eh?"

"As dead as Dickens," I said, but the voice wasn't my own. Mine was trying to burst through the top of my skull, screaming in horror.

CHAPTER 33

Hiram Henshaw was perched cross-legged on a deformed hassock in his living room, squinting at me like a myopic canary from behind his thick lenses. He was wearing a stained sleeveless undershirt and a pair of pegged pants the color of rotted apricots. Except to whistle once or twice he had not made a sound in the ten minutes I'd taken to tell him the story.

I wasn't sure why I was up there. My viscera were still rattling around like loose bolts, and I felt about as sociable as a hangman. It was well after nine o'clock.

He picked at a splotch of dried shaving lather in his left ear. "So you've been pacing the paranoic pavements ever since you left the law, like?"

"A couple hours. I had coffee just down the block—"

"Indeed, indeed, glad to be of sympathy. I can see how the circumstances would make a cat start gnawing on his nearest leg. Like rough. But man, you couldn't have been cognizant that crazy Turk would perforate the chick's pajama tops. Or that he'd do unto himself like he did."

"Okay, I guess I couldn't have been. But still, I—"

"Still you're dogged by dismal doubt. She came on with this parting bit about how she'd extemporized the whole solo, and you're sure she had to be just giving you the big razzoo—but you're not *that* sure—"

"You've got it, friend."

"Yet you voiced the conclusion yourself—the chick was the only one with motive for the mayhem, *n'est pas?* This is not reassuring enough for your caviling conscience?"

I shook my head. "I've got to come up with something concrete. If I could just prove she'd stolen the book—"

"Oh, yes. But she would have held flame to that script of old Loosh Vaulking's first thing—tell-tale page after tell-tale page, gone, gone. Alas, I dig your dilemma, I truly do."

"Yeah." I took a smoke. "How do writers work, Henny? Damn it, I suppose once a guy copied over a new draft of something he wouldn't have any reason at all to save the earlier version—"

Henshaw shrugged. "Like as not, not, like. But on the other hand since when does a cat need a *reason* to save things? Like I cherish three hundred and thirty-seven unpaid traffic tickets in a scented drawer, you know? And—"

He stopped abruptly, tilting his head to one side. His brow was wrinkled. After a minute he began to talk to himself. "In Vinnie's Place? Surely, in Vinnie's. Just making idle talk, and Loosh declared—hmmm, now what did Loosh declare? Like his pad had gone to pot since the domestic tranquillity had terminated. Like Fern had left his bed and board, his bed and broom, and that cat was such a slob he couldn't live in the same room with himself. So like he'd been—like—well, pull my daisy—"

He faced me again. He pursed his lips. Very slowly he got to his feet. "Now leave us not let hope spring too eternal, lad, but Loosh Vaulking had this brother. Upstate a ways—where, where? Dobbs Ferry, oh, yes. Oh, yes, indeed. And in his brother's pad are many mansions, you dig me? And like Loosh had taken to stashing stuff for storage—"

Henshaw giggled. And then he bowed from the waist. "Like I reiterate, there could be nothing up there but bags of old bread. But if you'll remember to make restitution for the long-distance chatter before you debouch, man, there's like a telephone on the floor under yon sagging chair—"

And it was that simple. That simple. The draft was sketchy, and far from finished, but it was indisputably the same novel. Roger Vaulking, his wife and a housemaid were able to swear it had been in a closet in their home, along with other possessions of Lucien's, for over two years. An immediate injunction was granted against sale of the Blalock edition, and Roger Vaulking told reporters he would eventually release the work through another firm, but not until its notoriety had substantially lessened. Review copies with Fern's name on them were around, of course, and Dana O'Dea got hold of one and sent it to me from San Francisco about a month later.

She'd hung around for a day or two, but my ribs got worse before they got better, and that baseball nostalgia goes only so far. I was sorry, but even Medwick had to leave potential scores on base once in a while. I rewrapped the book and mailed it to Sergeant DiMaggio that November, when Constantine and Ivan Klobb were indicted on assorted counts of prostitution.

Not that there was much point in the gesture. The sergeant probably never read it either.

photo by Johanna Markson

David Markson is the author of ten other books, including *Vanishing Point, This is Not a Novel,* and *Wittgenstein's Mistress,* heralded by David Foster Wallace as "pretty much the high point of experimental fiction in this country." Markson's work has also been praised by Kurt Vonnegut, Ann Beattie, William Kennedy, Gilbert Sorrentino, and many others. He lives in Greenwich Village.